Secrets *of* Clearwater Castle

BOOKS BY EMMA DAVIES

EMMA DAVIES

Secrets *of* Clearwater Castle

bookouture

Published by Bookouture in 2023

An imprint of Storyfire Ltd.
Carmelite House
50 Victoria Embankment
London EC4Y 0DZ

www.bookouture.com

ISBN: 978-1-83790-435-8
eBook ISBN: 978-1-83790-437-2

For Vic

1

In all the time that Alun's been gone, Jess has never told Lowri she'll feel better soon, or that time is a great healer. She just hugs her when she cries and tells her she's sorry she's having such a bad day. This never resorting to glib platitudes is one of the things Lowri loves about Jess. It isn't that her other friends don't care, but what *do* you say to a grieving widow? There's no manual for this kind of thing, particularly not for someone in their early thirties. It's awkward, so mostly people avoid the subject altogether, or worse, refrain from mentioning Alun's name, as if he never existed, as if his and Lowri's shared life simply never happened. They don't mean to be unkind, far from it, but given that death is the only certainty in life, Lowri sometimes wishes it wasn't such a taboo subject. So when she opens her front door to find Jess standing there, with a warm smile and a packet of chocolate biscuits, Lowri knows her friend has guessed how much she's dreading this day.

She should have sorted out Alun's things much sooner, she knows that, but when he died, she just couldn't face it. Their whole lives were still ahead of them; Lowri wasn't ready to be a widow. And with Wren so poorly too, Lowri had barely enough strength to look after her daughter and keep her world turning, let alone deal with anything else. So Lowri let time roll by. She moved Alun's things into the spare bedroom and there they've stayed, for two long years, until now.

Jess hands Lowri the biscuits, wiggling her shoulders. 'Blimey, it's freezing out here. It's April, for heaven's sake, shouldn't it be warm by now?' She grins, and steps into the hallway where she sheds her coat and bag, hanging them over the polished bannisters just like she always does. Lowri has a perfectly good cupboard in the hall but that's not Jess's style. Lowri does organised, Jess does clutter, that's just the way it is. Then Jess turns, and subjects Lowri to one of her long stares, the kind that misses nothing, the one that assesses all there is to know.

'I'm fine, honestly,' says Lowri, knowing Jess won't believe her.

Jess's eyes narrow. 'Hmm…' She regards Lowri for a second longer before her face brightens again. 'Right then, let's get the kettle on, shall we?' And, not waiting for an answer (she never does), she heads straight for the kitchen.

'How was Wren this morning?' asks Jess, taking down two mugs from a cupboard.

'Same as usual. Sailed through the school gate with a wide smile and scarcely a backward glance. That's one good thing at least.'

'So you think she'll be okay?'

Lowri nods. 'You know Wren, nothing much gets her down. She makes friends with everyone, so moving is just a big adventure for her. Plus, her Aunty Susan has always spoiled her rotten, so why wouldn't she want to live close by?'

Alun always said Lowri was small and mighty, but Lowri is nothing in comparison to Wren and it kills her how he'll never see the person Wren is turning out to be. Born too early, wrinkled and helpless, with huge eyes and pale blue-veined skin, her name chose her rather than the other way around. And she'll always be their little bird. She had to fight for the first three years of her life, struggling through chest infection after chest infection, her little lungs desperately trying to suck in enough air to stay alive. They thought they were going to lose her when pneumonia struck, but miraculously, Wren came through it, even though Alun didn't. After that, Wren got better and stayed better too, as if the universe decided to stop giving her a hard time. Lowri likes to think that Alun had a hand in that, though, as if when he died a tiny spark of him somehow found its way into his daughter. Now, Wren is small and mighty and fearless and Lowri wishes she was more like her.

Jess is quiet for a moment. 'Lowri, you know you don't have to go, don't you?' she says. 'Just because *Susan* declared it ought to be, doesn't mean there are no other options. I'm sure we can think of something.'

Jess's feelings about Lowri's sister are more or less the same as hers, but they both know they've exhausted all other possibilities. Just as they both know Jess would give anything to have Lowri stay. Lowri feels the same, but this really is for the best. She can't pay for this house any longer, however much she pretends she can, and it's time she moved on, emotionally as well as physically.

'It's not all bad,' Lowri replies, giving a weak smile. 'I'll be getting the Belfast sink I've always wanted.' It sounds better than it is. It's a cracked and very old sink in a tiny cottage, three doors down from Lowri's sister, which Susan and her husband Gary have owned for years. They'd rented it out for the past ten to a lovely lady with seven cats, and to say the place needs cleaning is somewhat of an understatement. But if Lowri helps them tidy it up a bit, she can have it for free, and it's really an offer she can't refuse. Lowri looks down at the packet of biscuits she's still clutching and lifts her chin a little. No more melancholia, she promised herself.

An hour later, they're already sidetracked, hijacked by an old shoebox full of stuff that Alun had kept from his childhood. Lowri hadn't wanted to open it, saying it was just rubbish, but Jess insisted, she isn't going to let Lowri off with a thing. Now, they're rolling around laughing at photos showing the series of awful haircuts Alun had as a child. Lowri takes one of the pictures, peering at the grainy image of the boy who'd grown into the man she fell in love with. She's never seen it before and it suddenly strikes her how few photos she's seen of this period of his life. How little, in fact, she knows about any of his early life. She knew there'd been a divorce. His dad did the dirty with another woman and it cleaved the family in two. Alun never liked to talk about it much, and Lowri respected this. His past wasn't a part of their present and that was that. Now though, she's wondering about the family who lost a son, his mother the only representative at the funeral, a woman Lowri had never met before.

Her thoughts are interrupted by another peal of laughter from Jess.

'Hey, look at this one. And we thought the haircuts were criminal.' She passes Lowri the photo.

Alun must have been in his early teens, dressed for a party or disco, perhaps a family event, in a truly appalling shirt and baggy jeans with silver high-top sneakers. Funny, he always had a thing about shoes.

'He never quite got the fashion thing, did he?' Lowri says, laughing. But then he was so unbelievably attractive she forgave him his habit of pairing random items of clothing.

It's been good to laugh but, even as Lowri thinks it, she can feel the threat of tears, just as she always does when she's filled with thoughts of him. She guesses it's always going to be this way – happy memories bringing home all that will never be again. She points at the box which sits on the floor between her and Jess. 'What else is in there?' she asks, in an effort to distract herself. They're nearing the bottom of the box now.

'Looks like old play programmes. There's one here for *An Inspector Calls* from Bristol uni. Is that where his hobby started?'

Lowri nods. 'Alun was roped into the dramatic society by a friend, got bitten by the bug, and the rest, as they say, is history.' She'd met Alun a couple of years after he graduated. By then he'd joined another amateur dramatic association in the small Welsh town where Lowri lived with her parents. Her mum had dragged her along to see the latest production, although it may have been so Lowri could give her a hand organising the refreshments. After the play finished, Alun and Lowri both reached for a custard cream at the same time, and she swears the lights flickered as they touched. At least, that's what she told Jess afterwards. She also told Jess she'd met the man she was going to marry; bored her rigid no doubt. But Jess never made fun of her – simply said she'd better get on a diet then as she'd want to be at least a size twelve by the time they bought her bridesmaid dress. She was a size ten, as Lowri recalls.

Lowri's still lost in those memories, a gentle smile on her face, when Jess pulls out the last piece of paper from the box. It's an envelope. 'Ooh, what have we here?' she says, raising an eyebrow. 'Rather official-looking, posh paper and everything. Is this the part where we discover Alun had a shady secret?'

'Don't even joke about stuff like that,' replies Lowri, trying to grab the envelope from her.

Jess snatches it away, holding it high above her head. 'Oh no, you don't. I'm going to read it first. And if Alun *did* have a shady secret, I'm going to lie and say it's just about an unpaid parking ticket and throw it on the fire before you can read it.'

Lowri sighs. 'Jess... come on, give it to me.'

Jess is reading the letter now, lips moving slightly as she does so. 'It's from a firm of solicitors,' she adds. 'Something about an inheritance.' Her eyes are wide. 'Shit, Lowri, this isn't the bit where we find out about Alun's dodgy dealings, it's the bit where we discover he had a hidden fortune.'

Lowri tuts. 'Believe me, I've looked for one, there was no such thing.' In fact, not even a life-insurance policy to help her out. She takes the paper, frowning at the unfamiliar firm of solicitors on the letterhead. Hope blooms momentarily, but then the penny drops. 'It's nothing,' she says. 'This is about one of Alun's relatives – on his father's side – so one of the dodgy ones. He left Alun a piece of land when he died, but it's worthless, just scrubland in the middle of nowhere. Alun told me about it.'

'But there's a house,' counters Jess. 'Look.' She snatches back the letter, scanning the text. 'See, there... it says land *and* property.'

Lowri looks to where Jess is pointing, squinting at the words on the page.

Dear Mr Morgan,

I write regarding the sad passing of Mr Stephen James Morgan, who died at home last month. Please accept my condolences for your loss.

As executor of the estate, it is my duty to inform you that you have been named as a beneficiary under the terms of Mr Morgan's will, and although the extent of the estate has not yet been finalised, the bequest includes both land and property. I would therefore be grateful if you could contact this office at your earliest convenience for further details and so that I might conduct the appropriate identity checks prior to the issuing of probate.

Yours sincerely

Lowri wrinkles her nose. '"Property" could mean anything.

And from the way Alun spoke about it, it's most likely a decrepit shed or something.' She does a quick sum in her head. 'See, the letter's dated over four years ago, and although Alun mentioned it, he dismissed it out of hand. As far as I can remember he never referred to it again.'

'But he must have followed it up otherwise how would he know it was worthless?' Jess frowns. 'And if he did, why is this the only letter that refers to it? And why is it here?'

'What do you mean?' asks Lowri, staring at Jess.

'Why did we find this letter stuffed in the bottom of a shoebox with a load of old photos and not in the study with all the other papers? The ones you and I had to wade through when Alun died. Why didn't we find anything else?'

It takes Lowri a second to process what Jess has just said. She's right. Alun might not have left her financially secure when he died, but he did leave everything in order – bank statements filed, mortgage details and everything to do with the house all neatly tucked away, even down to instruction booklets for the new cooker they'd put in after they moved. So why wasn't this letter among them? Why was there no mention of his inheritance anywhere else?

'Maybe Alun just kept this as a memento?' she suggests, pointing at the letter Jess still clutches. 'If the land wasn't worth anything, he wouldn't have wanted to put it with all the other important stuff. He wouldn't have thrown it away though either, and it had to go somewhere. Maybe this is just where it ended up.'

'Right at the bottom of a box?'

Lowri knows what Jess is getting at. 'You're saying he hid it there?'

Jess looks up at her through her lashes.

'Alun didn't have secrets from me,' Lowri replies. 'I don't know why he put the letter there, but don't go reading anything into this. You know I went through all his affairs with our solic-

itor when Alun died – you were there, it wasn't a happy occasion. And Simon didn't mention anything about this.'

'Yes, but he probably didn't know about it. Why would he?'

Lowri has no answer for that. The fact that Alun had made
a will was surprise enough and his estate was pretty simple.
He'd named Lowri his sole beneficiary, giving her the contents
of his personal bank account, the right to a teeny tiny pension in
a gazillion years, and that was pretty much it. If there had been
any land or property, then surely Alun would have written
them into his will? She checks the date on the letter again,
seeing that it predates the will by over two years. Jess is right,
their solicitor might not have known about it, but Alun certainly
did. So either he forgot about it, or he didn't think it was worth
including and Lowri can't help wondering why that was.

'Whether you think it's important or not, you still ought to
check it out,' adds Jess. 'It wouldn't hurt, would it? And you
never know, maybe whatever was worthless back then has
increased in value. It rightfully belongs to you now, Lowri, don't
dismiss it. For Wren's sake, if not yours.'

Jess's comment would have annoyed Lowri had it come
from anyone other than her. 'Look, I have no idea why Alun
stuffed this letter in the bottom of a shoebox, but I don't want to
get all worked up about something which will turn out to be
nothing. Alun wasn't daft, if there was anything in the bequest
he would have followed it up.'

'It wouldn't be getting worked up about something,' replies
Jess, 'it would be checking facts. The letter mentions property,
something you're very much in need of. At least see what it is. If
it's an old shed, fine, but what if it's not? Don't dismiss this
simply because you're trying to move on, it could be important.'

Jess has always had an uncanny ability to discern Lowri's
ulterior motives. And it's true, Lowri *doesn't* want to follow this
up. Sorting out Alun's things was meant to be cathartic. It was
meant to signal the end of a particular period of mourning, tran-

sitioning her into a different kind of emotional space, not one where she forgets him, but one where things aren't so raw, one where she stands a chance of living the rest of her life. She's scared that if she calls the solicitor on the letterhead she'll be dragged back down again. But Jess isn't about to let this go.

'Plus, we both know you don't really want to move to Monmouth. You'll be a stone's throw from Susan and she'll drive you mad in approximately two days. If there's any chance this could provide an alternative, you have to do it. You've come this far, Lowri, don't give up now because you think you can see light ahead. This could prove to be something even brighter.'

Damn, Jess is good. 'But it'll look like I'm clutching at straws. The grasping widow.'

'No, it won't,' replies Jess, rolling her eyes. 'I bet they don't even know Alun's dead. It will look like the sensible actions of a widow trying to finalise her husband's estate.' She hands Lowri the letter with a 'don't argue' expression on her face. 'Put this somewhere safe.'

It takes them several more hours to sort through Alun's life. To compartmentalise his existence into what could be thrown away, what might benefit a charity shop and what Lowri will keep with her until her dying day. There are tears, of course, though she'd been doing so well, even after the whole thing of Alun's mystery inheritance. It wasn't until they'd almost finished when it caught her. When Lowri suddenly realises, as she opens up yet another bin bag, that in a few minutes she'll have even less of Alun than she had before. Jess simply wraps her arms around Lowri as she has so many times before and then foists another chocolate biscuit on her.

By the time Jess goes, everything's pretty much back to normal. Lowri has hidden the bin bags in the garage, where Wren won't see them, and loaded those for the charity shop into the boot of her car. She's washed her face and put on a little make-up so that scary, crying mummy will be nowhere to be seen when she picks up Wren from school.

So, all in all, the day has been a success, and the evening is peaceful and happy enough too as Lowri listens to Wren's cheerful chatter about her day. She ignores a message from her sister and then switches off her phone for good measure so she can lie and say she hadn't realised it was out of battery. But, when it comes to it, and Wren is tucked up in bed, Lowri finds she can't ignore the letter about the land. She'd stuck it behind a packet of PG Tips in the kitchen cupboard and the end of it is poking out, taunting her as she reaches for a teabag for one last cuppa before bed. So she takes it down and reads it one more time. And, half an hour later, Lowri is still holding it, staring into space with a million possibilities whirling through her head.

It's just another 'what if' to add to those she's already collected. *What if* Alun hadn't been late for his meeting, would that have made a difference? *What if* he'd taken his car instead of hers because his was in the garage? *What if* the driver who hit him hadn't been distracted by a stupid sign at the side of the road? *What if, what if, what if...*

2

It takes Lowri two days, six messages and four missed calls from Jess before she finally rings the firm of solicitors about Alun's inheritance. It's ten past nine on Wednesday morning and in two days she will be moving to Drover's Cottage. She's got a heap of packing still to do, and a hundred and one other things to take care of, and she's not going to get any of it done moping around, staring at her phone as if it might detonate at any minute. *Just ring the solicitor, Lowri, how hard can it be?* The green eyes that return her look in the bathroom mirror are dull, much like her complexion, and her blonde hair is overdue for a wash. It's ridiculous; she has no time to fall apart, again, and over something which might turn out to be inconsequential.

She makes the call sitting on her bed, drawing comfort from the new quilt she treated herself to. She bought one for Wren as well. She can't afford it, but they will both need something nice to distract them from the dirty mustard paint on the walls of their new bedrooms. It might be a while before Lowri can get around to repainting them. She's going to need to start working again for one thing. Being freelance is great, it's given her the flexibility she's needed the last couple of years, but the small amount of money left from the sale of the house won't tide her over for long. She'll need to pick up her projects again as soon as she's settled.

Lowri should have known the phone call wouldn't be simple – that after an explanation from her, the response wouldn't be as you were, nothing to report, no change, forget you ever found the letter. The solicitor who dealt with the matter originally has since retired and so Lowri must wait a little longer for a resolution. It's not a problem, she's assured, someone will call her back, but both partners are with clients when she calls, and the receptionist, although apologetic, can't tell her when that will be. Lowri has no other choice than to go back downstairs and continue packing.

She's halfway through a cheese and pickle sandwich by the time one of the partners calls her back. He sounds a little bemused, and oddly embarrassed. Not by the mention of her dead husband, though she might conceivably burst into tears at any minute, but by the length of time that has gone by since the original bequest was made. A period of time during which 'things' should have been followed up, but weren't. When Lowri asks what that means, she's told it's a little difficult.

'Difficult how?' she asks, swallowing. She's feeling strangely as if she might have won the lottery but lost the ticket.

'The notes on file show that your husband made contact with us, indeed he was made fully aware of the details of his uncle's bequest, but for some reason a stewardship arrangement was put into place, one that seems to continue to this day.'

'A stewardship? What does that mean?'

'Your husband didn't wish to take physical ownership of the property, or be responsible for it, so he asked for a custodian to take care of it in his absence. That's not necessarily unusual, I've dealt with similar cases in the past, but it usually happens when there's some obvious reason for it, when the beneficiary is a child, for example, or resident in another country. That clearly wasn't the case here.'

Lowri thinks fast. 'No... So let me get this straight. There *is* a property involved, but it's being looked after by someone else, is that what you're saying?'

There's an awkward pause. 'Yes, but it's perhaps not quite so straightforward as it sounds. Would you be able to pay us a visit, Mrs Morgan? I think it might be better to explain in person. I have some space in my diary this afternoon,' he prompts, 'if that would suit?'

Lowri eyes the clock on the kitchen wall. 'I'm about an hour and a half away from you,' she replies. 'And I have a daughter at school, I'm not sure...' She begins the calculations in her head but it's half past twelve, there isn't a way she can do this that doesn't involve Jess.

'I understand,' soothes the solicitor. 'But it's in everyone's best interests to get this matter resolved as soon as possible.'

Lowri's desperate for this not to take up any more of her time. She'd had a feeling she'd be opening a can of worms. 'I might be able to ring a friend,' she suggests. 'If she can collect my daughter from school, I could be with you around... half past two?'

'Shall we say two forty-five? To give you a little extra wriggle room. Are you familiar with St Merrion, Mrs Morgan? Our office is just off the market square, we're easy enough to find, and there's a public car park just opposite.'

'I'm sure I'll be fine. Thank you.' She hangs up, blowing out her cheeks. What on earth is she getting herself into?

Jess readily agrees to pick up Wren, just as Lowri knew she would. She's even more desperate than Lowri to find out the details of the inheritance. So Lowri scurries around the house, tutting at the piles of boxes that litter every room. She should be sorting this lot out, not heading off on some wild goose chase. Twenty minutes later, however, she's entered the postcode for the solicitors' office into Google Maps and is reversing slowly out of the drive.

Lowri has lived in Pembrokeshire nearly her whole life, the little idyll in south-west Wales pretty much all she's ever known, but she's never been to St Merrion before. It's on the opposite side of the county from home, virtually on its southern tip, but is also quite close to Barafundle and everyone's been there. Lowri thinks it's possibly one of the most beautiful beaches there is, anywhere; living nearby could be really lovely. She focuses on the road ahead, navigating along the rows of parked cars. *Don't get ahead of yourself, Lowri,* she thinks.

Despite Jess's protestations of earlier in the week, the spring weather has been very kind, and April has seen more than its fair share of warmer days. Early mornings might still have a sharp nip to them, but once the sun's out, like today, the temperature begins to climb.

Lowri turns on her music and begins to relax into the drive. The traffic is quiet midweek and she makes good time, turning onto the road which leads to St Merrion much earlier than she needs to. She's greeted by a line of ice-cream-coloured houses as she enters the town, each a different flavour from its neighbour. They're typical of Pembrokeshire buildings, but her spirits never fail to lift at the sight of them, and she drives on, trying to ignore the first real burble of nerves she's experienced since leaving home. The solicitor could simply be being careful over a matter he thinks they haven't handled particularly well, but why would he ask her to come all this way over a piece of scrubby land and a dilapidated shack? The more Lowri thinks about it, the less it makes any sense. Alun wouldn't have lied to her about the bequest from his uncle, but there's something here which doesn't add up, and the thought of what that might be leaves her prickling with anxiety.

Taking a deep breath, Lowri pulls into the car park across from the solicitors' office. The building is painted a rather regal shade of purple, not everyone's first choice of colour, but at least it's conspicuous. Lowri wants this meeting over with. Whatever it's going to reveal, she's days away from moving house, she doesn't want any more hassle.

The receptionist has obviously been told to expect her and is out of her chair before Lowri is even fully through the door, ushering her to a waiting area which is – thankfully – not purple, but a restful shade of green.

'I'm quite a bit early,' says Lowri. 'Sorry. The roads were much quieter than I thought.'

'Mr Armstrong mentioned you'd be coming from a little way away,' the receptionist replies, smiling warmly. 'But it's no bother, I can get you a cup of tea while you wait, or coffee if you prefer?'

'Tea would be lovely, thank you,' Lowri replies. 'Just milk, please.' She adjusts her jacket and settles back into the squishy seat, looking around her. There's very little information about the company to be gleaned, just a series of tasteful watercolours to look at and a vase of pale-pink bunny tails on a table in the corner.

Lowri is checking her emails when the receptionist reappears. 'I'll take you through now,' she says. 'No point keeping you waiting, is there?' She smiles again, pausing until Lowri gets to her feet, before turning in the other direction to lead her down a long corridor and up a flight of stairs. 'It's just in here.' She gives a door on her left a perfunctory knock before pushing it open. 'I'll get that tea now.'

The man behind the mahogany desk is tall and good-looking in a rather patrician kind of way, but his smile is warm and his face friendly.

'Mrs Morgan...' he begins. 'Lovely to meet you.' He's around the desk in a jiffy, leading her to a table and an arrangement of chairs by the window. 'Shall we sit here? I always think business is far better conducted with a nice view to look at.'

Why this should make any difference, Lowri isn't sure, but he's right about the view. What she hadn't been able to see from the car park, or any of the roads through the town, is the curve of a beautiful river bending away to the left where it disappears from view amid a line of trees. Several buildings flank its far side, their stones glowing golden in the bright spring sunshine.

'The River Merrion,' says Gavin Armstrong, taking a seat opposite Lowri. 'From where the town gets its name. Lovely, isn't it?'

She nods. 'Beautiful. I've lived in Pembrokeshire most of my life but, strangely, I've never visited this corner. Perhaps I should.'

The solicitor's smile falters for a moment, his gaze flicking to the table. 'So you're not thinking of moving here then?' There's a file on the table, quite a slim volume.

'Should I be?'

He dips his head. 'We're getting ahead of ourselves.' He's about to continue when the door opens again and the receptionist reappears, manoeuvring a tray through the gap with one hand. She does so with ease, it's clearly a move she's perfected. 'Ah, excellent, thank you, Jayne.'

Lowri smiles as tea is placed in front of her, together with a plate of biscuits.

'Oh, and shortbread too. My favourite,' says Mr Armstrong.

Jayne blushes, with a quick look at the solicitor before immediately withdrawing. Lowri has the distinct feeling the biscuits are not a usual accompaniment and wonders why she's getting special treatment. Her stomach churns a little more.

Gavin waits until Lowri has her cup in her hand before clearing his throat. 'I'll get straight to the point, Mrs Morgan. Have you heard of Clearwater? More specifically, Clearwater House?'

'No, but I've a feeling you're about to enlighten me.'

He smiles. 'The name is somewhat misleading given the type of property it is, and of course it's fallen into a rather bad state of repair over the years, but...' He gets to his feet. 'Perhaps it's easier to simply show you.'

He's clearly waiting for Lowri to join him at the window, so she stands up, her teacup rattling alarmingly in the saucer. She smiles nervously, setting it down on the table.

He motions that she should move further to the right, shuffling towards her so that they're both standing at the window's edge, rather awkwardly given the lack of space. 'If you follow the line of the river away to the left, you'll see a row of cottages on the far side, followed by a long stretch of bank and then, some way in the distance a rather tall building. I'm sorry, you have to crane your neck a little.'

Lowri follows the direction of his finger, head cranked to one side, eyes peering into the distance. 'Yes, I can see it.'

'Well, that's Clearwater House.'

She stares at him. 'It's a castle...'

'It's a fortified house, actually, according to the record books. That's not quite the same thing, but I guess it amounts to as much.' He gives her an apologetic look. 'It is rather large, yes.'

'And you're showing that to me because...?'

The solicitor retakes his seat. 'Please, sit down.' He draws the file towards him. 'Clearwater House forms part of the bequest left to your husband, although – sadly – it is mostly now inhabitable. With an appropriate scheme of works, however, it could be returned to its former glory in time. It's a very well-known property around here. Something of a landmark.'

Lowri is still staring. 'It's a castle,' she repeats. 'Are you telling me my husband inherited a castle?'

'Not exactly...'

She wants to laugh. The very idea is preposterous but the

look on Gavin's face tells her he's deadly serious. 'But, I don't understand. I was told it was dilapidated. I imagined a shed or something...'

'Well, dilapidated isn't so far from the truth and, of course, the bequest was made quite a few years ago now. I'm afraid the property hasn't improved with age.' He smiles nervously. 'I'm rather at a loss to explain what might have happened over the last few years. You see, I've only been here for three, and the other partner only two. I think we just assumed Clearwater belonged to Bridie...' He breaks off, frowning. 'That's Bridie Turner, she's... well, the Turner family are well known hereabouts, they own a lot of property locally and, indeed, Bridie has been looking after Clearwater so...'

Lowri's lips purse at his explanation, thoughts beginning to churn in her head. 'So this Bridie person, she's the custodian appointed at my husband's request?'

'Yes, that's right.'

'But you all assumed she owned it?'

'Indeed.'

'Except she doesn't. My husband does... did.'

'That's also correct. But your husband's wishes were very clear, Mrs Morgan.' He riffles through the file. 'I can show you the original letter he wrote. He categorically states that he didn't wish to have, his words, anything to do with any of it. My colleague did urge him to think very carefully about his decision, but it seems your husband's mind was made up. Of course my colleague then retired and the file was effectively closed – only until further instruction was received, naturally,' he adds, with a tight smile.

'And no one's heard from my husband since that time?'

'No. I can assure you if we had, we would have placed any communication in the file and certainly acted upon his wishes, should they have changed in any way. But, once the initial arrangements were made, any contact from your husband would most likely have been with Bridie anyway so...' Gavin is clearly rattled.

She nods, signalling him to continue.

'From what you said on the telephone, however,' he says, 'you are your husband's sole beneficiary, which obviously changes things rather considerably. There will be certain formalities to go through, of course, but if everything is in hand, I don't see any reason why you shouldn't take ownership.'

'I brought a copy of my husband's will with me,' she says, reaching for her handbag. 'And the probate grant. My solicitor dealt with both, I'm sure he won't mind if I pass on his details.'

Gavin takes the offered papers, glancing over them. 'But these are dated nearly two years ago.'

'Yes, I... didn't I say?'

'I'm sorry, Mrs Morgan, I assumed your husband was only recently deceased.'

Perhaps that explains the biscuits, thinks Lowri. Maybe they might not have been so generous if they knew the real story. 'Does that make a difference?'

'A little... it's unusual more than anything, but...' He smiles warmly.

He doesn't want to say it, and Lowri is grateful for his tact, but he's right, this *is* something she should have known about when Alun first died. Clearwater House should have been included as part of his estate and for the life of her, she doesn't know why it wasn't.

He hands back the papers. 'We can get things rolling as soon as you like.'

'That all supposes I want this castle, though, this Clearwater House.'

'It does, but...' He trails off.

'*Should* I want this castle?' At the moment, all Lowri can see is an enormous chain around her neck, one which would also be an enormous drain on her finances. Money she doesn't have. 'I mean, if there's a perfectly good arrangement in place with this local woman, why change things?'

'That's one way to approach the situation, certainly, but I do think you should have a full understanding before reaching any decision.'

He smiles again and Lowri knows he's keen not to let history repeat itself. It's clear he's worried Alun was ill-advised and he doesn't want his partnership tarred with potential accusations like those. Lowri, however, is still thinking about his words.

'Hang on a minute... you said *not exactly* just now. That my husband hadn't *exactly* inherited a castle – fortified house. So what *exactly* did he inherit?'

Gavin's lips are pursed, his rather generous mouth now a thin colourless line. He's eyeing her cup of tea. 'We've got plenty of time,' he says. 'Perhaps you'd like to finish that.'

Procrastination, thinks Lowri. That can't be a good thing.

She picks up the cup, determined that it shouldn't rattle against the saucer. Ever tactful, Gavin looks away so she may manoeuvre her drink without the added pressure of his watchful gaze. It helps, but her hand still shakes as she grips the cup's handle. At least she manages to down it without slurping.

Once finished, Lowri looks up expectantly, ready for whatever he has to say, and is surprised to see him getting to his feet.

'It's really quite a beautiful day. Perhaps it might be better if I take you to visit Clearwater in person, so you can fully appreciate it.'

'Really? Oh...' This isn't going the way Lowri expected at all. Flustered, she stuffs her papers further into her handbag, trying to close it while simultaneously standing up. 'I don't want to put you to any trouble.'

'It's nothing, Mrs Morgan. All in a day's work.'

. . .

It's warm in Gavin's car and the leather upholstery fragrant. It's big and expensive and the road beneath the tyres is smooth, the noise from it just a whisper. If they'd been in Lowri's car, she'd be panicking about the suspension because, after the first few minutes, Gavin turns off the main road, manoeuvring through a gap in a hedge onto something which is definitely more farm track than public highway. There are no signs, no clues at all to where they're going, and Lowri's just wondering whether getting into a car with a man she's only just met is entirely sensible, even if he is a solicitor, when he draws to a halt, pulling up at the end of a field beside a five-bar gate amid a thicket of trees. A bright-orange loop of rope is slung around its topmost post, but if it was ever connected to anything, it certainly isn't now. The corresponding post, which should have held fixings to keep the gate secure, has rotted and split in half, leaving just a weathered stump.

'Right, here we are,' says Gavin, switching off the ignition.

Clutching her bag, Lowri climbs from the car, straining to see what's beyond the trees. 'Is this the way to the house?' she asks.

'To Clearwater, yes. The house itself has no driveway, as such, so it's easier to walk from here and... anyway, it's just through here. It's not far.' Gavin holds open the gate for her, lifting it slightly to stop it catching on the rough ground before following her through, and closing the gate carefully behind him. 'I must say it would be lovely to see work being done on the place. It has quite a history, and restored to its former glory, it would be quite something.'

Lowri nods, but 'work being done on the place' sounds expensive, not something she's in the market for. She's about to reply when they clear the treeline and the view ahead suddenly opens wide.

A sandy track curls away from them, at the end of which are two buildings, their tiled roofs glinting in the sun. They sit low, in a natural dip, to the right of which is an expanse of green and more bushes, but to Lowri's immediate left is another stone building. She takes a step forward, staring across at what doesn't seem possible given what she'd been led to believe. It's a beautiful cottage, only small, but with stone mullioned windows and an oak front door which—

Her thoughts grind to a halt as she realises that Gavin is now standing ahead of her, staring at something behind the cottage, shielding his eyes from the low glare of the sun. Tentatively, she joins him, moving past the angle of the cottage's thick stone walls and... Her mouth drops open. Just beyond the cottage, which she had already been mentally filling with furniture, is a tumble of stones and weeds and stumpy trees growing out of places where trees have no right to grow. Somehow it didn't look as bad from a distance. Or as big. The tower, when seen from the window of the solicitors' office, looked rough around the edges – unmistakeably a tower – but somehow small and manageable too. What she's looking at now is a wreck, a jaw-dropping pile of stones reaching for the sky, which look as if they might fall down at any moment. And attached to them—

'Isn't it beautiful?' says Gavin fondly.

Lowri turns back towards the cottage, which she now realises might be a gatehouse or something similar. She prays it's not just a façade. '*That's* beautiful. *This* is... chaos. Expensive chaos.'

'Admittedly, she's seen better days, but imagine how it would look restored. And the setting is stunning.'

Lowri casts her gaze beyond the pile of stones. 'What even is that?' There's water as far as the eye can see. Thick, dark and unmoving.

'The millpond,' Gavin replies. 'And over there...' He points to the low buildings at the end of the lane. 'The first building you can see is the original watermill, sadly no longer operational, and beyond it the building the textile business uses now.

Not quite as elegant, but functional. There's another cottage behind it, but I don't think that's habitable either, I'm afraid. Still, there's the land, and the wood, a huge swathe of river with fishing rights too, and—'

Lowri holds up a hand. 'Hang on a minute... what land? What mill? This is Clearwater, right?' She turns to indicate the cottage behind her, a cottage she can now see is tacked onto a ruin. 'Where does all the rest of it come into things?'

He smiles. 'This is Clearwater *House*,' he replies. 'That' – he sweeps his arm in front of him – 'is Clearwater. It isn't just a house, Mrs Morgan, it's an estate. It's all of this.' His arm stretches wide in an ever more expansive gesture as Lowri's mouth drops even lower.

In a daze, Lowri takes her phone from her back pocket. 'Jess,' she squeaks as her friend answers. 'Yes, I'm fine, honestly, it's just that...' Lowri stares out across the water in front of her and the range of buildings glowing golden in the afternoon sun. 'I wondered if you wouldn't mind hanging on to Wren for a little while longer after school. I might be back rather later than I'd planned...'

3

Belatedly, Lowri realises that Gavin is staring expectantly at her.

'Sorry, I was...' A helpless gesture is all she can manage.

He nods sympathetically. 'This is a lot to take in, I know. That's why I thought it better for you to see yourself what the bequest actually entailed. I'm not sure your husband ever understood...' He breaks off. 'I'm profusely sorry if he was never given sufficient information about the estate, although that seems unlikely.'

Now she understands the solicitor's earlier awkwardness, and his concerns that no one had been in touch with Alun recently. His inheritance wasn't some dilapidated tin-pot shed, it was a whole flipping estate.

She smiles as reassuringly as she can. 'Believe me, my husband would have checked the detail, he was that kind of man. And right now, even though I can't quite understand it myself, I'm sure he had his reasons for turning his back on all this. There was a lot of bad blood between him and his father, I assume that had something to do with it.'

'It happens,' replies Gavin. 'More often than you'd think.

Big families, fallings out, particularly where land and property are involved.'

She nods. 'Problem is, I don't quite know where this leaves me. I wasn't expecting to hear news like this today and... I don't have the kind of money to maintain an estate like this, let alone begin renovation works.'

'Well, I might be able to help you there. You see, there are several grants available and a property like this, with its history, I'm sure—'

Lowri holds up a hand, feeling suddenly overwhelmed. 'Sorry...'

The sympathetic smile is back in place. 'Mrs Morgan, there's no rush. I understand your concerns perfectly, and the reality is that the present custodial arrangement has been working well for a number of years. There's no reason why that shouldn't continue until you decide what you want to do.' He checks his watch. 'When we arranged our appointment today, I took the liberty of contacting Bridie Turner. Unfortunately, she's away on business or would have gladly come to meet you but, in her absence, she's asked Gordon Chapman to stand in. He oversees the textile operation here. I let him know to expect us on site and also warned him that you might like some time to look around. He's happy to give you a tour if you want, or you can simply wander at will, although I'd advise you to keep away from the ruins, obviously. I shall be in the office until six this evening, and only five minutes away. Give me a call when you've seen enough and I'll pop by and take you back to your car.'

Lowri is tempted to leave with him right now.

'Shall we find Gordon? Then I can leave you in his capable hands. He really does know far more about this place than I do. Is that all right?'

She nods although she's really not up to this. 'Mr

Armstrong, I'm very grateful, but you really didn't need to go to the trouble.'

'As I said before, Mrs Morgan, it's no bother.'

Lowri can see she'll have to go along with this. Gavin must already think she's weird. On being told they've inherited an estate, most people would probably dance with joy, but this is too much for Lowri. It belonged to Alun and for some reason he wanted nothing to do with it. If he'd wanted to share it with her he would have, so being here feels too much like she's going behind his back and she's finding that hard to handle. There's the financial aspect to it as well, never mind the fact that it isn't the kind of place Lowri could ever bring Wren, it's far too dangerous.

She shuts down her thoughts and gives a bright smile. 'Then that sounds perfect.'

Gordon reminds her alarmingly of her dad. Same height, same comb-over hairstyle, even the same gold-rimmed glasses, and is charm itself. He must be equally surprised by her sudden appearance but, if he is, he doesn't show it. He escorts them back outside almost immediately, apologising for the noise inside the low building – 'Once all the machines are running, there's a fair old clatter.'

'What is it you do here?' she asks.

'Textiles,' he replies. 'Tea towels and the like. We focus on traditional Welsh patterns, folks can't get enough of them.'

'And this is run by the estate, is it?'

'It is indeed. Clearwater textiles are what the estate was founded on. Of course, once upon a time, the business would have been centred around the watermill but that ceased operation well before my time. And when it did, the business moved here.' He pulls a handful of keys from his pocket. 'I'm afraid I can't show you around this building as it's a workplace – health and safety and all that – but I'm happy to give you a tour of the rest.' He looks between the two of them. 'Or I can leave the keys with you, whichever you prefer? You might not want an old duffer like me tagging along.'

'Not at all.' Lowri smiles, wondering how to say what she wants tactfully. 'But I think I might prefer to look around on my own, if that's okay? I think I'm still in shock and I could do with catching my breath without wasting your time.'

'Perfectly fine.' Gordon smiles and opens his palm, fishing through the keys. 'You'll work it out, but the blue tag is for the watermill, yellow for the gatehouse cottage, and green for the other cottage round the back, although that's usually left open – not much to lock, I'm afraid.' He eyes Lowri's shoes. 'And watch your step. Pop the keys back to me when you're done and I'll run you back to the office, if you like – save you the bother, Mr Armstrong.'

Gavin looks very pleased. 'Well then, that sounds like a plan. Excellent. And remember, there's no hurry at all, Mrs Morgan. Take your time.'

Lowri looks at the solicitor, who is already backing away. Despite his protestations to the contrary, she's no doubt he's a very busy man and has a pile of work waiting for him. She suddenly longs to be alone and holds out her hand for the keys. 'You're both very kind, thank you.'

With their goodbyes said, Lowri stands for a moment, overcome with indecision. The fact that everything as far as the eye can see now seemingly belongs to her is utterly overwhelming. The afternoon sun might be doing its best to make everything look rosy, but there's no hiding the fact that Clearwater House needs a substantial amount of work. And the castle is only one small part of the estate. The factory building looks tired and in need of attention, one of the cottages is derelict, and even though the other looks lovely from the outside, the inside might be a very different story. Then there's the watermill, the pond,

the river, woodland... none of which have probably seen any
kind of investment over recent years, let alone basic preserva-
tion. And they are also things about which she knows nothing;
she wouldn't even know where to start.

Sighing with frustration, Lowri looks back in the direction
of the castle and the gatehouse cottage which sits in its shadow.
She has no need of a mill, or a house with – by the sounds of
things – no door, but she *could* have need of somewhere to live.
She shakes her head. It's a crazy idea, but now she's agreed to
look around she might as well.

Walking back down the lane, she passes by the dark shadow
of the old mill building first. It's part timber-framed, part brick,
and would once have been quite handsome. Now, though, the
wooden waterwheel is all but gone, claimed by rot and moss,
with green mildew staining the brickwork of the building and
paths. Behind it, and above her, is the millpond she had seen
before and she shivers, its expanse of inky black water removing
any notion of romance from the setting.

Keeping her head averted, Lowri carries on by, happier once
she's out from under the gloomy shadow the mill casts. Ahead
of her is Clearwater House and, now that she's facing it, with
the buildings spread out left to right in front of her, it's much
easier to imagine how the castle and its grounds once would
have looked. The only habitable part, the tiny gatehouse
cottage, sits to her left, while the castle itself, and its once
majestic tower, lie to her right, the stones which once raised
them to the sky reduced to a pile of rubble amid weed-strewn
grass. Encircling the whole area are two huge defensive walls, or
what's left of them at least. Once, they would have kept everything safe within, but just like the castle, the walls lie toppled, in
one or two places only a few stones high, in others, gone
completely.

Avoiding the debris, Lowri makes her way towards the rear
of the gatehouse. It's really quite pretty, pale ochre stone criss-

crossed with thick wooden beams and with twin gables set high in the roof. Of the keys in the bunch, there's only one which could possibly fit the oak door she's walking towards; it's long, slender and made of iron.

To her surprise, the key turns easily and Lowri finds herself in a short, flagged hallway. It's so cold she can almost see her breath. There's another substantial door at the other end of the passage, and she pushes it open tentatively, gaping as it reveals, not just forward space, but upward space as well. She can see clear to the rafters.

Lowri is standing in a galleried living room which is, thankfully, much warmer than the frigid hallway. It's also furnished, which she hadn't expected at all and, as she gazes around at the room's details, she's even more surprised to see a young woman sprawled across a huge sofa in the middle of it. She has a magazine in her lap, a bar of chocolate poised an inch from her mouth, and a pair of headphones jammed over her ears, head nodding to whatever sound is coming from them.

There's a mad scramble of limbs as the woman lurches to her feet, ripping off the headphones as she does so. 'Shit...' Her chest is heaving. 'Sorry, I was...' Her eyes widen. 'Can I help you?'

Lowri dangles the keys at her. 'More to the point, can *I* help *you?*'

'Shit,' the woman says again. 'Did Bridie send you? I'm really sorry, I would never have...' Her arms flap at the various belongings around the room: discarded shoes, a can of Coke, and several items of crockery. 'It's just that she never said I couldn't, and it's not like... You won't tell her, will you?' She makes an ineffectual attempt to straighten some of the mess, but stops when she realises she's making no difference at all to the state of the room. She straightens, her arms hanging limply by her side. 'Please,' she says. 'I'll lose my job.'

Lowri is confused. 'Your job?'

'Yeah, I'm supposed to be the cleaner.' As she speaks, a pile of magazines on the table in front of the sofa slides slowly to the floor. 'Though doing a bit of a shit job, if truth be told.'

As their eyes meet, the young woman raises her brows with such perfect comedic timing that Lowri can't help but snort with laughter.

'Shall we start again?' she says. 'My name's Lowri.'

'Elin,' replies the young woman. She tucks a mixture of pink, purple and blue hair behind one ear. It suits her. 'And I really am sorry, no one told me you were coming. If they had, I'd have got the place a little more shipshape.'

'I didn't know I was coming myself before today,' replies Lowri. 'So, not to worry. And, as I didn't know what I was coming *to*, I really wasn't in a position to let anyone know.'

Elin looks at her, a puzzled expression on her face.

'It's a long story,' Lowri replies, looking around. The room might be a little messy, but it's beautiful. Rich, warm tones from the wood, mellow stone...

'So are you staying here then?' asks Elin. 'Only, no offence or nothing, but Bridie doesn't usually go in for visitors.'

Lowri's ears prick up at the mention of that name again. Doesn't anyone do anything around here without Bridie's say-so?

'It's a little hard to explain, but when my husband died, he—'

Elin looks horrified. 'Oh God...' She stands awkwardly, just like everyone does when Lowri mentions what happened, but then she lurches forward and hugs Lowri like a bear. 'I know we've only just met, but I'm so sorry... are you okay?' She pulls away, her eyes searching Lowri's.

Lowri is so surprised by Elin's actions she doesn't know what to say and, to her embarrassment, feels the tell-tale prickling in her nose that heralds tears. She has friends who've never even asked her that question. 'I'm fine, really... thank you. And it was over two years ago now so...' But the sympathetic look on Elin's face remains unchanged and Lowri manages a smile in return. 'Anyway, he inherited this place a few years before he died and I guess that makes it mine now.'

'No way!' Elin's mouth drops open. 'You own this place? Clearwater?'

'The estate, I gather, yes.'

Elin's face splits wide with a grin. 'This is priceless! Bridie's going to throw an actual fit when she finds out. I'd pay money to see the expression on her face.'

Lowri frowns. 'But she already knows. She would have met me here today but she's busy, so the solicitor handling the inheritance brought me over. A chap called Gordon met us. I think he works for Bridie?'

Elin's expression isn't giving anything away.

'He seems really nice,' Lowri prompts. 'Quite charming, I thought.'

'He's okay,' Elin replies. As Lowri waits in case she has anything further to add, Elin's face brightens. 'Hey, if you're Clearwater's new owner, that means you're my boss now too.'

'Well, I...' Lowri looks around the room. 'I'm not sure I'll actually need a cleaner. Sorry, but I—'

Elin is unperturbed. 'I don't mean here. I mean at the factory. You'll be everyone's boss.'

'The factory?'

'Yes, most likely where you found Gordon, he doesn't stray far. He's what you might call Bridie's... henchman?' Elin grins. 'Only kidding. But if you own the factory now, you could be the boss, couldn't you?'

'I suppose, but...' Lowri shakes her head. 'I'm really not sure if I'm coming to live here yet. Before today I didn't even know this place existed.'

'Oh, you'll love it. I can show you around, if you like.'

'Thank you. But, you know, even if I do move here, it might

be better to leave Bridie and Gordon in charge, for the time being at least,' Lowri adds, seeing Elin's face fall.

'Everyone would be on your side, I know they would. And it's a good little business.' Elin studies her for a moment, as if weighing something up, then sighs. 'I can't lie, it's actually shite. But it could be really good if they changed the things we make instead of the rubbish we do churn out. But *you* could do that. You could make it better.'

Elin looks so desperate, Lowri would love to believe her, but they're getting ahead of themselves.

'Elin, I'm sorry, but I only came for a look around the place.'

Lowri hasn't spoken to anyone but Jess about her current situation, yet something about Elin makes her want to confide. She must be Lowri's age, or a little younger, her fingers loaded with rings, wrists encircled by colourful beads. And, with her vibrant, baggy trousers and crocheted top, 'free spirit' is the description that comes to mind. And Lowri could do with a little of that right now.

'This cottage looks lovely though,' Lowri adds. 'Bit different to the pile of rocks outside.'

'It's gorgeous, I really love it and—' Elin breaks off. 'Sorry, I know it's not mine, but it seems really sad that no one lives here. Houses should be lived in, shouldn't they? Otherwise they get cold... I don't mean heat wise, more like cold in feeling, with no spirits inside to warm them up. That's all that's wrong with this place, so don't go believing any silly stories about it being haunted, it just needs a few bodies about. Shall I show you round now? It's plenty big enough for just you.'

'Oh, but I have daughter. Wren. She's six.'

A warm smile crosses Elin's face. 'What a beautiful name. I bet she was tiny when she was born, just like a little bird.'

Elin's words stop Lowri in her tracks. It's as if Elin has just repeated what Alun always said. 'She was... She was very poorly when she was little, but thankfully she's grown out of it now. Or maybe it's just that she's grown into herself.' Lowri is surprised. She's never thought that before, but it's true, it *is* as if Wren finally realised what she's meant to be. She smiles. 'Now she's quite fearless. And always smiling.'

'Well, don't worry, there'll be room for her too. It would be a lovely place for her to grow up, wouldn't it?'

Lowri is already thinking about that possibility, much to her annoyance. Could they come to live here? Might it work for them?

'I'm already supposed to be moving at the weekend,' she replies. 'Only to a cottage my sister owns, just down the road from her...'

Elin cocks her head to one side. 'Oh, I know that look. You're not sure you want to go, are you?' She nods. 'Family's great, but you don't always want to be in their pocket, do you? Not every minute of the day.'

Lowri has been struggling to admit it, but that's exactly what's been worrying her about this move. She gets on well with her sister, but she likes her privacy too and thinks their relationship works better *because* they don't see each other all that often. She's scared that moving so close will ruin what they have, not improve it.

'Come on then,' says Elin. 'You can't possibly make up your mind unless you've seen the place. It isn't huge – as you might have guessed, it would have been the gatehouse originally, but there are two good bedrooms.' She waves her arms around. 'This is the living room, obviously. And I know what you're thinking, but it isn't cold at all. The walls must be about two foot thick, so once it's warm, it stays warm, and the fire really chucks out the heat. I light it every now and again to keep the placed aired through.'

It isn't lit now, but it's one of the room's most impressive features, the inglenook so big Lowri could almost stand up in it.

'I'll take you upstairs first,' continues Elin, crossing in front of her. 'And you mustn't worry about Wren. I know it looks a long drop down from the landing, but the bottom of the bannister rail is solid, see? So there's no way she could fall through.'

Elin must be reading Lowri's mind. But she's right, the rail which curves around the galleried space has carved oak panels where it abuts the floor. They're beautiful too.

Upstairs, the rooms are cosy and surprisingly light. A third room is little more than a cupboard but then, Lowri supposes, every house needs somewhere to stuff the bits and pieces that don't belong anywhere else. She draws her line of thinking to a rapid close. This is far from being a done deal.

'The bathroom is downstairs,' continues Elin, leading them back down. 'Which is a little odd, but you get used to it, and the kitchen is through here.'

Elin takes Lowri through to a room which is easily two times smaller than her kitchen back home, but with considerably more charm. There's a huge fireplace which now houses an enamel stove, and beneath a stone-silled window, a double butler sink... Lowri swallows and tries to keep calm.

'So, what do you think you'll do?' asks Elin. 'Do you like it?'

'I love it,' Lowri replies. 'But it's not as simple as that. My husband gave me the impression that what he inherited was just a worthless piece of land. So to find all this... There's obviously been some sort of a misunderstanding, but it's come as quite a shock.' She pulls a face. 'I don't know what to think.'

Elin's look is warm. 'Everything happens for a reason,' she says. 'Maybe it simply wasn't the right time before. Maybe you weren't meant to find out about Clearwater until you really needed it. You *and* Wren.'

Lowri stares at her. 'Yes, maybe...'

'And just think, one day your daughter will own it too, how lovely is that?'

Lowri hadn't thought about it until now but, of course, any

decision isn't just about *her* future, but Wren's too. How could she have overlooked the possibilities this place could hold in store for her? 'It *is* a lovely thought,' she replies. 'I mean, Clearwater Castle, how many people can say they own something like that?'

'Clearwater Castle...' says Elin slowly. 'Yeah, I like the sound of that. It's much better.'

'Sorry?'

Elin grins. 'It's always been known as Clearwater House, and I never could figure out why. There can't be many houses that have a tower – *had* a tower.' She looks around the kitchen and nods. 'We should definitely call it a castle from now on.'

'But the castle, this house, they're only a tiny part of the estate,' says Lowri. 'What about the other stuff? The business, the watermill, all of that?'

'One thing at a time,' soothes Elin. 'You don't have to sort out everything all in one day. Just get yourself here, get settled, be happy and then you can sort the rest when you want. It isn't going anywhere.'

Lowri stares at the young woman in front of her. How did she get to be so wise?

The journey home is agony. Every mile seems to take an age to traverse even though the traffic is light and the journey without incident. Lowri's head is so full of things she needs to think about, but she's longing to be back with Wren too, to snuggle her close and breathe her in. And she could do with Jess's sage advice as well.

Aside from Jess, Lowri could number her friends on one hand, and she hasn't seen any of them for a while. She's shut herself away since Alun died, increasingly so, and Elin is the first new person Lowri feels she's connected with in all that time. She knows the road ahead of her might be a very difficult one, but there's a teeny tiny glimmer of hope and she knows it's no longer okay to let its embers grow dark. Instead, she wants to fan the spark until its flames burn bright. Could Elin be right? Is it simply fate which has brought Lowri to Clearwater now? Or is she simply deluding herself?

She waits until Wren is happily splashing about in the bath before confiding her fears to Jess.

'Alun lied to me,' she says. 'Or at least if he didn't outright lie then he withheld something pretty huge from me. He made out what his uncle left him was worthless. It's not without its problems, admittedly, but worthless isn't how I'd describe it. This could have been a real part of our future, Jess. Not just his and mine, but Wren's too, and he just turned his back on it.'

'He didn't get on with that side of the family though, did he?' she counters. 'You know how he felt about his father. Maybe that extended to his father's brother as well. Don't underestimate the power family feuds hold over people. They may seem petty and inconsequential to those outside of them, but on the inside... different story altogether.'

Lowri pauses, thinking. 'Perhaps, but if he really didn't want anything to do with his inheritance he could have taken claim of it and sold it on, not just left it there, ticking over in the hands of a custodian and gently rotting. That just seems... irresponsible.'

Jess nods gently. 'Lowri... you're never going to get answers to your questions, not now. Do you really want to keep beating yourself about the head with them? Or, knowing Alun like you did, just accept that he must have had a strong motive for his actions.'

Lowri sighs. Always the voice of reason. But Lowri has already thought those thoughts; she can't unthink them and shove them out of sight, hoping they'll go away.

Jess is watching her closely. 'What about the time he came

home having booked a holiday to Jamaica without even discussing it with you?'

'Yes, but that was different.'

'Maybe...' She eyes Lowri's expression. 'Yes, of course it was, but the point I'm trying to make is that Alun wasn't perfect. None of us are. There were things he did which drove you mad, and vice versa, but you didn't fixate on them. You knew they were only a part of who Alun was, and loving him meant loving *all* of him, good and bad.'

'So you think I've put him on a pedestal since he died?'

'I didn't say that...' Jess sighs. 'Okay, maybe just a little, but that's natural, everyone would do the same in your shoes. But just because you don't understand why Alun did something, doesn't mean you should think any less of him. I'm sure he had his reasons for keeping quiet about Clearwater and if you ever find out what they were, and disagree with them, then maybe have another conversation with yourself, but in the meantime...' She shrugs.

Lowri knows what she's getting at. Trust, that's what it boils down to. And she did trust Alun, implicitly.

'So what do you think you'll do?' asks Jess softly.

Lowri looks around her living room, a room which hasn't felt like home for a while now. A huge piece of it is missing and she's never going to get it back. She hasn't wanted to admit it, but it *is* time for something new. Something which is just about her, and Wren, something which living in her sister's pocket isn't ever going to give her.

'I'm going to go,' she says, swallowing hard. 'I'm going to make Clearwater Castle home.'

4

The insistent hammering on the door sounds again. 'Huw? You in there?'

Huw closes his eyes, as if to block out the noise. Whoever it is can go right back where they came from.

'I know you're in there,' comes the voice again. 'For God's sake, Huw, it's dark out here, and cold, and I could be plenty of other places instead of balancing on the end of your boat trying not to fall in the river.'

Growling, Huw removes the bottle from his lap, putting it down with exaggerated care on the table in front of him. Jamie had better want something good. He fumbles with the hatch, drawing back the bolt. 'I'm coming, okay? Quit banging on the door.'

'Why? You got a sore head?'

The boat rocks violently as Jamie swings through the opening and jumps down the steps, landing heavily on the floor of the narrowboat. Huw hates it when he does that.

'Jesus, it's cold in here.'

'Is it?' Huw stopped feeling it several hours ago.

Jamie eyes him, glance flicking to the table. 'Not surprising.'

He picks up the bottle and carries it to the sink, upending it. 'This is disgusting,' he murmurs.

'Hey!'

'And I hope that was the last of them,' adds Jamie, watching the liquid flow down the plug hole. 'You need to be sober to hear what I'm about to tell you.'

Huw smiles. 'Not much chance of that.'

Jamie stares at him for a moment and, even in his fuddled state, Huw can see anger flicking around his eyes. 'When are you going to get back out there and start living again, man?'

'When I damn well want to.'

'And when's that going to be? Jesus, mate, I know it's been rough, but you're never gonna find the answer at the bottom of a bottle.'

'It's as good a place to look as any,' replies Huw and hiccups. 'Don't you know by now there *are* no answers?'

Jamie ignores him. 'So do you want to know what I came to tell you or what?'

'I dunno, but it had better be good.'

'Clearwater House, Huw, that good enough for you?'

Huw shrugs. 'What about it?'

'Word has it some woman's arriving, and she's coming to turn the place around.'

'Yeah...? Where have I heard that before?'

Jamie mutters under his breath. 'Okay, looks like I'm going to have to spell it out for you. This could be a chance, Huw. An opportunity for you to do something you've always dreamed of. Ever since I've known you, you've wanted to see that place restored.'

'And what do you want me to do about that, Jamie? You know what happened last time so, like I said, I've heard it all before.'

'That was ages ago!'

'And? I still bust a gut over it. I still got my hopes up, and where did it get me? Nowhere.'

'But what if this is it? The last chance you might have. Are you really going to throw it away because you're *scared*?'

Huw lurches to his feet, eyes flashing in anger. 'That's a low blow, Jamie, even from you. I should bloody well throw you out.'

'Hit a nerve, did I? Good. Maybe now you'll listen.'

Huw swallows, placing a hand on the table to steady himself. 'I don't ever work for the Turners, you know that.'

'Who said anything about the Turners?'

'So who's this woman then?'

Jamie sighs. 'Listen, I shouldn't even be telling you this, you know how my dad hates it when I repeat things he's told me. But this is too good to keep to myself... Seems like the guy who owned Clearwater before is dead. This woman is his widow, apparently.'

'She'll probably be just the same as him.'

'Well, she's moving into the gatehouse at the end of the week so I don't see how. At least she'll *be* here. And, like I said, if she's looking to restore Clearwater, you need to get your arse round there before she gives the job to someone else.'

'Maybe she already has. Or most likely got someone lined up. What chance do I have?'

'Absolutely none if you carry on the way you are.' Jamie pauses a moment and Huw can feel the weight of his gaze. 'You know, being your best mate is a really shit job sometimes. I don't know why I bother.'

Huw can hear the disgust in his voice. Jamie's been his best mate since they were seven and he's been there for him, through it all. He's still here. Huw pushes him too far, he knows that. He feels his way back to the seat and sinks onto its cushions, closing his eyes. Jamie is still watching him, though, he can feel it.

'Right. Let's get some coffee on,' says Jamie. 'That's if you've got any.'

'You don't have to do this,' says Huw, eyes still closed. 'There's not many who would.'

'Jesus, don't go getting maudlin on me now. I know you're sorry, Huw, you've told me umpteen times how sorry you are. How about staying off the booze for a bit instead of apologising? Then maybe things might improve.'

Huw cranks open his eyes.

'The Huw of old would have given his eye teeth for an opportunity like this. Don't pass it up and then use it as an excuse to feel sorry for yourself all over again – actually do something about it this time. Because if you don't, I swear I won't bother you again.'

Huw holds up a hand, grimacing. 'Okay... okay, I get it.'

He takes a deep breath as Jamie's ferocious stare bores into him for a few more seconds before returning his attention to the drinks he's making. Jamie picks a couple of mugs off the drainer and peers at them suspiciously.

'Here,' he says after a few minutes, time during which Huw has tried to get his head a little clearer.

He clears his throat as he takes the mug of coffee. Clearwater House. Right. Focus... 'What have you heard?'

Jamie settles himself on the bench seat opposite. 'Only what I've told you. I don't know the details, but the point is that she's moving in in two days' time. I don't know what her plans are, but if she wants to restore Clearwater, she's gonna need someone to help her. She's going to need you. There's no one round here better qualified to do it.'

Once upon a time, restoring Clearwater was all Huw ever dreamed about. He thought he'd get the chance one day, and if it wasn't Clearwater then some place like it. So he worked shitty job after shitty job, trying to get some money saved, trying to learn as much as he could. He built up his skills, bit by bit, worked on bigger and bigger jobs, got a reputation for himself, a good one... Now it's all he can do to get out of bed in the morning.

'Mate, I haven't done anything like that in a long while, you know that.'

'And you think you'll have forgotten? Huw, all you need to do is clear the fog of booze from your brain and it'll all come flooding back. It's what you're good at.'

'Maybe...' Huw scratches his head.

'At least try.'

'But what about folks, and what they'll say?'

'That's a risk you were always going to have to take. Holing yourself up here hasn't stopped folks talking about you. In fact, it's made it worse. I reckon once you start showing your face again, you'll be yesterday's news before you know it. Besides, this woman's an incomer, she won't know all the town gossip, will she? Get in first and you'll be fine.'

Huw thinks for a moment. 'So what's going to happen to Bridie? And the factory?'

'Well, if this woman's got any sense she'll send her packing.'

'People like Bridie don't get sent packing, they dig their heels in, claws too.'

'Not your business, mate. Listen, there's no reason why any of that has to concern you. You won't be working for Bridie, will you? Don't get drawn into it and you'll have no problems. Simple.'

There's a faint but growing flicker of something deep inside Huw. Something he vaguely recognises, something he used to like.

'Come on...' urges Jamie. 'I can see it in your eyes. You know you want to. It's Clearwater House, fully restored and with your name on the foundation stone. This is the thing you've talked about ever since we were kids.'

'I know, it's just...'

'Scary as hell. I do know that. But if ever there was something to make you feel like living again, Huw, this is it. You need this, you know you do.'

Huw nods, taking a deep swallow of coffee. 'So what do you reckon I ought to do?'

'Sober up, scrub up, and then get yourself round there at the weekend – maybe give her a bit of time to get sorted, and then introduce yourself. But do it gently. Don't go all barging in, just be like how lovely it is to see someone new living there. How you've always loved the place, and wouldn't it be amazing to see it restored to its former glory? Then, when she agrees, you can offer her your card – I assume you've still got some? Offer to pop back and have a chat about what needs to be done.'

'I could find out about the grants and—' Huw breaks off, surprised at the surge of a feeling he's not felt in a long while.

'There you go, you've got it.'

Huw takes another swig of coffee, staring around him at the mess inside the boat. It probably doesn't smell all that sweet either. 'Jamie, I—'

But Jamie holds up his mug, clinking it against Huw's. 'No problem, mate. What are friends for?'

5

Susan isn't exactly overjoyed at the news of Lowri's change of heart when she calls her the next day. Lowri is in the middle of a rather difficult conversation with her, which isn't helped by the fact that Susan's husband, Gary, sounds as if he's putting up shelves. Lowri holds the phone away from her ear as another mechanical screech reaches it.

'I know it's short notice,' she says, 'but I couldn't physically have given you any more, Suse, I'm as surprised as you are.'

'*And* I've spent all day cleaning the place up for you.'

'Again, I'm sorry. But look on the bright side – at least you'll be able to get another tenant in the cottage now, someone who'll actually be paying you rent.'

'Yes, but we won't though, will we? Not without getting a whole heap of work done.'

Lowri's sure Susan doesn't mean it the way it sounds, but she can't help but wonder whether her sister is more concerned about the loss of some free labour than Lowri's well-being.

'Which will be more than worth it,' she comments, trying to keep the irritation from showing in her voice. 'Besides, whoever you get in will probably do a much better job than I would have.'

'There is that, I suppose.'

Thanks a million, Sis, thinks Lowri, closing her eyes wearily. 'And it isn't as if I haven't given it a huge amount of thought,' she adds. 'Well, as much as I could in the short space of time I've known about Clearwater. I'm still incredibly grateful for your offer of the cottage, you know that, but it's time for a fresh start, and I think to do that properly I need to stand on my own two feet.'

'Which is the other thing,' Susan replies. 'That all sounds wonderfully philosophical, but you don't know a thing about this place. Will you really be able to cope taking on all that? You haven't exactly been managing all that well as it is.'

Susan's cross. She doesn't mean that. And Lowri *has* been coping. She's been looking after Wren. And working. And cooking and cleaning and doing all the other things that being an adult entails. Susan should try doing those things when one half of your life has crumbled into dust without any warning.

With a superlative application of willpower, Lowri manages to bite her tongue. 'But I'm not taking anything on at the moment, Suse, I'm just moving to the gatehouse cottage. I can worry about the rest of the estate at a later date. Besides...' She hates herself but she's going for the pity card. 'Don't you find it odd that I find out about this just when Wren and I have need of somewhere to live? People say things happen for a reason, at a time when you need them most. Maybe this is Alun's way of looking after us. This inheritance is part of Wren's future too.'

Susan snorts. 'What I find odd is that Alun knew about his inheritance for the best part of two years and never spoke to you about it.'

Lowri sighs. There's no way she's going to win this one. 'There is that, Suse, thanks for mentioning it. I might be deluded but there it is and— listen, sorry, I've got to go, there's someone at the door. I think it's a delivery I've been waiting for. I'll speak to you soon, love you.' Lowri hangs up and takes a very deep, cleansing breath.

The removal company wasn't very happy about the change of plan either, but grudgingly agreed to move Lowri to a different address after she pointed out it was actually closer than the original one. So, now, two days after her visit to Clearwater, three very chirpy men have piled all Lowri's worldly goods into their van and she's left standing in the shell of what was once her home.

It was the first house she and Alun bought together, the one in which they made all their hopes and dreams, the one in which they made Wren. Lowri would like to take one last look around, to make sure she has all her memories with her, but she can sense the removal men are keen to get going. Perhaps it's for the best, she never did like goodbyes. As she closes the front door for the last time, Lowri reminds herself that even though those memories may have changed a little, they'll never be gone, no matter where she is. She holds them in her heart and always will.

Wren is waiting for Lowri on the path, her toy penguin tucked under her arm. This is hard for her too. Lowri smiles brightly to cover the ache inside. 'All right, sweetheart?'

Wren nods and picks up her rucksack from the ground. 'When will we have lunch?' she asks. 'Will we have to wait until we get there?'

'I've made us some sandwiches,' replies Lowri, nodding. 'Because I expect we'll be very busy and I might not be able to find the food. Or the plates,' she adds, pulling a funny face.

'We can have a carpet picnic,' replies Wren, a note of hope in her voice.

'What a brilliant idea. Come on, give Mum a big squish and then let's get going.'

'To the castle!' Wren laughs, throwing her arms around her.

Lowri hugs her close, loving how her daughter always finds the positive in everything. How when told she would still be moving to a new school just not the one she thought she would be moving to, Wren simply shrugged and whispered that the teacher smelled funny anyway so maybe this other new school would be better. Miss Ward's perfume was rather overpowering, it's true.

It doesn't hit Lowri until about halfway into their journey. The fact that she's turning aside the offer of a safety net and the chance to be close to her family, and instead striking out alone in a place she knows nothing about. And all on what is essentially a whim.

The last few days had been so busy, Lowri scarcely had time to draw breath, let alone dwell on what she was about to do. The sheer number of things which had to be put into place since she visited Clearwater have occupied nearly all her time. A change of school for Wren, cancelling services she'd already set up and moving them to a different address: electricity, water, phone, broadband, the list seemed endless. Now though, as she drives along roads which are becoming increasingly unfamiliar, she suddenly realises that not only has organising all these things made her feel in control, they've also provided a constant source of distraction. It's probably what her subconscious planned all along. She's forty minutes from their new home and a brand new life. It's frankly terrifying.

It's not helped by the fact that since Lowri's conversation with her sister yesterday there's been complete radio silence. She gets that Susan's miffed, but she had thought today might warrant a 'hope everything goes okay' kind of text message at the very least. Maybe Suse will contact her later, but Lowri can't help wondering whether she's crossed a line in their relationship, one she'll never be able to jump back over. The trouble is that Lowri has been forced to choose between Susan's very generous, but slightly claustrophobic offer, and a lifeline that seems to have been thrown to her by Alun. In hindsight, there was never a choice and Lowri hopes one day Suse might understand that.

Wren's chatter, which started off full of excitement, has become more and more intermittent the further they journey, and ceases altogether for the last ten miles or so. Her head is also angled permanently to the window so she can scan the road for clues to her new home, but it means Lowri can't see her face.

'Not far now,' Lowri says, navigating the final turning. 'Keep looking out for the castle's tower, you should be able to see it in a minute.'

Lowri is driving to the estate from a slightly different direction today, one which means she won't have to arrive via the broken-down gateway which served as her first introduction to the place. Instead, she can cross the threshold on the proper estate road, such as it is. It's still a track, but at least she can drive along it. As she bumps her way over the rutted ground, round one bend, and then another, past tree after tree after tree, it occurs to her that the woodland she can see in every direction belongs to her. It's a humbling, and rather terrifying thought. After a few moments, she reaches the tumbledown cottage, recognition kicking in for the first time since turning off the main road. Next comes the factory building with its collection of workers' cars outside, then the watermill, and, finally, Clearwater Castle.

The van has already arrived and as Lowri pulls up alongside, Wren's head whips around.

'Who's that?' she asks. 'There's someone waving at us.'

Lowri's heart lifts. It's Elin, bless her, a one-woman welcome party. And if ever there was the perfect person to distract Wren from any anxieties, it's Elin, already rushing over to greet them.

'Hello, hello!' she calls, as Lowri climbs from the car. She grins at Wren and then thrusts a picnic basket in Lowri's arms. 'It's so lovely to have you both here. Sorry, I can't stay long, I'm supposed to be at work, but when I saw the van go by I pretended I was popping out to the loo. I've put together a few things I thought you might need and I've left my phone number too, so if you need anything else you must ring me, okay?' To Lowri's surprise, Elin throws her arms around her and then, with a broad smile at Wren, rushes off, before turning and waving one last time.

'Who's that?' repeats Wren.

'She works here,' Lowri replies. 'She's the lady I told you about, the one who met me when I came to look around. Her name's Elin.'

Wren nods. 'I like her hair.'

Lowri likes Elin's hair too, but she's keen to head off any potential requests that Wren dye hers to match. She's at that age where she's beginning to take an interest in her appearance, and although Lowri is all for freedom of expression, she's not sure Wren's new school will take the same view.

'Tell you what,' Lowri says, handing Wren the basket. 'Why don't you have a peek at what's in there while I get our bag from the boot? Then we can go inside.' Wren has her head inside the flap before Lowri has even finished her sentence.

'Hey, pickled onion Monster Munch!' Wren exclaims, grinning. 'Can I have some, Mum, please? Just today, I'm starving. There's Coke too and chocolate chip cookies.'

Lowri steers her daughter around the back of the house, smiling at Elin's thoughtful choices. She'll be Wren's friend for life if she keeps that up. And pickled onion Monster Munch – Lowri has to stop herself from drooling.

'Oh...' says Wren, face falling as she catches sight of what lies beyond the cottage. 'Is that the castle?'

'Kind of,' Lowri replies. 'It's not really a castle like the ones you know, more like a big house with a tower. At least it was. Remember how I said it had mostly fallen down.'

Wren nods, wrinkling her nose. 'I still thought we were going to live in a bit of it.'

'We are,' Lowri replies, turning to face the ruins. 'See those piles of stones, they're what remains of a huge wall which would have formed a circle around the house and tower, keeping everyone safe inside. They would have joined up with our cottage too so that no one could get into the castle grounds without coming through our gatehouse first.'

'So we're the keepers of the castle?'

Lowri nods, smiling. 'We are.'

'Wow.' Wren turns, about to run into the house.

'Not so fast,' Lowri says, catching Wren's arm gently. 'Because this isn't like our old house, where you could just go in the garden whenever you wanted. There are a few rules.'

'Is there even a garden here?'

Lowri winces. 'Not right now, sweetheart, no. But there will be, as soon as I can sort things.' Her head is yelling not to make promises she can't keep, but Lowri so wants her daughter to be happy here. She's uprooted Wren from her friends, from the only memories she has of her dad, it's the least she deserves. 'Until then, though, you have to remember that our gatehouse has been repaired, so it's safe, but the rest of it is very, very old and all it wants to do is keep falling down. So you don't go there, okay? Not ever, and I won't be going there either.'

Wren looks up and down the space, chewing her cheek. 'So can I go to where our car is parked?'

'Yes, this little bit at the side is fine, and maybe up to that post there, but no further, okay?'

She nods. 'It's not a very big place to play.'

'No, but there are lots of other great places nearby, so we'll have to make sure we visit those instead.' She makes a mental note to ask Elin for some suggestions as soon as possible. 'And there's plenty of space to play in your bedroom. Shall we have a look?'

They have to make way for one of the removal men, but once inside, Wren gives a little hop of excitement. 'This is so big!' she says, staring up at the ceiling.

Lowri must not let the bannister worry her, must not let the bannister worry her... She thinks it might become her new mantra.

Thankfully, Wren takes a firm grip of the handrail before starting up the steps. 'Which bedroom is mine?'

This is something Lowri hopes the new house will score with at least. Wren's new room is twice as big as her old one.

To give Elin her due, there's not a sign that she'd ever been living here, and the place is spotless. A fire has been laid in the grate and when Lowri opens the fridge to add the sausage rolls she found in the bottom of Elin's basket, it's already half full: milk, butter, eggs, tomatoes, bacon, sausages and a pot of jam. A closer inspection of the kitchen cupboards also reveals a packet of chocolate biscuits, a loaf of bread and a tin with a slab of ginger cake inside. Lowri is pretty sure she and Elin are going to become very good friends. She's incredibly grateful to her, not only for her generosity and thoughtfulness but because to Lowri right now, she feels like a lantern in the dark.

It takes the removal men an astonishingly short amount of time to unpack the van, and after a bit of rearranging, Lowri has things pretty much where she wants them. She isn't too worried about the rest of the house, but she promised herself she'd get Wren's room looking cosy and comfortable today if it killed her. Fortunately, Wren is still excited enough to want to help, and pulls things from boxes, exclaiming over their contents as if she'd never seen them before. A couple of hours later, Lowri is settling Wren's two favourite teddies on her bed when a sing-song voice calls up the stairs.

'Anyone at home?'

It seems odd to hear it called that and Lowri guesses it will take a while before it truly feels as if this is their home, but she crosses onto the landing to greet their visitor. 'Hallo,' she calls. 'Sorry, I'll come down.'

Standing in the room below is a smiley-faced woman looking up at her. 'Ah, lovely, you're here,' she says. 'It's so good to finally meet you, Mrs Morgan, I've heard so much about you.'

Lowri takes the stairs two at a time, fairly certain she knows who this is; there can't be many people who know of their arrival.

'Welcome to Clearwater, Mrs Morgan.' The woman's hands are clasped in front of her as if she's excited, a broad smile on her face. She's probably the same age as Lowri's mum, and looks very elegant in a navy trouser suit. She also has on what Lowri's mum would call her 'full face', and has expertly styled, wavy brown hair. Lowri feels a little underdressed in her jeans and tee shirt, without so much as a lick of mascara.

'Thank you...' Lowri reaches out her hand as she crosses the room. 'But call me Lowri, please. You must be—'

'Bridie? Yes indeed. Bridie Turner.' She sweeps her gaze around the room. 'You'll have this place looking like home in no time, I'm sure. Is everything all right?'

Lowri isn't sure whether she means generally or with the house. 'Yes, wonderful. I—'

'And clean?'

'Yes, perfectly—'

'Excellent. And, as your solicitor requested, we made arrangements for the house contents to be moved into storage before your arrival, but you can get to those once you've had a chance to settle in. They all belong to you now, of course.' A sheepish look crosses her face. 'Now, before I say anything else,

I must apologise for walking straight in on you. What must you think of me? But the front door was unlocked and the gatehouse has no doorbell – something you might want to remedy now you're here – the door is so thick, knocking on it hardly makes a noise.'

'Oh... I hadn't thought.' And Lowri realises she must think. This isn't like her old house, with a door which locked behind them automatically, here she must turn the key to keep them safe inside. And buy a doorbell. Lowri adds it to the running list she has in her head of things they will need.

'I must also apologise for not being here on the day you first arrived,' continues Bridie. 'But business had already called by the time I heard you were coming, I'm afraid, and I was several hours away.'

'Honestly, it's fine, and everyone... Gordon looked after me perfectly well.' Lowri decides it's better to keep her meeting with Elin to herself. She'd hate to get her into trouble.

'Even so, I'm sorry. After all this time, it should have been the least I could do.'

'It must seem rather strange, me turning up out of the blue like this.' Stupidly, Lowri hadn't really given any thought to how Bridie and Gordon must be feeling about her arrival.

'It surprised us a little, yes, but only because we hadn't heard of your husband's passing. I'm so sorry. But Clearwater belongs to you now, Lowri, and if you want to be here, then you've every right to be. And you're very welcome, of course.'

Lowri is wondering what to say. Bridie is being so gracious, it seems only fair that she should make clear her intentions from the beginning and put Bridie's mind at ease. 'Thank you,' she says. 'And for everything you've done here too, you and everyone else who has been looking after Clearwater. I'm sorry, I don't really know who else... There's a lot I don't know.'

Bridie waves a dismissive hand.

'And I probably ought to say,' continues Lowri, 'that I

haven't come here to barge in and take over the reins – far from it, actually.' She smiles. 'The thought terrifies me.'

'But that's only because it's all so new and unfamiliar. Don't worry, you'll pick things up in no time, and if you want to leave everything as it stands for the time being, then that's fine as well. The estate is ticking along very nicely at the moment and I'd be delighted to carry on as custodian if you want the present arrangement to continue. Have a good think – get settled first, there's no rush – and when you're ready we can have a chat and I can tell you everything there is to know about Clearwater. Then you can decide how much or how little you want to become involved. How does that sound?'

Relief floods through Lowri. Bridie has every reason to be anxious about her arrival, even rather angry at her apparent upsetting of the proverbial apple cart but, thankfully, that doesn't seem to be the case at all. And it's bought Lowri some time. When she's ready, she can show polite interest in the estate and then leave the running of it to Bridie. It couldn't be simpler. Except...

'Sorry, there is just one thing I must ask you, Bridie, if that's okay? Only it's been playing on my mind ever since my first visit.' It hadn't occurred to Lowri until the day after she got home that having someone caretake the estate on Alun's behalf would incur costs, and she had a very sleepless night when it did. Fortunately, Gavin Armstrong was quick to respond to her questions so at least she understands the situation a little better. Even so...

She clears her throat. 'I'm guessing you're aware of the reasons why the stewardship of the estate came about in the first place, but I was wondering what impact that has here? On the business?' She isn't explaining herself very well, but it seems rather tactless to talk about money under the circumstances. Lowri is hoping that Bridie will come to her rescue.

'Ah, I see what you mean,' Bridie replies with a warm smile.

'Yes, it could be a little awkward, couldn't it, if I suddenly whipped out a very large bill for you to pay? But, you really mustn't worry, we're pretty self-sufficient here. The terms of the custodial duties were all agreed right at the beginning, and it's true, the cost *is* borne by the business, but not to its detriment. Thankfully, that's stayed the case so we've never had to alter the arrangement, but we'll put it on the list of things to discuss. Then you'll know exactly where you are with everything. Is that okay?'

'Oh, more than. Thank you.' Lowri is quick to respond and very happy to have one less thing to think about.

'Good. Well, shall I leave you to get on? I'm sure you must have lots to do without me getting in your way.' She pauses, tutting. 'I almost forgot... I have a little something for you in the car, I'll just pop and get it.'

The huge arrangement of flowers which Bridie returns with almost fills the doorway. 'These are just a little something to welcome you in.' She has to turn sideways to see her way into the room. 'Shall I put them on the coffee table? I wasn't sure if you would have any vases handy, so they're in a basket, I hope that's okay?'

'They're beautiful.' Lowri doesn't think she's ever seen such a grand arrangement. Admittedly, Alun wasn't a huge giver of flowers, but... 'I don't know what to say, except that you shouldn't have, but thank you so much.'

'It's my pleasure, Lowri. I hope you'll be very happy here.'

It's late by the time Lowri gets to bed, but a feeling of satisfied accomplishment has crept over her, despite her tiredness. Her furniture looks good here, different to how it looked in her old house, but good all the same, and in time she's sure it *will* begin to feel like home. Some of the boxes are unpacked, she has plates in her cupboard and clothes in her wardrobe, and that's enough to be going on with. She nestles her head deeper into her pillow and, pulling the covers up around her, gives a small smile.

The next thing Lowri knows, Wren's warm body is curled in next to hers, tucked under her arm.

'You okay, sweetheart?' she whispers. 'Couldn't you sleep?'

Wren snuggles closer. 'A bit... But then I woke up and it was strange. I didn't like it.'

'It's weird, isn't it?' Lowri replies. 'Being in a new place where everything feels topsy-turvy. But we'll soon get used to it.'

Wren is quiet for a moment and Lowri wonders if she's thinking about her dad, about the fact he's not here with them. 'Everything *is* going to be okay, isn't it?' she asks.

Lowri pulls her tighter, nuzzling her face against her hair. 'Everything is going to be wonderful. I promise.'

6

———

Elin arrives as promised at 11 a.m. the next day. So far, Wren and Lowri have had a lazy morning reading in bed, despite the number of things there are to do, but now that Elin has come to give them a grand tour of the estate, the boxes can wait. Wren starts her new school the day after tomorrow and Lowri doesn't want the next two days filled with nothing but chores and unpacking.

If Wren is worried about this new event in her life, though, she gives no sign of it, catching Elin's hand as she soon as she arrives. 'Would you like to look at my new bedroom?' she says, pulling Elin towards the stairs.

Elin exchanges a look with Lowri over the top of Wren's head. 'Ooh, yes, please.'

Lowri follows them up, smiling at her daughter's excited chatter. She had a feeling Wren would see Elin as a friend, but then again, Wren usually makes friends with everyone.

'Hey,' exclaims Elin, moments later. 'Look at this beautiful room! Is this all yours, Wren?'

She nods shyly. 'Do you like it?'

'I love it,' replies Elin. 'It's way better than my room at

home. And this is so pretty.' She runs her hand along the smooth surface of Wren's new duvet cover.

Wren's face lights up. 'Mum let me pick it myself.'

'Did she? Well, you did a fabulous job.' Elin looks around the room again. 'How's the rest of the house coming along?'

'Pretty much the same as the living room,' Lowri replies, pulling a face. 'Much more work required, but we'll get there.'

'And did you enjoy your picnic yesterday?' asks Elin, smiling down at Wren.

'Oh, yes,' she replies. 'It was the best.'

Elin grins. 'Pickled onion Monster Munch are the business, aren't they?'

Back downstairs, Lowri gathers her keys and jacket. 'Grab your coat, Wren, it's not that warm today.'

Yesterday's sunshine has disappeared behind banks of grey clouds and once they're outside, Lowri realises it's also quite misty in places. She pulls her coat around her. 'Do you get a lot of fog here from the river?'

Elin lifts her face to the sky. 'Not that often, but it's beautiful, isn't it? I love days like this. So still, sound muffled, the air so thick you could draw in it.'

Lowri gives her a wayward glance. 'If you say so.'

'No, honestly, it's lovely. You should see it at the beginning of autumn when the days start to get a bit of bite about them, first thing. The mist hangs low in the fields, with that wonderful slanting sunlight you only get at that time of year and—' She breaks off, grinning. 'You will get to see it now, won't you? I forgot. Spring and summer first though. That's beautiful too. You get heat hazes on the river then and the air vibrates with this incredible energy.'

Lowri is intrigued by the expression on Elin's face. She clearly means every word she says, enraptured by her thoughts, and Lowri suddenly envies her. She doesn't think she's ever felt that way about the places she's lived, not even with Alun. Try as she might though, she can't see what Elin sees – the day just looks dank and cold to her. She gives a slight shiver. 'So, where to first?' she asks.

'No contest,' says Elin. 'I've got to show you the watermill. It's not working now, of course, but the building is still in remarkably good nick, all things considered.'

'Are we allowed inside?' Lowri is hoping she'll say no.

'Yeah, there's nothing in there now, save for the machinery, and it won't turn without the wheel. It's quite safe.'

They cross over the rough patch where Lowri's car is parked and head out on to the lane which connects all the buildings on site.

'Do you know how old the mill is?' Lowri asks.

Elin shakes her head. 'It's been here longer than most folk can remember, but it hasn't been operational for twenty years or more. My mum would probably know, I could ask her if you like? Her dad worked here, I think, or maybe it was her dad's dad... Anyway, she's always been secretly pleased I'm carrying on the family tradition. Doesn't feel much like tradition to me, but there you go.'

Lowri frowns. 'Tradition? So it didn't originally grind corn then?'

Up ahead of her, Wren is skipping through the grass at the side of the track.

'No, it's always been a textile mill. This is Wales, remember? It's in our blood.' Elin grins as Lowri rolls her eyes. Of course...

Lowri pauses a moment beside the mill, staring at its forlorn wheel, and imagining how it would have looked when it was turning and alive with water. Now that same water has been curtailed and is not much more than a trickle, burbling gently along the mill race before heading back to the river. It's under their feet, she realises, passing beneath the lane to re-join the main body of water. Above them, level with the top of the building, is the millpond, and Lowri can feel the weight of it, restrained now by two enormous sluice gates, but when opened... She shivers.

Before she can stop her, Wren races up the steps cut into the grassy bank on the mill's left-hand side, eager to see what's there.

'Don't go near the water, okay?' she calls. 'Stop when you get to the top.' With a glance at Elin, Lowri hurries after her daughter, no idea how close they are.

A tight knot of fear gathers in her stomach when she sees there's literally only a single rail separating them from the millpond's dark expanse. She swallows. 'Come away, Wren, it isn't safe.'

They're on a bridge which spans the mill race, sitting above the wooden sluice gates. Water bubbles over the top of them, through them and around their sides. The gates themselves are almost black with age, pond weed clinging to them in slimy trails. Small tufted plants have made their home in cracks and crevices and Lowri can smell the cloying damp decay. The gates must be as ancient as the mill itself. They could give way at any time.

'But, Mum, it isn't even deep. Look, you can see the bottom here.' To Lowri's horror, Wren shoves her face through the railing, leaning forward. The water in the bottom of the mill race might be shallow, but on the other side the millpond waits serenely, and it isn't shallow at all.

'I don't care,' Lowri retorts, more sharply than she'd wanted.

Wren immediately recoils from the tone of her voice. 'Sorry,' she says, her pale face anxious.

Lowri holds out her hand, pulling Wren to her. 'No, I'm sorry, sweetheart. I just don't want you getting hurt, okay? I know it's going to be summer soon and the river will look lovely then, but it isn't somewhere you can play. It's dangerous.'

'Why don't we go inside the mill and I can show you what

the wheel does?' says Elin, coming forward to join them. 'It's broken now, but when it was working it did something quite miraculous.' She glances at Lowri with a smile, beckoning Wren back from the railing. Lowri nods in gratitude. 'Let's go back down the steps,' Elin adds. 'The entrance is on the other side of the building and you can have a proper look at the wheel as you go past, or rather what's left of it.'

The wheel is separated from the path at the front by a wooden gate and although its paddles have all but gone in places, the huge iron structure it was built around remains, rusted solid. Close up, it gives the air a tangy, pungent smell. Inside the mill, the smell is even stronger, but earthy now too, of damp and decay. Elin's right, though, the building is in surprisingly good condition.

Leading them through to the far end, Elin pushes open a rusty metal door. 'Although this is ground level, we're actually at the bottom of the mill now,' she says, 'so the water in the pond is above us. If you look through that hatch there you can see the wheel. Now, see that big metal spindle leading out from it? Look up.'

Their eyes follow its path as it disappears through a hatch in the ceiling or, from another perspective, a hatch in the floor of the room above.

'Keep that picture in your head,' adds Elin, 'while we go up these stairs here and you'll see what that machinery does. Careful though, the steps might be little slippy. Here, hold my hand.'

Wren does as she's told, and Lowri watches gratefully as Elin helps her daughter slowly up the stairs. They arrive in a lofty room with windows all along one side. In the far corner, the spindle rises through the floor to meet a huge cog hanging almost at ceiling height. From there, another spindle spans the whole width of the room, interspersed by more cogs.

'The weaving machines would have all been connected to

those cogs so that when the water turned the wheel, the spindles turned as well. Together, they powered the looms, all from just the water in the pond. How cool is that?'

Wren looks up with an awed expression on her face. 'Very cool,' she says.

Elin looks back at Lowri with a warm smile. 'And now everything here belongs to your mum. And although it isn't working now, one day it might. Your mum's right, though. It's okay to be in here now, or up on the bridge, but only because we're with you. It's not somewhere to be by yourself.'

Wren nods her head. 'I don't think I'd want to be here by myself,' she replies. 'It's very cool but it's pretty scary too.'

'There's a small garden up on the other side of the building,' adds Elin, turning to Lowri. 'It's a beautiful spot to sit in the summer, and nice and safe too. I can show you, if you like. It overlooks the millpond and is a great place for picnics.'

Lowri couldn't be more grateful to Elin. Since yesterday, it seems as if everything around Wren has come with a warning that it's not safe, and Lowri doesn't want this new start to be so negative. Elin has obviously thought the same. Lowri reckons she's in her mid twenties, so a little younger than she is and, although she hasn't mentioned any children of her own, she has a real affinity with Wren. Maybe she has nieces or nephews of a similar age.

The garden is only small but Lowri can see what Elin means. It's a pretty little space, sheltered and secluded, with a bench to sit on and tubs of bright spring flowers. There's also a fence enclosing it – not too high you can't see out, but high enough to make it safe. She wanders over to look at the water.

The afternoon has turned damp and grey and Lowri knows it's the light making it so, but the pond looks black, flat and lifeless, stretching ahead of her as far as the eye can see. For some reason it makes her shiver. She turns her head as something catches her eye. A bird perhaps? Whatever it was has disappeared into the thick bushes on the far side. Lowri watches for a moment but the line of the bank is dark and, although she strains to see, it remains motionless. She turns back to catch Elin watching her.

'Beautiful, isn't it?' she says. 'I love it here of an evening. It's so calm and peaceful.'

Lowri smiles, but can't agree. There's something here making her feel uneasy. Maybe it's just the endless water – she's not used to it and although others might think it tranquil, for her it's—

There it is again. Not a movement this time, but... a feeling. As if...

And this time, Elin sees it too. She tilts her head in the same direction. 'It's Seren,' she says. 'But you mustn't mind her, she means no harm.'

'Seren?'

So it wasn't a bird, or an animal, but a person. Someone is there, hiding themselves away in the bushes.

'Hmm... she often comes,' says Elin. 'The townsfolk all think she's weird, but don't pay them any attention. They like to gossip and they'll fill your head with stories given half the chance, none of them true. I think it's on account of her name.'

Lowri frowns. 'It means star, doesn't it?' she asks. 'Granted, it's not that common a name outside of Wales, but it's quite popular here. Why would people be wary of it?'

Elin glances at Wren and leans towards Lowri. 'It's not her first name they're bothered by – rumour has it her mum was the local witch,' she whispers. 'So obviously anyone with the surname Penoyre is bound to be trouble. I don't believe that either. Seren's just a bit of a loner, that's all. Hardly surprising, given what happened.'

Lowri stares at her. Elin's voice is matter-of-fact, but there's obviously a story here and Lowri isn't sure she's going to like it. 'Why? What did happen?'

Elin wanders back towards the bench, putting space between her and Wren, who seems quite content looking out at the water. She waits until Lowri sits beside her.

'She lost her mum, for one, when she was only fourteen.' Elin breaks off, shuddering. 'I can't imagine anything worse, can you? And at that age too. But what's worse is that no one really knows why her mum died, except that people reckon it was from a broken heart. Her little boy, Sorley, Seren's brother, disappeared one night. He'd gone to meet some friends and just never came home.'

Lowri feels a pang of loss ripple through her. She doesn't know what she would do if anything ever happened to Wren. 'That's awful, the poor woman... Do they know what happened to him?'

Elin shakes her head. 'No, technically he's still a missing person.'

'So Seren lost her brother and her mum all within the space of what?'

'Eighteen months,' supplies Elin. 'And her dad wasn't on the scene either. Rumour has it *he* was a married man.'

'So Seren had no one? She *has* no one?' Lowri can't begin to imagine how that must feel. 'When did this happen?' she whispers.

'About twenty years ago now. It's incredibly sad.'

Lowri considers Elin's words. 'But if Sorley disappeared that length of time ago...'

Elin nods sadly. 'Yeah, I know what you're thinking. Most folks reckon he must be dead. There was a huge investigation, pretty much the whole town turned out to help in the search, but he was never found. So he's either dead or...'

Lowri glances at Wren. 'Someone took him?' she murmurs, flinching at the thought.

'Neither of which bear thinking about.'

'So why does everyone think Seren weird?' she asks. 'Surely she needs help, not people being judgemental?'

'I know. I think a relative took her in for a few years until she was eighteen, but then she moved into her mum's old place and that's where she is now, virtually a recluse.'

It's easy enough to understand. Hasn't Lowri experienced something similar herself? People turning away because they're unable to handle her grief. Not knowing what to say, so they say nothing. Always thinking that someone else has surely stepped in to help, so they don't have to. It's no wonder that Seren sees little reason to connect with anyone, but the sadness of it is that it becomes a vicious circle – the more she stays away, the more people think her odd and treat her accordingly, which simply validates her withdrawal from the world. And so it goes on.

'So why does Seren come here?' Lowri asks.

Elin is thoughtful, her brow wrinkling. 'I'm not really sure, but apparently she and Sorley used to play by the river all the time when they were little, their mum's cottage backs on to it further upstream. I think Seren comes now to feel close to him.'

That makes sense. And Lowri wonders whether perhaps it's also a reminder of her childhood during happier times. It must have come to such a sudden and abrupt end. Lowri swallows, feeling guilt ripple through her. She can understand it, but Seren's presence still makes her feel uneasy. She doesn't like the thought of someone watching them, someone who obviously takes pains to keep themselves hidden, whatever the reason. It isn't just that though. It's the weight of grief which Lowri can't bear. She can feel it, heavy, like a cloak settling over the water.

After a moment, Elin leans gently into her side. 'Sorry,' she says, 'I didn't mean to spoil the mood.'

Lowri shakes her head. 'You didn't. It's sad, but I'm glad you told me.' She brightens her face. 'Shall we have a look at the factory now?' Calling for Wren, Lowri follows Elin back down the steps towards the lane. 'How long have you worked there?' she asks.

'About three years. After I finished my degree, I came back home with a head full of ideas but no job. So I took this as a means to an end while I followed up some other things, but sadly they all came to nothing and here I still am.'

'So what were you hoping to do?'

She grins. 'Well, I have a degree in textile design so... Actually, I wanted to work in restoration – I'm fascinated by period costumes and tapestries, that kind of thing. I had visions of working in a lovely old museum or a stately home, but no joy so far. Maybe one day...'

Lowri can't imagine such a colourful character as Elin working in what strikes her as rather staid environments, but she says nothing, simply nods and smiles.

A few minutes later, Elin leads them into the low stone building which sits on the far side of the watermill. She points to a door on her left as they enter. 'One boring office that way, the stockroom on the other side, and we're through here – the cutting edge of industry, well, me and about ten other women.' She heads straight for the door opposite, unlocking it and flicking on the lights. A bank of overhead fluorescents blink slowly to life.

'Well, this is it, for what it's worth.'

The room is frigid. Lowri knows the heating will be off for the weekend, but it's dark and feels damp.

'Lovely, isn't it?' says Elin.

Lowri turns slowly through three-sixty, taking in all the details. It's pretty bleak, and barren too, and Lowri wonders if it was always this empty. She can see the machines where Elin and her colleagues sit, some shelving units holding raw materials, and a couple of other cupboards pushed against the walls, but there's room for so much more. It's also quite devoid of comfort.

'So where do you go on your breaks?' she asks.

Elin's snort of laughter echoes around the space. 'What breaks?' she says.

'But you must have lunch, at least? And surely some sort of tea break?'

Elin shrugs. 'Most of us don't bother. In the summer it's not so bad, but...' She wrinkles her nose at Lowri's puzzled expression. 'You kind of hit the nail on the head,' she continues. 'There *is* nowhere to go on our breaks. And who wants to stand outside for half an hour when it's freezing or pouring with rain? Some of us sit in our cars, but even then, in winter it's flippin' cold.'

Lowri stares at her. She's not sure that's even legal. 'Has it always been that way?'

'Pretty much.'

Something Elin said the day before comes back to Lowri. 'When we arrived and you met us with the picnic basket, you said you couldn't stay long because you'd pretended to pop to the loo? You actually meant that, didn't you? I hardly dare ask, but where *is* the ladies?'

Elin grins. 'It's a rather lovely shed out back with a corrugated-tin roof. Quite the symphony when it rains.'

'A shed?' Lowri is disgusted.

'It's a very nice shed. Me and the girls did it up a bit. It's got curtains and everything. A nice rug on the floor...'

'That's beside the point,' Lowri counters.

Elin purses her lips. 'Well, I know that, and you know that, but...'

'For goodness' sake, you shouldn't have to go to the loo outside in a shed. It's the twenty-first century, not the Middle Ages.'

'Well, it's that or nothing. And when you're drinking cups of tea all day to try to keep warm, believe me, you'd rather go in a shed than not at all.'

Elin is trying to keep it light, but Lowri realises the longer she speaks, the more annoyed Lowri is becoming. This has been going on for years, clearly, and no one has done anything about it.

'Elin, I'm so sorry about this, I had no idea. And I'm sure my husband didn't either or he would have done something about it, he—' She breaks off. Would Alun have done something about it? Lowri almost flinches as the thought strikes her, marching in with doubt right behind it. Because family feud or no family feud, Alun must have found out some details about the estate before deciding to pass it over. So didn't he ask the right questions? Or wasn't he given the right answers? He wasn't stupid though, he— Lowri cuts off her thoughts mid train.

'There was a bit of a falling-out among his family,' she explains. 'He didn't get on with his father, wanted nothing to do with him. And it seems that was the case with his uncle too, because although it was him who left Clearwater to Alun, my husband decided he wanted no part of it. That's when Bridie was appointed custodian.'

'It's weird, because I always thought Bridie owned Clearwater – lots of folk do. But then again, her family do own a lot of property around here, so I guess people just assumed it was theirs.'

'Maybe, but what I'm trying to say is that this shouldn't have happened. You should have better working conditions than this and I feel as if that's our fault, mine and Alun's. I didn't twig straight away that having this place looked after by a custodian costs money, or that it would be paid from the business. I did ask Bridie about it and she said everything was ticking along nicely. Perhaps she was just trying to ease me in gently before giving me the warts-and-all version.' She gives Elin a warm smile. 'But I'll find out what's been happening, I promise.'

'It's okay, don't worry. Besides, I know how all this is going to work out. You're going to take over the running of the business, totally transform it, make a huge amount of money in the process and, as your right-hand woman, I'll naturally be promoted and my wages will go up as a result. See? Simple.' She grins. 'No pressure.'

It's a light-hearted comment, but Elin has also made a very good point. Lowri *is* now responsible for all the people who work on the estate, in whatever capacity. She was daft to think she could ignore that and allow things to carry on the way they had been. That might have worked if she was like Alun, and never set foot in the place, but she's not, she lives here and she can't in all conscience ignore what's going on right under her nose.

'Okay then,' she replies, grinning in amusement, 'I'll see what I can do.' There's no real need to stay any longer but there is one last thing Lowri wants to have a quick look at. 'Can I see what you make here?' she asks. The stone walls of the gatehouse are crying out for some colourful wall hangings.

Elin raises her eyebrows. 'Sure.' She locks the door behind them and then, pulling another key from the bunch she holds, opens another at the front of the building. It's dark and windowless. 'The light switch is just inside on the left,' she says, waiting while Lowri steps inside.

Lowri wonders why Elin makes no attempt to follow when she interrupts her thoughts.

'Bland, unimaginative and not particularly well made,' she says. 'These kind of things are ten-a-penny. Every tourist shop throughout the whole of Pembrokeshire stocks them in some form or another, and if they don't buy them from us, there are an abundance of manufacturers to choose from. We're nothing special.' Elin sniffs. 'But we're cheap.'

Lowri gazes at the array of products on the shelves – red dragon after red dragon after red dragon – on tea towels, flags and blankets. It's their national symbol, but she can't help but feel disappointed, she was hoping for so much more. And Elin clearly isn't impressed by what they make either.

Lowri turns to look at her, pulling a face. 'It's all a bit... twee,' she says, searching for a way to put it that doesn't sound incredibly rude. 'Sorry.'

'Oh, don't be,' replies Elin. 'I quite agree with you, but it is what it is, and it pays the bills.'

'Hmm... I suppose.'

They leave soon after that. There doesn't seem an awful lot more to say and it's Elin's day off, after all. Lowri doesn't imagine she wants to spend it talking about her job.

As if the weather has sensed their exit from such a dark and depressing place, the mists have lifted by the time they reach the lane and a thin sun warms the clouds.

Elin lifts her face to the sky once more. 'I won't bother taking you to see the other cottage, I'm sure you can use your imagination, but we could walk through the woods if you like? They belong to the estate as well. There are deer sometimes.'

'Deer?' says Wren. 'What, real ones?'

It seems an odd thing to ask, but Lowri realises Wren hasn't seen any which weren't in a book or on the television. Lowri grew up in the countryside, but all her daughter knows of the natural world is what she's seen in their old garden, a few local parks, and on odd days out. Maybe Clearwater does have something to offer a six-year-old after all.

With the early afternoon sun filtering through the green canopy overhead, it's a beautiful place to be and Wren is happy enough skipping along the paths among the trees. They don't see any deer, but plenty of birds, a few squirrels, and some very impressive fungi growing out from the trunk of a fallen oak. Lowri resolves to make these walks a regular thing; it will be good for them both.

Elin checks her watch as they approach the gatehouse once more. 'Right, that's me off. Back for my brother's birthday lunch down the pub. If I miss that, my mum will shoot me.'

'I can't thank you enough, Elin,' says Lowri. 'It's so good of you to come and show us around.' She raises her eyebrows. 'The solicitor gave me a map of the estate, but that didn't tell me anything.'

'No, I don't suppose it did. Anyway, plenty of food for thought, if nothing else.' Elin grins.

Lowri knows what she means. She knows why she said it too and, even though Elin's mostly teasing, Lowri suddenly feels swamped by her responsibilities. Was this why Alun had shunned them? Did he know what he would have been taking on? She dashes the thought from her head, she's sure he didn't.

Wren and Lowri wave Elin off as she drives away. Turning back to the cottage, Lowri realises there's someone else there, standing by the remains of the castle wall. The man is facing away from her, one hand running along the topmost stones in a manner that can only be described as possessive. And he's clearly surveying the land, maybe not with instruments, but his intent is obvious. Calling to Wren to go inside and that she'll only be a minute, Lowri takes a few tentative steps forward.

'Can I help you?'

At the sound of her voice, he turns. A huge figure, tall and broad as a bear, with thick, shaggy hair and a beard to match. He's the scariest-looking man Lowri has ever seen.

* * *

Her voice startles him. Something in the way she speaks sounding so familiar that for a minute Huw thinks it's Carys, until he remembers that it can't be. Bad enough to be standing here, thinking of the dreams he once held, lost in the past, and then to hear her voice...

But this isn't the past, and neither will it be his future. He needs to say something, but the sudden weight of everything he's lost is too much. The woman is staring at him, waiting for a reply, but everything he'd rehearsed is gone from his head. He struggles to recall Jamie's words of wisdom, but even those elude him. He dredges his memory for her name.

'Mrs Morgan?'

She's not what Huw expected. He didn't know what he expected, but she's not it. She's short for one thing, and the Turners are all lanky as bean poles. Her hands are on her hips though, so maybe she is related.

'Yes?'

He remembers to smile. 'My name's Huw. Huw Pritchard. I gather this is your place now?'

She frowns, clearly not quite sure what this has got to do with him. She asks again, 'Can I help you?'

Can she? 'Yeah, I... I'd like to rebuild Clearwater.'

'I see... Any particular reason?'

What? 'Because I'm a stonemason, a good one and I—'

'And what if I don't want it rebuilt?'

This is all going wrong, he's not explaining himself properly. Huw shakes his head. 'Sorry, I think you misunderstood. I heard you wanted to renovate the place and I came to offer my services. In case you hadn't taken anyone on yet.'

She's closer to him now, studying him, cat-like eyes flashing in the sun. He swallows.

'Well, you heard wrong. I don't have the money for one, and if I did want to restore the castle, I wouldn't ask a random man who turns up on my doorstep unannounced. You could be anybody.'

'But I told you my name, it's Huw Pritchard. Folk around here all know me.'

'Great. Except that I'm not from around here, so *I* don't know you. If you wanted to come and talk to me, you could have got in touch first.'

'And how was I supposed to do that when I didn't know how to get hold of you? No one knows *you*.'

She tuts. 'There are people who know me. Elin...' She pauses. 'Or Gordon, someone or other, I forget his last name. Bridie... everyone knows *her*.'

He bloody knew it. He knew it was too good to be true – she'd have to be in with the Turners, wouldn't she? Huw doesn't care what Jamie said, he's wasting his time here. 'Well, I'll be away home then, I'm sorry to have bothered you.'

He's nearly at the wall when her voice calls him back.

'Wait a minute, where are you going?'

What's she talking about now? 'Home.'

'The exit's that way,' she says, voice sharpened to a point. She waves at the lane which runs through the estate.

'Not when you live on the river, it's not.'

'I'm sorry? You live on the *river*?'

'Yeah, on a narrowboat, just a little way along and, before you ask, yes, I do have a permit. You're welcome to come along any time and inspect it.'

'A permit? Whatever for? And why on earth would I want to inspect it?'

'It's a residential permit, so I can live there,' he intones. 'And it states that I can moor up in any one spot for twelve consecutive days before moving on. I'm on day nine now, so don't worry, I'll be gone soon.'

She stares at the length of dark water behind him. 'And where will you go then?'

'Further down the river to a stretch you don't own and then I'll come back in another two weeks, only to the other side, just like I always do. It's all completely legal so there's nothing you can do about it. There's always been residential rights on the river.'

She looks flustered now. 'Has there? Oh... well that's fine then.'

'Yes, it is. Brilliant. Thank you so much.'

Huw turns on his heel, feeling her glare boring into the soft spot between the centre of his shoulder blades. He doesn't know why he even considered working on this place. It's always been nothing but trouble.

7

It hasn't been a good morning so far. There were no tears, but Wren still walked through the school gate with an unusually pale face. She looked so forlorn, it was all Lowri could do not to cry. She just hopes Wren has a good day. She just hopes she finds her spirit, and that others see it too. She just hopes...

And they'd had such a lovely time the day before. They went to the beach and it couldn't have been nicer. Except that, not really noticing how quiet Wren had fallen in the car on the way home, Lowri simply thought her daughter was tired. It wasn't until they were indoors that she realised it was much more than them having a long day. Lowri told herself it was just a little wobble, and only to be expected, but Wren's tears, which came after she was warm and snuggly from her bath, tugged sharply at Lowri's heartstrings. She knows she shouldn't blame herself, that moving here was something she had to do, but she's afraid she's asking too much of Wren – she's only little after all.

So, it probably isn't the best idea to call in to the factory, but Wren isn't the only thing on her mind, her conversations with Elin are also weighing heavy. Added to which there was that man who turned up out of the blue, rude and demanding, and because Lowri was feeling swamped by her responsibilities, and surprised by his assumption that she wanted to rebuild the castle, she'd become defensive and ended up being incredibly rude back, and that isn't like her at all.

Worse, is that Lowri now realises the estate hasn't been carrying on perfectly well without her, instead it's been slowly crumbling, and she's not sure she can let that happen any longer. She hadn't intended to do this. She'd told herself she didn't have to get involved with anything on the estate, but there are important things here: the buildings, the people, and the past... And whether Lowri likes it or not, she *does* have a responsibility.

Lowri only wants to make an initial appointment with Gordon but, to her surprise, he is not only happy to see her, but insists she stay so they can talk straight away. Lowri has nothing else planned other than a morning unpacking boxes so she readily accepts. The sooner she can put her mind at rest, the better.

As she suspected, the room at the front of the factory building is indeed Gordon's office and he indicates that Lowri should take a seat before crossing to the other side of his desk. He brings out a packet of chocolate biscuits from a drawer, opening them up and laying them on the desk in front of her before lifting out two more similar packets. 'Monday morning supplies,' he says. 'I bring these in for the staff from home. It's not much, but every little helps. Now, what will you have, tea or coffee? Although I warn you I don't drink tea, so I never know whether I make it like dishwater.' He gives Lowri a warm smile.

Lowri settles for the tea anyway, taking the opportunity of his absence to have a look around the office. It's incredibly neat. And clean. Nothing in the waste bin, papers in a neat pile on the desk. In fact, there isn't much in his office at all, save for his desk, a filing cabinet and two chairs. A couple of tea towels bearing the obligatory Welsh dragon are hung on the wall behind him, perhaps as decoration, or as an advertisement for their wares, but all the other walls are bare. You can see where things used to hang though, there are sticky tape marks left behind.

Clearing her throat nervously before Gordon returns, Lowri tries to remind herself it's perfectly okay for her to be there. She's being treated like a visitor, which is fine – actually she much prefers it that way. The last thing she wants is to come across as officious or demanding.

She thought of a few questions to ask last night after Wren had gone to bed, and is running them through her head when the door opens and Gordon returns, manhandling a tray awkwardly through the gap.

'I'm so pleased you called in this morning,' he says. 'I was hoping you would, even though I know you must have a hundred and one things to think about. How are you finding the gatehouse so far? Settling in okay?'

It's the last thing Lowri expects him to say. 'Oh, yes. Still got loads to unpack, you know how it is, but everything seems great, thank you.'

'And your daughter? Wren, is it? It must be her first day at school.' He smiles sympathetically. 'I bet you've had a tough morning. I remember when mine first started, quite a few years ago now, but they're still vivid memories. You never forget, do you? St Michael's is a brilliant school, though, you have nothing to worry about there.' He lowers the tray to the desk and places a cup and saucer in front of her. 'I hope the tea's okay and please, help yourself to a biscuit.' He pushes forward the packet, after taking one for himself. 'Now, what can I tell you about things here?'

For some reason, Lowri didn't expect him to be quite so open and obliging and she feels oddly on the back foot. There's no reason why he shouldn't be, of course, but she still feels as if she's poking her nose into things that don't concern her and she expects everyone else to think that way too. She smiles. 'Thank you. I don't want to take up too much of your time, but I guess what I want to know first is how the business is doing, if there's anything I should be concerned about.'

Gordon nods. 'Mmm, well, at least I can reassure you on that point. Everything is fine – not great, but those are the times we live in, I'm afraid.' He pauses. 'And this is absolutely no reflection on you, or your husband, but I have to be honest with you, Mrs Morgan, it will make the world of difference now you're here.'

'Oh?' Lowri smiles nervously. 'Will it?'

'Goodness, yes.' He clears his throat. 'We're rather constrained by our budget, you see. Having to take money from the pot for custodial duties, looking after the place as well as paying the staff wages, the cost of goods, heating...' He smiles. 'I could go on, but I'm sure you're as aware of these things as I am. The point is, it's left us rather short, as you can imagine. There were all kinds of plans in the beginning. I expect you've already seen for yourself – working conditions here aren't exactly top notch, and we'd love to have been able to improve them. In fact, we had drawn up plans to do so, but as time went on the money we'd earmarked got eaten away and it simply became impossible.'

Lowri winces. 'I wish I'd known, I'm sorry.'

'Not your fault at all. These were things in the past you had no control over. You're here now, that's what's important. Are conditions something you might want to think about first? We have good workers here and they've been incredibly loyal, despite circumstances.'

Lowri nods and smiles. But she still feels guilty.

'Although, there has been a marked downturn in business recently,' continues Gordon, 'which could make that a little difficult. There's been a marked downturn everywhere, I'm sure you're aware, so we're not trading at quite the level we were before, even a year ago. Still, I'm sure things will improve.' He looks at Lowri quizzically, then smiles. 'This is a little bit delicate, but... are you planning on drawing a salary from the business yourself? Only, it's something to bear in mind given where we are.'

A salary? Lowri had never even thought of such a thing, she already has a job. 'Um... I don't really know. But probably not, under the circumstances. If anything, I'd like to think my being here could reduce some of the custodial costs. Might that free up a little money? I'm sorry, I don't even know what those costs are.'

'Well, let me see...' Gordon's fingers lace together as he gazes off into the distance. 'There are the obvious – the salaries for managing the textile business, but the estate is quite complex. Always the case where there's land involved, and here we have a considerable stretch of river to manage *and* a large expanse of woodland. Both require differing approaches, so there are various third parties we enlist for support. Then there's the associated administration – permits, sub-lets, rights, etc., all of which have to negotiated and maintained. A bit closer to home there are considerable costs incurred in the upkeep of the old watermill and Clearwater House, both of which are listed, and then you have general repairs, grounds maintenance, cleaning... the list is quite extensive.'

'Yes, it certainly seems that way.' Lowri is beginning to panic on a grand scale. 'There's clearly a lot to consider so, perhaps, for now at least, we should leave things as they stand. Until I've had a chance to get to grips with things.' Lowri isn't backing away from her responsibilities, she really isn't, but she needs some time to think, to sit quietly and absorb it all, to fully understand what's required before she comes to any conclusions, or makes any decisions. Anything else would be foolish.

Gordon takes a sip of his coffee and nods. 'There's certainly a lot of truth in the saying "if it isn't broken, don't fix it", and we're not going anywhere, Mrs Morgan. What we have in place has been that way for a number of years, so there's no rush, is there? You can take your time and decide what will be right for you going forward.' He replaces his mug on the desk and smiles warmly. 'How does that sound?'

'A lot less scary,' she agrees. Lowri's trying to remember the questions she wanted to ask, but she's pretty sure they've all been covered, and the relief is immense. There is just one thing she wants to say, though, to press home the point, or her conscience will really give her a hard time. 'Even with the financial situation as it is, I still think we should make improving workplace conditions a priority. Having seen inside, it's obvious it isn't up to the standard it should be.'

Gordon nods. 'Absolutely, I totally agree. So let's make that our focus again. Of course, what we could really do with is an increase in revenue, so if you can think of any ways to improve our cash flow, for goodness' sake shout. Sometimes it takes a fresh pair of eyes to look at these things, doesn't it? To see what's been under our noses the whole time.'

Lowri nods again, thinking of something Elin said. She wonders whether she's ever mentioned it to anyone else. 'Just musing out loud,' she says, to make it clear her ideas aren't fully formed, 'but what about the products themselves? Is that something else we might look at?'

Gordon dips his head. 'Of course.' He pauses. 'Can I be absolutely honest with you, Mrs Morgan? There's a ready market for this kind of thing. Tourism is still a very important and lucrative area for Pembrokeshire and our products are tailor-made for that market. I think the quality is good and I think the range we offer more than compares with other manufacturers. Having said all that, however, I think it's also fair to say they are perhaps not the most original items I've ever seen. We make what we do because we've always made them. Our job here over the years has been to maintain the status quo, and it would have been quite wrong for us to alter the shape and structure of the company. Now you're here, all that changes. You can take the business in any direction you choose, and if you have new ideas, I'm sure everyone would be very excited to hear them.' He tilts his head slightly to one side. It really is quite extraordinary how much he reminds Lowri of her dad. 'So what else have you got planned for your day?' he asks. 'Something nice, I hope, it's such a beauty. And you should take some time to explore, the river's a lovely spot.'

It's clearly Lowri's cue to leave, but that's okay, she's taken up enough of his time. 'I have some unpacking still to do, but thanks, I will.' She looks around. 'And I'll have a think as well, see if I can come up with any bright ideas.'

He nods and gets to his feet. 'Excellent, and feel free to shout if you do.'

'I will, thank you, and...' She pauses a moment. 'I was just wondering... Do you think I should go and say hello to everyone? Introduce myself. People might think it odd otherwise.'

Gordon looks startled. 'Oh... I hadn't thought. I suppose it's not a bad idea, although Bridie has already briefed everyone about your arrival so if it's something you'd rather leave until later, then I'm sure that would be fine too.' He looks at Lowri, a slight smile of enquiry on his face. She gets the distinct impression he's against the idea.

'I won't be long,' she says, in case he was worried about keeping folk from their work. 'No more than a quick pop of my head around the door. I feel a bit rude not saying hello.' She gestures towards the door, an unspoken suggestion that he should lead the way.

'Yes, of course,' he murmurs. 'If you'd like to follow me.'

The whirr of machines is loud as they enter the workroom, but no more than a handful of seconds goes by before the first woman stops what she's doing, followed in quick succession by another, then another. In less than a minute there is complete silence. Lowri swallows. Maybe she hasn't quite thought this through.

She looks at Gordon for guidance, but his gaze is trained on the far wall. Surely he's going to introduce her and not leave her standing there like a lemon? The silence is becoming excruciating and, just at the point where Lowri doesn't think she can stand it any longer, Gordon gives a visible start and clears his throat. Wherever he went to just now, Lowri's pleased he appears to be back in the room.

'Ladies,' he says. 'Sorry to interrupt you, but as you know, Clearwater has a new owner. And she's come to say hello. Lowri?' He hands her the floor.

'Um... hi,' she says, feeling her insides swim restlessly. She'd hoped for a little more of an introduction. 'My name's Lowri, Lowri Morgan, and, yes, Clearwater seems to be mine now. It's a long story.' She laughs nervously. 'And, as you probably know, I've only just moved in and am still getting used to where things are and how they work. But I hope to be able to get to know you all soon. And the business, of course. In fact, I'd like to reassure everyone that I'm not here to start changing things left, right, and centre, although there are some obvious things which could be improved, and I'll try to look at those for you when I can.'

From the bottom of the room, Elin's smiling face beams out at her, but she's the only one in the room who looks remotely engaged. Everyone else appears either bored or disinterested. All apart from one woman, sitting on Lowri's left, who wears an expression which could curdle milk.

Lowri smiles again. 'So...' The word is drawn out, far longer than it needed to be. 'That's me anyway. Does anyone have any questions?'

The woman on the left raises her eyebrows. Maybe Lowri's reading it wrong, but it's almost as if she's mocking her. And the rest of the room is silent. Lowri wasn't sure what she was expecting, but she'd thought there might be a little more reaction. Gordon's suggestion to keep the status quo is looking more and more favourable by the second.

'Okay then, I'll let you get back to work. I'm only down at the gatehouse if you think of anything you want to know, or if you want to come for a chat...' She breaks off – *Don't be so stupid, Lowri* – and scuttles from the room as fast as she can.

Gordon follows momentarily, awkward and embarrassed. Lowri hopes to goodness he doesn't say *I told you so*.

He attempts a smile. 'They're a good bunch,' he says. 'Just... a little set in their ways, some of them. Don't like change, you know how it is.'

Lowri nods. 'Well, at least they can put a face to the name now.' It's the most positive thing she can think of to say.

'Oh, absolutely. It's always nice to do that. And now you've said hello, you can rest safe in the knowledge that you've done your bit and leave the rest to us.' He checks himself. 'Only if you want to, of course. How about you get in touch when you're more settled and we can have another chat?'

'Thank you, that would be good.' Lowri is desperate to be away.

'And have a think about those ideas. We'd be very pleased to hear them.' He ushers her towards the front door. 'Thanks so much for coming by, Mrs Morgan.'

'It's Lowri, please.'

He nods. 'Lowri, it is.'

Once outside, Lowri's first instinct is to swear, loudly and copiously. Either that, or cry and eat a huge amount of chocolate. But then she realises what just happened only lends more weight to the argument for staying out of the picture. Gordon's right – if it isn't broken, don't fix it. And although she feels a little foolish for not realising how much work was involved in running an estate, mostly she feels relieved that she can leave all that to someone else. Someone who can deal with a bunch of unfriendly women as well. And if she does have any ideas for how to improve business, then she can simply channel them through Gordon and Bridie, it couldn't be simpler.

She angles her head towards the sun. It *is* a beautiful day and she walks back to the gatehouse feeling considerably lighter of foot and heart.

* * *

'You didn't go looking like that, did you?'

As an opening greeting, Huw's heard better.

'No, Jamie, I didn't go looking like this.' Huw wipes his hands down his overalls. 'But my best bib and tucker isn't what I usually wear when cleaning out my bilge pump.' He points at the pile of smelly weed he's already fished out.

Jamie wrinkles his nose. 'Why don't you get a proper house like a normal person?'

Huw stares at him. Can he really have forgotten? He hasn't though, because very quickly a sheepish expression crosses his face.

'Sorry, but surely there are some places you can afford to rent? And once you get another job sorted out, you'll have no problem.'

'Have you seen the price of rentals, Jamie? Because if you had, you'd know I'd still only be able to afford the cheapest there is, which will more than likely belong to Bridie. No thanks, I'd rather sell my soul.' He pats the side of the boat. 'She might not be much, but she's mine and no one can tell me what to do on her. So are you coming in, or what?'

'Yeah, not for long though, I'm on my lunch break. Do you mind if I chomp on my ham and cheese while I'm here?' He brandishes a badly squashed sandwich and then climbs on board. 'So how did it go?' he asks, following Huw down the steps. 'With your woman?'

'If you're referring to the stuck-up cow at Clearwater, not all that well.'

Jamie sighs, and Huw knows that sound of old.

'What?' he adds. 'You gonna tell me what I did wrong? Even though you weren't there and didn't hear her practically bite my head off.'

'You're sounding a tad defensive there, Huw.'

And now it's his turn to sigh. 'She sounded like Carys, okay? Looked a bit like her too...'

'Oh, shit.'

'Yeah. So, I'm minding my own business, just running my hands along the stones, feeling their age, trying to imagine how they would look back in their rightful place. I wasn't doing anything wrong, just lost in my thoughts, when she barked at me, making me jump, this imperious "can I help you?" said like I was some unsavoury vagrant or something.'

'To be fair, you were standing on her land.'

'To offer my *help*, Jamie. I could hardly stand anywhere else, could I? But she wasn't interested anyway.'

'Did she actually say as much?'

Huw's struggling to recall the conversation, he's not sure they even got that far. 'She said she didn't have any money.'

'So then do it for free.'

'Yeah, great, Jamie. I don't have any money either. I need to make some, not give away my services for free. My *expert* services.'

'But there are grants and stuff, aren't there? You've always said there were, that they would virtually pay for the costs.'

'Some of them.'

Jamie's looking at Huw, weighing things up. 'I guess it all depends how much you want this, doesn't it? *It's all you've ever dreamed of, Huw*. And a project like this would make your name as a stonemason, as a conservationist. So think about it a

minute and ask yourself if a bit of free labour would be worth
what you'd gain in the end.'

Jamie has this really irritating habit of making things sound
really simple when they're far from it. He's munching away on
his sandwich like he's just found the solution for world peace.

'I love the world you live in, Jamie. The one where the right
things happen for all the right reasons. Here in the real world,
it's a little different. People aren't selfless or generous most of
the time.' Huw pauses. 'Make that *all* of the time. They're only
out for what they can get, only looking after number one. I'd
end up busting my gut for a considerable length of time, only to
watch her get all the glory when Clearwater's restored to its
former beauty.'

'You don't know that.'

'I pretty much do.' This is a conversation Jamie and Huw
have had far too many times now. 'Besides, it's immaterial
because she said she wasn't interested in restoring the place. I
can't make her if she doesn't want to. And if she was lying, then
she's more than likely the same as all the others, a woman with a
ton of money out to make a point. She won't care about the
place. If she's inherited that pile, all she's probably seeing are
pound signs.'

Jamie takes another bite of his sandwich. 'Why do you want
Clearwater so badly, Huw?'

'You know why.'

'Humour me.'

Huw tuts with frustration. 'Because it's part of our heritage.
A heritage that's slipping further and further away from us
every day. Because skills like mine are dying out. Because no
one's interested in spending time repairing something old when
they can just replace it with something new. Because she was
beautiful... And because buildings like that don't matter any
more, and it's about time they did. God knows there's little
enough beauty left in the world.'

Jamie is nodding, a slow smile spreading across his face. 'Which is exactly what you should tell her the next time you see her.'

* * *

It's lunchtime and Lowri has made good headway with the unpacking, but time is beginning to hang and she recognises the signs. If she doesn't heed them her mood will darken and she'll end up ruining what had turned out to be a surprisingly good morning. Lowri won't know if Wren has had a good day at school until she picks her up and no amount of supposition will give her an answer. And with no answer, all she'll do is fret. Much better then that she gets out for some fresh air and a change of scenery, and when she returns it will almost be time to fetch her daughter. At almost the very moment she has this thought, that's when she sees it, Clearwater Castle, looming large through her kitchen window. *I wonder...*

Lowri's feet carry her quickly outside until she's looking at the pile of stones, eyes tracing what remains of the tower up into the sky. It's still a beautiful day; a little blowy, but the sunshine is beginning to have real warmth to it now and the sight of it is cheering. It's been a long, hard winter, and not just in terms of the weather. It's also the first year since Alun died that Lowri has felt any sense of optimism and now she's here, with a brand-new start in front of her, rebuilding her life. Could she rebuild the castle too? *I wonder...*

Picking her way past the ruin, she makes for the field at its rear, heading in the direction of the town. It's unremarkable, scrubby grassland, but, on the other side, a stile takes her through a small thicket of trees and into a meadow. It's only early in the year but Lowri is astonished by what she sees. The whole area is a mass of colour – wild flowers, grasses, tall plumes of foliage, their colours still undeniably soft and spring-like, not yet reaching the vibrancy of summer, but it's beautiful. A path has been forged through the middle, and she joins it, walking more easily now, her fingers grazing the tops of the grasses as she goes. They're warm and silky to the touch. The path is drawing her closer to the river but her unease is tempered by the sight of buttercups, hundreds of them, clustered in bright clumps along the edge of the path. Keeping her eyes on their sunny-yellow colour, she walks on. *It's just a river*, Lowri tells herself. *And you had better get used to it.*

A black cat joins her after a few moments, weaving its sinuous way among the grasses, tail held tall, leaving them rippling in its wake. She bends for a moment to stroke its sleek head, smiling as it pushes against her hand with a loud, throaty purr. Then, with one final brush against her legs, it's off, trotting along the path.

'Hey, little one, where are you going?' Looking up, Lowri realises the cat is heading for a narrowboat moored a little distance away. She hadn't realised she was so close. Worse, as she watches, a figure appears on deck and turns in her direction as the cat trots merrily onwards. She has no idea what she's going to say, but she came here to say something so she had better do just that. To turn away now would be incredibly rude. Once was bad enough, twice would be unforgivable. If only he wasn't so big... or scary.

Once she's closer, however, she realises he's smiling. Whether at her or the cat, it's hard to tell, but she's grateful just the same. The cat hops effortlessly onto the deck and begins its sinuous dance all over again.

'Is he yours?' she calls. 'He's beautiful.'

'He is a she, but no, just a frequent visitor. She labours under the delusion that because I live on a boat I will always have a quantity of fish stashed on board. Not true, alas, but she still comes.'

There's a slightly awkward silence as both of them grapple with what to say next.

'What's she called?' Lowri asks, wondering how to begin.

'*Pugwash.*'

'*Pugwash?*' she repeats. 'That's a weird name for a cat.'

Huw's heavy brows knit together. 'Oh, sorry, I thought you meant the boat. No, the cat is called Boo, least that's what I call her. I first made her acquaintance at Halloween when she thought it might be fun to jump on my head as I came up the steps on the boat.'

'Ah, I see... and the boat's called *Pugwash.*'

The corners of his mouth twitch. 'It's a bit of an in-joke,' he replies. 'On account of this.' He tugs at the thick hair which covers his chin. 'Black beard?'

Lowri stares at him for a moment before the penny drops. 'Oh, of course! As in Captain *Pugwash?*'

'The very same. Though I'm not a pirate, obviously.'

Lowri would love to tell him he looks like one, but then they'd be back to square one.

'Do you want to come on board?' he asks.

She eyes the slick water in the gap between them. 'Maybe not. I'm not very good on boats.'

'She's pretty stable, hardly rocks at all,' he adds, mistaking her apprehension. 'Oh, and I'm sorry about the smell.'

'The smell?' Lowri wrinkles her nose.

Huw points to something on deck. 'I've been cleaning out my bilge pump and it stinks. One of those jobs you always tell yourself you'll do more often and then never do.'

Lowri has no idea what a bilge pump is, but it certainly doesn't sound very pleasant. 'Well, I can't smell anything, so...'

'Can't you?' He sniffs at his sleeve. 'Maybe it's me... Anyway, you're sure you don't want to come on board?'

She smiles awkwardly. 'I'm good, thanks.' Lowri embar-

rassed herself enough the other day, adding hysteria into the
mix wouldn't be a good move.

Huw studies her for a second. 'Fair enough, can't say I
blame you. You must think I'm some kind of Neanderthal, I...'

Bear, pirate, Neanderthal...

'I wanted to apologise for the other day,' he says. 'I wasn't at
my best and I went to Clearwater with a big speech all prepared
and I—' He smiles properly. 'Totally blew it.'

'You didn't, not really. In fact, I don't think I even let you
speak. I was a little overwhelmed by things, about the enormity
of what there is to do there. I'd just been hearing about conditions at the factory and then you came along and—'

'Touched a sore spot?'

She smiles. 'Something like that. I've only just got here and
a week ago I never even knew the place existed. It's been a bit of
a shock.'

He nods. 'Sounds complicated.'

'It is and there are lots of things to think about, so I—'

'You will think about it though? The castle?'

'Yes, I...' Lowri hesitates a moment, not quite sure how
much she should tell Huw. 'That's one of the reasons why I'm
here, actually. I wanted to apologise for being rude, but you also
obviously know a lot about Clearwater and I know nothing
about building or renovation. So I wanted to ask if it's possible.
Could the castle be rebuilt?'

'She definitely could. You've seen for yourself, a lot of the
stone is still there. It's worn, broken some of it, but I'm a stonemason, Mrs Morgan, that's what I do. It's local stone too, some
of it would have to be replaced, but when skilfully done... It
wouldn't be a perfect match, and really she needs time to
weather again, but – yes – she could be made whole.'

'So there are pictures, are there? Of how it looked before?'

'Maps, plans, drawings, descriptions...' He nods rapidly.
'I've got quite a collection myself.'

'Oh.' She's finding his enthusiasm a little unnerving for some reason. The pressure of it. 'I see, well, that's good at least. Of course, the money is an issue but—'

'There are grants,' he interrupts. 'All sorts of funding available and Clearwater was once an important building.'

She nods. 'Yes, my solicitor mentioned something. Perhaps I could look into it and see—'

'I'd be happy to do that for you. You'd need plans and specifications, a detailed bid written.'

He has such an earnest expression on his face, Lowri doesn't know what to say. 'That's a very helpful offer, Mr Pritchard—'

'Huw.'

'Huw, then.' She smiles. 'But you see, the thing is I'm still not sure if what I'm thinking will even work, and I guess I'm loath to get anyone's hopes up. This all sounds a bit... quick.' She pulls a face. 'Although, actually, speed would be of the essence.' She frowns, her brain racing ahead. 'I'm sorry, I haven't really thought this through.'

'There's time,' replies Huw. 'Really. Everything I've just described will take months. The decision to make a start might be a quick one, but the process itself...' He smiles.

Lowri's heart sinks. 'Ah. I was wondering about that. You see I need to raise some money and I thought Clearwater—'

Huw's head snaps back from where he's been staring down the river. 'You need to raise some money?'

Granted, Lowri doesn't know this man at all well, but that last comment sounded barbed. A prickle of irritation begins to stiffen her spine. 'Yes, I—'

'So you're gonna rebuild her, are you? Open her up? Turn the land around about into a car park? Build a twee little tea room and flog bara brith to tourists at exorbitant prices? Have a little shop too, no doubt, with Welsh dragons on anything you can think of. Oh, you already have that, don't you? In your factory, which everyone knows turns out inane crap instead of something which actually speaks to our heritage.'

The irritation is turning rapidly to anger. 'Hang on a minute! I never said anything about any of that. Besides, what's wrong with having people come to see the castle? For God's sake, every castle in the land is open to the public.' She stares at him, indignation kicking in. 'You don't even know why I raised the question in the first place. In fact, you know nothing at all about my intentions.'

'No? I can take a pretty good guess.'

Lowri isn't sure why this man has such a hugely inflated opinion of himself, but he doesn't own Clearwater – who the hell is he to tell her what to do with it? She doesn't owe him anything and her business is certainly none of his.

'How dare you!'

'How dare I?' His eyes flash in anger. 'I'll tell you, shall I? I dare because once upon a time Clearwater stood and guarded the whole village, who took shelter within its walls. It kept them safe, it kept them fed, and it kept them warm, their livestock too. It wasn't just some asset to be monetised and turned into a cheap and tawdry "experience". It had purpose, Mrs Morgan, that's why. It was important, and it meant something to the people who lived around here. What else can you say that about now? In a society where nothing is built to last, where we can throw stuff away without a second thought. You want to make a quick buck, do you? Well, there's no such thing. Things grow when you tend them, Mrs Morgan. Perhaps you should think about that instead of lying about your intentions.'

His words follow Lowri all the way home.

8

'Sounds as if Clearwater might be stealing your heart to me,' says Jess in that teasing way of hers. The one which always comes with a good dollop of truth. 'Even if the local menfolk are Neanderthal.'

'I'm not sure they all are,' replies Lowri, smiling. 'But one is enough.' Three days have gone by since Lowri's conversation with Huw and she's spent a good part of that time bristling with indignation at his accusations. 'He might have had a point,' she concedes. 'It probably did sound like I was cashing in on the castle's potential. But what *is* the point of having it on your doorstep if you don't do anything with it? And my motives weren't solely mercenary. That's what annoyed me the most – the fact that he jumped to conclusions without ever giving me the chance to explain. That's twice now. Besides, the castle is right outside my kitchen window, I see it every time I'm doing the washing up. I can't help but think about it.'

'Looking and thinking are very different from rebuilding though,' says Jess. 'So there must be something about it which is making you want to roll up your sleeves.'

Lowri sighs. 'I don't know, Jess. I swore I wasn't going to get involved with the running of the estate, but you should see the factory here, it's like something out of the Dark Ages. They desperately need an injection of cash, either that or a radical change of direction. Anyway, I'm not really getting involved. Gordon just asked me if I had any ideas, and anything I do think of can go through him, or Bridie.'

'Have you spoken to her about Alun yet?'

Lowri frowns. 'No... I've only met her once.' It's an odd question and throws Lowri for a minute. 'Spoken to her about him in what way?'

'I just wondered if she might have been able to shed some light on how things got to the point they're at now. Whether she'd had any contact with Alun at all.'

'Jess, if Alun had been in contact with anyone here, I'd have known about it.'

'Yes, of course you would. Ignore me. I'm just fishing for gossip.'

Jess is one for gossip, it's true, but she's also very shrewd. She wouldn't have asked a question like that for no reason. So *should* Lowri talk to Bridie? But Lowri already knows the answer to that.

'And talking of which, have you spoken to Susan yet?' asks Jess, changing the subject.

'I've spoken to her answerphone, that's not quite the same thing.'

'Ah...'

'I've been here nearly a week,' adds Lowri. 'I thought I might have had a "how's it going?" message at least. But nothing.'

'Maybe she's just been very busy?'

'Yeah, renovating a cottage I should have been sorting out for her.'

'Lowri...' warns Jess. 'You don't owe your sister anything. Offering her cottage to you was a lovely gesture, but your circumstances changed, and if she can't see how good that is for you, then—'

'Is it good for me though?'

Jess snorts. 'Of course it is! You've just spent the last ten minutes telling me about a castle you want to rebuild. And with a lightness in your voice that hasn't been there for a long while. Correct me if I'm wrong, but are you the same woman who swore she wouldn't get involved? Because rebuilding a castle doesn't sound like not getting involved.'

'I know,' replies Lowri, a wistful note to her voice. 'But it's all so sad. There are all these things at Clearwater, languishing, slowly slipping further and further into nothingness. It just struck me that the castle could be a way to bring them back to life.'

There's silence from the other end of the line.

Lowri stares at her phone, picturing the expression on Jess's face. 'What?' she asks.

'Nothing,' replies Jess blithely. 'Nothing at all.'

Lowri narrows her eyes but lets her comment go, a swift glance at her watch tells her she's running out of time. 'Listen, Jess, I'd better go. It's almost time to pick up Wren. She had her first play date after school tonight, can you believe it?'

'What a sweetheart!' sings Jess. 'God, I miss her. Give her a big squish from me, won't you?'

'I will. Of course I will.'

'And keep me posted too. I want to know everything that goes on.'

'Jess, you're incorrigible.'

'I know. That's why you love me so much.' Lowri can hear the smile in Jess's voice, but she's not wrong.

'Speak soon,' she says, hanging up with a smile on her face.

Wren's play date is with a girl in her class called Poppy, who she's talked about virtually non-stop since her first day at school. It might be the fact that Poppy has two rabbits and a new kitten which is proving so irresistible to Wren, but Lowri is incredibly relieved that Wren's first few days have been good ones.

Poppy's family live on the edge of town in a cul-de-sac of neat houses which, from the front at least, look quite similar to their old house. Lowri had no problem following the directions Poppy's mum gave her and ten minutes later, she knocks on their door. It's opened by a smiling woman who looks to be about Lowri's age.

'Hi, come in, you must be Lowri? I've heard so much about you.' She grins. 'Good stuff, don't worry. I'm Bethan.'

Lowri smiles back, stepping into the hallway, wondering who might have been talking about her, when she catches sight of a figure waving from what is obviously the kitchen at the far end of the hall. It's Elin, and as Bethan shouts up the stairs to Wren that her mum has arrived, Elin slips off the stool she was sitting on and comes to say hello.

'Small world, isn't it?' she says, grinning. 'Bethan's my sister – much older sister, obviously – and the more successful one. She has a house, a husband, kids and everything.'

Bethan rolls her eyes. 'None of which you want.'

'This is true,' replies Elin, grinning. 'And why would I, when I can come and squish your munchkin whenever I want?' She turns and beams at the two girls coming down the stairs.

'Hmm… pinch all my biscuits more like,' replies Bethan.

Lowri smiles at their easy relationship.

'How are you finding things up at Clearwater though? Settling in okay?' Bethan asks.

Lowri wonders what Elin has been telling her, but she nods. 'Yes, great, thanks. Slowly getting my bearings.'

'It's a lot to take on, but I've been saying to Elin for years it's about time there was a shake up.'

'Oh?' Lowri throws Elin a puzzled look, her eyebrows raised.

Elin grins sheepishly. 'Ah, yes... I might have mentioned my rather optimistic dreams for your domination of the empire.'

'But you told me—' Bethan stops. 'I might have known it was another one of your wild ideas.'

Elin throws up her hands. 'Guilty as charged. Although just because they're wild, it doesn't make them bad ideas.'

Given what's been on Lowri's mind, she's about to reply, when Bethan speaks again.

'In this case, I agree with you. They've been churning out the same old rubbish up at the factory for years. I honestly don't know how they're still in business.'

Lowri pulls a face. 'Sorry, I think that might be my fault.'

'It's not your fault,' argues Elin. 'You didn't know anything about it.'

'Maybe not, but when I spoke to Gordon on Monday he made the very good point that when the custodial arrangements were put into place their job, effectively, became to keep the business running as it has been in the past. Which explains why nothing's changed.'

Bethan nods and Lowri realises Elin has obviously explained the situation to her. She wonders if she minds, but then assumes it won't be long before the rest of the town finds out about her anyway. She's a newcomer, a source of potential interest; these things have a habit of getting around.

'But that isn't the case though,' says Bethan. 'You should ask our mum. The factory made all kinds of things in the past, better things. That's why she's always going on at Elin to show them her ideas. Bridie Turner bangs on about tradition and heritage all the time, but there's nothing traditional about churning out dross with a red dragon on it. Neither is it our heritage.'

Bethan's words seem to echo those of Huw rather too closely for comfort, but it's not the only interesting thing she said. Lowri is intrigued. 'What ideas are these, Elin?'

Bethan stares at her sister, an exasperated expression on her face. 'This is the part where Elin goes all coy and says they're nothing. But they're not nothing. Not at all.'

It's true, Lowri can see Elin squirming now she's on the spot. 'Well, whatever they are, have you shown them to Gordon?' she asks.

'For what it was worth, yeah.'

'And what did he say?'

'That they didn't fit with the current climate, whatever that means. Probably just that he thought they were shite.'

'They are not shite, Elin,' says Bethan. 'Gordon's no better than Bridie. The pair of them can't see what's in front of their faces. Or they choose not to, which is more likely the case.'

'Then it might interest you to know that the other thing Gordon and I spoke about was the general state of the business,' continues Lowri. 'And, his words, "if you have new ideas, I'm sure everyone would be very excited to hear them." We didn't talk specifics, but that doesn't sound like someone who isn't open to change. Perhaps now would be a good time to have another conversation.'

Elin tips her head to one side. 'Maybe...'

'You should show your designs to Lowri,' says Bethan. 'Go on, I can mind Wren for a while longer.' She turns to the girls who are standing side by side, waiting patiently. 'You won't mind stopping here for a bit, will you, Wren?' Bethan's expression is arch at the sight of the girls' lit-up faces. 'See? Mum's four doors down, Lowri. Elin has no excuse now.'

Lowri grins. 'Right, come on then, let's have a look.'

Up until that moment, Lowri would have said Elin was a confident woman – outgoing, easy to talk to, and with firm ideas and opinions – and yet as they walk along the road, Elin looks anything but. So where has that Elin gone? Lowri stops, forcing her to a halt too.

'The very first time I met you, you told me I'd end up being your boss, running the business and making everything right again.'

'Yeah, me and my big mouth.'

'But you must have meant it,' says Lowri. 'Out of all the things you could say to a complete stranger, you chose that, so it must have been important to you.'

Elin gives a rueful smile. 'I've probably watched too many Disney films,' she says. 'Where everything has a happy ending.'

'No, don't dismiss it... honestly, I'd really like to know.' Lowri pauses a moment, trying to work out what Elin is thinking. 'Put it another way then. You said before you didn't like the stuff you make at the factory.'

This, at least, receives a nod. 'If I never make another tea towel as long as I live it will be too soon.'

'So what would you like to make?' asks Lowri. 'If you had free rein. In an ideal world, if we didn't have to think about money and bills and whether it was possible. What would those things look like?'

A curious expression comes over Elin's face. Her features bloom for a moment, warmed by the heat of excitement, but then all too quickly are overtaken by the cooling drafts of reticence and they wilt once more.

'Go on,' urges Lowri. 'I really want to know.'

'Do you ever think about fabrics?' asks Elin. 'Because we have them next to our skins pretty much twenty-four hours a day.'

Lowri shakes her head. 'I can't say I do, no.'

'Well, I do, I think about them all the time.'

Lowri suddenly realises that Elin's wild and colourful clothes are all handmade, and she wants to give her the biggest hug, she's not sure why.

'And what I can't for the life of me understand,' continues Elin, 'is why, when there are so many different choices of material, so many patterns, so many colours, people choose the things they do.' She puts out a hand. 'Not you,' she adds quickly. 'You wear lovely things. But I'm not really even talking about that. I'm talking about the wider use of material, in our homes, as decoration, or even just practical stuff, like tea towels. Most of it is so utterly and incredibly boring.'

Lowri hasn't ever thought about it before, which is exactly Elin's point, and she wonders why that is. 'I guess most people are constrained by what's available to buy,' she replies. 'What's in fashion, what the latest trends are.'

'Exactly,' says Elin. 'Clothing manufacturers dictate what we wear because they only manufacture what's in fashion. But who makes those decisions? A bunch of people we've never met decide what we should all be wearing and then you just try and find anything different – you can't.'

Lowri nods. She's come across that problem herself.

'We're supposedly presented with a huge choice, but which is really no choice at all,' says Elin. 'We just have to go along with it. And the same is true of virtually any material we buy: curtains, bedding, you name it. Someone else decides what we can have and gives us a pretty paltry selection to choose from. But it doesn't have to be that way.' She sighs. 'This lack of imagi-nation is the thing which irritates me the most. If you trace the history of fabric, or fashion, you'll see very quickly that it wasn't always like that. People did incredible things with their clothes, they were ornate, embellished... Were they expensive? Yes. Practical? No. But that didn't stop them. I'm not saying that's what we have to do... I know those kinds of fabrics are expensive and out of reach of the vast majority – in itself that's wrong – but by making things accessible to everyone, we also water down choice, we make everything bland and homogenous simply because it's easy and cheap. I think there's a better way, that's all.'

Lowri stares at her. 'Wow,' she says.

Elin drops her head. 'Sorry... when I get on my soap box I get quite carried away.'

But Lowri shakes her head. 'No, that was wonderful. The products made at Clearwater aren't inspiring at all. I don't know much about textiles, but even I can see that. An opinion which seems to be shared by a lot of people.'

'They're shoddily made as well.'

'So what can we do to change that? It seems a big leap from what Clearwater is doing at the moment.'

'I know,' Elin says, resignation written across her face. 'That's the problem. But I can hope, can't I?'

Something in Elin's eyes tugs at Lowri. Up until Lowri's arrival at Clearwater, Elin had been working two jobs, one of them in pretty appalling conditions. She's given up the dreams she had for her future and instead works in a shitty factory making lack-lustre products. But she's also been unfailingly generous towards Lowri and her daughter from the moment she set foot in the place. Maybe Elin doesn't have much more than hope to keep her going, but wouldn't it be nice if every now and again that was enough?

Lowri smiles. 'You can, we both can. So would you show me your ideas now?'

Elin is suddenly shy as they arrive outside her house. Lowri knows her indecision comes from trepidation, anxiety that she'll be made fun of and have her ideas mocked, but she's humble too, not sure if what she makes actually has value, or whether she's inflated her own self-worth. But even if Elin isn't sure of those things, in an instant, Lowri knows that *she* is. She knows that what Elin wants to share with her is vital.

'Please, I'd love to see.'

Evidently still not sure whether she's doing the right thing, Elin leads Lowri through her hallway and upstairs to a bedroom which doesn't look all that different from Lowri's living room at the gatehouse when she first saw it. There's stuff everywhere:

clothes, magazines, empty mugs and, perhaps not surprisingly, a sewing machine and several folded piles of material.

Crossing the room to a chest of drawers on the other side, Elin pulls one open and lifts out a large sketchbook. She carries it to the bed and, shoving a stack of her things sideways, makes room for Lowri to sit down. Placing the sketchbook on Lowri's lap, Elin turns to the first page. 'These are some of my designs. The ones at the beginning are from uni mostly, but *these...*' She turns towards the back of the book. 'These are what I've been working on recently.'

She sits back and pushes the book further onto Lowri's lap as if to say, go on, look, and so Lowri does. She loses herself in the kaleidoscope of colours, in the patterns which she thinks are one thing, but then which change and become something else; in the emotions which assail her – joy, and awe and wonder; and in the thing which Elin has always put huge store by, hope. It shines from the pages of Elin's sketchbook. By the time Lowri has finished looking, and thinking, her head filling with visions, she knows that, more than anything, Elin should have her dream, and if she can, Lowri would like to be the one to make it come true.

'Do you like them?' asks Elin, even now, when she must have seen Lowri's expression, not sure if her work deserves praise.

'I don't think I've ever seen anything so beautiful,' Lowri replies. 'How do you do it? How do you make something like that?'

Elin goes back to the same chest of drawers and this time returns with something which Lowri thinks she might have been searching for her whole life. The thought makes her want to laugh, to dance, to shout that she never even knew she had this feeling inside of her. She reaches out and takes the weaving, gently, reverentially, eyes widening as she traces each tiny detail.

'It's a blanket,' says Elin, swallowing. 'Will be a blanket. Or a throw, a wall hanging. It could be lots of things really, depending on the size or the type of yarn you use. I only have a small frame, but...' She trails off, biting her lip. 'You get the idea.'

Lowri is lost in her thoughts. She *does* get the idea. She suddenly has lots of ideas. 'Can we make this? Could we make it? At the factory, I mean.'

Elin thinks for a moment, her nose wrinkling. 'Not right now. The machines are... well, they're all wrong for this type of thing. You need hand looms. But you could... you could simplify the designs to be made by machine.'

'I'm not sure I'd want to simplify the designs,' replies Lowri. 'So these hand looms, what are they like?'

'Pretty big, and they're actually operated by foot, well, hand and foot really. They're complex though, it takes a while to learn how to use them.'

'But you know how?'

Elin nods, tentatively.

'And you could teach the others?'

'In theory, but I... Yes,' she finishes, eyes shining. 'It could cause a lot of problems though.'

Lowri nods. 'I know, but problems have solutions.' She thinks for a moment, holding Elin's look. 'I would love to make this happen,' she says. '*We* need to make this happen. Will you help me? Because I had a crazy idea the other day and now I know why.' Lowri isn't sure she should be sharing this. She doesn't want to get Elin's hopes up, particularly given Huw's words that still echo through her brain, but suddenly everything seems to fit. 'If I tell you, though, you have to promise to keep it to yourself, for now at least.'

Elin nods. 'Of course.'

Lowri screws up her face. 'I must be mad,' she says, 'but when I spoke to Gordon the other day, he asked me if I could think of any ways to improve the business's cash flow. He said a fresh pair of eyes might see something which has been under their noses the whole time. And then I was looking out the window in my kitchen and I realised it was... The castle... I wondered if we could rebuild it.' She pulls a face. 'Don't laugh straight away, okay? Just pretend to humour me for a few moments and *then* try to dissuade me.'

Elin stares at her, beaming. 'Oh my God, that's a brilliant idea! It's just like that film with Kevin Costner in it... oh, what's it called? 'You know, the *If you build it, they will come* thing. It's something like that.' She looks wildly at Lowri.

'*Field of Dreams?*' she supplies.

'Yes! That's it... thank you. *If you build it, they will come.*'

Lowri screws up her face as if that might clear the confusion from her head. 'Elin, I haven't the faintest idea what you're talking about, but if by *they* you mean people, then yes, that's what I was wondering. Generally. Whether that might be a possibility...'

'People would come in their droves,' says Elin. 'That's what I've always said. Apart from the fact that it's part of our heritage, we've got Barafundle up the road a bit, Broad Haven, St Govan's Chapel...'

'Bosherton,' adds Lowri, nodding.

'Tourists have always flocked to this part of Pembrokeshire, why shouldn't Clearwater have a bit of that?'

'That's what I was thinking. Only...'

Elin tips her head to one side. Questioning.

'I wasn't sure if it was selling out,' adds Lowri. 'Cashing in on our heritage for all the wrong reasons. Would people think it was mercenary?'

'Who cares if they do?' Elin replies. 'Plenty of people would still want to visit. Besides, you're not just cashing in, are you? You'd only be doing it to take the estate back to its heritage.'

'True...' Lowri is still torn. 'It would take a long time though.

There are grants available, apparently, but no guarantees, and without them I couldn't even begin to think about restoration. I simply don't have the money for that kind of thing.'

'Changing what we make at the factory would take a long time too,' says Elin. 'I know there's no quick fix, but I think it could be worth it.' She pauses, tentative again. 'And I'm not just saying that. I know I could potentially profit from this, and seeing my ideas come to life would be incredible, but I think it could be good for you too. For your future and Wren's.'

'I think so as well,' says Lowri, a wistful note turning her voice almost to a whisper. A slow smile begins to creep up her face, growing suddenly wider as a rush of energy consumes her. 'So, what do we do now?'

'That's simple,' says Elin, suddenly leaning forward. 'You should go and see Huw, he—' She stops. 'No, scrub that, forget I ever said it. There must be other people around who can help you. Off the top of my head I don't know of any, but...' She trails off again, frowning when she sees the expression on Lowri's face. 'What?'

'There's just one little problem... I did ask Huw.'

'Ah... And how did that go?'

'Not well. I've met him twice now and on both occasions we ended up arguing.'

'I'm sorry, Lowri, but he's really bad news. I'd stay away if I were you.'

This isn't what Lowri wants to hear. She's so full of energy she feels invincible, utterly convinced that everything is going to be okay. It's a feeling she hasn't had in such a long time, a feeling she sometimes wondered if she'd ever experience again, so Elin's comment is akin to having a bucket of cold water poured over her head.

'I'm not sure he's that bad. Rude and arrogant yes, but, to be fair, on the first occasion we met he caught me in an off moment and I was pretty rude to him too. Maybe we just got started on the wrong foot.'

Elin pulls a face. 'I'm not sure there is a right foot, not now anyway. He used to be a really nice guy, but these last few years... I think he's been barred from just about every pub there is round here, falling down drunk, picking fights. The stories aren't good, Lowri.'

Lowri sighs. 'But he told me he's a good stonemason, and unfortunately I seem to have need of one of those just now. Or at least someone who can tell me what's possible. If I'm going to be applying for grants, I need to know what I'm talking about.'

'I'm not even sure he *is* a good stonemason any more. As far as I know, he hasn't worked for ages. Not after what happened. I know it was a horrible thing and—'

Lowri holds up her hand. 'No, don't tell me. I don't want to know what his problems are. If I know, I'll probably end up feeling sorry for him and that's the last thing I want to do.' She swears under her breath. 'So now what? This is so damned annoying. He tells me that rebuilding the castle is all he's ever wanted to do, and then the next moment virtually accuses me of trampling all over its heritage when I say I *do* want to see it restored. He can't have it both ways.' She practically growls. 'I'm going to have to speak to him, aren't I?'

Elin winces. 'I'm not sure you have any choice, but I'll go with you if you like. I've known Huw a long time, maybe that might help. And we can make it clear that we just want advice about the grant funding.'

'Okay... yes, please come with me. I'm not sure I want to do round three on my own. And on no account must we mention opening Clearwater to the public. That's what set him off the last time.'

9

At first, Huw thinks it's raining until he realises the hammering on the boat's roof is being made by something rather more substantial. By some*one*.

'Huw, you at home? It's Elin. Elin Hargreaves... Huw?'

An ominous silence is all that follows, but sure enough the hammering starts up again. He knew she hadn't gone away. Pulling himself upright, Huw swings his legs over the edge of the bunk and stands up, swaying alarmingly. He has no idea what time it is and, for a moment, no sense of what day it is either. Taking a deep breath, he tries to focus on the far end of the boat as he moves slowly down its length.

'Okay, okay... I'm coming. Keep your hair on.' He undoes the bolt and lifts the hatch lid, squinting in the sudden shaft of sunlight. He passes a hand through his shaggy hair and down over his face, rubbing at his bleary eyes. 'Can't a man get any sleep?' he grumbles.

'It's well past midday,' says Elin pointedly. 'Most normal people are up and about by now, even on the weekend.'

'Yeah, well I couldn't sleep, okay? Anyway, who designated

you my personal alarm clock? You don't normally come knocking at my door.'

Elin takes a couple of steps backwards so that he can see a second person standing on the bank.

He groans. 'I might have known. I thought I made my feelings clear the last time we spoke,' he adds, pulling at his beard.

'I wanted to ask you something,' Lowri replies, standing somewhat stiffly.

Huw looks from her, to Elin, and back again. 'You might as well come in,' he says, lifting the hatch and pushing it back over his head so it rests on the roof behind him. 'Although, unless you've had a complete change of heart, I probably shouldn't let you in at all.' He fumbles with the catch on the doors, pushing them wide.

It isn't until he descends the steps once more that Huw realises there's a warm fug inside the boat, and not a particularly pleasant one at that. Stale air, sweat, and something else... He moves to open a window.

'Have you been drinking?' asks Lowri.

The question assails him from behind. Jamie might possibly get away with asking him that, but not her.

Huw turns to face her. He's standing on the other side of the bench seating that surrounds a small table, and on which stands a bottle. He looks at it pointedly. 'That, is a bottle of beer,' he says. 'One. Singular. And it's only half full. In fact, I probably won't even finish it. So, no, I haven't been drinking. And if you're going to accuse me of doing so, at least do me the courtesy of getting your facts straight. *Drinking* is six or seven, maybe eight or nine, until I lose count. So, one, one is most definitely not drinking.' Huw isn't sure whether he meant that as a joke or not. Either way, the bottle's been there a couple of days. But Huw isn't going to tell her that, no point wasting his breath, it's clear what she thinks of him.

It's also clear from Lowri's expression she doesn't find his comment even remotely funny. So no sense of humour either, he thinks. Better and better.

'This is ridiculous,' Lowri says. 'You're right, Elin, we should never have come. Just forget it, it doesn't matter.'

Huw hates it when people say that. 'Clearly it does matter, or you wouldn't be here. And, as you've got me out of bed, maybe I think it matters too. So is this about Clearwater, or what?'

He catches Elin flashing Lowri a look which says, 'you first'.

'Yes, it's about Clearwater,' says Lowri, lifting her chin a little. 'I wanted to ask your advice.'

'Advice? You don't want her rebuilding then?'

'Well, yes, I do, but... look, I could do without your caustic comments about it being opened to the public. It's a castle, I'm not sure what you expect.'

'I never said you couldn't open it to the public.'

'Yes, you did,' argues Lowri. 'Your tone was pretty scathing, as I recall. About that, and the twee tea room I'm going to open as well, serving overpriced bara brith to tourists. Not forgetting the shop, of course, selling tat with Welsh dragons all over it.'

Elin stares at her. 'Did he really say that?'

Lowri nods. 'None of which is his business.'

Huw inhales audibly. There suddenly seems very little air in the boat. 'I didn't say you couldn't open the castle to the public, that isn't what I have a problem with. What I *implied* was that you'd most likely turn it into some glorified theme park, complete with souvenir pencils and mugs. *That's* what I have a problem with.'

'And, as I *implied*, you don't know a thing about my motives so your judgemental attitude isn't welcome. It's frankly none of your business what I do with the castle once it's restored. It belongs to me, not you.'

There's a moment when Huw thinks about forcibly ejecting her from the boat, but then he catches sight of Elin's face, wreathed in disappointment and something else... disgust? They used to get on well once upon a time. He used to get on with a lot of people. Overcome by an immense tiredness, he sits down heavily and, for a moment, holds his head in his hands. 'Okay, you win,' he says wearily. 'So, motives aside, what is it you want me to do?'

Another look passes between the two women.

'The last time we spoke you said there could potentially be grants available to help us rebuild the castle. How potential is potential?' asks Lowri.

Despite his tiredness, Huw tries very hard not to look as if all his Christmases have come at once, but this is the closest he's been in a very long while. 'Well, put it this way, the last time it looked like it might be on the cards, the folks at Cadw got very, very excited.' There's a lot more he could say but Huw's gonna leave it right there for now.

'Cadw?'

'They're the government department in Wales which looks after and protects our heritage. And I'm pretty confident you could light their fire again. I might still have the details of their main contact.' In fact, they're sitting on top of a pile of papers he was working on long into the night, but again, best to keep shtum for now.

'Okay,' says Lowri. 'So, assuming for a minute that Cadw *would* fund restoration, would this likely be limited solely to building costs of the castle? Or might money be available for other things on site?'

Huw narrows his eyes. 'Like what?'

'I don't know, the mill maybe or...'

She's trying to play it cool, thinks Huw, but that wasn't just a random question. Neither was her mention of the mill as off the top of her head as she wants him to believe.

'Cadw might go for restoration of the mill as well,' he says.

'Particularly if you're looking to recreate a working mill, supporting a heritage industry.'

'Yes, that's what I wondered...' Lowri purses her lips, her gaze dropping to the floor.

Huw watches her for a moment and then switches his attention to Elin, who looks away. There's something going on here they'd rather not share with him. Well, tough.

'Can I just clarify something?' he asks. 'Are we talking about the mill as in the textile factory?' He looks at Elin this time.

'No,' replies Lowri quickly. 'Sorry. I meant the old watermill, the original mill.' She gives a wry smile. 'I've been looking into the business a little,' she says, 'and although I haven't seen any accounts, it's obvious it's not doing too well. You only have to look at conditions in the factory to see that. The building isn't fit for purpose and that's the main issue I have. But, to replace it, or even repair it properly to bring it up to modern standards, is going to cost a whole heap of money, money I don't have and, I'm pretty certain, the business doesn't have.'

Huw nods and starts pacing up and down the boat. 'Then you really *do* need to think about the mill,' he says as he returns. 'The old mill, that is.'

Lowri gives him a quizzical look.

'It was designed as a textile mill,' he adds. 'It still is a textile mill, and it's far more fit for purpose than the building being used now. It would take a bit to get the wheel restored and working again, but once it was up and running, you'd have the means of powering your machines, some of them at least.'

'That might work,' says Elin, her face beginning to glow.

'We've been talking about changing what we produce,' Lowri explains. 'Possibly.' Clearly, she's not about to enlighten Huw. 'But, again, funding any changeover is going to be difficult, as is finding a suitable work environment. It occurred to me the watermill could be a fit, that's all.'

Elin nods rapidly. 'Maybe not for the machines we're running at the moment, but they're all wrong for what I showed you anyway. They're fast, automated. The piece I made was done on a small hand frame, but if I had a proper hand loom then...' She pulls a face. 'Trouble is, that wouldn't necessarily be commercially viable, the pieces take days to make and we'd have to charge too high a price. Maybe for exclusive pieces, but... Perhaps if we scaled the designs back a little, simplified them, they could be done by machine. The type of machines the mill *could* power.'

Huw raises his eyebrows. Reopening the watermill would be a smart move. Lowri would get new premises for her business, and have their renovation paid for by someone else, which would solve all her problems. Plus, she wouldn't have to resort to tacky marketing of the castle to raise her cash. Maybe she's not as daft as he thought she was. Or as bad...

'And weaving is one of the oldest trades there is,' remarks Elin, eyes gleaming. 'The estate could become the very thing it was always meant to be.'

'So where do we go from here?' asks Lowri. 'I need to speak with Bridie and Gordon, but I'm sure they'll be in favour of what I'm suggesting. Besides, nothing is a done deal yet anyway, we're far from that. But making some exploratory enquiries can't do any harm, can it?'

Huw isn't sure whether to say anything or not. Lowri has made it exceptionally clear that what happens at Clearwater is none of his business, but restoring the castle *could* be, and he needs this, he couldn't bear for anything to go wrong now. 'Maybe don't be too explicit about your plans,' he says. 'Like you said, works are a long way off yet and a lot can change in that time.'

He sees immediately he's said the wrong thing. Lowri doesn't actually say 'thanks, but I'm not stupid', she doesn't have to, it's written across her face.

'I just have a little history with Bridie,' he adds, trying to soften his comment. 'And she has a lot of connections around this town. If she doesn't like what you're doing, she can stir up a whole heap of trouble for you.'

'He's right, Lowri,' says Elin gently. 'She's really nice... until she isn't.'

Lowri nods. 'I'll be cautious,' she replies. 'But they'll have to be told something, they'll see you on site for one thing.'

Huw works hard to keep the grin from his face. He doesn't want to appear too keen. He also needs to choose his words carefully. 'About that... I did a bit of work for Cadw a while back,' he says. 'When the buildings here were being revalued. I'll have to hunt, but I might still have it. There were plans and several historical documents which would be useful.'

'Yes, please, anything you have,' says Lowri. She's quiet for a moment. 'Would I be right in thinking you'd be able to help me with any grant bids? Only, the technical details aren't something I know a great deal about.'

It was time for Huw to step up. 'Absolutely. I'd need to come on site, assess what's there, what's changed. Look at what their funding requirements are now and how potential bids should be pitched.'

'But you could do that?'

'I could.' Huw's look is unwavering. For once in what seems like forever he's managed to keep his eye and his mind focused.

Lowri nods, and swallows. She looks suddenly incredibly nervous. 'Okay then,' she says. 'I can't believe I'm even thinking this, but I reckon we should do it.' She holds up a hand in Elin's direction, quite possibly because she looks as if she's about to burst. 'There is just one more thing.' Lowri leans in towards Huw so she's good and close. He's to know she means business. That there can be absolutely no doubt she means what she says. 'I have a daughter,' she says. 'Who would probably like nothing more than to live in a castle like the princess she deserves to be. I will not let her get her hopes up and then see them dashed, do you understand me? So if we're going to do this thing, we do it properly. No more drinking, Huw. I might not be an expert, but even I know that building is a dangerous game and I will not risk either you, or anyone else, getting hurt. So you show up on site at nine sharp, Monday morning, and every day after that you're required to, and if I catch so much as a whiff of alcohol on your breath, you'll be off site faster than you can say "make mine a pint..." And you'll be taking your bloody boat with you. Do you understand me?'

'I can't believe I said that,' says Lowri as they walk back down the riverbank. 'I heard it coming out my mouth and I just couldn't stop it.' She feels mortified.

Elin, however, is grinning. 'I was a little surprised, but you go, girl, show 'em who's boss.'

Lowri groans. 'I don't want to be boss. I certainly don't want to be Huw's boss, and there were kinder ways of saying what I did.'

'I think he needed telling actually,' replies Elin. 'The whole boat stank of booze and I've told you how things are with him. Most people walk in the other direction when they see him now, he's upset far too many people. You're giving him a chance, which is more than most folk would do, but he has to know there are conditions attached. This is too important to mess up.'

'It is, isn't it?' Lowri stares across the water meadow. Even so, her cheeks still feel hot. 'Anyway, I've said it now, and if he doesn't show up on Monday, I'll know, won't I? And we'll just have to find someone else.'

'Oh, he'll show up,' Elin replies. 'Not sure what mood he'll be in, but he'll show up.'

Lowri nods her head in acknowledgement before glancing

at her watch. 'Are you sure your mum's all right having Wren for a while?'

'Yeah, I told you. Bethan does her big shop on a Saturday so Mum always minds Poppy, or I do. She'll probably be glad to have Wren there. Besides, I reckon you have masses to do.'

Lowri slides her a look. 'You got that right. But, thank you, Elin, really. I couldn't have done that without you. I don't think I'm going to be able to do any of this without you.'

Elin stares at her. '*You're* not gonna be able to do this? What about me? I thought I was going to be stuck in that factory freezing my arse off until the day I die.'

'You still might be.'

Elin shakes her head. 'Nah,' she says. 'Not now.'

She holds Lowri's look for a moment and Lowri wonders how she got so lucky in meeting Elin.

'So, what are you going to do now?' Lowri asks.

'Me? I'm going to get my sketchbooks out. I've got some dreaming to do.'

She grins at Lowri and together they walk back to Clearwater, saying their goodbyes by way of a warm hug as they reach the castle grounds. Lowri fishes out her keys for the gatehouse and is about to go inside when she stops, turning in the other direction. Pushing up her sleeves against the warmth of the beautiful late-spring sky, she turns onto the lane, heading for the watermill.

Inside, it's quiet, almost holy. She doesn't yet know every inch of the building, or what it will take to make her whole again, but she soon will. It's a thought which is both terrifying and exciting. She's been coming here most days while Wren is at school and, although she's not as scared of the water as she once was, she knows it's only because it's still. Soon it might come hurtling down the mill race, bubbling through the sluice gates to set the wheel turning. Then what will Lowri do? When the water moves so fast it makes her head spin too? She pushes the thought aside. That time is way off yet.

Picking her way back up the damp steps, Lowri's feet take her through a door in the side of the building and up another flight of steps, not damp this time, but warmed from the sun, and with tiny green shoots filling their cracks and crevasses. The garden is one of her favourite places to sit, perfect with a mug of coffee once she's tackled the morning's emails.

Lowri is getting used to the woman now. Seren. The woman who sits, watching from the far side of the millpond. Once or twice, Lowri has even caught a glimpse of her, but mostly the bushes at the water's edge keep her hidden from view. Lowri always knows when she's there though.

The feeling is much stronger today. The Welsh call it 'hiraeth'. A word which has no direct translation into English but whose meaning is still clear to those who take notice of it. Some call it homesickness, but for a land which no longer exists. Others say it's grief, but a nostalgic-like sadness for the loss of something inexplicable. Something which was, and which now is not. Lowri had found this feeling calming, being in a place where her emotions didn't need to be hidden or masked by something else. Instead, they fit right in, and she's found this acceptance of her oddly comforting. Today, though, Lowri can almost smell it, taste it, hold it. It's unnerving.

She doesn't know whether this feeling is connected to Seren, or if it's simply that she understands Seren feels it too, but without even thinking, Lowri moves through the garden and out the other side onto the path which leads into the wood.

The trees are greening all around her, as is the ground beneath her feet. New life is everywhere she looks, and she breathes it in for a moment, filling her lungs with the verdant air. A movement, off to her left, catches her eye and her head whips around, seeking the gentle brown flanks of the deer who roam wild here. But it was only a bird, nothing more.

She looks again, no, not just a bird, or rather, not only a bird, but a woman too, still and watching. Lowri raises her arm slowly, and smiles.

'I knew you'd come,' says the woman, shy, and skittish like the fawn Lowri thought she was.

Lowri nods, her calm acceptance of the woman's words surprising her. 'I thought it was time to say hello.'

The woman dips her head, acknowledging, but maybe not agreeing. She's slender, tall, unlike Lowri, but around the same age, with hair the colour of autumn leaves and she stands quietly, holding a bunch of pale flowers, the folds of her green smock dress billowing around her legs.

'I'm Lowri... and you're Seren, is that right?'

The woman nods. 'Seren Penoyre. You'll likely have heard of me.'

There are several things Lowri could say at this point, but she considers, perhaps, that Seren's words are a test. 'I've heard you're a witch,' she says. 'But I make my own mind up about the stories I'm told. Either way, I know that witches don't really fly around on broomsticks, or make potions with eye of newt and toe of frog, so it's nice to finally meet you.'

Seren nods in the direction of the castle. 'Is it true what they say? That you're rebuilding her?'

The question surprises Lowri. 'I'm hoping to.'

'And the watermill? Will you be setting the wheel working again?'

Lowri nods. 'Perhaps. If we can.'

Seren's expression is unchanging as she scrutinises Lowri's face for several moments, and Lowri is at a loss what to say next. It's impossible to fathom what Seren's green eyes are thinking and she has no idea whether her responses have found favour or not.

Eventually though, Seren nods. 'Good,' she says, 'it will help. The land around here has been sickly for so long.' She holds out the bunch of pale flowers she carries. 'I brought these for you, for luck. I hope it goes well.'

Lowri stares at her, suddenly and inexplicably close to tears. 'Thank you,' she says as she takes the bunched blooms, touched by this simple gesture. 'I hope so too.'

'I used to come here as a child,' adds Seren. 'It was different then. I could watch the water for hours – sometimes smooth and calm and, at others, wild and impatient – you wouldn't believe it was the same thing. But it was always alive and it's been dead for so long now, I've wondered whether it will ever heal.'

Bizarrely, Lowri understands exactly what she means. Is this what she feels? This loss? Is that why she feels strangely comforted, as if her own grief is being shared? 'The water terrifies me,' she says. 'Yet...'

'You find yourself beside it, the same as I. It draws us both.'

Seren is staring at her again, although, after a moment, Lowri realises she's no longer looking at her face. She raises her hand tentatively to her throat. 'I've always loved the moon,' she says, her fingers tracing the outline of the silver necklace she wears. 'My mum bought me this as a present.'

Seren smiles. 'She knew how well it would suit you.'

'Thank you.' Lowri nods, thinking she should add something. It feels awkward not to acknowledge something which Seren must know she's aware of. 'Elin told me about your family. About your mum and your brother. I'm so very sorry.'

'It was a long time ago,' says Seren. 'Things move on, the wheel turns.'

'Even so...' Lowri wants to offer her something, some small measure in return for what Seren has given her. 'You're very welcome to come to Clearwater any time you like. You don't have to stay on the river side. Come up to the castle if you want, and have a look around, not that there's much to look at yet, but... Come for a cup of tea, or just to sit in the garden if you'd rather.'

'Thank you,' Seren replies. 'Perhaps I will.'

But Lowri has the strongest feeling she won't, that it would take a great deal for Seren to come even as far as the garden.

'I should go now,' she says, just as Lowri knew she would. She's done what she came to do. 'But you should also have this...' Seren fishes out something from beneath the neckline of her smock and pulls it over her head. Whatever it is hangs from a length of blue cord.

Lowri weighs it in her palm, it's warm and solid. A small stone with a hole in it, just off centre, pale, with a tiny thread of glittering white running through it. She looks up into Seren's smiling face.

'It's a hag stone,' says Seren. 'From the river. People sometimes call them witches' stones, but they bring luck. They also let you see things for what they really are.'

Lowri slips it over her head without hesitation. 'I don't know what to say. Thank you.'

Seren shakes her head. 'There's no need.' Turning as if to go, Lowri sees her check herself. 'Incidentally,' she says, turning back, 'we do make potions from eye of newt and toe of frog... it's mustard seed and the humble buttercup.' She gives a wry smile. 'Just in case you were wondering.'

For the first fifteen minutes or so after Lowri leaves, Huw stomps about the boat, muttering under his breath. It rocks alarmingly beneath his weight, something which makes him even more cross as he realises that, given the way he feels, it's not a great idea. He should probably calm down. The bloody nerve of the woman though.

He fills the kettle, banging it down on the small gas hob, which he sets alight. He's about to grab a glass for water as well when he realises there are none. They're all in the sink, along with dishes and mugs and several inches of scummy water. He stares at it for a moment before raising his gaze to take in the rest of the boat – the overflowing bin bag full of bottles, the piles of clothing strewn about the place, none of it smelling too sweet either. The whole place looks grimy, with a foetid air that will take more than opening a window or two to get rid of.

Leaving the kettle for a moment, he sinks down onto one of the bench seats. It's all too much. He hasn't the energy to start sorting out the mess and, even if he did, what would be the point? He— His thoughts come to an abrupt halt. This is exactly the kind of thinking which got everything into such a state in the first place. He sits up a little straighter. Small steps, one foot in front of the other, that's what Jamie always says. Don't worry about all the things which have gone before, about all the things you've lost, just concentrate on the present, on where you're going next. One thing and then another. He can do that. He just has to keep from thinking about how much of it there is to do. Like when you're suffering from seasickness, you keep your eye on the horizon, not the whole ocean.

He'll start with the washing up. Then at least he can have a cup of coffee, and maybe something to eat. Put the rubbish out. Huw gets to his feet and heads down to his bunk, where he knows several more mugs are hiding. It's there that he sees what he was working on the night before and into the wee small hours of the morning. Clearwater... who'd have thought it? And as he stands there, losing himself in his memories once more, a slow smile spreads across his face. You'd never know it because of his beard, but soon Huw is smiling from ear to ear. He hasn't done that in a very long time.

10

Monday morning dawns bright and clear, something which ordinarily would fill Lowri's heart with optimism. She reminds herself the weather must surely be a good omen and the fact she has to see Bridie Turner this morning shouldn't detract from that, it's merely something to be attended to. So why she's appointing Bridie the role of monster under the bed, Lowri has no idea. Perhaps it's her guilty conscience. She strikes the thought from her head and finishes the tea she's making.

True to his word, or rather *her* word, Huw did indeed turn up at nine o'clock. In fact, he was a little earlier, carrying a canvas satchel over one shoulder. She didn't intend to watch him, but as the kitchen window overlooks the castle, washing the breakfast dishes put him directly in her line of sight. She still feels awful about her last words to him, but then again, perhaps it did need to be said. She has a feeling they're only going to get one shot at this.

For quite a few minutes, Huw did nothing, simply stood in the middle of what would have been the castle keep and stared up at what remained. Then, he moved to one of the walls, reduced by fallen stones to waist height, and laid down his bag.

Using the wall's width as an impromptu table, he opened up the bag and spread out several documents, securing them with a stone to stop them from blowing away. With one final look at the castle, he hitched the satchel back over his shoulder and turned for the gatehouse door.

* * *

Not surprisingly, Huw had hardly slept the night before. He'd given up trying to analyse the thoughts revolving around his brain in an endless cycle. Nothing new there, and he'd spent so long in the past attempting to make sense of them and move on that he knew it was pointless to try. So instead he simply lay there, listening to the sounds of the river, and waited for the dawn.

He looked old, haggard and dull-eyed when he awoke, but he had showered, was wearing clean clothes and, importantly, his breath smelled fresh. The day ahead of him is one he has waited for for a very long time and he's anxious to know what it will bring. It seems too much to hope that it will go well. But maybe... maybe just being at Clearwater will be enough.

He arrives early, but not too early, and had intended to announce his presence on site with a chipper good morning, but the sight of the castle rising up out of the spring sunshine stops him in his tracks. He nearly flees then, terrified of what he is about to do, fearful of the change he could be about to usher into his life. He will have to be the very best he can be and he isn't sure he even knows what that is any more, let alone be able to fulfil his potential. Gradually, though, as he stands there, gazing up at the ragged skyline, he begins to see order making sense of chaos, worn and broken being replaced by promise and rebirth. He can almost feel the tools in his hands, the heft of them, the fine balance as he works, and he longs to make them his once more.

Crossing to one of the walls, he opens his satchel and lays out a couple of sketches he's brought with him, fingers flattening the paper, tracing the outline of his pencil marks. He weights them down with several stones and takes a very deep breath. *You can do this, Huw. Don't think about the past. Don't think about whether you're up to this or not. Don't think. Just feel, remember, and get your arse over there to say hello.*

* * *

'Morning,' says Lowri with as welcoming a smile as she can manage. 'I've just put the kettle on. Can I get you a coffee, or tea?' She ushers him into the hallway.

'Thanks, but I'm good just now. Rather awash with the stuff, actually.'

So is Lowri. She's been downing coffee all morning and is so nervous she can hardly speak, but there's no way she's going to let Huw know that.

'Come in anyway,' she says. 'We probably should have a chat about how all this is going to work. Practicalities and so forth.'

Huw nods, looking around him as she leads him through the central sitting room. He stops for a moment, a curious expression on his face.

'It's a bit different from the pile of rubble out there, isn't it?' says Lowri. 'Although I'm incredibly grateful it is.' She looks up at the ceiling high above her. 'I had no idea what I was going to find when I arrived, but this is lovely.'

'Aye, I've been here once or twice. She turned out well.'

There's something rather closed about Huw's expression which doesn't invite further comment, so Lowri continues through to the kitchen, where her laptop is already set up on the table.

'I've been looking at the Cadw site,' she says. 'But I can't see any information about grants or... maybe it's just me,' she finishes.

'No, you won't,' Huw replies. 'There are layers upon layers to them, several different organisations who all part-fund grants, and the stipulations are pretty exacting too. As you might imagine they don't just hand out pots of money to anyone who wants one.'

'So how do I go about applying for a grant then?'

Huw weighs up her question for a minute and then gives a small smile. 'I thought that was where I came in?'

A hot flush hits Lowri's cheeks. 'Yes, of course, but I...' She scratches her head. 'I didn't want you to think I was leaving everything up to you.'

'Don't worry, you won't be.' He looks around the room, indicating a chair. 'May I?' he asks.

'Yes, of course.' She pushes her laptop out of the way.

Once settled, Huw opens up his bag and takes out a notebook, a sheaf of papers and an iPad. 'I brought you these,' he says, pushing the papers towards her. 'I wasn't sure if you even knew anything about Clearwater. Apologies if you do,' he adds carefully. 'But these are historical drawings, maps and plans of the site, together with more modern photos and renderings. You won't find these on the internet, they're mine, built up over time, so please...' He falters, clearing his throat a little. 'I'd appreciate it if you could look after them, they're the only ones I've got.'

Lowri nods, hardly daring to touch what's been placed in front of her, and she instinctively knows how much they mean to Huw.

'I take it you've got Wi-Fi?' he asks, opening his iPad. 'Would I be able to get the password?' Lowri pulls out her phone in order to share it with him. 'You do know this isn't going to be a particularly quick process, don't you?' he asks. 'Only there's a lot of work to do.'

She nods again. She has no idea about any of it. 'Perhaps you wouldn't mind explaining what needs to happen.' Her words sound pompous and formal but she has no idea how to make them any better.

Huw regards her for a moment. 'Well, the short story is that I'm going to spend the day looking at all the grant requirements so I can understand what might be available, and on what basis. Then I'm going to do a few sketches, make a few plans and write out a very long list of things which will need to be done. How does that sound?'

'Good, I think.' She's not sure how to ask this next question. 'And what do you need from me?' She has no idea what he expects. Whether he sees them working together at all.

'Nothing at the moment. That will all come later when we know what it is we're trying to achieve. For now, maybe just put Bridie in the picture? I think it might be wise to see to that sooner rather than later.' Huw drops his head to his iPad and Lowri wonders what he's thinking.

'Actually, I'm going to see her shortly,' she replies. 'Strike while the iron's hot and all that.' She cringes at her words. For goodness' sake, could she be any more jolly hockey sticks?

'Great. Oh, and give this guy a call. Michael Cornish. He's a mechanical engineer, a professor of industrial archaeology and a bloody good millwright at that. You'll need him on board to sort out the mill for you.' Huw swings his iPad round so Lowri can see the screen, then makes a note on a clean page from his pad and slides it across the table.

Lowri nods. 'Okay.'

'Right, I'll get going then. Make a start.'

He gets to his feet before Lowri can even register his words. And he's halfway to the door before she remembers what she wanted to say.

'Huw?' she calls him back. 'Sorry, I was... um. I was

wondering about practical things? Food and drink, and so on. If you need the loo...'

A second or two of silence beats out, Huw's body casting a large shadow against the far wall. 'I'll have a pee behind a wall if that's all right with you.' He gives her an amused look. 'I'll manage... but, thank you.'

Lowri nods, feeling incredibly foolish. He's a grown man for goodness' sake. 'I thought perhaps I'd just leave the gatehouse door unlocked,' she says. 'It's hard to hear if someone's knocking on it anyway, so maybe just come in and help yourself, if you need to.'

He nods. 'Okay then. And let me know how you go with Bridie. I'll see you later.'

After he leaves, Lowri lets out a very slow breath and closes her eyes, shaking her head for good measure. That had to be one of the most stilted, awkward conversations she's ever had. And in about half an hour she has to go and have another one with the monster under the bed.

Bridie Turner is wearing a chocolate-brown trouser suit today, ushering Lowri into Gordon's office with a beaming smile, her shoes clipping smartly across the tiled floor. 'You have moved at absolutely the best time of year,' she says. 'Spring at Clearwater is just a joy. How are you feeling now? A little more settled, I hope?'

'We've certainly been blessed with the weather,' replies Lowri. She smiles and nods hello to Gordon, who is behind his desk once more. 'It's been beautiful since I arrived.' As to whether she's feeling more settled, Lowri can't possibly answer, her heart is thundering in her chest. She knows she has every right to do the things she's doing, but she still can't escape from the feeling that her intentions are a slight on all Bridie and Gordon's work in the past.

'So, what can we do for you today, Mrs Morgan? Have you had a chance to think about your position here?'

'It's Lowri, please.'

Bridie shakes her head as if to chastise herself. 'Sorry, Lowri... do go on.' She looks expectantly up at her, but then changes her mind. 'Actually, before we start, I wondered whether we should make our meetings a regular thing? I wasn't sure if that would be something you'd find useful, but if it would help, I'm happy to put it in my diary.' She pauses. 'Maybe not weekly, but fortnightly? Monthly? Whatever you think best.'

'Oh... I hadn't really thought.' But now that Lowri has, she can see how useful an exercise it would be. At least that way she can keep everyone up to date with how things are moving. Miscommunication can spell disaster for any project. She should know, she says it to her clients so often she sounds like a stuck record. 'Monthly sounds good.'

Bridie nods. 'We'll fix the next date before we finish then. Of course, it depends on what you decide about your role here, but Gordon was very excited by your last conversation,' she adds, 'so I'm very much looking forward to hearing what you have to say. Anyway, have a seat, I'm gabbling on.'

Lowri sits down, feeling very much as if she's the new girl-friend been brought home to be interrogated by parents. She only hopes she doesn't disappoint.

'So, have you had some ideas?' asks Bridie without delay. 'Gordon mentioned you wanted to look at our rather horrible heap of a building.'

Her very accurate assessment surprises Lowri. 'Well, possi-bly... although nothing specific at this stage, I'm afraid. It's more some general thoughts about the estate.' She pauses. 'But I also want to say that I'm really very happy to leave our arrangement stand as it is at the moment. My ideas are some way off in the future yet, but I thought I should let you know what I'm think-ing, out of courtesy more than anything else.'

'Sounds very intriguing.' Bridie leans a little further forward. 'Go on.'

Lowri gathers herself, pressing the soles of her feet against the floor to stop her knees from jiggling up and down. 'Basically, I'd like to see the castle restored. I mean, I'm looking into it.'

'Goodness. Well, I don't think we were expecting that, were we, Gordon? But what a wonderful idea.' Bridie is clearly delighted. 'You know, I secretly hoped you would. I think that's perfect.' She sits back with a broad smile on her face.

'And do you see this as a money-making venture?' asks Gordon. 'Obviously, I wholeheartedly agree it's about time Clearwater was restored. But are you thinking it might help with our cash flow?'

Lowri swallows, Huw's very emphatic comments still fresh in her memory. 'Not entirely. Actually, I'm not really sure at the moment.'

'Because anything which can bring in revenue has to be good,' says Gordon.

'Yes, but these plans are a way off yet, obviously. And I think there are stipulations in some of the grant applications which might make this more difficult.'

'I'm impressed,' says Bridie. 'You *have* done your homework.'

Lowri smiles. 'Not really, or not yet anyway. It seems as if there's rather a lot of homework *to* do. And we also thought—'

'We?'

'Sorry, a figure of speech. I also thought that the old water-mill should figure in the restoration plans as well. There's the heritage angle, of course, but it could also prove a very practical move in terms of providing space for the business... potentially.'

Bridie's eyes narrow. 'To expand, you mean?'

Lowri really doesn't want to get into specifics just now. She nods. 'Or just to relocate. Like you said, the existing building is a bit of a heap, and so money to restore the mill could help us gain a space which is viable.'

Looks are being exchanged and Lowri can see something flicker between them.

'That could indeed provide a very useful alternative.' Bridie is quiet for a moment. 'It's possibly a little too early for this, but would you like me to enquire about potential contractors?' she asks. 'I know a lot of people hereabouts and have some very useful contacts I can call upon.'

'Thanks, but I've been given the name of someone who could most likely help with the mill, and—'

'Who by?'

Lowri is taken aback by the speed of the question. 'Oh... um... Huw Pritchard, actually. I've engaged him to look into the restoration of the castle.'

'Excellent,' replies Bridie. 'A very wise idea. I don't know much about him, but I've heard he's very talented.'

Lowri, who had been expecting abject warnings and doom-and-gloom prophecies about going anywhere near Huw, is a little confused.

'Let me know, though, if you need any more help on the people front,' adds Bridie.

Lowri nods. 'I will, although I don't anticipate that being for a while yet.'

'Of course.' Bridie smiles at Gordon. 'Having someone take an interest in Clearwater is a very welcome breath of fresh air, Lowri, I can tell you. Sorry, no disrespect to your husband, of course, but this all sounds wonderful.'

Bridie's comment was meant as a compliment, Lowri knows that, but she also heard the glib way those last words were delivered, as if they were merely an afterthought. And she cannot help but wonder if it was a deliberate gibe, or simply said without any real thought. She's not sure which is worse. Jess's question from the other day comes back to her. Maybe now would be the perfect opportunity to ask Bridie about Alun, except that Lowri knows she won't, and she's angry with herself because of it. What is she scared of anyway?

She's about to make her usual demure reply along the lines of 'it's really no problem', when she realises how irritated she's suddenly become. Words *do* matter and maybe she's just being sensitive, but it strikes her that by being so anxious to please, to keep the status quo and not upset either Bridie or Gordon, she's tacitly condoning the way the estate has been run. Even though it's been done with the best of intentions, from everything she's seen it really hasn't been run all that well. If Lowri wants things to change, it's down to her, and she can still be tactful and still be nice but, she reminds herself, she can also do whatever she likes.

She smiles. 'There is something else I thought I might run by you both. Only, looking at the history of the place and knowing how important the heritage angle is in trying to secure these grants, it got me thinking. No disrespect to what's being produced here at all, but it did make me wonder if it wasn't the perfect opportunity to try something a little different.'

'I see...' Bridie flashes Gordon a swift look. 'In what way?'

'Oh, I haven't the foggiest idea yet, it was just a thought that might be worth looking into.' Lowri is, of course, lying through her teeth, but she has no intention of bringing Elin's name, or her designs, into anything she discusses here today.

'Absolutely,' replies Gordon. 'I think we touched on this the other day. Conversations about product are always useful, but I think it's only right that I mention now what an incredibly tough market we're working in. The impact of any changes must be fully understood before being implemented.'

'Oh gosh, yes,' agrees Lowri. 'It could be a disaster otherwise. Has anything like this ever been discussed before? Or tried even? I'm afraid I don't know the history behind what's manufactured here.'

Gordon shakes his head. 'Not that I can recall in my time.'

'Okay,' Lowri replies lightly. 'I wouldn't want to come up with a brilliant idea only to find you've been there and done that.'

Gordon smirks. 'Bought the tee shirt even.'

It's just the kind of comment Lowri's dad would have made, his eyes twinkling at her because he knew just how rubbish a joke it was. It was a little game they played. Gordon, however, is not twinkling. Lowri thinks for a moment.

'Maybe when we're at that stage, I could bring any ideas to you and we could go through that process together? I obviously need to understand the existing business far more than I do at present, and I imagine there's heaps to learn.' She gives him a warm smile. 'In fact, I know you're very busy, but would we be able to make a start on that reasonably soon? I just feel the more I know, the better.'

'Let's put something in the diary,' suggests Bridie, cutting in. 'We're nearly in May now, so how about something towards the end of the month? When you've had a chance to look at the restoration grants.'

Lowri pulls out her phone. 'Let's see, where are we now?' She calls up her diary. 'It's only the nineteenth of April now though, so the end of May is quite a long way away. How about the third? That's a Monday too, would that work?' She wrinkles her nose. 'Actually, that's only two weeks away... If it's easier, I could take some stuff away with me and look through it in my own time. Even if it's just the profit and loss account. I know how busy you must be.'

There's a large hardback book on the edge of Gordon's desk and he pulls it closer. 'It's really no trouble. Let me see how the third is looking.' A thin ribbon peeps from the bottom of the pages and Gordon uses it to pull open the diary. It's just a little too far away for Lowri to see clearly. Removing a pen from his desk drawer, he makes a quick mark before shutting the book. 'I can make room for that, no problem,' he says. 'All sorted.'

'Well, that's excellent,' says Bridie, and something in her tone communicates that it's time Lowri was on her way. But that's fine, she's said what she came to say.

'I can't thank you enough. Really.' Lowri drops her head a little. 'I was a bit worried that you'd resent my coming here and interfering.'

'Not at all, Lowri. I know I speak for Gordon as well, but we've looked after Clearwater for quite some time and she steals a little bit of your heart, if truth be told. It's been – how shall we say? – a little frustrating at times not being able to do those things we thought needed doing, so anything which improves the situation here, for the estate, our workers, has to be a good thing. I don't see that as interfering at all.' Bridie finishes with a warm smile.

'Right then, I'd better be going,' says Lowri, getting to her feet. She holds out her hand and shakes first Gordon's and then Bridie's. 'I'll keep you posted.'

A few moments later, Lowri leaves the office and heads back into the sunshine. What she wouldn't give to be a fly on the wall right now.

She takes her time walking back to the gatehouse, pausing by the mill to run her eyes over its handsome lines. On a whim, she takes the steps up into the garden and stands at the rail for a moment, looking out over the millpond. As she searches the riverbank on the far side, her hand instinctively moves to the warmth of the stone around her neck. But she knows Seren's not there, not today.

She feels relieved that her meeting went well, that her decisions were received with such good grace, but there's something else... something she can't yet put her finger on, but which is sitting uneasily. Would Gordon have remembered that Elin had been to see him once upon a time? Full of ideas about how they might transform the business. He certainly should have done. And if he did, then why didn't he mention it? Perhaps it was just Bridie's comment about Alun which unsettled her, but Lowri isn't sure.

She thinks a moment, analysing the emotions which are running through her, those on the surface and those that run deeper. Words *do* matter, they matter a great deal, and she feels the sudden sharp sting of those she said to Huw. They were inexcusable. So maybe he liked a drink a little too much. Whatever his problems, it wasn't her right to berate him about it, to belittle him and treat him like a child. What she should have done was show him some understanding, some compassion. She told Elin she didn't want to know what his problems were because then she'd have to care about them, but, with a sudden pang of shame, she realises that's exactly what she should be doing. She's incredibly lucky he even turned up on site this morning. If she were him, she'd have told her very firmly where to stick it. She shakes her head as if trying to clear it. Lowri has some new words to say and now would be as good a time as any to say them.

But, as she approaches the gatehouse and looks towards the castle keep, she realises now is not the time to say them at all. Huw is standing, just as he was this morning, square to the building, his face tilted to the sky. There's something about his stance though, which catches her eye. The way his hands hang limply by his sides, the way his legs seem almost unable to bear his weight. And she doesn't need to see his face, or speak to him, to understand the emotion which courses through him, his shaking shoulders are words enough.

Silently, she moves on past and slips inside her hallway, where she closes the heavy oak door ever so quietly.

When she dares to look again, Huw has recovered himself and is moving slowly, almost reverentially through the site. He stops to examine stone after stone, some he moves and others he leaves where they fell. A while after that, she sees him sitting cross-legged on the scrubby grass, a pad in his lap, committing something to paper with quick strokes. By mid afternoon, he's leaning up against the wall, studying something on his iPad. He stays that way for a very long time.

It's late by the time Huw finally leaves, the sun already fading from the day. She turns from where she's been making herself and Wren their tea to find him standing in the kitchen doorway, a tentative smile on his face.

'I just wanted to say thank you,' he says. 'For letting me come here today.' He's holding a piece of paper in his hand, his fingers pulling out the creases as he speaks. 'I don't doubt Elin has told you plenty of stories about me and I'm not proud that most of them are true. But I do care about Clearwater. And I'll do a good job for you, I promise you that.' He turns slightly as if to look back at the remains of the building. 'Maybe I care too much, and that's my problem.'

Lowri doesn't know what to say. 'I was watching you earlier... And you seemed, it's hard to describe, but peaceful maybe?'

He nods. 'I lose myself when I'm here, I don't know why.' His eyes suddenly roam her face. 'Some folk reckon this is a thin place. I'm not sure if I hold with that, but there's something about it all the same.'

'Well, you're welcome to come back,' she says. 'Anytime, not just when you're working.' She pauses. 'In fact, I was thinking about your boat. Because if your mooring licence is administered by the estate then, in theory, I could alter the terms, couldn't I? Given that I now own it.'

'I guess you could, yes...'

'In which case, it seems ridiculous that you keep having to move. Why don't you just stay where you are? Or better still, moor closer? Especially now that you're going to be on site so much.'

Lowri can't clearly see his expression, hidden as it is behind his huge beard, but she can see the way his eyes light up.

'Thank you, I will. It's much quieter than upriver, where I'm closer to the town. Bridie is going to hate it though...' He pauses. 'But, she won't be able to do a thing about it, will she? Oh, sweet joy of joys.'

Lowri grins at his choice of words. 'She seems perfectly reasonable to me. What's she ever done to you?'

'Maybe another time,' he says. 'But really, thank you.'

Lowri doesn't say it, but the thought of having someone keeping an eye on Clearwater is also quite appealing, even if it is Huw. 'You're welcome. And if there are any problems with Bridie, I'll sort them out.' It's bravado she doesn't have, but it seems the right thing to say. 'Although I can't see why it would be a problem. Why does it matter where you moor?'

Huw shrugs. 'I dunno. And I've never seen the point in asking. It wouldn't change anything and she'd just say it was standard terms. Most boaters *do* need residential permits.'

'So, are there quite a few people living on the river then?'

Huw shakes his head. 'As far as I know, I'm the only one.'

'Then it's hardly a money-making exercise, is it? I'm just wondering why Bridie insists you keep moving...' She suddenly has an impish desire to tease him. 'Unless you're a real trouble-maker, of course.'

And the slow smile which works its way up his face totally transforms it.

11

The week has whizzed by. It's late Friday afternoon, and the three of them are sitting around the kitchen table. Lowri is writing a shopping list, Huw is busy on his laptop, using a program which seems impenetrable to Lowri, but will allow him to produce all manner of plans, and Wren is sitting by his side, drawing a picture of a castle. Every now and again, she nudges him to show some new detail and he smiles, giving her a thumbs up. Several times he's had Wren in fits of giggles, showing her a drawing he's made on his laptop, but infuriatingly he won't let Lowri see. Just lowers the lid when she tries to look and raises his eyebrows at her.

Two weeks ago, Lowri really wasn't sure how to introduce Huw to her daughter, wondering how she would cope with having a strange man in her house, and one who looked so big and scary at that. But she needn't have worried. Huw kept his movements slow and his voice low, as if she was a young foal and easily spooked and, as the days went by, the quick glances became longer and the wary expressions became smiles. Now, they chat away like old friends – most often with him at one end of the table, huge and hairy, and she at the other, small and fairylike. A most peculiar pair of bookends.

The days may be flying by, but they have a way to go yet before they'll be in a position to submit a grant bid. The requirements are extensive and time-consuming, and they're really going to be up against it if they're to meet the submission deadline. Michael Cornish, the millwright, can't come to see them for another week yet and much depends on what he has to say. All they can do, meanwhile, is carry on, putting flesh on their plans and researching what they can.

This afternoon, Lowri has spent time looking at other renovation projects around the country, trying to come up with a unique selling point for Clearwater. It's clear from the grant requirements that, once finished, the restored buildings must add something to the local community, being a draw for tourists is simply not enough. There's the watermill too, of course – visitors to the site could potentially have two attractions to see – but even that doesn't make them stand out from any other historical site. They need something special, but at this precise moment Lowri has no idea what. Her attention wandering from her shopping list, she's about to ask Huw a question when a sudden frantic banging on the kitchen window has her nearly leaping out of her skin. It's true that anyone knocking on the front door is often unheard, but a gentle tap would suffice. Honestly…

Lowri swings around in her seat, a scowl on her face, until she realises the person outside is Seren. And she does not look happy.

She bangs again, even though she has Lowri's full attention. 'Please!' she shouts. 'Is Huw there?'

Lowri can only just hear her, but at the mention of his name, Huw jumps to his feet and goes crashing through the kitchen door.

'Stay here, sweetheart,' Lowri murmurs to Wren, slipping from her chair and following quickly in his wake.

'I was in the garden,' says Seren, her voice full of anguish. 'Please, you need to come.' Seren snatches at Huw's arm, her frame tiny beside his. 'It's your boat, Huw...'

At first glance, Lowri thinks Seren is still in her nightie. Her feet are bare, and the white fabric of it hangs to just below her knees. But then, Lowri realises she's simply wearing a cotton smocked dress, the hem of which has clearly snagged on something in her haste to get here.

Seren is still pulling at Huw's arm. 'Please, it's sinking!'

With a look at Lowri, Huw takes off, running through the gate at speed, leaving her and Seren behind.

'I didn't know what to do,' Seren says, her chest still heaving. 'I was weeding, in the garden, and I looked up to see it was listing. Lowri, they sink so fast, all I could think of was to get here as quickly as I could.'

Lowri nods. 'I'm sure you did the right thing.' It's an automatic response, trying to bring comfort, but also because Lowri has no clue what to do either. 'Should we call the police? The fire brigade?'

'There's no time, she'll be gone. And all his things are on board!'

Suddenly realising the enormity of Seren's sentence, Lowri looks back to the gatehouse, torn. 'Wren is still here.' Should she ask her to stay behind? Or take her along when she has no idea what she's running into? Dashing back to the kitchen, she snatches up her phone from beside the cooker. 'Wren, sweetheart, come with me. Quick as you can, lovely.' She takes her daughter's hand, leading her around the table.

'What's the matter, Mummy?'

'We need to run, okay? To the river, but you hold my hand.'

Back outside, Seren is hobbling across the stones in the pitted lane, making for the grassy verge as quickly as she can. 'I'll raise the alarm,' she says, pointing at the factory. 'Maybe some others can help?'

Lowri nods, not at all sure how Seren will manage it, her feet will be cut to pieces. But she can't worry about that now. Grasping Wren tightly, Lowri pulls her towards the gate. 'Come on, sweetheart, let's see how fast we can run.'

Together, they take off across the fields, Wren stumbling a little on the uneven ground.

'What's the matter?' she asks again. 'Where's Huw gone?'

'To the river, so we have to hurry.' Lowri has neither the time nor the breath to answer Wren's questions, but she does the best she can, trying not to alarm her. 'Come on, we're almost there.'

She can see the boat now, lying serenely in the sunshine, but as they near, it becomes immediately obvious that this is no pretty waterside scene. The boat is in big trouble. The rear deck is almost underwater, and Huw himself is ankle-deep as he grapples with the door hatch.

'Huw!' she yells. But if he hears, he takes no notice.

As Lowri watches, to her horror, Huw disappears inside the boat, reappearing seconds later with an armful of belongings which he manhandles through the opening. On reaching the deck, he flings them towards the riverbank.

Lowri stops, dropping to her knees until she's facing Wren. 'You stay here, okay? You don't come any further forward.' She waits until her daughter's anxious face nods silently before getting to her feet again and running closer to the boat. Fear floods her face with heat; she has no idea what to do. She races to pick up the clothing Huw has thrown, pulling it away from the bank, but no sooner has she done so than he's back with another arm load, panting with exertion.

'Lowri, here, take these!'

She looks up in horror – at his hands reaching out to her – at the water swelling over the deck and pouring down the steps into the boat. It swirls in a torrent, fast and getting faster still.

'Quickly!'

Huw's sharp voice cuts across her, but she can't do this, the water is too much. She stares at him helplessly, at his puzzled face. His home is fast disappearing and she's doing nothing to help. Gritting her teeth, she leaps onto the gunwale, which is still above the water line, grabbing a rope and pulling herself onto the boat. She will need to step down into the water if she's going to save any of his things.

The next second, a bundle is thrust at her and she has no choice but to jump down onto the deck and take it. Huw is already launching himself back through the door, jumping the steps to land in water up to his knees. The boat lurches sickeningly as he does so and, for a moment, Lowri is thrown completely off balance. She throws out a hand to the roof, steadying herself, shuddering as the freezing river laps over her feet.

She jumps to the bank, flinging her cargo from her arms, with no thought for Huw's possessions other than to get them out of her hands. She's about to jump back on the boat when she sees Wren running forward to pick up what she's just thrown.

'Wren, no! Just leave them, okay? They'll be fine.' She sees her daughter hesitate, wanting to help, but knowing she should do as she's told. 'Stay there!'

With one final check, Lowri launches herself back at the boat, collecting another armful of belongings, scrabbling to keep hold of them before jumping back on land. Over and over she does this, and each time she deposits his things safely, she realises it's taking him longer and longer to return to her. He reaches her again, his tee shirt wet well above his waist, his beard dripping with water. His eyes are panicked, wild and fearful, and she wonders how she looks to him. Can he feel her terror too, or is he just locked within his own?

The minutes click by as books, clothes, mugs... a saucepan, all make it safely to the bank. A shout goes up as she flings a pile of papers onto the grass. They're wet and bedraggled but suddenly several hands appear, taking them from her, making them safe, people picking up other things and moving them further away. She returns to the boat.

The next time she swings around, the bank is massed with people and she searches among them frantically. Where is Wren? A cry from behind pulls her away, and she rushes to the steps. Huw has fallen, missed his footing and is all but submerged. He lurches to his feet, spitting water from his mouth and shaking his head. Blood trickles from a gash on the side of it.

'Huw! Come out!' Lowri reaches forward with her hand, but he ignores her, pushing himself upright and wading back down the boat. 'Huw!'

The water is now over the gunwale and Lowri can no longer see where to put her feet. She can feel it tugging at her, wanting her, but she can't leave yet. Huw is still down there, lost from sight. A sudden shift throws her off balance, and it's only the rope on the roof which saves her from toppling backwards. But the water is coming faster now. The tipping point is fast approaching.

'Lowri!' It's Elin, shouting from the bank, her voice almost lost among the others. A hand is thrust towards her. 'Jump! Come on!'

Lowri looks frantically back down the steps. 'Huw, come on, that's it now, there's no time. Huw, *please!*' With a desperate shout, Lowri turns, inching her foot forward, trying to find the edge of the deck as the water swirls around her knees. She can't find the gunwale, and she must step onto it first if she's to jump over it without catching her feet.

'Lowri!' Elin's voice comes again, her hand wiggling, stretching out, trying to close the inches between them.

Lowri's foot makes contact, she steps, and misses, her knee

bashing painfully against steel. Her hand grapples the air and then...

'I've got you!'

There's a wrench and Lowri feels herself falling forward.

'It's okay, I've got you...'

Lowri's hands grapple for the bank, for the arms trying to pull her up. She's trying to stand but the grass is wet, slick with water.

'Mummy!'

Lowri hears Wren's anxious cry, sees her face, rushing closer, too close, too fast. Lowri is trying to stand, to hold Wren, but her foot is slipping, slipping... She's falling, holding, pulling... and, as if in slow motion, she feels them both toppling, falling backwards. Their tipping point has been reached.

There's a shock of cold and then water closes over her head. And all is silent.

Moments later, Lowri tears through the water, pushing her head above its surface. She drags in a breath. 'Wren!'

She has let go.

She kicks out, her arms and legs flailing, trying to find substance, but finding only the strong grip of the river. She splutters, eyes filling with water, blinking, spitting... *Wren, where is Wren?*

Then, suddenly, Seren is beside her, a hand under her chin, her face only inches from Lowri's. 'It's okay,' she murmurs, 'It's okay.'

For a moment, Lowri knows how safety feels, but then it's gone and she's left with nothing to hold, and for the second time the water claims her.

The next thing she knows, strong arms are around her, pulling her upwards. Her head breaks the surface and Elin is there again, laying on the riverbank, flat on her stomach, hauling at Lowri's arms. Someone else joins her and with a grunt, Lowri is grounded on the bank, like a fish, gasping for air.

She rolls onto her back, struggling to sit. 'Where's Wren!?'

Elin's arms are around her. 'It's okay,' she croons. 'She's safe. Seren has her. Lowri, it's okay.'

Lowri's head whips back and forth, her eyes raking the water beyond the boat. There's only half of it left now, the rear submerged, drawn into the river. And then she sees them, a little distance away.

'Jesus, the current's too strong...'

Lowri hears the voice behind her, panicked, and, as she watches, she realises that one of Seren's arms is flailing wildly, the other under Wren's armpit as she struggles to keep her afloat.

'Shit... Someone get in there...'

'No, don't, it's not safe, you'll all drown!'

The words aren't hers. She doesn't know whose they are, but Lowri wants to yell at them. To plead. To beg. To do whatever it takes. Only *please* do something...

Another shout goes up and, as her attention wavers, she sees the impossible out of the corner of her eye. Someone is walking on water. No, not someone... Huw.

As Lowri turns, Huw staggers, exhausted, and it's only when she realises he must be standing on the roof of the boat that he plunges, headfirst, into the water. She thinks he's fallen, but then as the noise around her rises, she realises he's swimming, his arms arcing overhead as he closes the distance between the boat and to where Seren is still struggling with Wren.

Lowri sees Wren's arms go around Huw's neck, Seren's feet kicking fiercely and, slowly, slowly, the three of them inch closer to the bank.

Moments later, Wren's tiny body is pressed up against hers, shaking, shivering, but alive. Lowri sinks into the warm huddle of arms around her, and holds her daughter as if she'll never let her go.

. . .

'She's asleep,' says Lowri, coming back down the stairs into the living room. 'Tucked up with her two favourite teddies and a few extra for good measure.'

Despite the relative warmth of the spring evening, a fire is roaring in the grate and Lowri feels it's soothing heat wrap around her as she sits down on the sofa. She wasn't sure she'd ever feel warm again.

It's nearly half past seven and just three of them are left in the gatehouse: herself, Elin and Huw. Countless people offered Huw a bed for the night, including Elin's mum, Mari, but Lowri was fierce in her insistence that he stay with her. He's lost almost everything he has, yet in saving Wren, given her everything she could ever want. She will not hear of him going anywhere else.

Elin has made another round of drinks and a plateful of hot, buttered toast with jam, which she's placed on the sofa between them. After the shock of the last few hours they all feel suddenly ravenous, the sweet saltiness of this simple fare absolutely what they crave.

They've all been checked over by one of the GPs from the local practice who, after hearing the news, very kindly called in on his way home. Apart from warmth and plenty of rest, no other prescriptions were necessary. He didn't need to tell them how lucky they all were.

'Right,' says Elin.

It's the third time she's said it in the space of ten minutes, and each time she has, Lowri has met her look expectantly, yet Elin remained exactly where she was, staring into space. This time, however, she stirs herself.

'I really should get going,' she adds. 'Are you sure there's nothing else I can do?'

Lowri shakes her head. 'Honestly, Elin, thank you, but I think all we need now is some sleep and a new day.'

'Hmm, well make sure you do what the doctor said, get plenty of rest now.'

'I will,' replies Lowri, walking Elin to the door. 'Promise.'

Huw's belongings, or what's left of them, are piled outside, ferried there by a succession of people who all wanted to help. Many of them are sodden and may never recover, and all of them will need a home at some point. But, for now, Lowri's porch is as good a place as any. Most importantly, his laptop, notebooks, and satchel full of maps, plans and drawings is still in her kitchen. He's thanked God more than once they're all safe.

Elin picks her way through the assortment of possessions. 'What's he going to do?' she whispers.

'I have no idea,' replies Lowri. 'Except take one day at a time.'

Elin nods. 'Well, if you need a hand, just let me know. I'll catch up with you tomorrow anyhow.' She holds out her arms for a hug. 'Are you sure you're okay?'

'I'm fine, Elin, honestly,' Lowri replies, pulling away. It's perhaps the eighth or ninth time Elin has asked the question. 'And thank you, really, for everything you've done to help.'

Elin gives her a stern look. 'It's no bother. And make sure you give Wren a big squidge from me.'

'I'll give her two.' Lowri smiles. 'Night, Elin.'

As much as she loves her, Lowri's quite glad to be, finally, almost, on her own. She's overwhelmingly tired. With any luck, Huw won't be in the mood to talk either.

When she returns to the living room, however, she finds Huw frowning, his brow furrowed in response to some internal conversation he's clearly wrestling with. And she realises he's been this way for the last hour or so; preoccupied, there with them in the room, but not there, lost in his thoughts. It's perfectly understandable, but Lowri wonders if it isn't just the obvious which is bothering him.

'What is it?' she asks. 'Something's the matter.' She grimaces. 'Sorry, that was really tactless. Aside from having your boat sink, that is.'

Huw thinks for a moment, his fingers pulling at one side of his beard. It's something he often does, she's noticed. 'I guess it's just that there aren't many ways you can sink a narrowboat.' He blinks at her. 'That's not strictly true, there are plenty of ways accidents happen. Locks are the riskiest places. Unwary boaters can easily get the bow end caught on a lock gate and when the water level drops...' He makes a slanted angle with his arm. 'It doesn't end well.'

'But you were nowhere near a lock.'

'Exactly, nor a weir or on a tidal river. Boat ropes not too tight against a rising river level—' He breaks off, studying her face.

Lowri frowns. 'So what are you saying?'

Huw pushes a hand through his hair. 'I don't know really, I guess I'm just tired.' He looks weary to the bone.

'But?'

'One of the easier ways to scupper a narrowboat is to open the weed hatch. Looks like an accident, something a novice boater might do... something a drunken boater might do in a forgetful moment...'

Lowri sits up a little straighter. 'But you didn't leave the weed hatch open?'

Huw shakes his head. No trace of doubt in his mind. She studies him a moment. 'So what you're saying is that someone sank your boat on purpose?'

Huw doesn't reply. He doesn't need to.

'But who on earth would do something like that?'

He gives an easy shrug. 'I can think of a few folk. I've not made many friends the last couple of years.'

'Yes, but...' Lowri is astounded by how well he seems to be taking this. She'd be leaping up and down, cursing whoever did it to kingdom come. 'Even so, there's no excuse for doing something like that.' And all she can think is that she's incredibly glad Huw wasn't on board when it went down; asleep, or in a drunken stupor... It doesn't bear thinking about. 'So what will you do now?' she asks softly.

'I'll find something, don't worry.'

But Lowri does worry. If Huw hasn't made many friends of late, it's not very likely there'll be queues of people falling over themselves to put him up. The answer is patently obvious, but it might be the rashest thing Lowri has ever done.

'You can stay here,' she says. 'And don't look at me like that, I mean it.' She pauses. 'I can't offer you more than the sofa, I'm afraid, but you're very welcome to that.'

Huw's look is a mixture of things, some of which are hard to identify. He dips his head. 'We'll see,' he says. 'But I'll be very grateful for it tonight.'

He closes his eyes briefly, and Lowri gets the sense that this is a conversation he's reluctant to continue. She can understand that. But she's also very conscious that she doesn't want their chat to end altogether. Despite the circumstances, she feels quite peaceful sitting here in the dimly lit room.

'I wish Seren had stayed,' she says, trying to guide them towards a safer topic. 'I don't like the thought of her being alone tonight.'

'But that's because you're not Seren,' replies Huw. 'I think the last thing she would want is a horde of people around her. Solitude isn't always lonely. And for Seren, it's also a place of safety. She's been on her own a long time, Lowri.'

His words surprise her, but Lowri can see the truth in them. She still finds it sad though, because although Seren *has* been on her own a long time, it doesn't mean she chose it as a way of life. Surely it was forced on her by circumstance? Lowri shivers, remembering the tragedy in Seren's past. In *her* past too… And how close they both came to it again today.

She closes her eyes, forcing back the image that has always haunted her, one she recognises might not even be real, but it makes no difference. Whether it's purely an invention of her brain, or not, the effect is still the same.

The trouble with emotions though, is that sometimes they won't be told. Sometimes they won't be well-behaved and stay in the boxes Lowri puts them in. And, at times, when she's over-tired, or feeling under the weather, when her resistance is low, they're even harder to control. Times like this evening.

Without warning, Lowri's eyes fill with tears, and before she can blink them away, change the subject and pretend nothing is happening, one spills from the corner of her eye and traces its way down her cheek.

Flustered, she scrabbles for a tissue. She usually has one in a pocket somewhere… 'I'm sorry, I… Oh God, this is ridiculous.' She wipes furiously under her eye, sniffing as she tries to control herself. 'I was just thinking about what happened to Seren when she was younger and… I'm sorry,' she repeats.

But Huw's hand is on her arm. 'You should cry,' he says. 'It'll help.' His eyes are soft on hers. 'You've been more scared today than I'm guessing you have been for a very long time, that has to go somewhere.'

Lowri manages to nod, furious with herself, but she's still determined not to let herself go.

'And I'm sorry too,' he adds.

Lowri stares at him. 'You big eejit, what on earth are you sorry for?' she asks, embarrassed now.

His eyes flick to hers and away again, uncertain. 'I would never have asked you to help if I knew you couldn't swim.'

His words hang in the air, their size increasing until they've outgrown the space allotted to them, expanding to fill the whole room and taking the air with them.

Lowri swallows. 'I... I never learned, and I should, I know, it's terrible for Wren. I should have taken her when she was little, but I just couldn't bear it. I did go once, but I had a panic attack and never went back.' She hangs her head. 'She could have died today and it would have been all my fault.'

'No,' says Huw, firmly, 'it wouldn't. Wren's small and the current is strong in that section of river. It's wide and most people don't realise. Seren's a strong swimmer, and even she struggled.'

'Then *she* might have drowned too and...' Even the thought makes the back of Lowri's neck heat unbearably.

'But she didn't. What happened today is a terrible, scary thing, Lowri, but no one was hurt. And I know you're thinking of what happened to Seren's brother, but it was a long time ago now and if Seren couldn't cope with the memories she wouldn't choose to live by the river. Despite the fact that she looks as if a puff of wind would blow her over, she's a tough cookie. She'll be okay.' He smiles. 'And so are you.'

But Lowri won't be comforted. 'No, you don't understand...' The moment the words are out of her mouth she wants to take them back. She doesn't want anyone to understand. She doesn't want to have to tell anyone what happened, and why she feels so guilty. Jess is the only person who knows.

Huw nods. It's a tiny movement, a weighing up of the words which came out of her mouth compared with what her body is saying. 'You could tell me,' he says quietly. 'Sometimes we think that's the last thing we want to do, when actually the opposite is true. And if you ask yourself that question I think you'll have your answer.'

It's as if something inside Lowri unlocks. She gives a nod of her own, breathing in the wisdom of Huw's words. 'Wren's dad... my husband, Alun, died in a car accident two years ago. He was driving home to us, coming over the bridge into the village, when a four-by-four coming the other way took it too fast. There's a sharp bend, you see, just as you come off it and as the other driver swerved, he hit Alun. Alun crashed through the bridge and into the water, nose first, the rear end of the car hung up on the bridge support. His door jammed, and although they managed to get him out eventually, he'd been under the water too long and he died later in hospital.' Another silent tear rolls down Lowri's cheek.

'I sometimes wonder if that's why I've always been afraid of water – that somehow I always knew I would lose someone to it. It's as if I knew what fate had in store for me and all my life I've feared it. So when Alun died... I sometimes think that's my fault too,' she whispers. 'That if Alun had never met me, he'd still be alive. That was my curse – that someone close to me had to drown. I fell in love with him, but in doing so I condemned him to death.'

Huw is quiet, and if he's embarrassed by Lowri's tears or made to feel awkward, he doesn't show it. 'But if you'd never met Alun, your life would be so different in so many ways. Who knows if that would have been bad or good. And without him, little Wren would not be here.' He studies her face. 'You know, the same is also true in reverse, that fate may not have been working solely for you when it brought Alun to you, but also for him. Have you ever considered that? That perhaps he was your fate too?' He lays a hand on her arm. Just one. Gentle, and undemanding. Warm.

Lowri blinks. She's never thought of it like that. 'Even so, what happened today...' She shivers. 'I've been afraid of water all my life, and I've seen first-hand what it can do, heard what it can do as well. Mine isn't the only life that's been changed irrevocably. And now yours has too. Sometimes, I can't work out why I thought moving here would be a good idea. I'm surrounded by the very thing I hate.'

Huw tips his head at her. 'Seren once told me that the river has a spirit. She says a lot of things that don't hold with a lot of folk, but I've always thought there to be some truth in that. She said that just as the river has a spirit, so does the air, the ground... and each work in harmony with one another.'

'Yes, she told me our plans to restore the watermill were a good thing. She said it would help heal the land.'

Huw nods. 'Mmm. They're supposed to exist in balance, you see, and without that balance, things don't happen as they're meant to, they can't. She says the day the millwheel stopped turning is the day the problems started. It denies the river its energy, its spirit, and without that, it dies. The river is powerful. She can be cruel, you've seen what she's taken today, but she can also be kind. She takes life, but she also gives life to others.'

'Do you believe that?'

He shrugs. 'At one time I'd have said Seren was as batty as they come. Now? Now it makes as much sense as anything else I've heard. I also know something else.'

'What's that?'

He nods towards the stone still hanging around Lowri's neck. 'If Seren has given you that, she thinks you're in the right place, Lowri. You're where you're meant to be, you *and* little Wren. There's comfort in that, I think.'

Lowri nods. She *does* feel oddly comforted.

He smiles, his face not half as scary in the flickering light from the fire. 'Now, promise me something? Promise me you'll think about this and not just reject it out of hand. I won't be the slightest bit offended if you say no, but don't say no because you're embarrassed or because I'm...' He looks down at his chest. '... an oaf. But if you would like, and we take things slowly, go at your pace, I will teach you and little Wren how to swim.'

12

Bridie is poised and welcoming when Lowri arrives at the factory on Monday morning, opening the office door wide with a bright smile. She looks a good deal fresher than Lowri, who hasn't had much sleep.

'Lowri, come in. Goodness, you must be exhausted. Come and sit down. Gordon has gone to organise some drinks, but first tell me how you are? And Wren, of course, the poor mite. I did wonder if you would be able to come this morning, I can't imagine how you must be feeling. And Huw's boat too... what a horrible thing to have happened.'

'Um...' Lowri reels under a tumult of emotions. 'Yes, we've all been very lucky.' She nods. 'And we're okay. Tired, ache in places I didn't know we could ache, but—'

'So who's looking after little Wren?'

Lowri blinks. 'Sorry? Oh, no one, she wanted to go to school.'

'Did she? Oh... goodness.' Bridie's hand is hovering near her heart. 'She must be a plucky little thing.'

'Yes, she...' Irritation flickers through Lowri. She doesn't want Bridie referring to her daughter as little Wren, or little anything. It's *her* endearment and hearing it from Bridie's lips is wrong. It's over-familiar, too close to home, especially from someone Lowri hardly knows. 'I was expecting to keep her home, but she got herself up and ready for school as usual so it seemed better to stick with routine. I don't want to make a big deal over what happened.'

'Yes, quite.' Bridie nods. 'Well, anyway, I'm pleased to hear you're both all right. Ah, here's Gordon with the drinks.' She moves a couple of envelopes to one side of the desk, and replaces a pen in the pot. 'Pop them down here, Gordon, that's lovely. And biscuits too, excellent idea.'

'I thought they might be needed this morning,' he says, laying down a tray on the desk with a smile at Lowri. 'Tea, no sugar, if I remember rightly?'

Lowri nods. 'Yes, thank you.' She takes the proffered mug, wrapping her hands around it gratefully.

'Now then, the accounts,' says Bridie, smoothing down her skirt, as if to brush off unwanted crumbs. 'I've printed out the last full year's trading profit and loss statement, and also our current year to date, although given that we're only in early May that's only a month. Our accounting year runs with the tax year,' she adds, passing some papers across to Lowri. 'So that's April to the end of March.'

Lowri has to resist the impulse to roll her eyes.

'Shall I run through what these statements say? They can look a bit like gobbledegook.' Bridie points to the headings on the page. 'The most important line is this one – the bottom line – that shows the profit or loss the business has made and, happily, as you can see, we're turning in a profit, not a large one, but profit nonetheless. This section here, however, details expenditure...'

Lowri listens to her drone on about the nitty-gritty of the figures on the page, only half listening. She's tired and preoccupied, but that isn't it. Everything Bridie's saying is meaningless.

She's trying to make it sound like the document in front of Lowri is the Holy Grail, but without the supporting paperwork, the figures don't show anything. They don't even include budgets, let alone any variances to them. The business might be making a modest profit, but there's no real indication of how they arrived there, nor is there any indication where there might be room for improvement.

Lowri isn't naïve enough to think that any funding they're lucky enough to secure will pay for everything. They're going to need money for all manner of things, not least of all because Lowri has all but promised Elin her dream. But if they don't secure funding for the watermill, as well as the castle, then without a decent building, how can she ever realise it? And then there's Huw, he... Lowri stops, feeling the space his name occupies inside her head. Smiling at the space he occupies inside her home, too much at times, but...

Dragging her attention back to what Bridie is saying, Lowri realises she's waiting for an answer from her. And she has no idea what she's just been asked.

'It's a lot to take in, I know,' says Bridie. 'I can go through it again, if you like?'

'No, no,' says Lowri quickly. 'That's great. Thank you.' Flustered, she tries to remember what she wanted to say. 'So where can I find all the paperwork that goes with this?' she asks.

'Sorry, I'm not sure I understand,' says Bridie.

'Well, what you've shown me is really useful, a great summary of where the business is at, but how do I find out more? For example, where you show the admin costs here, made up of stationery, postage, telephone bills, etc., where do I find the detail on all of these?'

Bridie is beginning to look a little irritated. 'I hadn't realised you wanted to see so much information. Are you sure? It's rather complex.'

Lowri nods. 'I didn't think I did, when I first arrived, but now I've been thinking a bit further ahead, I've realised that I can't make any suggestions about how we run the business without understanding it more fully.'

'I see.' Bridie flashes a glance at Gordon. 'So does this mean you're also thinking about taking over the reins?'

'Goodness, no, nothing like that.'

'Only the accounts are all computerised. It really isn't that easy.'

Lowri pauses. 'Oh... Well, in that case, how about I ask my accountant to have a look? Actually, he isn't mine, he used to look after Alun's affairs, but he said it didn't matter what accounting software Alun used, as he was pretty familiar with them all. I bet he could help. You could just give him access and then I could ask *him* if I have any questions, save bothering you with them all the time. He's kind of a family friend, I'm sure he wouldn't mind.' Lowri smiles brightly, as if she just had the most marvellous idea.

Bridie, on the other hand, is just beginning to twig that maybe Lowri knows a little more about accounting than she's been letting on. She sits back in her chair. 'Why don't you have a chat with him then,' she replies. 'Then have him call me, that's the easiest thing. I'm sure we can work something out.'

Lowri stares at the shelves over Bridie's right shoulder. The shelves which are still empty. 'I will. Brilliant.' She gives an apologetic smile. 'Alun sometimes used to say I was a bit of a control freak, but it isn't that, just that I've got rather a lot of things in my head that all want thinking about. And I cope better when I have everything laid out just so.'

Bridie nods. 'Of course.'

Lowri can tell she's itching to stand up, a signal for her to go. So Lowri does it for her.

'I guess I'd better be off,' she says. 'Only I promised Huw I'd help him sort out his things.' She holds Bridie's look, curious to see her reaction now she's mentioned Huw's name. 'But, thanks so much for this morning.'

Gordon clears his throat. 'Terrible business yesterday. What an awful shock.'

'Yes, it was. But at least I still have a roof over my head.' She pauses. 'It's ironic, really, as Huw's boat was one of the things I wanted to talk to you about today.'

'Oh?' That got Bridie's attention.

Lowri nods. 'Yes, I wanted to look into changing the terms of his mooring permit. I wanted to extend it. It seems daft to me that he has to move every twelve days, particularly given that he's going to be working at Clearwater on an ongoing basis.'

'Indeed... And that would have been fine if the land belonged to Clearwater, but as it doesn't...' Bridie gives a small smile. 'Anyway, like you said, sadly it's rather academic now, isn't it?'

'I'm sorry?' A noise similar to a buzzing bee fills Lowri's head. 'What do you mean the land doesn't belong to Clearwater? I'm talking about the river meadow, just up from the castle.'

'Yes, that's right.'

'But it's on the map the solicitor gave me. It's part of Clearwater.'

'It used to be, yes, right up until the point I bought it.'

Something lurches in Lowri's stomach. '*You* bought it?'

Bridie frowns, looking first at Gordon, then back at Lowri. 'Oh dear, I thought you knew. How embarrassing. I should ask—'

'But how can you own it?' demands Lowri. 'Alun would never have sold part of the estate. Besides, he's had nothing to do with it. How could you possibly—'

'Goodness, this is unfortunate,' Bridie soothes in response to Lowri's raised voice. 'I'm so sorry, but Alun never owned it in the first place. The executors of his uncle's estate needed to liquidise some assets to pay for inheritance tax, so I bought that parcel of land before your husband even received his bequest. I thought you would have known. And the solicitor certainly should have made you aware of it.'

'Yes, he should...' Lowri is so shocked – and angry – she can hardly speak.

Bridie is looking at her, an expression on her face which she no doubt thinks is sympathetic, but which Lowri sees as pitying. The poor little wife whose husband kept details of his inheritance from her, and who now doesn't even own what she thought she did. She's been made into a laughing stock.

'I need to go,' she blusters. 'I promised I'd be back to help Huw.' It's all she can do to keep from running for the door. Anything to be out from under Bridie's oh-so-understanding gaze.

Lowri is almost at the door when Bridie clears her throat. 'Erm... actually, Lowri, I wonder if... Oh dear. I didn't want to say anything before when you first mentioned Huw because I know you're only trying to help, and I know you're looking into the possibility of restoring Clearwater House, but when you're new to a place it can take a little while to get to know what's what and who's who. Goodness, this is difficult... but I think I really should sound a little note of caution about something which might save you a great deal of embarrassment in the future. I like you, Lowri, and, as I said at our first meeting, it's been wonderful having someone come here full of fresh new ideas, and I absolutely want you to make a success of things. So, I hope you won't mind me saying this, but are you absolutely sure that carrying on with Huw Pritchard is a good idea? He's—'

Lowri is about to bite back. *Carrying on? Who the hell says I'm carrying on?* Anger is burning through the fog in her brain and, as she stares at Bridie's perfectly styled hair and her pale-pink nail polish, she realises exactly what's going on. And then her anger burns even brighter.

'He's an excellent stonemason,' she replies, deliberately misunderstanding. 'Yes, I did know.'

Bridie gives a tight smile. 'He has quite a past.'

'He does.' Lowri smiles. 'I know, he's told me all about it. I know he hasn't worked in a while, but he explained why, and I understand. I'm prepared to give him a chance.'

To her surprise, Bridie looks distinctly uncomfortable. She studies Lowri, as if weighing up what to say. 'I'm sure he's told you *something*... whether it's the truth is another matter.'

Lowri can't help herself. 'And what's that supposed to mean?'

'I'd hate it if he's misled you in any way, Lowri. Perhaps when you get a minute, you should ask him what his real motives are around Clearwater.'

The evening can't come soon enough for Lowri. It seems ridiculous when she thinks about it, skulking about in the dark dead of night on land that actually *is* hers, but as she walks towards the factory, she still keeps her torch pointed at the ground. Her daughter is tucked up safe and warm in bed, and although she rarely wakes, Lowri still feels guilty about leaving her, even if Huw is at home. She feels it, but still she goes. There's something not right here and she has far too many unanswered questions.

The key turns easily in the lock and Lowri slips through the door without a sound. Elin has already told her there's no alarm system – it wasn't a huge surprise to learn that Elin also cleans the factory and is therefore privy to such information – and it's a relief not to have to contend with one. Seconds later, she's in Gordon's office.

It looks much as it did before, and the first thing Lowri does is sweep her torch light over the empty shelves. It wouldn't have been so obvious in the daylight, but under the bright beam the pattern of dust on the shelves is plain to see. So something *has* been moved. It occurred to her shortly after she left the office earlier how bare it was and, as a quick message to Elin confirmed, until very recently these shelves housed the company accounts. Lowri doesn't know where they are now, but she's beginning to suspect why they were moved in the first place.

The number of hiding places is relatively few. There's the desk, an obvious place to start, a filing cabinet, and a cupboard in one corner, all of which are locked, as a waggle of drawers and door knobs confirms. It's possible Gordon has taken the keys home with him, in which case this is going to be a very short search, but if he hasn't, then the chances are they'll be somewhere easy to find.

Lowri reaches for Gordon's in-tray, lifting the topmost layer of papers to search beneath them, but there's nothing there apart from a random paperclip. She does the same with the rest of the trays, but they too are empty. Lowri's been in enough offices, however, to know the little places people hide things, desk keys in particular. She used to do it herself once upon a time. So when her eyes alight on the pen pot, she smiles in triumph. *Gotcha*, she thinks.

Lowri spills the pot's contents on the desktop, banging her hand down on the desk as a pen makes a dash for the edge. Her reaction isn't quick enough though, and it clatters on the tiles. She winces at the sound it makes, unnaturally loud in the silent building, and then laughs at the vision of herself behaving like a cat burglar. Dropping to her knees, she retrieves the pen from under the desk and, as a sudden thought strikes her, swings her torch upwards to check the underside in case the key might be taped there. For goodness' sake, now she's behaving like James Bond.

* * *

There's barely any moon tonight but Huw doesn't need the light to know the castle is there. He can remember almost every stone. And just standing here helps, it reminds him why he's doing this, drives the bad away from the good.

It's been an odd day. Yesterday, he lost almost everything he owns, not to mention the only place he could call home. Today, his insurers informed him they'll be sending out a claims adjuster to look into the sinking of his boat – routine – but Huw's already pretty sure they'll turn down his claim. So, all in all, he should feel an awful lot worse than he does, and he's pretty sure he knows why that is.

'Hello, Huw.'

The voice comes from behind him, like a whisper on the wind. And at one time he would have given anything to hear it again.

'So the rumours are true. I heard you were finally getting your wish.'

Don't bite, Huw, he warns himself, but he isn't sure it's going to be enough. 'You're on private property,' he growls, turning around, breath catching in his throat.

'So are you,' she replies, staring up at the house. 'Although, by the looks of things, you seem to have got your feet well and truly under the table.'

'Yeah, well my boat sank. But I expect you've heard that too.'

Her eyes are glinting in the light from the kitchen window, its glow turning her blonde hair to gold.

'What are you doing here, Carys?'

'Oh, you know, taking care of business. Much like you.'

'You're nothing like me. Last time I checked I had a heart.'

'Yeah? I heard yours got broken.'

'Stay away from here,' he warns.

'Or what? You'll have to tell Mrs Morgan the truth of why

you're here. Or should I call her Lowri? I expect that's what you do.'

'She knows the truth.'

'Does she? I'd be very surprised if she does. Shall we see?'

Huw steps forward. There's no way he's letting her knock at the door. 'She isn't here,' he says, keeping his voice low. 'And it's late, you'll wake her daughter.' He only hopes Lowri can't hear them.

'Oh, well, never mind.' Carys looks back at the kitchen window. 'I can always pop round for a chat another time. I'm sure she'd love to know some of Clearwater's history.'

Huw doesn't want to beg, but he's lost almost everything else, why should his dignity matter? Not when there are things more important.

Carys laughs. 'Anyway, I must get going. It's good to see you, Huw. No doubt I'll catch you around.' And with that, she turns on her heel and walks back around the front of the house.

For several long minutes, Huw stands, staring after her, blood rushing in his ears. He doesn't move until he finally hears her car drive away and, even then, it takes a very long time for his heart to quit jumping around in his chest. He turns to look back at the tower, tracing its outline against the sky. All he ever wanted was to put things right. How can that be so difficult?

But the tower has no answers for him and, after a moment, he turns away, thinking about what Jamie once said to him. *One day at a time, Huw, one day at a time.* Great advice. At least it was, before Carys came back on the scene. Huw needs a drink.

He's about to head back inside when his attention is caught by a faint flicker, just on the periphery of his vision. He turns back, scanning the dark night.

Maybe he shouldn't, but Huw knows every inch of Clearwater. He's equally aware, however, that he's not the only one and, still shaking from his encounter with Carys, the sight of a torch light flickering around the factory can only mean trouble.

Following the path of the light, he realises that whoever the torch belongs to is now inside the building. Huw quickens his pace, intent on surprise.

Fleetingly, it occurs to him that the front door has been unlocked rather than forced open, and he's pondering why that might be, when movement inside the office claims his attention. What on earth would someone be doing in there? He peers through the darkness, straining to make sense of what he sees. Surely that can't be right?

He moves closer, eyes narrowing, cat-like. For such a big man he makes very little noise...

All at once, the figure crouching beneath the desk scrabbles to its feet, head banging against it in the process. Huw has been spotted.

'Jesus, you made me jump! Don't do that, sneaking up on people.'

Huw stares at Lowri in surprise. 'I wasn't sneaking, but if you will go walking around with all the lights off, I can see how it might look. Besides,' he continues, 'when *I* saw someone sneaking around, I thought it best if my arrival were a little low-key. Just in case I needed to call upon the element of surprise, jump on whoever it was, and pin them to the floor until the cops got here.'

'Okay, well...' Lowri trails off. He's embarrassed her. And if he could see her properly, Huw knows her cheeks would be flaming. They do that at times, when she's flustered, or angry. 'Look, I didn't want to announce my presence, okay? Anyway, what the hell are you doing here?'

Huw grins. 'You first.' His adrenaline-filled body is still geared up for fight or flight, and his brain, on finding neither are required, suddenly finds the situation absurdly funny. 'Maybe I'm reading this all wrong,' he continues, smirking, 'but doesn't this place belong to you? In which case, why all the skulking around?'

'I was not skulking. Nor sneaking,' Lowri declares, although her guilty expression would say otherwise.

'No? You have a torch when you could just flick on the lights. You'd be able to see so much better if you do.' He moves to the switch on the wall, an impish smile on his face.

'No!' Lowri lurches towards him. 'Look, I'm not skulking, okay? But neither am I wanting to shout my presence from the rooftops. People talk and, for now, I'd rather keep the fact that I've been here to myself.'

'But there's no one about. Who's to see?' Lowri must never find out that Carys has been here.

'I know, I'm just not taking any chances.'

'Okay...' His voice is still amused. 'So what are you looking for then?'

'I'm not sure that's any of your business.'

Huw is silent for a moment. 'True,' he says eventually, stretching the word far beyond its natural extent. 'Odd then, that when I saw what I thought was someone breaking into this place I decided it *was* my business. Maybe I should have just continued on my merry way and not bothered to investigate. Let the intruder have their wicked way, steal whatever they could lay their hands on, damage things which might cost a fortune to repair...'

Lowri sighs. 'Okay. I'm here because—' She stops herself, clearly wondering whether she should come clean. She flashes her light at the empty shelves. 'See those? They should be full. They used to be. Files, ledgers... In short, a whole bunch of stuff relating to the company accounts. That's what I'm looking for.'

Huw's lips twitch. 'You could ask for them. Wouldn't that be easier?'

'I have asked for them,' Lowri retorts, rolling her eyes. 'And was told everything was computerised, that it was too difficult. Call me cynical, but I don't believe that for a minute. And why the sudden disappearance of everything that was on the shelves? I need to find some answers.'

'Are you always this impatient?'

'Are you always this rude?'

Huw ignores her question. 'I'm just wondering why the hurry... and the subterfuge. Are you worried they're squandering your millions?' He hopes the amusement is still clear in his voice.

'Yes, actually,' she retorts, although he's pleased to see a mischievous glint in her eye. 'Although I sincerely doubt we're talking millions.'

'Lowri, look around you. This is an *estate*. Of course we're talking millions.'

Lowri stares at him, heat rising from her boots and flushing her cheeks.

'Okay, maybe not millions,' Huw continues, 'but it's got to be worth a very large amount of money.'

Lowri sits on the edge of the table, lowers her torch and lets it lie limply in her hands. It sounds ridiculous, but it's never occurred to her how much the estate might actually be worth. When everything is so run down or derelict, it's hard to imagine it having any value at all, but of course it does. And now she *is* thinking about it, the weight of what Alun kept from her hits her square in the chest. Did any of this ever occur to him? Did he even bother to find out what his uncle had left him? She's not sure which is worse – that he might not have checked the details of his inheritance because of some stupid family feud, or that he did find out and decided he could still turn his back on it, denying it, not only for himself, but for his family too. For her and little Wren.

The seconds tick past, and she can feel the weight of Huw's

gaze on her. She'd really rather he wouldn't stare at her like that, she doesn't want him to see her cry. Again.

'Sorry, *are* you worried they're squandering your millions? Genuine question.' He clears his throat, a tentative sound. 'You really didn't know about its value, did you?' he adds quietly, studying her face quite intently. He looks confused and, to her surprise, touches the sleeve of her coat gently. 'How could you not have any idea?'

Lowri swallows and gives a tight smile. 'It's complicated. As to whether I'm worried Bridie and Gordon are on the take... Not really,' she replies. 'I don't know. It's just that...' She points to the shelves behind her. 'Since I arrived, all the files seem to have mysteriously disappeared off the premises, and it seems far too much of a coincidence to me.' Lowri also wonders just how much she should say. 'I want to check a few things out, that's all.'

Huw nods, expelling his breath in a long sigh. 'Okay. And I'm sorry, I was being flippant when I shouldn't have. But you know, this place belongs to you. You have every right to be here, every right to ask about the accounts.' He bangs a hand against his head. 'As for why I sounded like I was sticking up for Bridie, I've no idea. I loathe the woman. I don't trust her either.'

For some reason, it's suddenly very important to Lowri that Huw understands the reason she's here. She hardly knows him, yet she still doesn't want him to think badly of her. 'Thank you, and I know there's nothing wrong with my being here, but...' She cocks her head to one side. 'Perhaps I'm just trying not to scare the horses.'

'Ah, now I get you.'

'According to Elin, this is where the accounts have always been kept and I *am* trying to find out if my millions are being squandered, but not because they could be diddling me out of money, but because, if that's what's been happening, then they've been neglecting to spend it where they should. The staff here should have a decent place to work so that they don't have to go to the loo in an outhouse. They should have decent salaries too, and I bet that's just the start of it. Plus, if things are ever going to change, if I'm ever going to secure a future for everyone, then I need to know exactly what I'm dealing with. Exactly *who* I'm dealing with.' She thinks for a moment. 'Did you speak to your insurers about your boat today?' she asks.

'I did...' Huw frowns. 'But nothing is going to be settled for a while yet. Why the question?'

'Because I found out today that the river meadow doesn't belong to Clearwater, it belongs to Bridie. She bought it when Alun's uncle died and the executors of his estate sold it off to pay inheritance tax.' She holds up a hand against Huw's interruption. 'That hardly matters though. What matters is that, despite Bridie's "I'm your new best friend routine", I don't think she's anything of the sort. I only found out about the river meadow because I mentioned changing the terms of your mooring permit, and she took great delight in telling me I couldn't have, regardless of your boat sinking, because the rights belonged to her. Which was when I remembered your notion that your boat might have been scuppered...'

Huw's eyes widen, dark before, but now darker still. 'And you think the two are connected?'

Lowri shakes her head. 'I don't know. But there's something funny going on here. And when she warned me off working with you as well, then—'

'She did *what*?'

Lowri pulls a face. Huw looks justifiably furious. 'Her words: was I sure that carrying on with you was a good idea. She knows she can't stop me, but it's as if she doesn't want me getting involved with anything relating to Clearwater. I have no idea why, but I'd really like to find out.' She sighs. 'Maybe I'm just being silly but I can't help how I feel and—'

'I don't think you're being silly at all,' replies Huw with a voice that could sharpen knives. 'Believe me, Bridie's good at playing games. The trick is knowing which one.' His eyes stay on hers. 'Which all goes to show what a jolly good job it is I showed up just now.'

Lowri gives him a quizzical look.

'Because, if what you're looking for has been hidden away then it's most likely in that filing cabinet, or the cupboard, and you might need some help getting it out.' He smiles then, grim and determined.

Though it's dark, and his face covered with a mass of hair, Lowri still thinks how differently he looks when he smiles.

'I've been looking for some keys,' she replies, before Huw can prise open any drawers with his bare hands. She's in no doubt he could. 'I don't want Gordon to know that anything's been obviously disturbed here. I thought if I found where the accounts have been moved to, I could come back another day and go through them. I need some time to look properly before I go shooting my mouth off.'

Huw takes a long, slow look around the room. 'Gordon's a stumpy guy, isn't he?'

Lowri, who, despite her doubts, still considers Gordon and her father to be peas in a pod, bristles slightly in defence of his stature, but she nods anyway.

'So he'd want the keys somewhere he can reach them without too much of a stretch. Otherwise it's just irritating.' He peers at a spot over her head before moving to join her on the other side of the desk.

'I've checked the pen pot, and the desk tray,' remarks Lowri. 'And looked on the underside of the desk.'

'I did wonder what you were doing down there, but I think that's a little too much of a secret-agent vibe for Gordon. I don't think he's anywhere near as imaginative.' Huw reaches past her head and, for a moment, Lowri thinks he means to pluck something from her hair, but instead he lifts one corner of a tea towel which hangs on the wall. 'Now, what have we here...?'

The fabric has been tethered to a cup hook screwed into the wall and, as Huw lifts it clear, a silver-coloured jump ring appears, dangling from which is a long slender key.

Huw grins. 'Bingo,' he says. 'And judging by the shape of it, the cupboard would seem to be the hiding place of choice. Shall we have a look?'

The files slide out the moment the door is opened, and Lowri guesses they'd been pushed inside in a hurry. She bends to her knees to sort through them, noting the labels affixed to the sides, opening one or two briefly to check inside.

'Are they what you're looking for?' asks Huw as she continues to riffle.

'Partly...' She sits back on her heels. 'There's some of what I need here, but it's very probable the rest is on that computer.' She points to the one on Gordon's desk. 'Or worse, on someone else's computer.' Her brows knit together in consternation. 'And I don't know why, but I feel like I'm being given a royal runaround.' Lowri rearranges the files to resemble their original positions as closely as she can, and then closes the door on them, toeing the last couple back inside. 'Thanks, Huw, but I think that's all we can do for now. I can come back and do a little digging, but if the balance accounts are computerised, I'm going to have to come up with a Plan B.'

Huw regards her silently for a moment before looking away, eyes narrowing as if he's spotted something of interest. He nods. 'Best put the key back then.'

Surprised at her disappointment, Lowri gives a resigned shrug. There's nothing more she can do for now. With one last look around the office, she indicates they should leave and leading them both outside, she locks the door behind her. The night seems to have grown heavier and its damp chill closes around her. Her thoughts return straight to Wren and she longs to be back inside, in the warm, dim glow of the house. She feels as if she should say something but she doesn't know what, and the silence is beginning to feel a little awkward.

Lifting her head as if scenting the river, Lowri stares out into the night. The water is there, somewhere, but she can neither hear it, nor see it. She's suddenly thinking about Alun, and Huw's boat, about Wren and the feeling of the water as it closed over their heads. It binds them all, and she shivers.

13

Three days pass before Lowri can get back to look at the accounts. Checking where the files were in the dead of night was one thing, but if she wants to keep her perusal of them a secret, then she will need to do this after hours, and with Wren to think about, that isn't so simple. She could easily ask Huw to keep an eye on Wren, but somehow that doesn't feel right, so it isn't until Elin asks how she got on that she's able to take up her offer of babysitting and make some plans.

'What will you do?' asks Elin once they've sorted out the arrangements. 'If you find anything, I mean.'

Lowri has been trying not to think about that and purses her lips. 'Well, if there's dodgy stuff going on, I'll just have to put a stop to it, won't I?' Which is fine to say before the event when she's feeling brave and heroic, but what if she does find something, what then? The answer is obvious, but Lowri knows she doesn't have the nerve, not really. And for some reason, talking further with Bridie is becoming a more and more terrifying prospect as time goes by.

Once in Gordon's office, it takes only minutes to open the cupboard door and spread the files across his desk. She has every right to be here, she reminds herself and, with a deep breath, she settles down to work.

Lowri has no idea what, if anything, she's going to find, and no idea where to start looking first, but she's hoping her nose might spot something which seems out of place, or some discrepancy she can't resolve. Until recently, Lowri wouldn't have described herself as an inherently suspicious person, but now she's dreaming up all manner of scenarios, most of them far-fetched. She does pause for a moment to consider if she's deluding herself, looking for something that isn't there simply out of a desire to help Elin and the other staff at the factory. The business might not be making any money and that's all there is to it but, either way, a good look through the nuts and bolts of it won't hurt. She is the owner now, after all.

It takes a while to become accustomed to what's normal. She has no knowledge of how the textile operation works, who their suppliers are, and what production costs they incur. Neither does she know who their customers are, or how they distribute their goods. Then there are running costs, administration, staff salaries, and myriad other services too, all of which could be completely legitimate. Without access to the finalised accounts either, Lowri is unable to follow any of the paper trail, or see in which areas the business might be overspending, but what she's banking on is a little luck.

Forty-seven minutes later, it finds her. It takes another twenty-four for the next break and only sixteen for the third.

The walk back to the gatehouse is grim. Sometimes, Lowri hates it when she's right.

* * *

'Sorry, mate,' says Jamie, slipping into the seat opposite Huw. 'I couldn't get away. Clare wanted me to look at pushchairs with her.' He rolls his eyes. 'Do all babies need this amount of kit?'

Huw shrugs. 'I'm not really the person to ask, am I?'

'Guess not,' Jamie replies, grinning. 'Anyway, what's so urgent it couldn't wait until the weekend? I had to tell Clare I was popping out to see a client.' He eyes Huw's glass. 'So, lemonade for me, or else. What are you drinking?'

Huw pauses. Meeting Jamie in the pub wasn't the greatest idea he's ever had, but he couldn't think of where else to go. He and Clare didn't exactly see eye to eye. Talk about temptation though. He'd just drunk half a pint of Coke and wished it was whiskey with every mouthful. 'I'll have another Coke,' he replies pointedly.

Jamie's lips quirk. 'Blimey... things must be serious if you're—'

'Carys is back,' interrupts Huw.

Jamie's mouth forms her name but no sound comes out of it. He stares at Huw. 'Since when?'

'I have no idea. She just turned up at the house on Monday night.'

'What house? You mean Clearwater?'

Huw nods.

'Shit.' Jamie thinks for a moment. 'And what did she do? Did she speak to Lowri?'

'No, but only because I happened to be outside when she showed up. If I hadn't, then God only knows what she might have done.'

'So Lowri has no idea who she is?'

'No, and I aim to keep it that way. But, Jamie, you know Carys, if she's back, she's back for a reason. And whatever it is, it's bad news.'

Jamie's expression is grim. 'So why now?'

Huw shrugs. 'I wondered whether Clare might have—'

'Well, she hasn't. She hasn't mentioned her, Huw. I'm pretty sure I'd know if they'd met up.'

Huw swallows. Jamie's been his best mate for as long as he

can remember, but there's only so much he can ask of him. This is important, though, he needs to know. 'Do you think you could maybe ask Clare—'

'No! Come on, you're not serious?'

'You don't have to be blatant about it,' argues Huw. 'Just say something like you thought you saw Carys the other day. See how Clare responds.'

Jamie is torn. 'Mate, I really don't need this. Clare's two months away from giving birth and she doesn't like you much as it is. Bringing up the subject of Carys again is asking for trouble.'

Huw regards him coldly. 'You're saying that like what happened with her was my fault.'

Jamie looks instantly contrite. 'Sorry. I didn't mean it like that, you know I didn't, but Clare's a bit emotional right now. She has a lot on her plate and Carys was her best friend. It's tricky. I still think she misses her.'

Huw nods. 'Okay.' He runs a hand through his hair. 'I understand, Jamie. I'm sorry, I should never have asked.'

But Jamie isn't the kind of mate to do nothing. 'I'll keep my ears open, all right? I'm not promising anything, but if I get the opportunity, I'll ask.' He frowns. 'And someone must know why Carys is back. Hey... you don't suppose she had anything to do with your boat, do you?'

Huw raises his eyebrows. 'I think it's odd we both came to that conclusion. Proving it though, that's something else entirely.'

'I can ask around,' replies Jamie. 'You never know, someone might have seen something. Maybe not Carys, but someone...'

'Thanks. I'm not holding out much hope. But that's not the only thing though. Before Lowri's husband inherited Clearwater, they had to sell off some land to pay for death duties. And guess who bought it?'

Jamie winces. 'I hardly dare ask.'

'Yep, Bridie. She's desperate to get hold of Clearwater, one way or another. She's up to something, Jamie, I'd lay money on it. And now Carys is back too...' He looks down, playing idly with a beer mat. 'I'm pushing my luck here, but I wondered if you could do something else for me as well?'

Jamie picks up Huw's glass. 'Are you sure you don't want a pint?'

Huw is sitting with Elin by the time Lowri returns, nursing a cup of tea. One look at her face tells him it hasn't gone well. 'I'll put the kettle on,' he says.

'Is it bad news?' asks Elin once Lowri is settled at the table.

Lowri gives a wry smile. 'It depends on your point of view. It's good news if you're trying to work out where all the money has gone, but not so good if your name is Bridie or Gordon.'

'I'd say it's very good news then,' cuts in Huw. 'How long have they been on the make?'

Lowri shakes her head. 'I've no idea. It could be years. And when I think of how much money could be involved, and what could have been done with that money... I feel awful. If I hadn't turned up when I did, it could have continued for a good few more.'

'Lowri, you weren't to know.' Huw studies her closely, the way she looks when she's feeling vulnerable. The way she—

'It's complicated,' she adds, as if he'd asked her a question.

'You don't need to tell me,' he says, 'it's none of my business.' He's pretty sure she's referring to Alun, and a conversation about him is something he'd rather not have either.

Lowri considers his statement. 'I just wonder how Alun could have been so trusting,' she says to Elin. 'He might not have had any reason to think anything amiss, of course, but had he ever bothered to check on how the estate was being administered? Would I, if I was in his position?'

She's musing out loud, even Elin has no answer for her.

'So what *have* they been up to?' Huw asks.

Lowri's eyes narrow. 'I still need to check one or two things but...' She stops as a thought comes to her. 'Actually, you could help me out. There's a business in town... Castle Crafts?'

'Yeah, they stock our stuff,' answers Elin.

'But did you know it was owned by Bridie?'

Elin looks at Huw. 'Is it?'

He shakes his head. 'It's a tacky gift shop. I wouldn't have thought it was her cup of tea at all.'

'Well, whether it is or it isn't, she's been selling Clearwater's goods to them for a fraction of the price the other retailers are charged. She'd probably say it's a discretionary price given that they're a local business, but that doesn't wash when you find out she owns it.'

'But that's surely illegal?' counters Huw.

'Frowned upon certainly, but it happens. Which is why company directors are always asked to disclose any interest they might have in another business, to prevent this kind of thing from happening.'

'Bridie isn't a company director though,' comments Elin.

'Exactly. And she's been clever. You have to look damned hard to find any connection to her. I only spotted it because I've been googling her, and I recognised part of an address for Castle Crafts' head office. The address belongs to another business that Bridie owns, or part owns... there's rather a confusing paper trail I haven't got to the bottom of yet.'

'So Bridie's creaming money off the business?' exclaims Elin. 'The thieving—'

Lowri holds up her hand. 'I don't know that. Not for certain, anyway, and I can't go shouting about my suspicions until I have absolute proof, and that could take a while. I also don't know whether Gordon is involved or not, although I deeply suspect he is. He's signed off on the invoices and...' She turns to look directly at Huw. 'The other night when I went to the office, you came to investigate because you saw my torch light. Why did you do that?'

Huw's puzzled. He should have thought that was obvious.

She tuts, no doubt seeing his expression. 'No, I meant, why did you think there was something wrong? I could have just been out for a walk. Or conceivably, someone else could have been.'

It's a small distinction, but he thinks he knows what she's getting at. 'Because it was unusual, that's all. I'm not used to seeing lights at Clearwater.'

'But how would you know?'

And now he does understand, although he still has no idea why she's asking. 'Because when I was on my boat there's a direct line of sight to here, and all I usually saw was blackness.' Huw knows this because he was in the habit of taking a little air on deck before he went to bed, but on no account must Lowri find out that actually means having one last pee before he hits the sack. 'Admittedly, I wasn't always moored where I have been and, further round the bend in the river you can't see the place, but—'

'You've been there often enough to know with some degree of certainty?'

'I'd say so, yes.'

'Why are you asking?' says Elin. 'Is there something wrong with that?'

Lowri nods. 'Only that when I was looking through the invoices, I spotted several raised by a security company. Money owed for, among other things, a night patrol. Now, I might be wrong, but wouldn't there be lights if someone was walking the premises at night?'

Elin frowns. 'Lights and a bloody big dog...'

'It's one of the oldest tricks in the book if you want to defraud a company – invoicing for fake services. And in this case, apart from you on occasion, Elin, there's been no one living at Clearwater to either corroborate or refute the fact that these patrols have taken place. So supposing an accountant did query the bills, who else would know if it was a bona-fide service or not? Answer, nobody. And Gordon, Bridie, whoever, could simply provide some fake details and Bob's your uncle.'

Huw can feel his anger beginning to burn. He and Bridie have history, but this, this is something else.

'So what do we do now?' asks Elin sharply. 'Bridie can't be allowed to get away with what she's done.'

'I know,' replies Lowri, and Huw can see she's trying to play this down. 'But if I'm going to tackle her, I need to be absolutely sure my accusations are valid. Because, if I'm right about what Bridie's been doing, all kinds of very unpleasant things will happen and the long and the short of it is that I'll end up running the business.' She sighs. 'That's probably going to happen anyway, given what I want for its future, but I hadn't banked on it happening so soon.'

'So you really want to do what we talked about?' asks Elin, eyes lit up like sparklers despite the situation.

Lowri nods and smiles. 'Yes, I really want to do it. Clearwater deserves better, as does everyone who works here, but until I can get my hands on the full accounts, I won't really know what we're looking at, or what I can do to improve things. Putting a stop to leaking money will help our situation, but it won't dramatically turn the business around and I think that's what's needed. If we want to make a success of it then we need to think of doing things differently. Better.' She swallows. 'So for now, I think we keep on doing what we're doing. Let's carry on making our application for funding the best it can be and take it from there.'

Huw nods. 'I don't see we have any other choice. Plus, Michael Cornish will be here on Monday and that will help no end.'

Elin grins from ear to ear. 'I'd best get home then,' she says. 'I've got dreams to dream.'

Huw smiles as Elin rushes around the table to give Lowri a hug. He's always liked her, they used to get on well before... before he made an arse of himself. She can sometimes be a little exuberant, but— his thoughts crash to a halt as Elin throws her arms around him too.

'Oh, this is too exciting!' she exclaims and, with a wave from the kitchen doorway, she's gone.

'Someone's happy,' he remarks.

'I hope so,' replies Lowri. 'Because I'm counting on her. I don't know much about weaving, but I know good stuff when I see it and she's been working on the most incredible designs. She deserves for them to see the light of day.' She laces her fingers around her mug and then, as he watches her, takes a thoughtful sip.

'Penny for them?' he says quietly.

She looks up, anxiety clouding her bright-blue eyes. Anxiety, and something else. 'I'm just worried,' she says. 'I don't know what we're dealing with here, but whatever it is has the potential to make things very difficult. Our project, rebuilding the castle, it's only just got off the ground, we don't need these kinds of complications.' She holds his look. 'I know how much Clearwater means to you.'

Huw remains silent, suddenly realising what lay behind Lowri's earlier expression. It was empathy. Understanding of a shared feeling. 'Correct me if I'm wrong, but it means a lot to you too, doesn't it?'

Lowri smiles. Bashful, as if she's been found out. 'I didn't plan it that way, but she's under my skin, that's for sure.'

And Huw wonders if perhaps he'd got it wrong about her all along... Her use of the words 'our' and 'we' – it's been a very long time since Huw's been a part of anything. She meant it too, he can see that from the light in her eyes. He'd been holding back, trying not to get too close. Telling himself that she was just the same as all the rest, telling himself not to get involved. Just do the job, get in, get out. It made life so much easier. So, now what's he going to do? Now that things have changed?

He wasn't going to mention this but... 'I went to see my mate, Jamie, this evening. He works for a communications company doing something incomprehensible with computers. I'd tell you what his official title is, but even that makes no sense to me. What he can do, however, is get into virtually any computer, and I wondered if he might be willing to help... if ever such a thing were needed.' He raises his eyebrows a tad.

'Get into, as in hack?'

'Essentially, yes.'

Lowri is clearly thinking about the possibilities, her face becoming more animated as she does so. 'That could prove very useful... And what did he say? Did he agree?'

Huw arches his eyebrows even higher. 'He's not a fan of Bridie's either. He said he'd be happy to, just say the word.'

Lowri's mouth curves into a warm smile as she holds his look, eyes twinkling. 'Well, that's excellent. I think we should keep it under our hats for now, don't you? But roll it out as a nice surprise if we need to.'

Huw nods, pleased she's thinking the way he is. 'Just one thing though,' he says. 'How come you know all this stuff? The accounts, about suppliers, profit and loss, running a business? I wouldn't have the first idea.'

'Oh, didn't I say? It's what I do for a living. I work with start-up companies, helping them put together their business plans, securing capital and/or loans, and then work alongside them for a little while, just until they're on their feet. It's problem solving mostly.'

'And Bridie and Gordon don't know a thing about that, do they?'

Lowri meets his smile with another of her own. 'Nope.'

14

'So, how are things going?' asks Elin. 'Do you think you'll be able to make the bid deadline?'

Lowri pulls a face. 'It's going to be tight, but I think so.'

They're sitting in Elin's kitchen drinking tea and eating bacon sandwiches, courtesy of Elin's mum, who wouldn't take Lowri's refusal for an answer.

'It's Sunday morning,' she said. 'Everyone has bacon sandwiches on Sunday morning.'

Lowri, who never has, found herself presented with a two-inch-thick butty which, by the time she was halfway through, had already made her alter her opinion. These were going on the menu every weekend from now on.

'I can't believe how fast the days are flying by,' adds Lowri. 'Huw seems pretty confident he can produce plans which fit the brief, but it's the other aspects we're struggling with, or rather *I'm* struggling with.'

'And how is Huw?' asks Elin in pointed fashion.

'He's fine,' replies Lowri lightly. 'Other than being homeless and losing most of his belongings. He wasn't insured either.' She pulls a face. 'Or rather the boat was, but that's the only thing, and even that might not be worth the paper it was printed on.' She can't believe that after everything he's been through the insurers may not pay out if the boat is deemed to have sunk through negligence rather than an accident or vandalism.

'Scumbags,' says Elin, which just about sums up how Lowri feels.

She nods. 'He's remarkably sanguine about it. I'm not sure I would be quite so cool in his position, but until he hears for certain what caused *Pugwash* to sink, there's nothing much he can do anyway.'

'Maybe he's more your strong and silent type,' says Elin.

Lowri tuts. 'Would you tell your daughter to behave?' she says as she catches Mari Hargreaves's eye. 'Huw is sleeping on my sofa and that's it, end of. In fact, most of the time you'd hardly know he was there.'

Lowri is well aware what Elin's loaded comment was all about, but she refuses to play her game. It's bad enough having to contend with her own thoughts, let alone Elin's teasing questions. Questions she'd already had to parry from Jess during their last phone call.

Elin flashes her a mischievous smile. 'I don't believe that for a minute. How can you miss someone that size?'

Lowri concedes with a small smile. 'He's outside so much I *do* forget he's there, until I suddenly realise the space in the room is considerably reduced.' Lowri can feel her cheeks growing hot at the thought of the polite 'dance' she and Huw are forced to play around her kitchen. *After you... no, after you...* 'But he *is* being a perfect house guest, so I can't complain.'

'Okay,' says Elin, in a voice which lets Lowri know she isn't off the hook yet at all, that Elin's just biding her time. She takes another bite of her sandwich. 'So what are these other aspects of the brief you're struggling with?'

'We need a community angle for it. Apparently, it's no good just opening the place to the public and allowing them to take in the majesty of our heritage, we have to provide some kind of what they call "added value". Looking at what other successful projects are doing, they all include some benefit to the local area, either by involving local groups, or providing some kind of service.'

'How about a crèche?' asks Elin, grinning as a particularly loud shout of laughter comes from the room next door, where Wren is playing with Poppy.

'I think Huw is quite keen for the building to remain standing, rather than having a bunch of small children tear down the place, but I'll bear it in mind.' Lowri smirks. 'Trouble is, I don't really know what goes on around here yet, so it's hard to know if there's a gap we might fill.'

Elin wrinkles her nose. 'Won't the renovation of the watermill help?'

'It will,' agrees Lowri, 'because then we'll have two attractions, which makes the heritage angle even stronger. I did wonder if when the mill is in operation – a long way off yet, I know – whether we could open it for tours to see the weaving in action. An exploration of traditional crafts, you know the kind of thing.'

Predictably, Elin pulls a face. 'But that would mean I'd have to be on my best behaviour all the time, and you know how much I'd hate that.'

'I'm sure we could work something out,' replies Lowri with a raised eyebrow. 'Aside from that, however, I'm a bit stumped for ideas. The only other thought I had was whether we could make more of the wildlife along the river. Bridie might own the river meadow, but there's still a public footpath along part of its length. And with the millpond and the woodland as well, I thought we could open them up, offer walks, or maybe even turn it into a nature reserve?'

'Hey, that's not a bad idea,' replies Elin. 'Seren would be

able to help with that, I'm sure. There isn't much she doesn't know.'

Which is exactly what Lowri had thought. She'd also thought it might be a good opportunity for Seren to get to know folks a bit better, and for them to get to know *her*.

'What do you think, Mum?' asks Elin. 'You know what goes on in the town better than I do. Or rather what *doesn't* go on.'

'It's still quite a busy little town though,' Mari replies. 'And you know how much I'd like to see the mill restored and you making proper things again, instead of the rubbish you churn out at the minute. Textiles were bread and butter for a lot of folk round here once upon a time, and I'd love to see more of that – traditional crafts and whatnot.'

'So maybe even workshops, that kind of thing?'

'That's a good idea,' says Elin. 'I like that.'

'There's also a good argument for more outdoor spaces,' continues Mari. 'Especially those which are family-friendly. The council closed the big park in the town a couple of years ago due to health and safety issues, and there are very few places you can walk now. Folks don't exactly resent it, but the fact that the estate owns quite a chunk of the riverside rankles with a few people – I think you'd get a lot of local support if you offered something like that.' She looks at the tea towel she's holding. 'Mind you, I suppose the new houses would scupper that idea though, wouldn't they?'

Lowri, who has just shoved the last sandwich crust in her mouth, looks up, and throws Elin a look. She chews fast. 'What houses?' she manages after a moment.

Elin's head also swivels in her mum's direction. 'Yeah, Mum, what houses?'

Mari Hargreaves looks instantly contrite. 'Oh dear, maybe I've got that wrong, but I'm sure that's what Rose said...'

'Who's Rose?' asks Lowri, swallowing hard.

'Wife of the local publican,' supplies Elin. 'Shameful gossip and general busybody but that doesn't mean she's wrong.' She grimaces at Lowri. 'So, what exactly did Rose say, Mum? And where are these houses?'

'Up along the river, in the meadow. Bridie Turner's building them, apparently. Well, not personally, of course, but she's got some fancy company interested. One of their blokes was in the pub a few months back, said he'd been over the site again.'

'But that can't be right,' argues Elin. 'How come no one knows about this?'

Mari shakes her head. 'I've no idea, love, I'm just repeating what I heard.'

'But to build houses she'd have to get planning permission,' counters Elin. She looks at Lowri, who nods her head.

'She would, but more to the point she'd need to be able to access the meadow in the first place. The only way to do that is to cross land which *does* belong to Clearwater. And I'm certainly not about to give her permission.'

'You'd think Bridie would have mentioned it though,' says Elin.

'Hmm... you would, wouldn't you?' Lowri's lips narrow. 'And when I speak to her, I'm sure she'll have a smart answer.' Lowri knows without a shadow of doubt she will.

'But what will you do?' asks Elin. 'If what Mum says is true?'

Lowri would love to say something bold and feisty – that she'll be putting a stop to it and showing Bridie who's boss, but she has a horrible feeling she'll be polite and altogether far too timid. She isn't the most assertive person at the best of times, but there's also a gnawing anxiety at the back of her mind. One she doesn't even want to acknowledge. She checks her watch.

'I should get going,' she says. 'Thanks so much for the sandwich, Mari, I haven't had one of those in such a long time. It was delicious.'

Despite her words, Mari looks troubled. 'I'm sorry if I've stirred something up,' she says. 'I didn't mean to.'

Lowri shakes her head. 'No, you've done me a favour. Who knows how far this might have gone if you hadn't said anything? I'd much rather know.' She smiles. 'Forewarned is forearmed.' But this is a battle Lowri really doesn't want to fight.

'Tell you what,' says Elin. 'Why don't I drop Wren back later? She and Poppy are quite happy playing and I'm sure you have a hundred and one things to do.'

Lowri readily agrees and with the arrangements sorted, she heads back to Clearwater. Her head is full of questions, not least of all how she's ever going to break the news to Huw about Bridie's plans for the river meadow. Apart from the horror of yet another piece of beautiful countryside being torn up to make way for houses, the building of them would spell disaster for their plans to rebuild Clearwater. Who on earth would give funding to renovate a castle and open it to the public when there's a housing estate being built right behind it? Huw will be devastated. This isn't what Clearwater is about. It can't be.

Her heart is decidedly heavy as she reaches the gatehouse and climbs from the car, feeling inordinately weary. All she wanted was a home for herself and Wren, and for the first time in a long while she had begun to feel a little optimism and hope for her future. Is that so very wrong? In her preoccupied state, it takes her quite a few moments to register something different about the house. Something which definitely wasn't there when she left that morning.

The most amazing smell is filling the hallway, and as she wanders through to the kitchen, she finds the table laid for three. Huw is standing at the cooker wearing an apron, of all things. It's such an unexpected sight, she almost laughs. Instead, she clears her throat.

Huw spins around, a wooden spoon in his hand and an odd

expression on his face. It's a mixture of guilt, anxiety and hope. 'I thought I'd cook us lunch,' he says. 'I hope that's okay?'

Lowri, who isn't at all hungry after her bacon sandwich, can only nod and smile. 'It's very okay. And it smells wonderful. But you really didn't need to go to the trouble, Huw.'

He glances at his feet. 'It's a thank you, for putting up with me, and putting me up.'

Lowri finds herself surprisingly touched by the gesture. 'Even so... and you're very welcome. Wren and I don't usually bother on Sundays any more, not since there's just been the two of us. This is lovely.'

She registers Huw's face falling.

'She's not with you?' he asks.

'Ah... no, sorry, she's staying at Elin's, playing with Poppy.' She glances at the table and gives a sheepish smile.

'Right... well, never mind.' Huw's clearly disappointed, but then he grins. 'I hope you're hungry, because there's rather a lot of roasties. My portion control is a little rusty.'

'Mine's never been good, particularly with pasta for some reason.' She smiles, eyeing the large number of pots and pans on the side. 'Do you like cooking?'

'Aye, I do. Got out of the habit lately though.'

'I imagine it's not that easy on a narrowboat.'

'They're fully kitted out, but it's more that space is lacking, especially for someone like me. I spent half my time bent double.' He looks around the kitchen. 'This turned out well though.'

It's an odd thing to say, and she's about to ask what he means when he waves an arm at a bottle on the table.

'I wasn't sure if you usually had wine with Sunday lunch, so I bought you a bottle just in case.' His face falls. 'Although maybe that's not such a good idea, if you have to pick up Wren?'

'Elin's bringing her home, actually.' Lowri doesn't normally drink during the day, hardly at all really. 'I'll open it, shall I?' she asks. 'Is there anything else I can do?'

Huw shakes his head. 'Nope, it's all under control. Sit down and catch your breath for a few minutes, it's been a busy week.'

The food looks so good, perhaps Lowri does have an appetite, after all. Or maybe it's just that no one apart from her mum has ever cooked her dinner. Alun never did, even before they were married. She loads up her fork and takes a mouthful, smiling with pleasure. It tastes as good as it looks.

'This is incredible,' she says, her mouth still full. 'Although I'm not sure I'm going to manage it all.'

'No problem,' says Huw lightly. 'I did give you rather a plateful.' He picks up his wine glass. 'To Clearwater.'

His toast tugs at her heart even more. Huw has gone to so much trouble, how can she possibly tell him what she learned today? It would be like throwing everything he's done back in his face. But she doesn't feel comfortable toasting to Clearwater either. It's such a normal thing to do, among family and friends, that is, but Huw is neither of those things. Not really. Sure, they've been getting along fine, but she mustn't... She pushes the thought from her head and focuses her attention back on her dinner. 'To Clearwater,' she mumbles.

The conversation flows easily enough, and the wine helps, although she notices Huw only has half a glass, yet it still comes as a surprise when somewhere in between her first two roast potatoes and, God help her, pudding, Lowri finds she's really rather enjoying herself. She can't remember the last time she had such a companionable meal. It's usually just her and Wren and her head fizzing with a multitude of things which need doing.

'This is nice,' she says, before she can stop herself. Lowri isn't talking about the apple crumble and they both know it.

Huw's hand, which holds a spoon halfway between his bowl and his mouth, pauses. 'Good, I'm glad you like it.'

She could kick herself, knowing instantly that she's blown the mood. She's brought something to the mix that didn't need to be there, and now it sits between them, an enormous elephant in the room. Lowri doesn't know much about Huw's past, but you don't get to be living alone on a narrowboat, drinking yourself stupid, without a good deal of baggage weighing you down. She hasn't shared a meal with another man, however innocent, for a very long time, and she'd lay money on the fact that it's a similar situation for Huw as well. She groans inwardly. How could she have been so stupid?

The remains of dessert are eaten in near silence, and despite her offer to help with the washing up, Huw steadfastly refuses. It seems rude to just up and leave the kitchen, however, so Lowri sits at the table, pulls her laptop towards her and pretends to work. Idly, she types Bridie Turner's name into a search engine and is amazed at the number of returns which come back. Ten minutes later, she's all but forgotten how she'd been feeling.

Lowri isn't sure how Huw normally spends his Sundays but, shortly after lunch, he announces he's off out for a walk. It's a walk which must have taken him halfway around the county judging by the amount of time it takes him. Wren has long since returned home by then, had a bath and hair-wash ready for school in the morning, and is snuggled on the sofa, practising her spellings.

If Huw is still dwelling on Lowri's stupidity, however, you'd never know it.

'I'll take over if you like?' he says easily, sitting down beside Wren.

Lowri, who is ironing school uniform, readily agrees.

'I bet you're gooderer at spelling than I am,' he adds, picking up Wren's schoolbook.

Wren grins. 'Gooderer, what kind of a word is that?'

Huw pretends confusion. 'Is it not a real one then?'

She nudges his arm. 'No, silly, you just made it up!'

'I did not!' But he winks. 'Right, how do you spell "house"?'

After a moment, Lowri tunes out. There's plenty more occupying her mind and most of it she'd like to discuss with Huw. But how *do* you tell someone their project might be over before it's begun?

15

Michael Cornish is a fizzing ball of energy. Or so it seems to Lowri. From the minute he shakes her hand to the moment he first sees the watermill, his eyes miss nothing, darting to and fro, catching every tiny detail. His head nods as he takes in each new piece of information and there's an eagerness about him which even he seemingly has to restrain.

Having heard Huw wax lyrical about Michael's expertise, Lowri really wasn't sure what to expect, but a man wearing jeans, a thrash-metal tee shirt and trainers with more hole than sole wasn't it. Now that he's here, however, she can see why Huw thinks so much of him. Mixed with his energy is a very precise, enquiring mind, and he soon picks up what they're trying to achieve.

'I've done my homework,' he says as they head outside, 'but nothing can replace being on site. So many factors affect the way the mill works, or rather how it will work in the future.'

'So, you do think it's possible to get her going again?' asks Lowri.

Michael's eyes twinkle. 'Oh, yes, the question is more how long is it going to take, and how much money is it going to cost?

Actually, that's two questions, but never mind.' He smiles at his words. 'Essentially, you have a very valuable piece of history here and I'm pretty confident we can get funding, provided we fine-tune our bid to the right frequency. And make no mistake, the funding agencies all have one, and it changes year on year, but hit the sweet spot and you're in business.'

Lowri smiles at his use of musical metaphors – she can imagine him playing in a band, the drummer quite possibly.

'So what do you need to see first?' asks Huw, as Michael stares up at the castle ruins.

'That's quite something, isn't it?' he replies. 'I've seen pictures, of course, but nothing quite prepares you for the majesty of sites like these. You have your work cut out though, Huw...' He gives an impish grin. 'Although I guess you already know that.' He looks around him. 'Right, let's have a look at the mill, shall we? Always start with the main event. I want to hear your plans, Lowri, first-hand, not written in an email, it's never the same.'

She nods and together they approach the mill, Michael bouncing on the balls of his feet as if he needs to stop himself from running. He pauses as they reach the steps, eyes scouring the building.

'Okay, inside, please.'

Some days the smell seems less strong than on others, but this morning as Lowri opens the door, it's alive with a rich earthy tang. It's odd, but it's rapidly becoming something she looks forward to every time she comes down here.

Without a word, Michael strides into the centre of the room and stands motionless, only for a few seconds, but it's enough for Lowri to sense he feels it too, as if he's making the kind of connection she has. He inhales deeply and turns to her.

'Have you ever done this?' he asks. 'Stood quietly and let the building come to you?'

With a quick glance at Huw, Lowri realises that's exactly

what she does. As if somehow it has a message for her. She thought she was being silly, but Huw nods too. Encouraged, she smiles. 'I do... I can't really explain it, and I'm still not sure it isn't the first sign of madness. But when I stand here, my head fills with pictures of how it might have looked, filled with people, full of industry.' She laughs. 'But then I wonder if what I see isn't the past, but the future.'

Michael holds her look for a second. 'Excellent.' He gestures around the room. 'So, tell me what you see in this future of yours. What are your dreams for this place?'

Lowri isn't sure whether they started off as her dreams or Elin's, but somewhere along the line, they've merged into one. She pauses, anxious that what she wants to say sounds daft. 'It's weird, but I hear laughter. I see bustle and energy, a group of people all working together, loving what they create. Maybe this sounds silly, but that feeling when you do a job that doesn't feel like a job, does that make sense? That's what my dream is, that the people here are doing what they love, not just turning up for work every day because someone tells them they have to.'

Michael smiles and holds up his hands in front of him, turning them one way and then the other. 'See these?' he says. 'I enjoy most parts of my job, but what I love the most is when these are covered in muck. When I'm down and dirty, deep in the bones of the machinery. That's when I feel the potential of what I'm doing the most, knowing that I can make inanimate objects come to life, when I can create something from nothing. So, yes, I know exactly what you mean.' He pauses. 'And up here is where you see the weaving taking place, is it?'

'Yes, I thought the looms along here, staggered so they're not in an exact line, that way people can still see each other. Then storage here for the yarns, and over here, where it's lightest, a long table for laying out the cloth. I thought...' She stops suddenly, realising just how much detail she can see, has always seen. 'Well, something like that anyway.'

'And downstairs?'

'Areas for finishing and packing. We're going to be producing pieces of the highest quality, individual, some possibly even bespoke, so we need to treat them like that. Our finishing processes, everything we do, even the boxes we send our goods out in have to give that same message.' She turns around to indicate the area behind the staircase on the lower floor. 'And these products will speak to our heritage as well, so we could accommodate visitors at times, channelling them safely through areas away from the machinery, but still giving them a clear view of what we're doing.'

Lowri isn't sure how much detail she should provide at this stage, but Michael looks happy with what she's saying.

'If it ain't broke, don't fix it,' he says, nodding. 'What you describe fits almost exactly with how the mill would have operated. We can get to the nitty-gritty later, but it helps to see how you envisage the work space.'

Throughout the whole time Lowri has been speaking, Huw hasn't said a word. In fact, he's been strangely quiet, deferring to her to answer Michael's questions. Now she's aware that he's staring at her, a warm smile on his face. He looks pleased. In fact, more than that. He looks proud... Proud of *her*? It's an odd sensation, but Lowri feels warmed by it, inordinately happy to think he approves. And she smiles back in return, holding his look.

'Right, that's enough in here then,' chimes Michael. 'I've delayed my gratification for long enough, let's have a look at the wheel.' Beaming at both her and Huw, he all but gallops out the door and down the steps.

Following him around the front of the building, they arrive to find Michael leaning over the railing at a precarious angle to get closer to the metal structure. He pulls himself back and straightens.

'Can you give me a hand with the sluices, Huw? There's

still a good deal of water in the bottom there and we might as well get as much out as we can.'

Climbing the steps back up to the level of the millpond, they each lean on one of the paddles which hold the sluice gates closed, forcing them together until the water is completely shut off.

'Has she ever been fully dried out?' Michael asks, running back down to where Lowri is standing.

'I can't be certain, but I'd say not,' replies Huw, watching as Michael leans precariously over the railing again.

'I can't find record of any major restorations,' says Michael. 'But that doesn't mean there haven't been any.' He looks at his watch. 'We'll give her a few minutes to drain and then I'll have a look, but first glance, she looks in surprisingly good nick for her age.' He unbends himself from the railing and grins. 'I'm looking forward to working on this one. She's a very fine wheel indeed. So finely balanced that all it took to set her moving was less than a quarter bucketful of water. Hopefully, I can get her back in the same kind of shape.'

Lowri is about to ask how long it might take to restore the mill when Michael gives his watch another look, tuts and ducks under the railing, jumping straight down into the water.

'Patience never was my strong point,' he says.

The water isn't particularly deep, but it still reaches almost to his knees, and it's muddy water at that. He wades along the channel's length until he's standing almost directly under the wheel. And suddenly, what hadn't looked all that large from the safety of the bridge, now looks enormous when compared to Michael's body. It towers over him.

As Lowri watches, Michael runs his hands over the structure, reverent, almost as if he's stroking it. He stoops, stretches, cranes his neck this way and that, and drops to his haunches like a doctor assessing a patient, his backside only just clearing the water. Huw comes to stand beside her, his arms resting, as hers do, on the railing. They're so close, they're almost touching.

'This is incredible, isn't it?' he whispers, leaning in. 'I told you Michael was good.'

The level of the water has dropped now, draining away along the tail race as she's learned to call it, and for the first time in quite a few years, Lowri imagines, more of the structure becomes visible.

'This will be the worst section,' says Michael. 'Where the wheel has been constantly under water. Rather ironic given that water used to be its friend, but it's now turned enemy, rusting the metal. Not the easiest thing to get at either as the wheel pit is full of silt.' He plunges his hands into the water, scooping out handfuls of muck. 'Doesn't smell too pleasant either, but there you go.'

He straightens, and inches his way along the side of the wheel, reaching down once more to investigate. 'There's something stuck under the very bottom bucket – a rock or something, I think. You get all sorts chucked in the river and, unfortunately, however careful you are, some of it makes its way down here. Then again, with the wheel stationary, anything could be in here. Ponds are a bit like canals, folk just love throwing stuff in. We're not quite in supermarket-trolley territory, but you get the idea.' He grunts with exertion. 'And whatever it is has got itself wedged good and tight.'

Swearing under his breath, Michael finally lifts whatever it is clear, and holds it up. 'Got the little bugger.' He swipes his thumb across the hard surface, wiping away accumulated muck and filth. 'It's not stone. Not sure what it is.' He bends down to swish it through the small amount of water that still lies in the bottom of the race.

When he lifts it clear, Lowri thinks her heart might actually stop. Michael Cornish has his thumb through what is unmistakably an eye socket. He's holding a human skull.

Lowri doesn't even think about what happens next. All she wants to do is turn away, away from the sheer horror of what this must surely mean. And, as she does so, Huw's strong arms reach out so that she's pulled into the space between them. His skin is warm, and smells of soap.

'Dear God!' She pulls away as Michael's voice rasps from below her. 'Oh, this is... this is awful.'

She's aware of Huw reaching out, grasping Michael's hand and hauling him back up onto the bridge. He's still holding the skull, as if it's glued to him and he couldn't free himself from it even if he tried.

'What do we do?' she whispers, staring at the horror he holds.

'Call the police,' says Huw. 'But we mustn't touch anything. Anything *else*... There's no way of knowing how long this has been down there, but they'll want to—'

But Lowri is no longer listening. Her thoughts have been pulled elsewhere, out beyond the watermill and across the pond to the far side, where a young woman often sits and watches. Seren.

She hadn't even realised she'd said Seren's name out loud, but she must have because, suddenly, Huw has turned with her. He knows Seren's story just as well as she does, better perhaps. And he's seen the skull, it's gleaming white structure too small to be that of a fully grown adult. Instead, more like a child's...

Lowri looks up at him, tears welling in her eyes. 'It can't be, can it?' she asks. 'What happened was so long ago.'

'Poor Seren...' Huw doesn't even contradict her, she realises. 'Someone should fetch her.'

'No, don't, not right now. The police will want to—'

'Huw, she has to come,' Lowri argues. 'That's her *brother*... How will Seren feel hearing what's been found via the town gossip? Or perhaps hearing the police sirens and wondering what's amiss? Knowing that other people were here first, before she even knew. If this is Sorley, then this mill race isn't just a crime scene to be cordoned off and examined inch by inch. It's a grave, Huw. It's where Sorley died. Please, we have to go fetch her.'

Huw's eyes are searching her face. 'We don't know that, the skull could have come from anywhere, it could've—'

No,' says Lowri emphatically. 'It didn't. I *know* it's Sorley... I've always known.' She frowns at how easily the truth comes to her.

Michael is still standing, wordless, on the bridge. Very slowly, he bends down and places the skull on the ground, taking several steps backwards. 'Did you know this person?' he asks incredulously. 'You know who it might be?'

Lowri nods. 'A friend of ours. Her brother died about twenty years ago when he was a little boy. People always said he'd drowned, but his body was never found.' She looks at Huw, imploring him. 'I'll go fetch her,' she says. 'Seren has to be here, Huw, you know it.'

But he shakes his head. 'No.' His eyes wrinkle. 'I mean, I'm not letting you do this by yourself, Lowri. I'm coming with you.' And, to her surprise, he takes her hand. 'Michael, we won't be long, can you stay here? Make sure no one else comes.'

'Well, I can but...' He looks confused. 'Shouldn't I call the police?'

'No,' Lowri implores. 'Not yet. Please, just wait until we get back. What difference will it make?'

Reluctantly, he nods.

It's all the confirmation Lowri needs. 'Come on,' she says, pulling at Huw's hand. She hadn't even realised she was still holding it.

To her surprise, he stops her. 'No, not by car. It's quicker through the woods. Come on, I'll show you.'

Lowri hasn't a clue where they're going, but she races after Huw, blinking in the sudden darkness after the bright sunshine of before. It's taking too long though, and what if Seren isn't there? What if she's shopping? Or... She thrusts the thoughts away. She'll be there.

Seren's house is like a gingerbread cottage. Lowri has never been there before but, now that she's seen it, she realises Seren could never live anywhere else. It's only small, red-bricked, with a window either side of a green door, and baskets of flowers hanging in between. A chimney stack completes its chocolate-box image. She stops, thinking. What on earth is she going to say?

She's about to make her way along the path to the front door when she realises that Huw is heading in a different direction.

'She'll be in the garden,' he says, waiting until Lowri joins him. Without speaking, he holds back, knowing that Lowri will want to go first. 'Are you okay?' he asks, his eyes warm on hers. 'You don't have to do this, you know. I could go, I...' He trails off when he sees that Lowri's mind is made up and he smiles and dips his head as if to tell her she's doing the right thing.

Swallowing, Lowri nods, and tentatively opens the gate.

The path to the back garden is burgeoning with flowers, so much so that Lowri has to brush against them as she walks, dislodging the bees which cling to them. She wasn't sure what to expect, but there's only a tiny lawn here, the rest is planted with every colour flower Lowri can imagine. A smile of wonder pulls at her lips despite the circumstances.

Seren is standing right at the bottom of the garden, facing the river. Still and silent. But almost as if some sixth sense guides her, she turns as Lowri approaches.

Lowri tries to remind herself they don't know for certain the skull they found belongs to Sorley. And it would be quite wrong to give Seren a misleading impression but, as the other woman faces her, Lowri sees very clearly that she already knows.

She takes a step forward. 'Seren, I'm so sorry...'

'You found him.' It's not a question, Lowri realises.

She nods. 'I think you should come. We found something I think you'll want to see.' Lowri can't bring herself to say the word 'skull'. It's too clinical, too harsh. It holds nothing of Seren's brother.

To Lowri's surprise, Seren smiles, soft and gentle, full of love. 'Ever since I heard you were restoring the mill, I've wondered,' she says. 'And, in a way, I'm glad you've found him. I think, like me, he's been waiting a long time too.' She looks past Lowri to Huw, who is standing a little awkwardly a few paces back. 'Thank you for coming. It isn't easy to bring news of a death when grief still walks beside you.'

Lowri has no idea whether she means her or Huw. But she's right, it is hard. Lowri can clearly remember the face of the young police officer who brought her the news. And it troubles her that what she can't remember is how she behaved when she learned that Alun had died. Did she scream, or cry out? Was she rude? It's a blank space and she knows she will never get it back.

'Will you show me?' asks Seren. 'Take me to where he is?'

She holds out her hand and wordlessly, Lowri pulls her into a hug. She can feel Seren's body trembling through the thin cotton of her dress.

'Come on,' she murmurs.

Michael is still standing where they left him, only now cradling the skull in his arms as if he didn't think it right that it should sit on the ground. He makes an incongruous sight, with his tee shirt which says one thing and his stance and manner saying something very different. He's obviously never met Seren, and is clearly uncomfortable, but he hands her the skull as if it's a new-born child. Seren's hands are shaking as she takes it.

'Are you sure this is the right thing to do?' Michael whispers as Seren walks away. 'We don't actually know whose remains those are.' He winces. 'That sounds uncaring and I don't mean it that way, but shouldn't we wait until the police arrive?'

Lowri knows he's being sensible, but for Seren's sake she has to try. 'What evidence is there to collect?' she whispers back. 'The skull's most likely been down there for years, in the muck and water. If there was anything to be gleaned, it's long gone. Let Seren have these moments, *please*. They may be all she'll have.' She looks to Huw for support and realises he's close to tears.

Seeing him, Michael nods.

Seren has taken the skull to the edge of the millpond and, as Lowri watches, she sinks to the ground, sitting down to cradle the skull in her lap. She runs her fingers along it just as if she were stroking her brother's hair. Lowri's breath catches in her throat, but she's careful not to make a sound. Nothing must disturb Seren. Nothing must take away these last moments she will have with him.

At first, she sits quietly but, gradually, Lowri becomes aware of a strange noise and realises it's Seren, a keening sound rising from within her as the dam she has built to hold everything back for so long, finally breaks. She rocks her brother's remains back and forth, the pain of everything she's lost tearing through her. It isn't just him, but her mother, her childhood, and all the years since which should have been so different. It's all she's lost and all she will never have.

Swallowing, Lowri turns to Huw. It's too much. Seeing Seren's pain, so raw even after all these years, is far too close to home. She knows what it's like to have all hope suddenly shattered. And even though it brings closure, it also brings the pain of an ending so absolute there is nothing left and Lowri isn't sure which is worse – to live with just the faintest glimmer of hope, or to know with finality that you will never see the person you loved alive again.

It's exactly how she felt when they told her that Alun was

alive, that they had managed to free his body from the car. The worst thing possible had happened but he had survived, he would be coming home to her. And even though she knew how poorly he was, she still had hope on her side. She still believed everything would be okay. But then it wasn't. Sometime in the night, Alun took a turn for the worst, and Lowri knew she had reached the point. The point when, for just a few minutes, fate hung in the balance, resting on the axis between hope and despair. It was the very worst kind of torture but, sometimes, she still wishes she was there, locked in those moments, because at least she had something. When they were over, she had nothing.

She doesn't even realise she's crying until she feels Huw's arms go around her. And she knows he isn't Alun, she knows it's so very different from the hugs her husband used to give her, but Lowri's been holding herself up for so long now, to have someone else take the weight of everything pulling her down is the nicest feeling. And, as her arms creep slowly around Huw's back, she wonders if perhaps that's what he needs too, someone to hold, someone to hold *him*.

16

News of Sorley's discovery travels fast, and within half an hour it seems as if the whole world wants to know what's happened. Escaping with Seren in tow, Lowri retreats to the safety of the gatehouse, rather cowardly leaving all the questions for Huw to answer. She makes tea and settles Seren on the sofa who, despite insisting she is okay, looks pale and still trembles even though the afternoon is warm.

'What will happen now?' she asks Lowri.

'I'm honestly not sure,' she replies. 'But I expect the police will explain once their investigation is underway. They've already placed a cordon around the mill.' She only knows this because Huw has messaged her to suggest that Seren be kept from seeing it.

'But I will be allowed to bury him, won't I?'

Lowri nods, her heart aching at the question. 'I'm sure you will. But they need to make sure first, Seren, that it is Sorley we found...' She breaks off. 'It might not be.'

Seren shakes her head. 'Don't,' she says. 'Don't let me think it might not be. He's gone, Lowri. I need to believe that. I've had twenty-odd years of ifs and buts and maybes.' Her eyes search

Lowri's face. 'Besides, I know it's him, just as I've always known the river would give up its secret one day.'

Lowri knows Seren is right. She has no idea how she knows this, but she does. And her thoughts go back to the day when she first met Seren, standing looking out across the millpond and feeling the weight of everything which had happened there. 'There might have to be an inquiry though,' she adds. 'And how long before that happens I guess depends on the time it takes to establish Sorley's identity. But I'm sure they'll work as quickly as they can.'

'They'll want to speak to me, won't they? The police, I mean.'

Lowri nods. 'I expect so,' she replies, as gently as she can. 'But you don't have to be on your own, I can be with you. Or Elin can, Huw even. Any one of us would be happy to help.' She smiles. 'You're not alone now, Seren.'

Seren looks down at her hands, clasped around the mug she holds but hasn't drunk from. 'The worst thing is thinking they don't believe me. Thinking it was me who had something to do with Sorley's disappearance.'

Lowri is shocked. It never even occurred to her that might be the case. That the police would think Sorley's death was anything other than an accident. 'But you've done nothing wrong, Seren. You were a child yourself when he went missing.'

'Does that make a difference?' she asks.

Lowri has no answer. She doesn't know whether the police suspected a crime had been committed, or whether they simply ruled the case as misadventure, and now clearly isn't the time to ask.

They both fall silent for a moment and, finally, Seren drinks her tea. She drains the mug as if she suddenly realises she's thirsty, turning anxiously to Lowri when she's finished.

'You will still restore the mill, won't you?' she says, her eyes bright with tears. 'You mustn't let this put you off.'

'We will if we can,' replies Lowri. She's been thinking about this too and there's no point in lying. 'It just might take a little longer than we first thought, that's all. The police investigation could mean we miss the funding application deadline, but some things are more important.'

'*The mill* is important,' Seren replies. 'You must do it. And the castle.'

Her urgency surprises Lowri. 'Okay,' she says lightly, not wanting to promise what she might not be able to deliver. 'I'm sure everything will work out fine.'

She's about to ask whether Seren would like another cup of tea when her phone beeps with a text message. It's from Elin.

Sorry, I know this is really bad timing, but Gordon's gone to the bank and things are kicking off over here.

Lowri frowns. *Kicking off? What does that mean?*

Elin types back. *Loudmouthed Gwen. I don't suppose you could pop over, could you? They won't listen to me.*

Lowri has no idea who Gwen is. *Why? What will happen if they don't?*

There's a long pause and then: *The whole bloody lot will walk out.*

Lowri sighs. Oh, for heaven's sake... Her fingers fly over the keys. *I'll be two minutes.*

With apologies and assurances to Seren that she won't be long, Lowri rushes over to the factory, where she's met at the door by a very anxious-looking Elin.

'It's Gwen,' she says. 'She doesn't need any excuse to down tools, and I only managed to keep her here by saying you were coming over.' She pulls a face. 'Sorry, I think I may have rather set you up. I didn't think. I just couldn't bear the thought of them all standing around the mill, gawping.'

Lowri nods. 'That's okay, I'm in agreement with you there. That's the last thing the police need. Or anyone else for that matter.' She takes a deep breath.

Not a single machine is working as Lowri walks onto the factory floor. She positions herself carefully, sitting as casually as she can on the edge of a table near the front of the room. All eyes are on her.

'Hi, everyone. If you could please listen a minute, I'll try to explain what's going on.' She smiles.

'Gwen says someone's dead,' calls a voice from the back of the room.

'Well, not exactly...' Lowri winces. 'I'm sure there are lots of questions and speculation but I just want to reassure you that everything is okay.' She clears her throat. 'I've been looking at having some restoration work done on the old watermill, and in the course of that work, I'm afraid some remains were found. Human remains...' A flurry of voices rises up. 'However...' She pauses while the noise settles back down. 'However, it's very likely that they've been there some time so, although the area has been cordoned off by the police, there's absolutely nothing to worry about.'

A woman halfway down the room nods in knowing fashion, arms folded across her chest. 'Told you,' she says. 'It's that weird one's brother, the one who lives up by the river, floats about in silly dresses, the one whose mother was a witch. She died as well... reckon there's something right funny going on. Everyone always said the brother had gone in the river... Well, they were right, weren't they?' She looks around triumphantly.

Lowri's voice cuts across the resultant murmurings. 'Sorry, I don't know your name.'

'It's Gwen.' It's also a challenge.

Lowri gives her a smile that is ninety-nine-per-cent fake. 'As to who the remains belong to, it's a little too early to say as yet. And for Seren's sake, and Sorley's too, it would be nice if we weren't the source of needless gossip. I imagine it's hard enough losing a brother and not knowing what happened to him, without receiving sudden confirmation that he might be dead. Horrible, actually. Anyway... does anyone have any questions?'

She looks around the room, carefully avoiding Elin's eye.

A hand raises to her right. 'Hi,' she says, indicating that they should talk.

'You said about the mill just now. Is it true you're going to open it back up again and sack us all?'

'Sack you?' Lowri's mouth drops open. She has no idea where this conversation is going. Or why. 'Sorry, why do you think I'm going to sack you?'

She isn't meant to see it, but there are heads turning in the periphery of her vision and they're all looking at Gwen. It's pretty obvious who started this particular rumour. Lowri focuses on the woman who spoke, eyebrows raised.

'I dunno. Not sure where I heard it now, but stands to reason, doesn't it?' She shrugs.

Lowri shakes her head. 'I'm confused... because surely the only person who could sack any of you is me. And, as I haven't spoken to you, I don't see how that can be right. But...' She smiles. 'I'm really glad you've brought the subject up because now I can tell you a little of what I've been thinking. And you're not to worry, any of you. I'm going to need you all, and that's not going to change. What I would like to do is make things a little better around here, working conditions, salaries too, if I can manage it. It's early days, but one of the ways we might do this is by renovating the mill and moving everyone into that building. So that's what I've been looking into. And that's it really. Nothing sinister.' Another smile. 'But I'll absolutely keep you updated with developments as they happen, *if* they happen. Does that answer your question?'

There's a mumbled acknowledgement that it does.

'Great,' says Lowri, beaming. 'Does anyone else want to ask anything? Feel free, I don't mind.'

Predictably, the room is silent.

'Okay, then I'll let you all get on, but please don't worry about what's taking place outside. The police won't need to come in here, or ask questions of any of you, nothing like that. So you can all just go about your work as usual.'

A chair scrapes across the floor, Gwen's arms are folded even tighter.

'Not sure I *can* work, knowing what's happened. Gives me the shivers... All this time we've been working here with a skeleton practically under our noses. This place is creepy enough as it is, without that.'

'It's been a big shock,' agrees Lowri. 'But there's nothing nasty to see and the police have assured me they'll be gone quite soon.'

'Well, I don't know, my head's in a right tizzy...'

'Understandable,' Lowri replies, with a quick check on the time. 'Of course, if you feel that upset by the news, by all means go home, there's only a few hours left to go as it is and—'

The chair scrapes even further as Gwen snatches up her bag from the floor. 'Reckon I might do that then. I think I'll feel better at home.'

'Of course...' Lowri smiles, and waits as Gwen gathers herself. 'See you tomorrow then, Gwen.'

Gwen's head comes up. 'Oh, right... yes, see you tomorrow. Thanks.' And with that, she virtually runs from the room.

Lowri gets to her feet. 'Is everyone else feeling okay? Maybe you should have a quick break? Tea and biscuits maybe.'

'Biscuits?' snorts someone. 'That'll be the day.'

Lowri frowns. 'Oh, well... we could have a cuppa at least.' She looks around the room. 'Sorry, I don't know anyone's name but, Elin? Could you give me a hand? Carry on, everyone, we'll bring them round.'

Moments later, Elin joins her at the top of the room. 'Lowri, sorry, but what are you doing?'

She gives the side of her nose a small tap. 'Humour me,' she says in a hushed voice. 'Let's just get these drinks made, shall we? And while I'm doing that, *you* can have a wander on the pretext of asking everyone what they'd like to drink, and listen to anything that's being said.' She looks up at Elin from under her lashes, smiling at her surprised expression. 'I'm pretty sure Gwen's the one who's been spouting off about people getting the sack, but what I want to know is who put the idea in *her* head?'

It takes a few moments, but machines soon start up again and murmurs of conversation with them. Most of it's just general chat and Lowri turns her back on it, busying herself with the kettle and the motley collection of mugs.

'Very interesting...' murmurs Elin, sidling up to her a few minutes later.

'Don't tell me now,' says Lowri. 'You can fill me in later.' She raises her voice a little. 'So that's how many coffees?'

Ten minutes later, she meets Elin outside.

'I didn't catch much,' Elin says in answer to Lowri's question. 'But I did hear someone say, and I quote, "far too thick with Bridie". Do you reckon that's who it was?'

'I'd lay money on it,' replies Lowri. 'It can't really be anyone else, can it? The only people who know what I've been looking into are you, Gordon and Bridie, and I know it wasn't you,' she adds quickly. 'But I'm beginning to get very irritated by that woman.'

Elin pulls a face. 'You don't want to go getting on the wrong side of Gwen though either,' she says. 'She can make trouble for you and she's one of the worst gossips there is. Most people side with her because they're scared if they don't, *they'll* be the ones being talked about next. And if she thinks you're being soft, she'll take every opportunity there is to be off sick or at the doctor's. Then, before you know it, they'll all be at it.'

Lowri smiles. 'But I'm not being soft, Elin. One day very soon, people are going to have to choose – whether they like my version of the future, or Bridie's, and I'd quite like to know how that will go so I can be prepared. I don't want anyone here who isn't fully committed to what we'll be doing. So if they're not, then I'd rather they weren't here at all.'

'Ooh...' Elin's eyes widen. 'You go get 'em, girl.'

'And if Gwen thinks it's okay to call Seren "that weird one" in front of me, then she can think again.'

'Lowri Morgan, you dark horse, you. But I'm liking your style.' She grins.

'I'm pissed off,' Lowri replies. 'And people like Gwen wind me up. That's never a good idea. Mind you...' She stops and wrinkles her nose. 'It's all well and good talking about reno-vating the mill, but I have no idea how long the police will be here. They haven't assured me of anything and I'm pretty certain they'll take as long as they want. Which means that Michael can't get in and assess what state the wheel is in, nor the building for that matter. And if he can't do that...'

'You won't get the funding bid in on time.' Elin's face is grim. 'But you can still carry on with the castle though, right?'

'We can, but all our research suggests we stand far more chance of being successful if we incorporate the mill into our plans. But if we can't, we can't. And I have to think about Seren too. She was adamant earlier that we go ahead, but I don't want to do anything which might cause her more pain than she's already in.' She glances back towards the gatehouse. 'Actually, Elin, I should go. Seren's there and I don't want to leave her on her own for too long. Although...' Lowri has spotted a car approaching, her eyes narrowing as she sees who's driving. 'I don't suppose five more minutes would hurt.'

With a quick hug, Lowri moves off to intercept Gordon as he steps from his car. He looks understandably confused.

'What's going on?' he asks as soon as he sees her. 'Has there been an accident?'

Lowri shakes her head, not really knowing quite how to

explain. 'There's no easy way to say this, but we found a skull, in the bottom of the wheel pit. We've no idea how long it's been there, but it's human... and we think it might be Sorley Penoyre.'

Gordon's eyes widen. 'After all this time. Dear God... how awful. Is there anything we can do?'

'No, the police have everything under control. Huw is talking to them, and a chap called Michael Cornish, who's been here looking at the mill for us. I think it's probably better if the rest of us just let them get on with it.'

'Yes, indeed.' Gordon glances towards the factory. 'Goodness, this is hard to take in... I'm assuming everyone else knows?'

'I've just been over speaking to them. Gwen's gone home, she wasn't feeling very well, but the rest seem okay.'

He gives a grim nod. 'Right, well, I'd best get on then. See what's what.'

'Before you go, Gordon...' Lowri gives an apologetic smile. 'Bridie obviously isn't here today, but I do need to speak to her rather urgently. Do you know where I can find her? I've just realised I don't even have her phone number.'

'Bridie?' he says, as if he hasn't the faintest idea who Lowri is talking about. 'Oh, yes, now let me see, what day is it today?' His brow furrows in consternation. 'Monday... Oh, well I think she might be away, I'm not sure.'

'Oh, that's a shame. Although, once Bridie finds out what's happened here today, I'm sure she'll call in, won't she? Or phone at the very least. So when she does, would you mind passing on a message and say I'll be over to see her at ten thirty in the morning?'

Panic crosses Gordon's face. 'Ten thirty? I'm not sure—'

'It really is quite urgent,' says Lowri, still smiling.

'Right, well, I'm sure that will be okay. Leave it with me.'

'Thanks, Gordon, you're a star. Listen, I'd better dash, I need to get back to the gatehouse.'

Lowri hates being disingenuous, but she's not sure there's any other way. There's no doubt in her mind now that Bridie, and quite possibly Gordon, are leading her a merry dance, and by the time she gets home, she's built up a good head of steam. She pauses a moment before going in, however, swallowing down her anger, breathing deeply in an attempt to instil some calm. Now is not the time to lose her temper, Seren deserves better than that.

To her surprise, only Huw is sitting at the kitchen table, there's no sign of Seren.

'She's gone,' he says as Lowri enters. 'But she gave me strict instructions to tell you not to worry. She's only gone to fetch some herbs from her garden. Said she wants to make us all a tisane, whatever that is. One of her potions, no doubt.'

Lowri smiles. 'It's a humble herbal tea, nothing too scary.' She thinks back to the day she and Seren first met when she joked about eye of newt and toe of frog. 'Is that what she does? Grows herbs?'

'Among other things, I believe. Like most folk, I'm not really sure what Seren does.'

'But she must have some way of supporting herself?'

'I guess...' He pauses, eyes on hers. 'That's a curious look.'

'I was just thinking about something. Never mind.' There's a germ of an idea here that Lowri would love to breathe life into. 'Her garden looked amazing.'

Huw nods. 'She grows all sorts. Flowers, herbs, vegetables, and fruit too. She used to bring me a few things on occasion as well. At least, I think it was her.'

Lowri gives him a quizzical look.

'She'd leave things on the roof of the boat for me to find. I tried to thank her on several occasions but Seren is very good at hiding if she doesn't want to be found.'

'Is that sad?' muses Lowri. 'Or just clever? I'm beginning to think she might have the right idea. Keeping out of people's way sounds rather appealing just now.'

'Oh?'

Lowri shakes her head. She mustn't get herself worked up again. 'Just a wee problem over at the factory, one which I'm pretty sure has been engineered by Bridie.'

Huw studies her for a moment. 'You look tired,' he says. 'Come and sit down and have some tea. It's common or garden builder's brew, I'm afraid. I thought I'd get some in before Seren returns. Not sure how me and a tisane are going to get along.'

'Sounds wonderful.' Lowri sinks down onto a chair, suddenly overcome with weariness. Laying her arms on the table, she leans forward until her head rests on them. 'What a day,' she says, closing her eyes. 'Poor Seren.'

'I had to send Michael away,' says Huw.

Lowri's head springs back up. 'Oh God, of course, what did he say?'

'Just that we should keep in touch. And he'll happily come back as soon as we're given the all-clear by the police.'

She nods, feeling suddenly awkward. 'About earlier...' she begins. How does she apologise for hugging him, without saying the word hugging? 'I'm sorry. For crying all over you. It's just—'

Huw holds up his hand. 'There's no need to apologise, I think I was crying too. It was all so unexpected.'

'I know, but... I'm sorry if I made you feel awkward.' She doesn't want to say how nice it felt. Or how she wondered if Huw felt the same.

Huw dips his head. 'Not at all.' He swallows. 'No harm done.'

Damn, thinks Lowri. He *looks* awkward, his eyes flicking to the floor, lips pursed a little. And she doesn't want him thinking she's thrown herself at the nearest available man— Stop, Lowri, for goodness' sake. Alun died two years ago, it's not as if— Sudden heat floods her face.

'Good... well, that's all okay then.' She smiles and tuts for good measure. 'And there's me thinking it was all going so well.' *Blimey, Lowri, now he's going to think you meant him and you, not the project. You're digging yourself an even bigger hole...*

'It *is* going well,' Huw replies, smiling now, meeting her look.

Lowri frowns. Does Huw mean him and her, or does he mean the project? She groans inwardly. *He just means the project, don't be silly, so make out like that's what you mean too. But it* is *what she means, isn't it...?* Jeez, now she's confusing herself.

'Maybe not completely, one-hundred-per-cent well,' adds Huw. 'But, with any luck, we should still be able to apply for the mill funding.'

Lowri breathes a sigh of relief. He *did* mean the project after all. She nods. 'And I guess, for Seren, what happened today is a good thing. It could bring years of speculation to an end and allow her to finally lay her brother to rest. That has to be a positive outcome. I'm tired, I know, but I can't help feeling as if I've been promising you something I might not be able to deliver. What if we can't get the bids in on time?'

Huw lifts the teapot and pours Lowri a cup. 'Listen, I'm here because I want to be. I made a promise to you, and one to myself, so I'm in this for the duration. Let's not paint the devil on the wall, count our chickens or any other cliché we can think of. Let's not do any of those things until we know what the situation actually is, not what we think it might be.'

Lowri gives a small nod, but it's only so Huw thinks she's paying attention, that she agrees with his stance. She doesn't, not at all. Because she's pretty sure she knows what the situation is and she can't bear to talk about their plans, to see the hope and excitement on people's faces, knowing that it could all come to naught. It's the first time she's dared to dream since Alun died. It's also, aside from Jess, the first time she's felt the warmth of friends around her. People like Elin, with her incredible talent, and Seren, with whom she feels such affinity. People like Huw... and she'll be damned if she'll let one woman spoil all that. Whatever game Bridie is playing, Lowri needs to know now, she's tired of waiting.

'Huw, I'm sorry, will you excuse me for a bit? I've remembered something I need to do, and if I don't do it now...' She picks up her mug and takes several mouthfuls. 'Sorry,' she says again, indicating the rest of her tea. 'But I've got to go. Tell Seren I won't be long.'

And, with that, she practically runs from the kitchen in case Huw tries to stop her.

17

It occurs to her the moment she leaves that Huw will more than likely know where Bridie lives, but in the split second Lowri thinks it, she realises she will never ask him. Too much history lies between him and Bridie, that much is obvious and, for some reason, she wants to have this conversation with Bridie without anyone knowing. Gordon, too, is off the list of people to ask. She still isn't sure how much she can trust him, and has a sneaking suspicion that, even if he did tell Lowri where to find Bridie, he'd ring and warn her the moment Lowri leaves to seek her out. Which rather means she's out of options.

Her car heads in the direction of the town before she even thinks clearly about where she's going but, as she pulls up in the market square's car park, she realises there's a way to find out the information she needs and, if she's lucky, rattle Bridie's cage as well.

From the outside, Castle Crafts looks smart and well-cared for. It's one of a row of pastel-coloured buildings, painted a soft pink in this case and, despite the earliness of the season, already sports several baskets of hanging flowers outside. Inside, however, it's virtually the same as any other gift shop Lowri has ever been in.

It occurs to her that she really ought to check their stock before marching up to the counter, but then again, she isn't interested in a soft approach. Confident and direct is the only way to go. Even so, Lowri's heart still thumps uncomfortably as she heads for the till.

The woman standing there barely has time to register Lowri's presence.

'Hi, I have a message for Bridie Turner,' she says. 'Is she here?'

Predictably, the woman looks confused. But she also looks anxious. 'Bridie Turner?'

Lowri doesn't reply.

'Sorry, I'm not quite sure who that is.'

Lowri stands her ground. 'Everybody round here knows who Bridie Turner is. And, given that she owns this business, I would imagine you know her quite well.'

'But Bridie doesn't own...' The woman trails off, perhaps realising her mistake, perhaps a little intimidated by the glint in Lowri's eye.

'Right, so you do know her then,' Lowri replies. 'And you can deny it all you want, but I know for a fact Bridie owns this place. I'd be happy to show you how I know, if you need a little reminder. So is she here or not?'

The woman shakes her head. 'She emails mostly. Or phones...'

'That's okay then. I'll catch her at home if you can tell me where that is.'

'I'm not really sure I should.'

'There are plenty of other people I could ask,' says Lowri. 'So you could just save me the bother.' She smiles. 'And if you're worried, I won't mention who told me.'

Another few seconds pass as the woman tries to decide

whether she really can divulge her employer's whereabouts, or, indeed, if she believes Lowri. It's killing her, but Lowri can wait if she has to. She tries another smile.

The woman tucks her hair behind her ears. Then pushes a bangle further up her wrist. 'It's the big house,' she says eventually. 'Up the top of the road by the church. You can't miss it.'

Lowri lets her eyes linger on a rack of items for sale beside the till. 'I really appreciate it. Thank you so much.' She taps a finger on top of the display stand. 'Nice tea towels, by the way.'

Bridie's house looks just as Lowri imagines it will, right down to the topiary box plants flanking the elegant front door. A door on which she knocks politely. She really doesn't think Bridie will be home or, if she is, that she will answer. It's somewhat unnerving, therefore, when the door is opened almost immediately.

'Lowri. Good heavens, this is a surprise. I was just on my way over to Clearwater, as it happens. Gordon telephoned to let me know the awful news. You must all be dreadfully shocked.' If Gordon told her anything else, like perhaps their meeting scheduled for the morning, Bridie isn't about to say. She regards Lowri steadily.

'Yes, we were rather, and it's one of the things I wanted to talk to you about.' Lowri is determined not to be sidetracked.

'Yes, of course. I'll do anything I can to help, although I was under the impression the police are dealing with it all.'

'They are. But when Gordon popped out to the bank, some of the staff were a little upset, understandably so, but—'

'Gordon will have a chat with Gwen,' replies Bridie, smiling warmly. 'She'll be back at her machine tomorrow, so no real harm done. She takes advantage at times, I'm afraid, but you weren't to know that.'

'I'm not bothered about Gwen going home,' says Lowri, eyeing the hallway behind Bridie. 'Sorry, can I come in? I'd feel much happier talking about this somewhere other than the doorstep.' She smiles sweetly.

Bridie opens the door wide. 'Of course.' She leads Lowri down the wide entrance way. 'Let's pop into my study.' She indicates a door immediately to her left. 'Although, you'll have to excuse the state of my desk. I'm a little busy.'

Lowri smiles politely as she takes the seat Bridie indicates. 'I'm sorry, I don't even know what it is you do? Outside of Clearwater, that is.'

'Don't you? Oh... We have a haulage firm. My husband and I started it years ago. He's dead now, I'm sad to say, but it still keeps us going.' She moves a stack of papers to one side of the desk. 'Now, I'm all yours.'

Lowri takes a deep breath. 'Going back to the staff at the factory for a moment... Gwen's leaving aside, I'm more concerned that she, and therefore most of the rest of the staff, seem to have got the wrong idea about the watermill restoration. They were under the impression they were about to be sacked.'

'Oh dear.' Bridie sighs. 'That's Gwen for you. I can see how it happened.' She lays her palms flat on the table, pale-pink polish gleaming on the tips of her nails. 'How can I put this? Gwen is a troublemaker. Every business has one and she's ours, I'm afraid. She also has a most irritating habit of loitering where she shouldn't – dreadful gossip – and, unfortunately, when she overheard Gordon and I talking about the mill a couple of days ago, she jumped to her usual wild conclusions. Now, granted, it would have been better had she not been privy to what we were discussing, but then again, I didn't think the mill's restoration was a secret. Or perhaps I've got that wrong?'

Lowri doesn't answer.

'In any case, I spoke to Gwen at the time and made it very clear that, as far as I knew, her job was not on the line but, unfortunately, Gwen has always been happy to twist what's said for her own invention.'

'Well, that's one explanation for how it happened,' replies Lowri.

Bridie is beginning to look a little uncomfortable. 'I'm not sure I understand.'

'No, me neither.' Lowri lets the seconds tick by. 'Because I don't remember raising the subject of sacking anyone. So I'm wondering what it was Gwen overheard that made her leap to her wild conclusion. As far as I'm concerned, there shouldn't have been a need to reassure anyone their job was, or wasn't, on the line. As far as you knew.'

'I know, ridiculous isn't it? But that's Gwen for you.' Bridie smiles. Complicit. 'You know, I sometimes wonder if she's just looking for an excuse to be sacked.'

'Really? People are so strange, aren't they? Well, let's just hope Gwen doesn't overhear that.' Lowri uncrosses and recrosses her legs to stop them from jiggling. 'Let's make it clear then, shall we, in case anyone else asks, that I'm not thinking about changing staffing levels. But, if I do, I'll make it a priority to talk to everyone myself. How's that? Does that help? In case you have any more Gwens on the staff. You can tell them that and then we all know where we are.'

'Excellent.' Bridie smooths down her hair. 'Well, I'm glad we've had the opportunity to chat about this. It's so easy for misunderstandings to get out of hand, isn't it?'

Lowri nods. 'Indeed it is. So you're not telling me about your plan to build houses on the river meadow... that's a misunderstanding, is it?'

Lowri hates the surge of triumph she feels at Bridie's reddening face.

'A misunderstanding?' Bridie recovers quickly. 'Hardly that. I wasn't aware I had to inform you of my every decision. It's early days yet, the planning application has only just gone in.'

A ripple of shock makes Lowri flinch. This is so much worse than she thought. 'Even so,' she replies, trying to keep her voice even, 'it seems rather too important a subject matter to have been left out of our conversations. I should have thought common courtesy would suggest I ought to know. Surely you can see the potential conflict of interests here?'

'Left out?' retorts Bridie. 'But I didn't leave it out, I simply assumed you weren't ready to discuss it yet. Forgive me, Lowri, but you don't seem particularly well informed. I thought that from the moment you arrived.'

Lowri ignores her gibe. 'So you're not denying it then?'

Bridie looks confused. 'Why should I deny it?' She rearranges her hair. 'Oh dear... Are you telling me you didn't know about the plans for that parcel of land?'

Damn, Lowri walked into that one. But she still won't give Bridie the satisfaction of agreeing. 'Only if houses *were* to be built on that land, you'd need access to it. Access which would have to be granted by the Clearwater estate.'

'Yes, that's right,' replies Bridie smoothly.

'Access which would have to be granted by me.'

Bridie gives her a pitying look. 'Ah... Now I can see where the confusion has arisen from. You see, I don't need permission from you, Lowri, because I already have it. From your husband. He signed a contract before he died.'

Lowri wonders if her heart has stopped beating. It must have, she can't feel it. In fact, her whole body feels numb. She forces herself to think. Bridie must be bluffing. There can't be any contract because Alun hadn't had any dealings with the estate for years. This is just another of her twisted games.

'I have all the email correspondence here,' adds Bridie, getting to her feet. 'One moment...' She crosses to the filing cabinet in the corner of the room.

Breathe, Lowri, breathe...

'Sorry, what am I thinking?' says Bridie, turning back. 'They won't be here. I have them in a file in my other office, but I'd be very happy to show them to you.'

'I'll get the contract revoked,' blusters Lowri.

'I'm sorry, but you won't,' replies Bridie, a smug smile flickering around her mouth. 'Haven't you ever heard the expression, "the contracts of the dead survive to haunt the living"? There's nothing you can do about it.'

'What is it with you?' Lowri argues, getting to her feet. 'Ever since I've arrived, you've tried to trip me up. Hiding your true intentions beneath a sugary-sweet veneer. I appreciate you're getting some kind of kick out of all this, that, in fact, you're not a very nice person. I can accept that, some people aren't. But what I don't get, is why? Why don't you want to see me succeed? Why don't you want to see the castle restored?'

Bridie's eyes flick upwards. 'I should have thought that was obvious. It's just a pile of rocks, Lowri. Any splendour it might once have had is long gone. In the past. And even though a few sad individuals think we should all still live there, I'm not one of them. Times move on. I should have thought you of all people would understand that. And I look set to make a very large amount of money from the sale of those houses. Money I've had coming to me for years. Money I should have had in the first place. I've even had to babysit Clearwater's pathetic little business while I've been waiting. Well, I won't have to wait much longer. The houses *will* go ahead, Lowri, I've made sure of that. And there's nothing you can do to stop me.'

Lowri opens her mouth to retaliate and then closes it again. She was about to play her trump card, but something stopped her. 'You think you've won, don't you?' she says instead. 'Well, go ahead and think it. There's plenty I can do to stop you, so let me just make it clear, Bridie. There will never be houses on Clearwater land, not while I live and breathe. So if it's a fight you're looking for, you've got one.'

Somehow, Lowri manages to stumble from the room, out of the front door and back to her car. She fumbles with her keys, knowing she should stop and calm down, that driving in the state she's in isn't a good idea, but she can't bear the thought that Bridie might be watching her, laughing at her. So she starts the car and roars off the drive as if she's in perfect control.

A sleek silver sports car is coming towards her at speed, and she just manages to slam on her brakes as it tears past, taking the place on the drive she's just vacated. Lowri has a fleeting impression of sunglasses and blonde hair and then the car is gone from view, leaving her gasping for breath, her chest heaving. She pulls over and it takes her a full ten minutes before she can even think of driving home, guilt over what might have happened coursing through her.

For a few minutes, Lowri really has no idea where she's driving, taking streets through the town she has no recollection of, circling round, first one way and then back the other. Part of her wishes she could stay this way forever, so she won't have to deal with everything that's coming, but all that does is make her angrier – that Bridie thinks she can trample over the shoots of Lowri's new life without a care. That she can also trample over Alun's memory.

This last thought twists inside her, writhing and tormented. Because, up until a few weeks ago, Lowri knew nothing of Clearwater and would have told anyone with conviction that the same was true for Alun. Now she's not so sure. Doubt has crept in.

She'd known it was there, just beyond the corner of her eye, waiting until it could ambush her with its suspicions. And exactly when she let her guard slip she doesn't know. But she did, and it took advantage of her. Now it has her in its grip, and she's not even sure whether if faced with the question of building houses on his land, Alun would have outright rejected the notion like she supposed, or even held an opinion. Because, let's face it, isn't proof of his turning a blind eye everywhere she looks, even in the shape of his employees who have to go to the loo in an outhouse? Worse, if what Bridie said about permission for the land is true, it means Alun had been lying to her all along. His memory won't be the only thing tarnished, their marriage will be too.

A few minutes later, she's back at Clearwater. Despite everything, it's the only place she can find peace. Rounding the gatehouse, she spots Seren standing in the castle keep. Her face is upturned to the sky as she turns in a slow circle. Waiting until Seren catches sight of her, Lowri crosses the space to join her.

'I must look a sight,' says Seren, a shy smile on her face. 'No wonder people think I'm mad.'

But Lowri doesn't think she's mad, or looks a sight either. With her red hair streaming out behind her, bright copper in the sunshine, Lowri wishes she could look as free.

'I feel better when I'm outside,' adds Seren. 'So I was trying to decide where a garden could go.'

Lowri walks forward and draws her into a hug. It feels the most natural thing in the world. 'I'd like a garden,' she says. 'In fact, I'd been thinking I should ask you to make one for us here.' She pauses. 'But you probably knew that.'

'Were you?' asks Seren, but her smile is knowing. 'Of course, there would have been one here, once upon a time. Quite a sizeable one too. Vegetables from it would have supplied the castle, but also a good deal of the village, particularly during times of harsh weather when people sought shelter within its walls, or if they were under siege. Castles were remarkably self-sufficient places.'

'I hadn't really thought of that, but yes, I guess they must have been.'

'I need to get the orientation right though,' adds Seren. 'That's why I was spinning – to check where the moon appears at different times of the year. Then I can work out which areas face the waxing moon and which the waning.'

'The moon?'

'Yes, I always garden according to moon cycles. I could plant the garden anywhere, but if you can manage it somewhere the light actually shines so much the better.'

Lowri nods, although she doesn't really understand. 'And does that work? Does it help things to grow?'

Seren is amused. 'Lowri, when I first met you, you were wearing a silver moon about your throat. People don't like to admit it, because then it means they're someone like me, but a lot of people are instinctively governed by it.'

'I suppose so, but...'

'Think of the sea,' continues Seren. 'The vastness of the oceans, all moved by the power of the moon. Each wave which crashes upon a shore has the moon's influence to thank. So the way I look at it, human beings are eighty per cent water, why shouldn't the moon exert its influence over us too? Plants as well, they're mostly water.'

Lowri stares at her. 'That makes perfect sense.'

'It does. But you'd be amazed how many people refuse to admit it.'

Lowri looks around the keep. 'So what would they have grown here?'

'All sorts of things. Vegetables, obviously, and lots of herbs too. They used them for flavouring, but it wasn't unusual to plant an apothecary garden which they used solely for medicinal purposes. No paracetamol back then, so a plentiful supply of healing plants was an absolute necessity. They grew flowers as well though. Quite a few are edible but they loved them for their scent and decoration, just like we do.'

Her words prickle at Lowri's thoughts of earlier in the day. 'Seren, would you really be able to create a garden here? I don't mean that as in are you capable, I know you are. But I wondered if you'll have the time? Sorry, this is going to come out wrong however I say it, so I'll just add the rider that I'm not being nosey, or derisory in any way, but you must have some way of supporting yourself, some sort of employment. How do you survive?'

'I have an Etsy shop.'

Lowri can't help her snort of surprise. 'That's the last thing I expected you to say.'

Seren gives her a surprisingly cheeky grin. 'I might have my head in the clouds most of the time, but my feet are firmly on the ground. I sell all sorts of things. Dried flowers for decoration, garlands, herbs for healing, and I make my own creams too.'

'Which is exactly my point. All of that must take time, and creating a garden here will be a big job. I don't want to take you away from anything else you need to do.'

'Perhaps this *is* something I need to do,' Seren replies, smiling softly. 'Keeping busy, it's what we all do, don't we, in times of stress? But it will help, I think, draw me onward into the future and that's what I need now. I've spent so many years thinking about what happened to Sorley, whether he was still alive, if I would ever see him again. It's like living in limbo, like one long dream you're not sure you'll ever be free from. And I've wasted so many years because of it, Lowri. Finally knowing Sorley's gone is horrible, but there's a weird kind of peace in it too, an acceptance. Getting my teeth stuck into something new is just what I need to help me move on.'

Lowri nods. 'I can understand that, but just as long as you're sure.' Her head is whirling with thoughts. 'And have you ever wanted to expand your business? Maybe even have a physical shop one day?'

'No.' Seren's reply is quick and decisive, and Lowri feels her heart sink. Seren's eyes search hers. 'I live a simple life, Lowri, partly through necessity, but also partly through choice. What I take from the soil, I give back. I sell what I need to pay my bills and eat, with a little left over, but I don't want any more. I don't have need for an endless amount of things, and... Anyway, sorry, but no, what you describe isn't for me.'

'Okay, I just thought I'd ask.' Lowri gives her a sheepish smile.

'What I will do, however, is teach you to do what I do, if it will help.' A mischievous look crosses her face. 'I know what you're trying to do here, Lowri. This land is important to me, and I know what you're facing. And before you go wondering how on earth I could possibly know, I got talking with Huw the other day, and he explained about the conditions of the funding you're applying for.' She grins. 'I may be many things, but I'm not psychic.'

Lowri shakes her head in amusement at Seren's words, yet she almost wishes she were. Perhaps then she could tell Lowri everything is going to be okay. Her head is beginning to teem with the possibilities of what the funding could mean for them all, what they could achieve, and the thought that it might all come to nothing is almost too much to bear. 'Seren, I know you have a lot of things on your mind right now, but just suppose we did get the funding. How do you think we should use the space here?'

'I hadn't really thought about it,' she replies. 'But we *could* think about it, if you want to?' She cocks her head to one side. 'Would you walk with me for a few minutes, out along the river?'

It's the last place Lowri wants to go, or so she thinks, but then immediately on its tail comes another thought, much stronger, and she realises the river meadow is exactly where she wants to go. With Bridie's words still ringing in her ears, and her doubts about Alun snagging her conscience, she needs to see this space again, to feel it, and what it means to her.

'Tell me where your thoughts have been going,' says Seren after a few minutes companionable walking.

'They're a bit all over the place, but in order to get the

funding we want, we need to think of a community angle for the restoration and—' Lowri suddenly stops. 'Seren, how come I never realised before how beautiful this is?' She indicates the meadow in front of her. The sun is warm in a gentle blue sky, the barest of breezes rippling the tall strands of grass. She can smell them, sweet and full of summer's promise. The colours are just emerging, shy and soft, and in a few more months, more blooms will spring forth, vibrant and full of life.

She stares at Seren. 'I've been going about this all wrong,' she says. 'I've been searching for ideas on the basis of need, when what I should have been doing is thinking about what I *want*. And why has it taken me so long to understand they're one and the same?'

'Things come to us at the right time,' says Seren, her face tipped upwards to the sky. 'The trick is realising when that is.' She smiles warmly. 'And you would appear to have done so.'

Lowri shields her eyes as a clutch of birds swoop by, making for the soft riverbanks. She follows their path, squinting against the sun.

'They're sand martins,' says Seren. 'They come every year from March to October, a marker that the wheel of the year is turning.'

'It's so gloriously simple,' says Lowri, stunned by her sudden revelation. 'This is it. *This* is what I want. A life filled with all these wonderful things. One that other people can share in.' She's now more determined than ever that Bridie's plans should never come to fruition.

'But you have it,' replies Seren, laughing. 'This belongs to you, Lowri, or have you only just twigged?'

Lowri so longs to confide in Seren, to voice all her fears and doubts. But she can't, she must speak to Huw first, she owes him that much. 'Wouldn't it be wonderful if this could be a place for everyone to enjoy?' she muses, her voice growing wistful. 'We could have a community garden, we could teach people how to grow things, how to use them, in all sorts of ways... You could hold workshops or, *something*... I'm talking off the top of my head here, but there are loads of possibilities.' Lowri's face falls as she sees Seren's expression.

'Lowri, I'm sorry, but I don't think I could do that. I've lived my life away from people for good reason. I don't think I'm ready to embrace them just yet.' She holds out a hand to touch Lowri's arm. 'But these are still good ideas. In fact, they're wonderful ideas and there's no reason why you couldn't do all the things you say. But, please, don't stick me in front of a whole crowd of people, that's all I ask. Other than that, I will help you all I can.'

Lowri nods, feeling a little foolish for her outburst. 'Sorry,' she says. 'I get a bit carried away. But, thank you. There's the seed of something here, I'm sure of it.'

'And that is all you need.'

Lowri looks back the way they came, at the castle, and the millpond beyond it. 'Will you be okay, Seren?' she asks gently.

For a moment, Seren doesn't speak, but then she nods, her eyes seeking Lowri's. 'We're all going to be okay,' she replies. 'It's time for us all to heal.'

Lowri finds Huw where she left him, sitting at the kitchen table, staring intently at his laptop. He must have made himself another cup of tea and then forgotten about it, because it sits beside him, a film of milk settling over the surface.

'Hi,' she says, taking a seat quietly beside him. 'How's it going?'

When he turns to her his face is weary. 'Good, but I'm getting bogged down in some of the costings nitty-gritty. Necessary, but not exactly scintillating. Anyway, how about you, did you get it sorted?'

Lowri looks at him quizzically. 'Sorry?'

'Whatever it is you needed to do,' he replies. 'When you rushed off earlier.'

It's hard to remember that she and Huw only spoke a short while ago, so much seems to have happened since. Lowri looks down at the table, her eyes tracing the pattern of swirling grain. 'I did what I set out to do,' she replies. 'But I'm afraid things are far from sorted.' She inhales a long slow breath. 'I went to see Bridie,' she adds. 'To see if a rumour I heard was true.'

'Oh?' Huw is alert to the tone of her voice.

'And, sadly, it was.' She stares up at him. 'Huw, Bridie is planning to build houses on the river meadow. She's just applied for planning. I'm so sorry.'

For a moment, Lowri thinks Huw hasn't heard her, his eyes are locked on hers, staring but unseeing. She isn't sure she can bear to say it again.

Then he tears his gaze away. 'Of course she is,' he replies. 'Bridie never does anything without good reason. I should have guessed she'd be up to something like this.'

'I thought it might have been gossip,' adds Lowri. 'A friend of Elin's mum overheard. Rose, it was, she's the—'

'Aye, I know all about Rose.'

'Well, she heard someone in the pub mentioning they'd been to look at the land again. It must have been someone from the planning office. Or a developer even.'

Huw's brows knot together. 'How long ago was this?'

'I've no idea. Why?'

'I haven't seen anyone, that's all. And my boat's a pretty good place to spot folks from.'

'Oh...' It's a good point. Lowri wonders whether he's telling her this is the reason why his boat might have been scuppered. 'I get the feeling it was a while ago,' she says. 'Maybe a few weeks back.' She doesn't want to mention that in all likelihood Huw wouldn't have seen anyone, not when he'd been slumped inside in a drunken stupor. She slaps down her thought. *Stop it,*

Lowri, this isn't Huw's fault. You know exactly whose fault this is.

Huw is still thinking, remarkably calm under the circum-stances, although... Lowri studies his face. He isn't calm at all, there's anger there, but something else too, something she can't quite put her finger on. She's going to have to tell him. It won't be long before he works it out for himself and—

'I think Alun gave her permission,' she blurts out. 'I can't believe it, but maybe he did. Maybe he...' She trails off as a wave of grief assails her. How could Alun have done this? He wasn't like that, he... he cared about things for one. He cared about people. But the little voice in her head is telling her maybe he didn't. Maybe she never really knew her husband at all.

'Alun did?' Huw's eyes flick to hers and then away again. 'I'm sorry, Lowri, I—'

'*You're* sorry? Why are *you* sorry? It's my husband who... But the castle, Huw! And everything else we have planned. We can hardly argue the sanctity of our heritage when twenty bloody houses are being built in our back yard. Who's going to give us funding knowing that when she's finished, Clearwater castle will be overlooking a housing estate?'

'Your husband gave Bridie rights of access to the meadow, is that what you're saying?'

Lowri nods, taking a deep breath, trying to slow down the river of noise in her head. 'That's what Bridie told me. But I can't believe Alun would have done something like that. Or maybe I do, I don't know,' she adds sadly. 'I thought Bridie was bluffing, playing one of her games, but why would she lie? Either she has access to the meadow, or she doesn't, and she can't get planning without it, surely?'

'Not a chance. She might not get it anyway. It's a traditional river meadow, on an historic site. I've never had much faith in the local council myself, but even so, I can't see the planning department running with it.'

'Bridie told me the houses *would* be built. She said she'd made sure of it.'

Huw's mouth settles in a hard line. 'Hmm, I wouldn't put it past her to have nobbled someone on the planning committee. That's exactly the way she works.'

'So what can we do?' urges Lowri. 'There must be some way we can stop her.'

'Due process, I believe it's called,' replies Huw, his voice flat. 'The right to object.'

'But what difference will that make if Bridie *has* got someone on the planning committee in her pocket?'

'None whatsoever.'

A wall of silence opens up between them.

'I'm so sorry,' says Lowri again.

But Huw makes no reply.

18

It's Elin who brings the proof, breezing through the door on her way home from work. She drops off a folder from Bridie and it's clear from her manner she has no idea what it contains. Lowri, however, lays it on the side in the kitchen, where it taunts her throughout the whole of dinner. Red, the colour of danger.

When Lowri finally opens it – after a surprisingly good-humoured meal, after they have washed up amid much chatter, after she has listened to Wren read and left her doing a jigsaw with Seren before she has her bath, after she has walked up the stairs to her room, and carefully closed the door, after she has sat on the edge of the bed, and after she has composed herself – that's when she finds out her marriage was a lie.

One of the worst things is that she had no idea. Lowri wasn't a wife who was suspicious of her husband having an affair, who lived a life full of lies and questions, disbelieving and hurt. She and Alun may have had a few small disagreements, but Alun was her best friend, her best confidante, her best self. *Her best.* They lived their lives with trust and openness, with love.

Except that now Lowri can no longer claim any of that, because only she was living that life, Alun had chosen not to.

What Lowri still can't understand, even when faced with concrete evidence of Alun's deceit, is why. Why had he lied to her? Why had he kept Clearwater secret from her as if he had something to hide? *Did* he have something to hide? The thought impales her, sharp as a pin.

In the folder are seven emails. None of them are particularly long, and all of them are only part of a larger conversation, but they prove, without a doubt, that Alun had given Bridie access to the river meadow across Clearwater land. He had even wished her well with her endeavours.

Perhaps the most curious thing is that they came from an email address Lowri doesn't recognise. It wasn't his main account, or the one he used for business, and it wasn't the more private one he used for family and friends. Its existence is unsettling enough even before she considers it might not be the only thing she knows nothing about.

She is still sitting on the side of the bed, her legs clamped together, jaw clenched and hands trembling. Not very far away, beneath her, is a box. It's not a very big box, but it contains several things of Alun's which she couldn't bear to either throw or give away. And one of these is his laptop. She knows the password, Alun had never been secretive about it, and although she can't access much, sometimes just opening it is enough. Because when she does, the first thing she sees is the photo Alun chose for his background wallpaper and she knows how much he loved them. It's a close-up picture of herself and Wren, taken during one hot summer when they were playing in their local park. Both of them are grinning at the camera as they try to eat the rapidly melting ice creams they hold. Wren is wearing most of hers, but her impish smile lights up the photo and Lowri herself looks blissful, carefree, relaxed. It's such a vivid memory and she can almost, if she holds her breath and breathes shallowly, almost see him in front of her, laughing at Wren and smiling at her. That smile... Now, she isn't sure if she can bear to look at it.

But she gets on her hands and knees and pulls out the box anyway, lifting the laptop clear and returning with it to sit in her original position. She runs her hands over its surface, thinking for a moment. The laptop isn't charged, but if she plugs it in, within minutes she could have access to it. She could potentially see all the emails that Alun exchanged with Bridie. And she has to ask herself what she wants most. Is it to remain in ignorance and in doing so hope to contain what's she's feeling now? Or does she want to find out everything she can, and open herself up to the possibility of more hurt? Two seconds later, she opens the laptop lid. This may be the only way she can stop the building of the houses going ahead. There are other people's fortunes at stake here, not just her own.

She's fishing for the charger when there's a polite tap at her door.

'Hello?' It's Huw, holding a bundle of clothes.

'Hi, sorry... I was just wondering if I could put on a load of washing? I'm almost out of tee shirts. I probably don't quite have a full load though if there's anything you want to add?' He peers at Lowri. 'Are you okay? You look... Like you've gone somewhere...'

Lowri licks her lips, wondering if she's been crying or not. Sometimes she doesn't always realise. 'Fine, just...' She should tell Huw about the emails. But that would mean sharing things which, even if she doesn't make them explicit, throw light on her marriage. She clears her throat. 'When we were looking for the accounts, you mentioned your friend, Jamie, the one who's good with computers?'

Huw's gaze drops to the laptop in her hands. 'Have you got a problem?' he asks.

'This isn't mine. It belonged to Alun.' She swallows. 'And I wanted to check something. Some emails... only I'm not sure how I can access them, *if* I can access them.'

Huw studies her face for a second, but thankfully doesn't ask the question he probably wants to. He nods, lightly, tactfully. He isn't going to pry. But, perversely, it makes Lowri want to tell him even more.

'When I spoke to Bridie today she told me she had proof that Alun had granted her access to the river meadow. Despite everything, I still wasn't sure I believed her, but...' She indicates the folder lying on the bed. 'She did.'

Huw looks anxious, his eyes fixed on the thin metal case she holds. 'So you want to go through his emails, to see what else you didn't know?'

She looks at him quizzically. Is he disappointed in her? 'I don't *want* to go through them, no, but I think we need to know the extent of what has been planned for the land. At least then we might see how to stop it.'

She looks away as tears burn at the back of her eyes. Shit... She thought Huw might understand, but it almost seems as if he's suggesting this is her fault.

He checks himself then, looking awkward. 'Thing is, I'm not sure how Jamie can help. Without the password, email accounts are incredibly secure. It's also illegal to hack them.'

'Huw, my husband is *dead*, who do you think is going to report you?' She frowns. 'And I thought you said Jamie was some kind of whizz?'

'He is, but... I'm not sure he's up to cracking passwords.' He shifts uncomfortably. 'I could ask his advice, if you like? But all he might say is to check whether Alun used a password manager or not. If you can guess the password to the account... or if he used autofill, then you might be able to get in yourself.'

'I would like you to ask him, please, if it's not too much trouble. This is important, Huw.' Her eyes bore into his. Why is he being like this? She'd thought he would want to help.

He adjusts his grip on the bundle under his arm. 'Sure, I'll go ask him now.' His hand is on the door, ready to pull it closed. 'Oh, is it okay?' He indicates his washing.

'Yes, Huw, use the machine, do your laundry, it's fine.'

* * *

Damn, damn, damn... Huw swears on every step of the stairs. He should have known something like this would happen. And he should have come clean right from the very beginning. But how could he have? He didn't know what Lowri's situation was when he first met her, and by then he'd already asked her if he could restore the castle. It wasn't the kind of thing to drop casually into the conversation. She'd never have spoken to him again, and he sure as hell would have lost his only chance to do the one thing he ever desired. He stops. Not the *only* thing he ever desired...

He's about to swear again when he realises that Seren and Wren are still in the living room. He smiles and walks on through to the kitchen as quickly as he can. The last thing he needs is someone else asking him questions.

* * *

Lowri could kick herself. There was no need to make such a fuss about contacting Jamie. If she'd stopped to think for just a minute she would have realised there was every chance she could access the emails herself. But she isn't thinking straight and now her stupidity has made her cross at Huw when he's done nothing wrong.

She plugs in the laptop and impatiently waits out the seconds until she can boot it up. It's old, and was already well used when Alun died, so is also interminably slow. Or perhaps it just feels that way. Eventually, she's looking at the home screen, carefully letting her eyes bounce off the wallpaper photo instead of sucking it in like she would have done before. She opens an internet tab and navigates to the iCloud home page, a provider that Alun had never used for his emails, or so she thought. Could it really be as easy as typing in his email address and letting his laptop do the rest? She checks the printed pages in the folder Elin gave her and enters the characters, one by one...

Forty minutes later, when Lowri has read as much as she can bear, she realises why Alun didn't keep any paperwork concerning Clearwater. He didn't need to. He'd stored everything electronically, and hidden it where she wouldn't find it, even after he died. All he had left behind was a letter, buried at the bottom of a box of mementoes, his guilty little secret. If it hadn't been for that, Lowri wouldn't be sitting in her bedroom at the gatehouse, contemplating all manner of things for her future. Instead she'd be living two doors down from her sister in blissful ignorance.

The screen blurs over as tears fill Lowri's eyes. Almost as hurtful as being lied to is the question of why Alun felt he couldn't share Clearwater with her, or didn't want to. What possible motive could he have for doing that? She had no idea how much Clearwater was worth, but they certainly hadn't been rolling in money when Alun was alive, and when he died, she'd been forced to move because she couldn't afford the very modest house she and Wren were living in. Money isn't everything, of course not, and she knew how difficult Alun's relationship with his father had been. Had she known about Clearwater, though, the choices they made for the estate may not have been any different, but at least they could have made them together.

Scrolling back, Lowri finds the very first email, the one sent to the solicitor who advised Alun of his inheritance, the one where he states very clearly, as she had been told, that he didn't want anything to do with Clearwater. Lowri had never thought to ask all those weeks ago if she could see that email. If she had, she would have noticed it had come from an unfamiliar email address. She could have found out everything before she even arrived. Lowri stares at the wall opposite. Would she even have come?

But the answer, she knows, isn't the one she wants to hear. Because if she'd never come, she'd never have met Elin and be contemplating a bright new future, she'd never have helped Seren lay to rest a mystery about her family that has haunted her for years, and she and Huw certainly wouldn't— Her thoughts come to an abrupt halt. She closes her eyes and swallows. Because she wouldn't want to lose any of what she has now.

* * *

The silence is becoming unbearable. Like a tangible thing which Huw can feel emanating from Lowri's room, pulsing through the walls as if it cannot be contained within the space. He has stayed resolutely in the kitchen, coward that he is, and now he is waiting.

Lowri emerged once, to give Wren her bath and put her to bed, laughing and giggling with her daughter, blowing raspberries on her belly as if nothing is wrong. But Huw knows differently. He knows how Lowri's voice sounds when she's happy, or anxious – and he certainly knows how it sounds when she's cross. This evening, it has a bright brittle edge to it that doesn't belong to her.

Huw knows what it is to be lied to. To be let down by the one person you loved and who you thought loved you, the one person you trusted. And Huw feels ashamed, because he knows he should try to talk to Lowri and yet he does not, scared, not of how Lowri is feeling, but of what it will awaken in himself.

Eventually, he gets up from the table where he's been pretending to read and thinks about making some tea. He's noticed Lowri often has a cup after dinner but, today, has gone without. He could make her one, take her a biscuit too. But then again, now that Seren has agreed to stay the night and been offered Wren's room, Wren will more than likely be curled up beside Lowri, and the last thing he wants to do is wake her. Lowri is perfectly capable of coming down if she wants a drink.

Wracked with indecision, Huw seeks out Seren instead. She's sitting in the living room, tucked into one corner of the sofa in front of the fire, her hair glowing bright copper from the dancing flames. With her legs curled beneath her, and a pad of paper resting on her lap, she looks peaceful and perfectly at home.

'Would you like some tea?' he asks, cringing at the banality of his question. He's known Seren a long time, since when did he find it so hard to start a conversation?

But, if she notices the slightly forced tone in his voice, she doesn't show it. After a second or two, her pencil stills and she looks up, smiling. 'Sorry, I was miles away.'

When he looks, Huw sees she's been idly doodling, not making notes or a list as he'd imagined. 'Penny for them?'

'I'd intended to write down all the plants I have in my garden,' she says. 'But my mind won't sit still. It does that at times, it's really quite annoying.'

Huw smiles. 'I know the feeling.'

Seren acknowledges his words with a nod. 'Trouble is, I might find out tomorrow if that really was Sorley you found, and if it was, what that means.'

Huw sits down. 'I hadn't realised it would be that soon,' he says. 'I'm sorry.'

'They took DNA samples when he first went missing,' Seren replies. 'And apparently bone is one of the easiest things to check, so... I keep wondering if knowing he's dead will change things. Change my memories. I guess it makes sense if he drowned, but I really can't remember what happened the night he went missing and I think if I could, it might help me to piece it together.'

'But...' Huw breaks off, wondering whether he should ask the question. 'But even if they do confirm it's him, you still won't know *how* he died, will you?'

Seren shakes her head. 'Until they find the rest of his body they won't have any idea, and even then, it's unlikely. It will depend on where the body is found and what condition it's in. Same for the skull. There's some damage to it, but most likely that was made after death, by the waterwheel.'

Huw is amazed how calm and rational Seren is. 'Do *you* think he drowned?'

She thinks for a moment. 'It makes the most sense,' she says. 'And yet it doesn't because Sorley was a strong swimmer. We grew up alongside the river, and Mum taught us to swim practically when we were babies. We were in and out of the water all the time.'

Huw frowns. Is Seren trying to tell him that Sorley's death wasn't an accident?

'It was a horrible night though, lashing rain, that I do remember. And Sorely hated arguments, he—'

'There was an argument?'

Seren grimaces. 'There were always arguments. You don't realise when you're a child, do you, that what happens in your house isn't necessarily what happens in others? And I don't think I ever realised we didn't have a proper dad. That ours came and went, while other children's fathers stayed with them, all the time. It wasn't until I was much older that I worked out the arguments were always about him staying. Choosing my mum over his wife, Anna. It took me even longer to realise that "Anna" and my Aunty Anna were one and the same.'

'What?' Huw is astonished. 'Your dad was having an affair with his wife's sister? How did I not know that?'

Seren smiles. 'I don't suppose they advertised it. And you were a child back then too, just like me, so of course you didn't know. No one knew. That's why they were able to carry on for so many years. Until my aunty found out and, boom!' She makes a gesture like a bomb blowing up.

'And that was the night Sorley disappeared?'

'No, she found out a few weeks after. But I think his disappearance was the catalyst. Mum was obviously beside herself, but my dad was cut up too and I think that's how Aunty Anna knew there was something fishy going on. An uncle wouldn't have been anything like as upset as he was, but if one of his own children had gone missing...'

'So what happened then?'

'It split the family apart. Aunty Anna and my mum had never got on – people called her a witch, as you know, and I think my aunt almost believed it too, like Mum had seduced my dad by means of a magic potion or something. In any case, Anna moved away with her child, and my dad took off too, didn't want to stick around and face the music. So that just left Mum and me, and pretty soon it was just me.'

'But couldn't you have gone somewhere else?'

'My uncle and aunt on my dad's side of the family both offered to have me. I wanted to stay with Uncle Stephen and be close to Mum and Sorley, but my aunt thought that was a terrible idea. She and Stephen argued, but in the end, Aunt Deirdre won and so I went to live with her and her husband near St Davids.' She pulls a face. 'Which I hated. So as soon as I turned eighteen, I came home.'

Huw swallows. 'Jesus, Seren, I had no idea. I'm so sorry.'

'Well, there's still a lot of folk around here who do know. *I* want to know if it was Sorley in the river. I want to know he's no longer lost, but I don't suppose we'll ever know the truth of what happened to him. And when people don't know the truth they invariably make something up. That's what worries me.'

'And you don't want that something to be about you?'

'It was bad enough before, but I was a child then, I didn't understand a lot of what was being said.'

'Well, this time you're not on your own, Seren. Let folk say what they want, they'll have Lowri and me to put them straight. Elin too.'

Seren studies his face for a moment, her eyes glistening in the dimming light. 'No one's ever said anything like that to me before,' she says. 'I don't know what to say. Except thank you, of course. Sorry, I'm not very good with people, I guess.'

Huw smiles. 'You're doing just fine, Seren, just fine.'

She nods, a little shy. 'I was in the castle keep earlier, chatting to Lowri about the garden that once would have been there. She'd like me to recreate it. She talked about all kinds of plans she has for Clearwater, plans she wants to involve me in. She talked about having a community garden, possibly holding workshops to teach people some of the things I know.' Her eyes flick to her lap. 'I've never been asked to take part in anything before, and when she first said it, I told her I'd never be able to do it, but now... I think at least I ought to try. Do you think she would still be interested?'

And suddenly Huw sees a way out of his current predicament. Here is the perfect opportunity to find out how Lowri is feeling. 'I'm sure she would,' he replies, glancing up at the door to her room, high above them. 'I tell you what, why don't we ask her?'

Moments later, he's outside, standing on the threshold, his stomach in knots. Mindful of Wren, he taps softly.

Lowri comes to the door almost immediately, pulling it open just a little, but she's standing in its shadow and he can't see her face.

'Hi,' he whispers. 'I was about to make Seren and I some tea. Would you like a cup?'

To his relief, he sees a glimmer of a smile and, with a backward glance, she slips through the door.

'Thanks,' she says softly. 'I'd like that.' She looks tired, and although her eyes are clear, the skin around them seems puckered and a little redder than usual. He'd swear she'd been crying.

Conscious of Seren's proximity below them, Huw smiles, anxious to keep the conversation away from difficult subjects. 'Is Wren asleep?' he asks.

'Out like a light. I've just been listening to her breathing, like I used to when she was little, and very poorly. It used to terrify me, now it's rather soothing – lovely, actually.'

He leads the way down the stairs. 'Seren and I have just been chatting,' he says. 'About Sorley, but also about your plans for this place. She mentioned you're thinking about a community garden?'

'Hmm, among other things.' She smiles then, properly. 'I got a bit carried away. Probably frightened the life out of Seren,' she adds, as Seren looks up.

'I think she's still with us,' replies Huw. 'I'll go put the kettle on.'

Lowri moves as if to take a seat on the sofa and then checks herself. 'Actually, I'll come with you. I've got some flapjack in a tin and I don't know about you, but I really fancy some. Seren?'

'Not for me, thanks. I ate far too much pasta, I'm still full.'

'I'll have some,' says Huw. The flapjack he can handle, he just isn't sure about Lowri. But he should say something about what happened earlier, or she'll only think it odd.

As it happens, she beats him to it. 'I'm really sorry about before,' she says as soon as they're alone in the kitchen. 'I bit your head off and I shouldn't have. I thought you were being awkward, when you were just being sensible.'

'Don't,' he says. 'There's really no need to apologise.'

'But I could have put your friend in a really awkward position.'

'It's fine, Lowri, honestly. I had to leave a message for Jamie, and he hasn't got back to me yet,' replies Huw. 'So when he does, I'll let him know not to worry.' It's not quite the truth, but Lowri doesn't need to know that.

She looks down at her feet. 'As it happens, I followed your very wise advice and managed to look at the messages I needed to anyway.' She's making light of it but Huw can see the hurt there. 'All of which showed that Bridie was right. Alun *did* grant her access to the river meadow, but there is also a string of emails between him and Bridie dating from when he first learned he'd inherited his uncle's estate. At the time, Alun told me he wanted nothing to do with Clearwater and, in fact, as I was told when I first came here, Alun did email Stephen's solicitor to say as much. That's when he asked for a custodian to be put in place.'

'Stephen?' The name trips his memory.

Lowri nods. 'Alun's uncle. Unfortunately, that's where it all goes a bit adrift because, obviously, the solicitor assumed that was the end of the matter. He set up the agreement with Bridie and that was that, except, unbeknown to him, to all of us, Alun and Bridie kept in touch.' She lifts her chin a little and Huw can see the threat of tears just behind her eyes.

He swallows, his heart thumping uncomfortably. Lowri is standing only inches away from him. His hand wavers, uncertain. She didn't ask for any of this. She came here in good faith, she... He does put out his hand then, touching hers lightly. 'I'm sorry,' he says. 'I know what it's like to be lied to.'

* * *

Lowri jumps as if she's been burned. Just the touch of Huw's hand. The look on his face. 'Do you?' she whispers. But she can see that he does. Suddenly, she can feel his pain, almost as if it belongs to her. Or is something they *share...* She pulls back slightly, scared by the strength of her emotion.

'Am I allowed to change my mind about the flapjack?' asks Seren, coming into the kitchen.

Lowri sees her opportunity and quickly moves away, reaching up to one of the cupboards. 'Of course. It's too tempt-ing, isn't it?' She takes a deep, slow, quiet breath. Thank heavens Seren came in when she did. Behind her she can hear Huw clattering about with cups and the kettle. 'I'll just bring the tin through, shall I?' she adds. 'Then we can all tuck in.' She turns and smiles a little cheekily at Seren. 'And talk some more about gardens.'

By the time Huw returns with the drinks, Lowri and Seren are already chatting and she thinks she has herself back under control. All Huw needs to do now is simply sit down and join in, and with any luck, that's exactly what he will do.

'The thing is,' says Seren, 'I've never done anything like what you suggested before, I wouldn't even know where to start.'

'Me neither,' admits Lowri. 'But it could be fun finding out.' She glances up at Huw. 'Would now be a good time to tell you my wild ideas?' Despite the predicament they're in, she needs this – time to dream, time to put distance between herself and Alun's betrayal, to think that they might all still have a future at Clearwater.

Huw smiles and sets down the drinks on the coffee table. 'As good a time as any. Let me snaffle one of these first.' He takes a flapjack and sits back expectantly in a chair.

'We really should have Elin here as well,' begins Lowri. 'Although I already know she'd be up for what I'm thinking. In fact, it was her family who partly gave me the ideas.'

Seren and Huw exchange glances.

'See, when I was talking to Elin about the state of affairs at the factory, both her mum and her sister spoke about the business, not as it is now, sewing tourist tea towels, but how it was originally, with its foundation in traditional weaving. Elin has a degree in textiles and apart from creating some of the most beautiful work I think I've ever seen, she's really interested in the history of fabrics, in their conservation too. And what better place to explore all those things than on the site of a traditional watermill?'

Huw leans forward. 'Go on...'

'When I think of the mill, in my head it's always been about its weaving heritage, but weaving isn't the only ancient skill we've got at Clearwater. We have you, Huw, a traditional stonemason, and you, Seren, a herbalist, and it struck me that there couldn't be many places where such skills have come together. I walked out to the river meadow with Seren today, itself a type of landscape under threat, and I suddenly saw Clearwater for what it was, a place steeped in history and tradition. That's what I want to share, more than anything – with our local community and with visitors too.'

'Is that where the teaching comes in?' asks Seren.

Lowri smiles. 'Yes, although I'm sorry I threw that one at you. I hope I didn't scare you. Listening to you talk about the garden that would have once existed within the castle walls... Seren, I've seen your garden and the first time I met you, you teased me about eye of newt and toe of frog – mustard seeds and buttercups. You have so much knowledge. Knowledge which could be shared with people for whom our ancient skills are important too. The same goes for weaving, stonemasonry, and anything else we can bring into the mix.'

'So we'd be like a centre for these things?' says Huw.

'That's exactly what we'd be,' replies Lowri, feeling energy begin to flow through her again. 'A place where people can come and see these things... the castle, the watermill, and the meadow, but also where they could come and learn about them too, if they wished. Who knows, we might even have room for ye olde traditional tea shoppe and sell them a bit of bara brith too...' She holds Huw's look for a moment. 'I'm kidding,' she says but, to her surprise, he smiles.

'If it's as good as your flapjack, we definitely should.'

'What do you think?' she asks them both. 'Could we do this? Could we bring Clearwater back to life again?'

Huw nods slowly, several times, a smile beginning to tug the edges of his beard upwards. 'I think this could be just what our funding application needs,' he replies. But then his face falls again. 'There's just one problem, Lowri, and I hate to be the one to pour cold water on your ideas, but—'

'The houses, I know,' replies Lowri, forestalling his concern. 'But I'm damned if I'm going to let Bridie have her way over that land. My husband might have sanctioned her plans, but he's not here now, I am. And I don't sanction them. I didn't think about it before, mainly because Bridie told me the contract was irreversible, but there must be some way of proving that the agreement between her and Alun can no longer stand, legally I mean, now that he's dead.'

'You could ask his solicitor, he would know,' says Huw.

Out of the corner of her eye, Lowri can see Seren's urgent look.

'What houses?' she asks. 'What are you talking about?'

Lowri pulls a face. 'I'm sorry, I should have said. But I only found out about Bridie's plans earlier today, and I honestly wasn't sure if I believed them. Or maybe it's that I didn't want to.' She quickly explains the gist of what's happened. 'And I wouldn't have known about it at all, had Elin's mum not let slip about some gossip she'd heard. But it turned out to be true. Worse, my husband was probably the only one who could have put paid to Bridie's plans before they'd even got off the ground, but he chose to help her instead. Something else he managed to keep to himself.'

Seren looks between her and Huw. 'And these houses are definitely planned for the water meadow?'

Lowri nods. 'Bridie took great delight in telling me she's just filed her planning application. But I have to stop her. Apart from the obvious problems it would cause for *our* plans, tearing up the water meadow to build houses on would be, would be...' She casts about for a suitably strong adjective.

'Impossible...' supplies Seren.

'I'd like to think so, but sadly I suspect it's all too possible.'

'No, it really is impossible,' she adds. 'Because of *Cypripedium calceolus*.'

Lowri stares at Huw quizzically, but he clearly has no idea what Seren is talking about either. 'Come again?' she says.

'*Cypripedium calceolus*,' repeats Seren. 'Better known as lady's slipper. A beautiful and joyously rare orchid. And one of the very few places it grows in the country is in the water meadow. It's a protected species, there's no way Bridie can build houses there.'

19

Lowri stares down at her laptop, a wave of sudden heat prickling the back of her neck as her stomach drops away in shock. 'Shit...' she murmurs. 'Shit, shit...' How could she have been so stupid? The planning application was the first thing she should have checked.

A sudden whistling from her phone makes her jump. Tearing her eyes away from the screen, she reads the message, brows drawing together in consternation. It's only ten past ten, Elin can only have been at work for just over an hour, what can possibly have gone wrong? She reads the message again.

Lowri, I'm so sorry, but you need to get over here.

This is all Lowri needs. Reluctantly, she closes her laptop and hurries down the lane towards the factory, pausing only briefly to register the cars outside.

'Where's Bridie?'

Gordon looks up from his desk, a panicked look crossing his face. 'Um... I'm sorry, I passed your message on, but...'

Lowri stares at him. She still hasn't worked out Gordon's

role in all this. 'Why does everyone around here insist on lying to me?' she asks. 'Her car is in the car park, so she's here, somewhere. I'd like to know where.'

Gordon bristles. 'She's on the factory floor, but she—'

Lowri isn't listening, she's already on her way, but, as she pushes open the door, the hum of machines is suspiciously absent. Bridie is standing at the top of the room, her audience in thrall. Only one person isn't paying attention to what she's saying. Instead, Elin is sitting quietly at the back of the room, head bent.

'Obviously, I'll do my very best to find out what's going on, but it isn't looking good, I'm afraid. There might be openings for one or two of you, possibly more, but I can't see...' Bridie's voice trails away as she catches sight of Lowri.

Lowri doesn't know what's going on, but somehow, and given her stance she's certain of it, Bridie has outmanoeuvred her.

'Mrs Morgan,' says Bridie, taking a few steps back so that Lowri is, involuntarily, in the limelight. 'I was explaining to our ladies here your new plans and how it affects them. Perhaps you might like to take over. It's only fair, given how it's you who's planning on making them redundant.'

'But that isn't true!'

'Come now, at least be honest. Kid yourself they're not really lies in the comfort of your own home, but don't do that here, not in front of the very people who have worked so hard for you.'

Lowri stares at her, open-mouthed. Bridie hasn't so much as thrown down the gauntlet, she's withdrawn her sword for good measure.

'Okay, well I'd like to start by refuting what you've just been told. I'm not planning on making anyone redundant. When we spoke yesterday, I told you about my plans to renovate the mill and potentially relocate the business, and that's still the case. I must also stress that my reasons for doing so are to improve working conditions and, importantly, provide a future for the business, one it currently doesn't have.'

'A future for the business?' says Bridie. 'Correct me if I'm wrong, but you're looking to substantially change the business. And not only that, you'll be ending contracts the company has negotiated over time, good contracts, and striking out on your own without so much as a firm order on your books. And into a potentially very risky market as well.'

Lowri's heart sinks, and she immediately knows where Bridie has got her information from, the abject look of misery on Elin's face is clue enough. But that hardly matters now. What matters is that Lowri is woefully underprepared and she's made a massive error of judgement. It isn't that she's been deliberately keeping her plans for the mill secret, it's just that her time has been occupied by other things, namely getting the bid and their plans finalised in the first place. But she should have thought more about the practicalities of what she was trying to achieve. Thought about them, and communicated them. And now she's been called out. She swallows.

'You're absolutely right, Mrs Turner,' she says. 'That's exactly what I'm planning to do.' She holds up her hand. 'But... *but*, I have very good reasons for doing so. And I'll tell you why.

'It doesn't much matter about the circumstances, but up until a few weeks ago, I didn't even know Clearwater existed. I came here to live, with my daughter, because we had need of a home. And that's it. A simple story, the sum of my intentions. Except that when I arrived, I realised I couldn't ignore what was going on here.' From the corner of her eye she can see Bridie working up to another tirade and she turns to face her. 'No,' she says. 'You don't interrupt. I have been patient. I have given you the benefit of the doubt, and I've more than let you have your say. But I've been lied to since the day I got here, so you *will* let me finish.'

She turns back to the other women. 'Before I moved here, I worked freelance for an enterprise group which supports people to set up small businesses. I helped these businesses form their ideas, helped them obtain finance, and then worked alongside them every step of the way until they were up and running, and well on the way to succeeding. So I *do* know what I'm talking about, and I *can* see a business in trouble when I walk into it. You might not want to hear it, but as Bridie said, *do* let's be honest. You have no proper breaks, no kitchen facilities besides a kettle thrown in the corner, and you work in a building which looks as if it might fall down at any minute, one – I might add – that doesn't even have a toilet. Are you really happy with that?' She stares at the faces around the room.

'And, while we're on the subject of being happy, who here likes the products they make? Who is proud to make them? I'm asking because since arriving at Clearwater, everyone in town I've spoken to has told me what they think, and it isn't very complimentary. I'm not sure about you, but I'm not the kind of person who can be happy with that. So I started to think about what might make it better. I've seen some designs recently, which—'

'Yeah, Miss Fancy Pants over there,' someone shouts. 'We know all about that.' It's Gwen. Lowri might have known she wouldn't be able to keep her mouth shut for long. But Lowri has had enough of other people's unhelpful attitude.

'So having aspirations is wrong, is it? To have incredible talent is wrong? When I looked at Elin's designs, they blew me away, and I'm not ashamed to admit that I don't have that much creativity in the tip of my fingernail. Maybe you should ask yourself the same question and give credit where it's due rather than bad-mouthing one of your colleagues. There's nothing wrong in dreaming, but there's everything wrong with compla-cency. And I'd rather not make room for that here.' She draws in a deep breath. 'So... I want to restore the watermill. I want to relocate the business there because the building will be better suited to what I'd like us to do, and because it will also give us the opportunity to tap into the textile industry's heritage and begin creating things we can be proud of.'

'Like what? Posher tea towels?' Someone giggles.

'Woven fabrics,' replies Lowri. 'Woven, not sewn. Now, I don't know a thing about weaving, *yet*... but I will find out. I do, however, know how to run a business. As it currently stands, Clearwater Textiles is not making any money. It makes just about enough to pay you all, but it's a lousy wage with no benefits, and I don't believe that's right. What's worse is that there's very little that can be done to change this if the business remains as is, so that's it, pretty much forever. The alternative is to create a business which *is* able to pay you properly for your expertise, one which will grow and, as it does, the rewards will also grow. But this is going to be hard, make no mistake. It means changing the way we do a lot of things, and it also means changing what we make. You will all have new skills to learn, and some of you might find that easier than others, but I'm still intending to employ you all.' She smiles. 'And, don't forget, this is a way off in the future yet, and also dependent on us receiving funding to renovate the building. It's not a done deal by any means.'

'So what do we do in the meantime?' asks Gwen.

'We carry on. Doing what we do now.'

'But are you going to be running the show though?' It's someone else this time.

Lowri swallows, fighting down the urge to look at Bridie. 'I'm yet to have that conversation,' she says. 'But it's very possible.' Her heart is hammering in her chest.

'And what do we do if we don't want to accept all your fancy new rules and plans?' It's Gwen again.

Lowri purses her lips, and lifts her chin. She has to do this. 'Then you're perfectly entitled to leave,' she says. 'This is a partnership, after all. And in return for my providing you with certain things, I expect certain other things in return, and one of those is honesty. Honesty, commitment and hard work. It might not be the kind of relationship you have now, but it's how things are going to be in the future.' Lowri pauses, waiting for any response, although she'd be very surprised to hear one. 'Does anyone have any questions?'

Vague mutterings fill the floor.

'Yeah... I've got one. Supposing we do what you want us to, will you be able to pay us from the start?' It's another woman this time, one who hasn't spoken before.

'Yes. I will guarantee everyone who wants to stay the same wage they're on now. But I also want to be honest about that because what I can't guarantee is how long I can pay this for. It's a risk, I know. I understand you have families and commitments, and bills to pay. So, again, if this is something you don't want to live with, there will be absolutely no hard feelings if you want to look for another job elsewhere. I hope you won't, but I will understand if you do. However, if you do decide to take that risk, alongside me, then I will increase your wages just as soon as I'm able, when the business is stable and established enough to do that. It will be hard. It will take a lot of work. I will need everyone to give one hundred per cent, but I wouldn't be asking you for those things if I didn't think it was worth it.'

'It's all just talk,' shouts Gwen. 'You and your fancy words. It doesn't mean anything, it's just giving us the sack dressed up as something else.'

'Thank you, Gwen,' says Bridie before Lowri can respond, 'I couldn't have put it better myself.' Bridie stares out at the group of women, her perfectly styled hair not the slightest bit out of place. She looks calm, composed and triumphant.

'Of course, you're perfectly entitled to feel that way,' says Lowri. 'I don't suppose you've ever had anyone allow you to believe things could be different. I understand that. And what I don't want are people here who don't trust me. I can't make it any plainer than I have. You either believe me, or you don't. It's up to you now.'

There's a moment's silence during which Lowri can almost hear the thoughts of those in the room as they weigh up what's been said, think about who to believe. But then the sharp screech of a chair leg against the floor echoes around the room and Lowri realises there was never any question of what would happen. Gwen is the first to her feet, followed in quick succession by two more women.

'Come on,' shouts Gwen. 'You heard what Bridie said. She's got jobs for us all if we want them. Proper jobs, with more money and a guaranteed bonus. I'm not staying here a minute longer. I get enough lies from my kids at home.'

By the time everyone has made their decision, only two women aside from Elin remain seated, two women she hardly knows – Rhian and Nia – but whom she owes a debt of gratitude. She quietly thanks them, reassuring them as best she can, and then, with as much dignity as she can muster, she walks from the room.

Once outside, she pulls her phone from her pocket and is still typing out the first line of her message to Elin when the front door opens and she comes hurtling across the space. She stands in front of Lowri, almost hopping from leg to leg, tears having tracked their way down her face.

'I'm so sorry, Lowri,' she blurts. 'All I was doing was drawing, I didn't think Bridie would jump on me the way she did. And then when she started talking to everyone... It's all my fault.' Her arms hang, redundant by her sides.

Lowri tuts, and takes them in her hands. 'Elin, I can see you're upset, but slow down. I don't really understand what's gone on here.'

Elin pulls away. 'I've ruined everything.'

'I sincerely doubt that you have.'

'But I have!' Elin stares at her, white-faced. 'I'm supposed to be your friend and I've played right into Bridie's hands. Now she knows everything you're planning and—'

'She would have found out sooner rather than later. And it's all rather immaterial now.'

'But she's turned everyone against you.'

Lowri shrugs. 'Maybe, but I've said all I could. And none of this is your fault, Elin. I should have kept you in the loop about what's been happening but...' She rubs a hand across her eyes. 'Things are moving so fast. That's no excuse, though, and Bridie showed her true colours long before today. The gloves are off and as far as the staff here go, let them leave with Bridie if they think she's offering something better. I don't want those kinds of people here anyway. What we're planning is too important to have people on board who aren't totally committed to what we'll be doing. It's going to be tough, and a challenge, and we all will have to work harder than we ever have. But I think it's worth it, and I know you do too.'

'I do, but—'

'No buts. Give me a hug.'

Elin sniffs, wiping her eyes. 'I don't know why you're being so nice, you should be shouting at me.'

'Why on earth would I want to do that?'

'Because of Bridie... Because...'

Lowri touches the stone which still hangs around her neck. 'Elin, I know who my friends are. And who's honest. Just as I know who's been trying to milk Clearwater for all it's worth. Maybe we didn't want things to go the way they have, but perhaps it's better. At least we all know where we stand.'

'So what do I do now?' asks Elin. 'Please don't make me go back in there, I don't think I can.'

'I wouldn't dream of it. Besides, we need to have a catch-up, there's a lot I need to tell you. I need your help too.'

Elin gives her a quizzical look. 'Are you okay?'

Lowri shrugs. 'Not exactly. Look, I'll meet you back at the gatehouse in fifteen minutes or so... I just need to have a few words with Bridie. But don't worry, I won't be long. And if I don't appear, call the police – it's quite possible I'll have committed murder.'

'That's not even funny,' says Elin.

'Fifteen minutes,' Lowri replies and, gritting her teeth, heads back inside.

A gaggle of women crowd the entrance hall, their strident voices falling silent as she enters. Pushing through them, she marches back into the office. 'Enjoy that, did you?'

Bridie is there, in mid-flow, waving her arms about as Gordon looks on helplessly, something approaching fear in his eyes.

'Lowri, I really don't know where you're coming from,' Bridie says. 'I thought folk had a right to know what's going on. You of all people should know it's far better to tell the truth.'

'Me, tell the truth?' spits Lowri. 'That's rich. I don't think you've told me the truth since the day I got here – when you waxed lyrical about how wonderful it was to finally have someone take an interest in Clearwater. At which point you carefully omitted the fact that my husband had been taking an interest for years before he died.'

Bridie smiles. 'Ah... I see you read through the folder I sent across yesterday.'

'What's in this for you, Bridie? Is it just the money, or do you get some kind of thrill having everyone think you run this place? I bet you jumped for joy when you heard Alun was dead, didn't you? You could carry on using Clearwater for your own purposes with no one to stop you. Well, I have news for you, Bridie, there is someone to stop you now. So just in case you think you can still go ahead and build houses on the water meadow, think again. I don't care what kind of contract Alun signed with you, I'll fight any agreement he made and, if that isn't enough, then I will do everything else I can think of to stop you going ahead. I'm sure there's a good part of our community who will have something to say about your destruction of a natural habitat like the river meadow.'

Bridie's eyes are ablaze. 'You won't win, you know. You're out of time, Lowri, and you know it. I'm not sure who you think you are, but you should know who you're up against before you go throwing your weight around. Speak to anyone in this town and they'll tell you who the Turners are. I know a lot of people. People in all sorts of places. People who could make your life a real misery if I wanted them to. I think you'll find, when it comes to it, that people will side with me. They generally do.'

Lowri snorts. 'Well, you've made your position very clear, but before you go throwing *your* weight around, let me make it clear that you don't know me either, you don't know me at all. And it goes without saying that your role here is over. Effective immediately. As in right now, this second.' She smiles sweetly.

There's a fraction of a second when Lowri thinks Bridie is going to argue again, but then she smiles, graciously, as if leaving had been her idea all along.

'Right, come on then, Gordon, get your coat. Madam here has obviously decided she wants to play Miss High and Mighty, so it would seem our services are no longer required. We won't hold you up by bothering to explain how a single thing here works, you're so knowledgeable I'm sure you'll figure it out.'

'Hang on a minute,' says Lowri, frowning. 'We? I asked *you* to leave. I didn't say anything about Gordon.'

Bridie rolls her eyes. 'Oh, for heaven's sake. Are you blind, or just stupid? Do you honestly think he'll want to stay and work for you? Come on, Gordon.'

But Gordon hasn't moved. He is staring at the blotter on his desk, hands clasped loosely in front of him, lips pursed as if deep in thought. After a moment, he releases a hand to readjust his glasses so they sit more squarely on his nose. 'After careful consideration, I think I'd like to stay, if that's all right with you, Mrs Morgan?'

'It is,' replies Lowri, smiling. 'Only none of this "Mrs Morgan" rubbish. It's Lowri, please.' She turns to Bridie. 'We'll take it from here, thanks. You and the rest of your coven outside can go. And if you step foot inside here again, I'll be calling the police to tell them you're trespassing.'

'Big words, Lowri. But don't say them unless you really mean them. Not when you don't even know the truth yet. So before you carry on making a fool of yourself, ask yourself *why* your precious husband didn't want you to know about Clearwater? Perhaps it's time you found out a little more about his past, and his *real* connection to Clearwater. Better yet, ask Huw, since he's the one who's been keeping your husband's secrets.'

Lowri stands in the lane for quite some time before returning to the gatehouse. From her position, she can see the mill, quiet now, the fluttering police tape gone, but soon teeming with life again, she hopes. She can see the castle with the tower beyond, the river with its meadow, and her cottage, the one which she and Wren came to live in when they had nothing. And in very short order all these things have come to mean more than anything she's had in a very long time. Not because of the buildings, or the land, or the value they might have, but because of the people she's found along with them. And the thought of losing any of them brings a sudden choking sob to her throat.

Lowri knows what Bridie has told her is true. For the most part her stock in trade is lies and deceit, but Lowri has learned now that Bridie picks and chooses her moments, that when she wants to, when she knows it really matters, when only that will serve her best, she tells the truth.

And her truth means that Huw has lied. Is lying still. Unaccountably, and much to her surprise, she realises that this huge man, whom she once found scary and belligerent, and who still takes up far too much space in her kitchen, has also taken up a space in her heart.

Her phone whistles again, interrupting her thoughts.

Time's up! Are you on the run yet or shall I put the kettle on?

It's Elin, bless her, who always seems to be around just when Lowri needs her. Swiping at her eyes, she hurries back to the gatehouse.

'Is Huw here?' she asks Elin as she arrives in the kitchen. His name sounds peculiar, as if her mouth can no longer form it.

'No, he left a note to say he's gone into town to see Jamie. Why, what's the matter?'

Lowri opens her mouth to speak but she can't explain, she wouldn't know how to. But she also doesn't want to say aloud words which will make what she fears become real, so with a superhuman effort, she forces a smile on her face. 'Nothing, I just wanted to ask him something, that's all.' She checks her watch. 'Listen, Elin, this is crazy, but we don't have much time. You'd better come and sit down.'

She waits until Elin is settled, using the time to gather her thoughts. Her head is spinning. 'I need your help,' she begins. 'Because not only is it true that Bridie wants to build houses on the river meadow, she's actually lodged a planning application to do so.'

'But she can't,' objects Elin. 'You said she'd need permission from the estate. Something to do with access.'

'Yes, that's right. But it turns out I don't even figure in the equation because Bridie has all the permission she needs. Alun gave it to her.'

Elin's eyes widen. 'Alun did? Your Alun? Oh, Lowri...' Her expression changes in an instant. 'What a total bast— Sorry, I shouldn't say that, but—'

'Oh, don't worry, I quite agree with you,' replies Lowri, her mouth a grim line. 'I've called Alun all the names under the sun. Cried far too many tears as well. But the fact of the matter is that it's done and I have proof as well. Bridie very kindly provided me with that.'

Elin closes her eyes. 'The red folder I brought over for you.'

'You weren't to know,' replies Lowri. 'And it almost doesn't matter any more.'

'But it does!' replies Elin. 'There must be something we can do. Challenge the contract, and if that doesn't work then object to the planning. When local people get to hear about the plans I'm sure that—'

Lowri lays a hand gently on her arm. 'Elin, we're almost out of time.' She winces. 'I thought we were safe. Seren told me and Huw there's a rare orchid growing in the meadow. She says it's a protected species and that the planners will never allow the application to go through—'

'See, there you go. I knew there'd be something.' Elin stares at her, hope in her eyes, which quickly dies when she sees Lowri's expression. 'What?' she asks.

'Bridie has played me for a fool yet again,' murmurs Lowri, feeling suddenly, almost overwhelmingly tired. 'When I challenged her about the houses she told me she'd just submitted her planning application and, aside from what Seren told us, I've been busy thinking of everything else we could do to challenge the application. Involve the local community, all sorts. What I should have been doing, however, was *checking* Bridie's application. She hasn't just submitted it at all, Elin. It was done nearly three weeks ago. We only have two days left to object.'

Elin stares at her. 'What? That can't be right.'

'I was looking at the planning regulations before you called me over to the factory. It's all there on the council's website, clear and concise. There are three weeks granted for receipt of objections and that's it. Not one day more.' She lets out a long breath. 'I'm not sure what we can possibly do in the time.'

'But we have to try.' Elin grabs at her hand. 'Lowri? We have to give it a go.'

Lowri gives a sad smile. 'I'm tired of fighting, Elin. Of everything always being an uphill battle. I never wanted all this.'

'I know.' Elin drops her head. 'And I think that might be my fault. If I hadn't badgered you about becoming the boss in the first place then none of this would have happened.'

'It would,' replies Lowri. 'I just wouldn't have known about it.' She swallows. 'I'm beginning to see why Alun thought ignorance is bliss.'

Elin shakes her head. 'No,' she says. 'I won't let you give up. Not when you've come this far. There are still things we can do. Seren must know someone who can identify the orchids – formally, I mean. Like an official report or something. We can lodge that at least. And I'm sure if we tell them how urgent it is then...' She pauses, looking around. 'Where is Seren anyway?'

'She's gone to see the police family liaison officer,' replies Lowri softly.

Elin's face sags as she registers Lowri's words, and their meaning. 'Oh, poor Seren,' she says. 'Shouldn't one of us have gone with her?'

'Huw and I offered,' replies Lowri. 'But she wanted to go by herself. She's pretty sure they'll tell her the skull we found belonged to Sorley, and I think she just wanted some time on her own.'

Elin nods. 'I can understand that. She's waited a long time for this news.'

'She has. And although it's closure of sorts, I can't help feeling we ought to do something. I wondered whether she might like to have a ceremony for him here, in remembrance. Do you think she'd like that?'

A soft expression comes over Elin's face. 'I think that's a beautiful idea. And I'm certain Seren will think so too.'

'I thought she might like to hold it by the river, and if she does, I'd like to give her a gift. It sounds silly, but something which says that Sorley has my blessing too, that he's welcome to stay at Clearwater. Do you know what I mean? I thought it might help Seren to know that.'

Elin smiles softly. 'I know exactly what you mean. The river has always been a big part of her life, but not always for the right reasons. Saying goodbye to him properly, and laying his spirit to rest is incredibly important to her.'

'Well, I hope it brings her some small measure of peace too. To lose her family when she was so young – I can't even begin to imagine what that must be like.'

Elin shakes her head. 'It's the living with uncertainty that would get me. Not knowing whether Sorley was dead or alive. Forever wondering if he might turn up one day out of the blue. Perhaps there's some relief in knowing there are no what ifs any more.'

Lowri sighs. She knows exactly how that feels. 'How did her mum die?' she asks.

'I'm not sure I ever knew. I was even younger than Seren was when it happened. I remember my mum saying it was from a broken heart, but what that means, I don't know.'

'Losing a child though...' Lowri shivers, thinking of the countless times when she sat watching little Wren, praying she would keep breathing.

'Hmm... Bad enough. But she lost the love of her life too and, whatever the reason for her death, I don't suppose that helped.'

Lowri gives her a quizzical look.

'She and Seren's dad weren't married, even though they'd been together years. He was already married, you see, and there was a big bust up when his wife discovered his secret. She threw him out, but I think Sorley's death hit him really hard and, rather than stay with Seren and her mum, he took off.'

'And Seren doesn't know where he is?'

'Nope. He left the child he had with his wife behind as well, so it seems he had a talent for it. Poor Seren was left with no one.'

Lowri looks up, a name swimming into her consciousness. 'Was that child a girl too?'

'No, a little boy I think. Why?'

And suddenly the air is full of names. Names Lowri hardly knows, some only spoken once or twice, others only recently heard, but now they twist and turn, entwine with one another and rearrange themselves, like wind-blown leaves, like leaves on a tree, a family tree...

All at once Lowri sees it, as plain as day. She sees it all. She sees what Clearwater really is, and she knows exactly why her husband kept the truth from her. Because he was afraid. Afraid of what that truth might do.

20

'I have no idea,' says Elin. 'She just went pale, and then rushed off. I thought she was going to be sick. But I don't think she's ill... I think she's crying.'

Lowri can hear Elin and Huw's voices clearly through the door. And she can picture them both, pacing up and down the landing, wracked with indecision. Do they disturb her or not? If left to her own devices, Lowri knows Elin would tap on the door and check she's okay, and Lowri would probably open it. But Huw's presence makes Elin more cautious than she would otherwise be. She'll think it rude to leave him standing on the landing because she also knows that Lowri won't want to see both of them, that she'll more than likely be embarrassed of her tears in front of Huw. So Elin doesn't knock. As for Huw, Lowri knows he won't knock. She doesn't think he'd dare and, in any case, she certainly wouldn't let him in if he did. She doesn't want to listen to any more of his lies.

It was one of the first things she did when she reached the safety of her room – pull up Alun's laptop and go back to his emails. Because she'd checked the more recent ones, and she'd checked the first one when Alun told the solicitor he wanted nothing to do with Clearwater, but what she hadn't done was sift through the ones in between. And, as soon as she did, there it was: Huw's name, clear as day. And now she has all the pieces of the jigsaw, the ones which Bridie had gleefully provided for her.

She's become aware of Huw's voice, and now he's speaking again, telling Elin he knows why Lowri is upset. *Yeah, I bet he does.* He's telling Elin that it's all right, that she can leave and he'll look after her. Elin isn't sure. She argues she should really check if Lowri is okay, but Huw is firm. Please, he tells her. He can't explain now, but he will just as soon as he can. And, yes, in answer to her next question, he'll make sure that Lowri gets in touch with Elin just as soon as possible.

Elin calls out to her, telling Lowri she hopes she'll be okay. That she understands if she wants some time to herself, whatever the reason, but that she'll be there waiting with a big hug when Lowri is ready. And although Lowri would like nothing more than to have the comfort of Elin's arms around her, she stays quiet because she wants to disappear. Then maybe Huw will go away too.

She isn't sure how long it is before she hears his soft knock at the door.

'Lowri, come on, we need to talk.'

She ignores him.

'I know you've figured out that this isn't the first time I've been asked to rebuild Clearwater, that your husband asked me too. And I know you think this means I lied to you, but I haven't. You need to let me explain.'

She almost shouts out then. Bitter words, full of derision. But she doesn't, she bites them back and throws them on the pile of all the others she wants to say.

'Lowri?'

More minutes go by. Each one of them thick with silence.

He knocks on the door again. Calls her name. Hammers louder. But Lowri ignores it all.

Eventually she hears a huffing sigh and Huw's weary voice. 'Fine, I'll leave you to it then. I have a bid to finalise, so I may as well do something useful. If you decide you want to talk, I'll be outside.'

She hears his footsteps travel down the stairs and the front door banging shut, most likely slammed in anger. She doesn't care. She doesn't care how he's feeling. Except that she does, and that angers her even more.

A few more minutes tick past as she listens to the silent house. She wants a drink and she needs the loo. Huw said he would be outside, meaning by the castle, surely, and only the kitchen window overlooks it. If she's careful, she can get a glass and fill it with water without him ever realising she's left her room.

Quietly, she opens her door and creeps down the stairs, listening. But all she can hear is silence reverberating around her, and she knows she's alone.

She crosses the living room and slips into the kitchen. It even occurs to her she should be angry about that as well – for having to tiptoe about her own house, when Huw is just a guest. When he—

Lowri stops dead, staring at the man who is sitting at her kitchen table. It's Huw, but not Huw. And she heard the door slam. Did he *trick* her? Did he make out he'd gone when he hadn't? She stares at him. At his face, which she has always seen covered in hair, and which is now pale and open and... beautiful. Her anger surges, bringing self-pity in its wake. How can this happen to her now?

'I think you should leave,' she says coldly. She has no choice, she must push him away.

'And I think I should stay,' he replies. 'So we appear to have a bit of a problem.'

'A bit of a problem? Is that what you call it?'

'I can call it something else if you prefer, but I'm not sure that's really going to help.'

'Don't be clever, Huw. That's just insulting. You lied to me.'

'I kept the fact that your husband was a shit from you. What would you rather me do?'

Her mouth drops open. 'How dare you!'

'What? Speak the truth? And don't look at me like that, all indignant because I've had the gall to criticise him. Don't you dare defend him either, you think exactly the same as I do – which might be the only thing we currently agree on – and you're angry at me because you just want to be angry. You want to let out all the hurt and hurl it at someone, but that person shouldn't be me. I'm not the one who's hurt you here. Alun kept Clearwater from you, he's the one who lied.'

'But you should have told me about Alun. You could have, right when I first met you. Then it wouldn't have mattered if Alun lied because I—' She breaks off, ashamed of what she was going to say.

'Because you wouldn't have fallen in love with Clearwater by then,' Huw supplies, knowing he's right. 'It only matters now because you have.'

'I never wanted to get involved with this place,' argues Lowri. 'You let me believe that restoring Clearwater was all you ever wanted. You made me fall in love with her too. With all the plans and drawings, talk about how it could be.'

'I didn't make you do anything. You did it all by yourself, Lowri. Because you're the kind of person who cares, who notices when things are wrong, who sees potential, and beauty, and can't fail to be moved by these things. I've never put any ideas in your head. I never once persuaded you to take any course of action. I didn't need to.'

Lowri swallows. She doesn't think she can bear it if he's nice to her.

'You still should have told me.' It's the only argument she has, and she knows it.

'Lowri, what was I to do?' he says gently. 'When you arrived, reeling in shock from what you'd discovered here, you must have questioned why Alun never told you about it. But because you didn't want to be hurt, because you didn't want to think badly of someone you loved, you did what we'd all do in the circumstances – you told yourself his reasons for not doing so must have been good ones. We've all done that. We've all kidded ourselves a wrong was right, even though we knew deep down it wasn't. Even when later circumstances make it absolutely clear it wasn't, we still want to hang on to the good in someone. There's nothing wrong with that, but I didn't want to be the one to point it out. I didn't want to hurt you, Lowri. That's all this is.'

How did she never realise how expressionate his face could be? 'So you've played it cool, bully for you.'

'I haven't played it cool at all, Lowri. Maybe you think so, but if you knew how hard it was for me to be here, you wouldn't say that.'

A sudden image comes back to her, of Huw staring up at the castle, his shoulders shaking with emotion.

'Lowri, why don't you sit down and I'll make you some tea? There's...' He hesitates, and for the first time Lowri sees a new emotion on his face. It makes her suddenly scared.

'I know about Alun's dad,' she blurts out. 'And Seren.'

He nods, eyes warm. 'I wondered if you'd make the connection, but I didn't know how much you knew of Seren's past. I only realised myself when I was talking to her yesterday and she mentioned her Uncle Stephen. Then when you mentioned the same name in regard to Alun's inheritance, I realised they could be one and the same.'

'Which means that she and Alun were half-brother and sister...'

Huw smiles. 'As are you now.'

Lowri's hand instinctively reaches for the stone around her neck. 'There's a reason why we're drawn to one another, I can see that now.' Tears well in her eyes as another thought comes to her. 'Seren doesn't know,' she says. 'She has no idea who my husband was, who I am.'

'Perhaps not,' replies Huw. 'Although I think she probably does. Some things you just know to be true. Just like she knew it was Sorley we found. I don't think this news will surprise her. But, Lowri... Let me make that tea. There's something else I need you to know. Clearwater means too much to me to be here under false pretences of any kind.' He swallows and his gaze drops to the floor, almost as if he's said too much. He opens his mouth to speak again but then closes it and smiles, almost sadly, she thinks.

It seems to take an age before the tea is ready, and several times Lowri thinks she should tell him to simply forget their drinks. To come back to the table and start talking. The agony of waiting, with apprehension building all the while, seems almost cruel but then, as she watches him, his broad back facing her, she realises that perhaps he needs to take this time for himself. And, when he eventually turns back to her, she's certain of it.

She's never seen Huw look so small. Without his beard, and his hair cut to half its previous length, he looks less fierce and imposing, but that isn't the only reason. As he puts down her mug, it's as if he's shrunk into himself. Despite her anger, which still simmers, something about his manner implores her to be kind.

'I first came to Clearwater when I was five,' he says, clutching his mug as if his life depends on it. 'And I thought it was the most wonderful place I'd ever seen. My dad brought me, one summer's evening, when it must have been way past my bedtime, but that didn't seem to matter. It felt like we had all the time in world, just sitting there, beside the river. We came a lot that summer, and the next, the one after too, and by that time I'd learned what my dad did all day when he went to work. He was a stonemason. He used to talk about the castle as if it was still newly built, telling me stories about the people who lived there, who worked there too. He told me you'd always be safe if you had the castle at your back. And I thought so as well, until four years later when he died. It had always been his dream to see it rebuilt, and on the day of his funeral, I vowed that I would make it happen in my lifetime.'

Lowri isn't sure how old Huw is now, but if twenty years had gone by since that time she wouldn't be surprised, yet it might have happened yesterday for all the emotion still present in his voice. She suddenly longs to take his hand.

'And then, one day, Carys came along.' His jaw clenches at the memory. 'I was a stonemason too by then. I'd learned my trade, done my apprenticeship, and was working on a commission in Cornwall. My reputation was growing, but I hadn't even set my sights on Clearwater then, I knew she was out of my league. But my best mate was getting married, so I packed a bag, and hopped on a train for his stag do – two days of drunken festivities back home. I met Carys that very first evening.

'I'd done my duty as best man and made sure that Jamie got safely to bed before going back down to the bar of the hotel we were staying in. One last nightcap, I'd thought. Carys was there, nursing a vodka and Coke. I bought her another drink and we talked until dawn.' He gives a rueful smile. 'And then I went back to Cornwall. Should have stayed there too, but as stag dos are invariably followed by weddings, three months later I was back.' He stares into his mug for a moment before closing his eyes against the heat and taking a swallow. When he looks back up, bitterness has crept into his eyes.

'I'll spare you all the gory details, but eight months later Carys and I were head over heels in love, and it was only then that I found out Clearwater was to be hers.'

Lowri frowns, and is about to ask a question when Huw holds up his hand. 'Please, just let me get this out.' He takes a deep breath. 'Things were getting serious between Carys and I, and we were talking about moving in together when she mentioned her step-dad had offered a place to her. It needed some work, but if we could raise the cash and were prepared to do it, it could be ours. I will never forget the day she brought me here.'

Lowri's eyes widen as realisation strikes. '*Here?*' she whispers.

Huw nods. 'I built this kitchen. I laid every stone in this building. The gatehouse was supposed to be mine. Mine and Carys's. And with it, of course, came the castle.'

Lowri hardly dare ask. 'What happened?' she asks.

'I don't know... Carys's step-dad died and—'

But Lowri knows what he's going to say even before he says it. 'Stephen left Clearwater to Alun instead.'

There's a stunned silence. A moment where time expands, filling the room, and taking all the air with it. And when the bubble suddenly bursts, Lowri's breath comes rushing back, a tide of anger riding alongside.

'So when you heard that Alun had died and his wife was moving to Clearwater, you saw your chance, did you? Another opportunity to have a crack at the jackpot? Oh, well played, Huw, well played.'

Huw chokes. 'No, Lowri I wouldn't do that. Please... It's not what you think.' He runs his hands over his face, as if looking to seek comfort from the hair that is no longer there.

Well, let him seek it. 'No doubt you thought it was justice well-served too. You obviously broke up with Carys because she couldn't give you Clearwater after all, and here you are, feet right under the table, getting exactly what you wanted all along.'

'No! Jesus...' Huw lurches up from the table. 'It wasn't like that.'

'Oh, come on, Huw. You knew all of this, the whole time. About Alun, about everything. What do you expect me to believe? I've been crying tears over a husband who lied to me, who betrayed everything we'd built between us, and you're no better. Great sob story, by the way, you almost had me—'

She stops, caught by the look on his face. He's angry. Angrier than she's ever seen him before. His eyes bore into hers.

'Before you go and vent all your anger on me, let me tell you you're not the only one who's been lied to.' He practically spits the words at her. 'Not the only one who has been betrayed and had their future pulled out from under them. This isn't all about *you*.'

'No?' She glares at him. 'Well, right now it is. It is all about me because this is *my* house.' She points a trembling finger towards the door. 'Get out,' she says. It's the last thing she manages before she bursts into tears.

21

'I can't believe Huw would do that!' From beside Lowri in the car, Elin is indignant.

'Well, he did. The whole time lying to me, just like Alun did. He'd even spoken to Alun, discussed the possibility of rebuilding the castle so, right at the beginning, when I turned up oblivious to everything about Clearwater, Huw knew that Alun must have kept it from me. But did he tell me? No, he just carried on lying. They're both as bad as one another.' Lowri turns her head to check for traffic as she pulls away from Clearwater, catching sight of Elin's face as she does so. 'Don't make excuses for him, Elin,' she warns.

'I'm not going to, it's just that... I like Huw. I didn't think him capable of anything like that.'

'I like him too, that's why I'm so bloody angry!' She sighs. 'Sorry.'

Elin reaches out to give Lowri's arm a quick rub. 'It's been a bit of a bumpy few days, hasn't it?'

'Isn't that the truth? I guess it stands to reason though. You even warned me off Huw, said he was bad news.'

'Yeah, but that was because of the booze. Like most people I didn't stop to think about the reason behind the drinking. And there must have been one.'

'Guilt, most like,' mutters Lowri. 'But, whatever the reason, the past is no excuse for your actions in the present and—' She stops. 'God, it is, isn't it? It's all about what's happened in the past. Am I ever going to be free of it?'

'Well, let's hope Mum can shed some light on the matter. Then at least you might be able to put Alun's skeletons firmly back in the closet.'

Lowri nods. 'It's ridiculous that I came here never realising St Merrion is where he grew up.'

'Or that he had a half-sister...'

'Yes,' says Lowri quietly, a warm smile softening her face as she thinks of Seren. 'You and she are the only good things to have come out of all this.'

'Did you manage to get hold of her?' asks Elin.

Lowri shakes her head. 'I had to leave a message. I imagine she has enough on her plate right now.'

'Hmm. That's not true, though, about me and Seren,' says Elin, and Lowri can hear the smile in her voice. 'It's lovely, but it's not true. We're not the only good things. You and Wren have found a home. You've *come* home.'

Lowri risks a glance across at her. 'You're right, I have.' She smiles again. 'You've been right about a lot of things, from the very beginning.'

'I know.' Elin gives a snort of amusement. 'It's a special talent I have.'

'And, thankfully, not the only one,' adds Lowri. 'Because with virtually no staff left at the factory, we need to start thinking seriously about what we do now. We can carry on as we are for a little while – Gordon's pretty sure we can still fulfil the orders we have, but it makes no sense to do that indefinitely. Why don't we start exploring some new possibilities?' Out of the corner of her eye, she can see Elin staring at her in astonishment. 'Yes, really,' she adds. 'The sooner we make a start, the sooner we can be up and running, *if* we get the grant, that is.'

'*When* we get the grant,' replies Elin. '*When.*'

'Mum, I told you we were coming over, couldn't the painting wait?'

Mari Hargreaves is halfway up a stepladder in the dining room, a dripping paint roller in her hand. 'Elin, I'm slapping on a bit of magnolia, it's not the Sistine Chapel. Besides, I want to get this finished before your dad gets home from work. He's promised faithfully he'll put up my new curtains tonight.'

'We can come back,' says Lowri. 'Honestly, it's all right.'

'Don't be daft, you're here now. And I'm not sure there's that much I can tell you anyway. I didn't know the Morgans all that well.'

'I can't believe Alun's family lived at the other end of the road though,' adds Elin. 'I don't remember them at all.'

'You were only little when they moved away. People come and people go, and there have been six families in that house since they left. I think most folk were happier when they went too. It put an end to the gossip, so what happened soon became old news.'

'Still a coincidence though – that you knew them, I mean.'

'Elin, I've lived in this town most of my life, I know a lot of people.'

Elin grins, acceding her mother's point. 'So how well *did* you know Alun's mum?'

Mari puts down the paint roller and picks up a small brush instead. 'I didn't. She was a bit...' She slides Lowri a glance. 'No offence, but Anna was a bit of a snob. Kept herself to herself most of the time. We all had little 'uns then, but she didn't really mix with the rest of us. Most of the kids in the street were in and out of each other's houses all day long, but I don't remember ever really seeing Alun. I wasn't surprised when she moved away – despite what happened, I reckon she'd been looking for an excuse to leave. Where did they end up?'

'Cardigan,' replies Lowri. 'I don't know much more myself.' She's trying to recall what she can of the solitary figure who attended Alun's funeral. But the fact that his mother never even properly introduced herself to Lowri was perhaps the biggest indicator of the kind of woman she was. Lowri's grasp on the day was pretty slender anyway and she never even noticed when Anna slipped away.

'Do you remember much about the night when Sorley went missing?' she asks Mari.

'Not really. Beyond everyone knocking on doors to drum up a search party. Your father went, Elin, but I had to stay at home to look after you lot. All us mums did. No one wanted another child to go missing.' She gives them a pointed look.

'It must have been awful.' Lowri shakes her head. 'Panicked, desperate. I don't want to think about how I would feel in that situation.'

'Even the search party caused argument,' adds Mari. 'You'll likely know the stories about Seren's mum? Well, some folk wouldn't even turn out to help look. That's how shameful it was. I didn't really know Judith either, but I always used to think the gossip was nonsense. I ask you, whoever heard of a witch called Judith? And whatever she got up to, her little boy was lost. Every man and woman who was free that night should have helped look...' She frowns, perhaps reliving her own role in events, wondering if her conscience is clear. She turns away, dabbing at a patch on the wall.

'I guess the thing is, whatever the circumstances, no one ever really believes the worst, do they? Not until it happens,' says Lowri.

'That's certainly true,' says Mari, turning back around. 'And to this day, no one knows what *did* happen. Despite everything the police have done.'

'People must have talked about it though, Mum. Traded theories?'

'God, did they. Morning, noon and night, it seemed. And when they found out what Alun's father had done, you can imagine. The stories were rife. Some even said he'd killed the little boy himself. I don't think that for a minute, but I can see how they got the idea in their heads.'

Lowri exchanges a look with Elin. 'The thing is, Alun never told me anything about Clearwater. He kept the whole thing a secret from me.'

Mari is watching her carefully. 'Aye, Elin told me.'

'And I can't help wondering if the reason for that was because he was scared in some way. Perhaps of his connection with St Merrion coming to light. I never even knew he lived here.'

'You're not thinking he had something to do with it?'

'I don't know. I'm just trying to understand it.'

'But he was just a boy. And he and Sorley were friends, I'm sure they were. Although... There is one thing...' She squints, as if peering into the past itself. 'I remember Ffion saying how upset Alun was at school. How he said it was his fault Sorley died.'

'Ffion?' queries Lowri.

'Mum's friend,' supplies Elin. 'Local primary school teacher.'

'Why, what did she say?' Lowri's heart begins to pick up pace.

Mari scratches at her chin, leaving a streak of paint behind. 'I'm just trying to remember. I know it had something to do with Alun being an only child. That's it... She told me how upset he'd been because he'd wished Sorley dead. I don't think it was anything more than that, though.'

Elin frowns. 'But what does that have to do with Alun being an only child?'

'Just that Ffion was pretty sure Alun knew his dad was having an affair with Sorley's mum. Kids aren't daft, are they? Maybe Sorley told him, who knows? But I think she thought it was a touch of jealousy on Alun's part, that Sorley was taking his father's attention away from him. With no siblings to play with, I guess that must have hurt.'

Lowri nods. *Could that be it?* she wonders. That Alun had wished Sorley dead and, when he did die, had heaped all the guilt upon himself as only a child can. Tears begin to prickle at the back of her eyes. What a lost, lonely child he must have been at times.

* * *

'Hello, Carys.' Huw slips into the seating booth beside her, the angle of the table in front of them effectively cutting off her exit. 'I don't think I know your friends.' He looks pointedly at the two other people sitting opposite. 'Aren't you going to introduce us?'

It's busy in the pub for a lunchtime and Huw can't quite catch what she says. But he can guess.

'You're quite happy to turn up on other people's doorsteps, aren't you? But not so pleased when someone does it to you.' He pauses. 'And still no introductions?' He turns to the two men, smiling awkwardly. 'Okay, let's just call you accomplice number one and accomplice number two.'

'You're hilarious,' says Carys, her face stony.

'Aren't I? Well, you've done very well for yourself since we last met. Not talking about the other day, you understand, but the time before that, when it all went ka-boom... Anyway, I see you've got a good little business going now. Property develop-ment. I almost didn't twig it was you when I looked at the plan-

ning application – you've changed your name.' His eyes drift to
her hands. 'Ah, married, I see. Who's the poor bastard?' He
looks across, smiling at the two other men, one of whom is also
wearing a wedding ring. 'Oh, oops. I should take that back. I'm
sure you'll both be very happy.' He waves a hand. 'I'm getting
sidetracked...'

'Are you drunk?' hisses Carys.

'Not at all... Maybe... Just a little bit.' He holds up his
thumb and forefinger with barely a gap between them. 'But
back to the property thing... Lucky I spotted you just now.
Were you on your way to look at the site? Over by the river?
It's a beautiful spot, isn't it? I bet you were there so you could
think about all that lovely money you're going to make.' He
burps slightly. 'Course you scarpered as soon as you saw Lowri
and Seren. They're there with a very nice lady from the
National Botanic Garden. I was there too but, luckily, you
didn't see me, otherwise I wouldn't have been able to follow
you.'

Huw wasn't strictly with them, he hadn't been invited to
the meeting, but he was there just the same, lurking in the
bushes at the edge of the field. Carys didn't need to know that
though.

'I'm sure that's fascinating.'

'Oh, it is. You see, the very nice lady is there because we
have a little flower growing in the river meadow. Quite rare, I
forget the name. *Cypri...* ladies-something-or-other. Anyway, it's
rare, did I say that? And this lady is going to make sure you
never build a single house in that field, Carys. It's a protected
species, you see.'

Carys tries to squirm her way out the other end of the
booth. 'Come on, Rob, let's go. We don't have to sit here and
listen to this pathetic drunk. You don't know what you're
talking about, Huw.'

But Rob is really quite interested, Huw can see that.

Rob frowns at Carys. 'He might be drunk, but none of our surveys came up with that information.'

'He's bluffing, Rob. He's just pissed at me for being successful when he is clearly not.' She inhales sharply. 'Move, Huw! Get out of my way.'

'In a minute, in a minute...' Huw thinks for a moment. 'See, what I can't figure out is why you sank my boat. I understand the whole buying the land, making a pile of money, and finally getting what you think you deserve thing, but where do I come into it? Is it just that you didn't think your prospective house buyers would like looking out on *Pugwash* every morning? Or did you think that if I was homeless, and even more broke than you left me, I wouldn't be in a position to rebuild Clearwater at all?' He holds up a finger. 'One last thought... Could it be that you're not a very nice person and you can't stand to see me being happy at Clearwater, so you thought you'd try to bring my little world crashing down? How am I doing?'

'I don't know what you're talking about.'

Huw mouths at the two men opposite, 'Sorry.' And then he smiles. 'Carys and I have a bit of history, but then maybe you already know that. Thing is, Carys, you know my mate, Jamie? Of course you do. His dad's the local solicitor. Pillar of the community. Expert badminton player and also coordinator of the local Neighbourhood Watch scheme. And he's been asking around. Seems you were spotted, up on *Pugwash*'s deck...'

Carys flashes her husband a sharp look.

'Or maybe it wasn't you. Maybe it was Rob? The man walking his dog said the person he saw was quite tall. But no beard... so it couldn't have been me. Which one of you was it then?'

'He's just trying to rile us, Rob. Don't pay him any attention.'

'Oh, I would, if I were you. You sank my boat and I can prove it.'

'What utter rubbish.' Carys has struggled to her feet and leans in close, towering over Huw. 'You're a loser, Huw, you know that. Always have been, always will be. A pathetic drunk who can't even sit up straight for God's sake, look at you. I would imagine you're quite capable of leaving that smelly hatch thing off, the state you're in most of the time. I'm surprised you haven't fallen in the river by now and drowned. Now there's a thought... No insurer is going to believe you over me, so leave me alone, Huw, I mean it. Oh, and I win. Again.'

Huw watches her leave, muttering furiously to Rob, who takes Carys's arm, steering her out of the pub at speed. Accomplice number two trails behind, very probably wondering what on earth just happened. But Huw doesn't really care how rude he's been, he's successfully rattled their cages, so mission accomplished. And it was a pretty good performance, he reckons. That's one good thing about being known as a drunk. No one thinks for a minute you're putting it on.

After a moment, he takes his phone from his pocket and taps at the screen as a slow smile works its way up his face.

* * *

'Oh, there she is... so pretty.'

'So Seren's right,' says Lowri. 'It *is* the slipper lady thing. Sorry, I know that's not the right name.'

The woman in front of them smiles, getting up from her knees. '*Cypripedium calceolus*. Yes, indeed it is. And there's quite a large colony of them here. Beautiful.'

'It's not the only place they grow,' adds Seren. 'There are more on the other side of the path there.'

Sally Wainwright looks to where Seren is pointing. Lowri had no idea what a botanist would look like, but if she had to guess, Sally would be spot on. With her long, flowered skirt, pale-pink tee shirt and hair wound up in a messy bun, she looks perfectly at home in the river meadow.

'I see. And from what you've told me, there's a public right of access across this land, is that right?'

Lowri nods. 'The meadow used to be part of the Clearwater estate, but was sold off a few years ago. I can show you on the map I have.' She fishes in her bag and pulls out the one the solicitor gave her. 'So this is the road from the town. There's a layby right around here, which is where the footpath comes in. It cuts through the meadow and then follows the line of the river for some distance, as you can see.'

'And that's the only access, is it?'

Lowri pulls a face. 'Well, it was. Unfortunately, the developer applied for a right of access across another part of the Clearwater estate and it was granted. I'm sorry, I don't have all the details yet – it's a long story – but surely that doesn't really make a difference if they can't build here anyway because of the orchids?'

'Ah...' Sally looks down at the map and back up again. 'I think I see the confusion here. From the planning application it looks as if the proposed houses are to be built in this area.' She taps a spot on Lowri's map, which Lowri had already marked.

'Yes, that's right.'

'In which case there probably won't be an issue.'

Lowri stares at Seren before looking back at Sally. 'Sorry, what do you mean, won't be an issue?'

'Well, the orchid colonies are here, well away from the curtilage of the properties. So as long as the developer sticks to the plans, and is mindful of the site in general, then I don't see there's a problem.'

'But what about all the lorries?' asks Seren, her voice rising. 'All the people trampling about. Building sites aren't pretty and these people aren't the sort to pay a small orchid any heed.'

Sally shrugs. 'There's always an element of risk about these things which the planning committee might see as being too great, but as long as contingencies are put into place by the developers, then they'll probably be able to argue successfully.'

Seren looks as if she's about to cry. And Lowri feels sick. She can't believe that having got the botanist here against all the odds, with only one day to go until the deadline for planning objections, she can tell them the orchids make no difference at all. 'But what about the access?' Lowri says. 'What if it's in the wrong place?'

'Well then you might have a case. You said you don't have all the details though?'

Lowri nods. 'My husband was the one who granted the rights of access, but he died a few years ago. According to what I've been told, that contract will still be binding. But I've only recently found out it exists and I don't have a copy of it yet.'

'Then I hope you find it. It might be your only real hope of overturning the planning application.' She smiles reassuringly, but there's a finality about it too. Sally Wainwright has done what she was asked to do. She has other jobs and a life to get back to.

Lowri knows how lucky they were to even get her here today, which almost makes it worse. That they could come so far and fall at their last source of hope. She'll beg if she has to.

'Mrs Wainwright, you have children, don't you?'

Sally looks immediately wary.

'I couldn't help but notice the toys in your car,' adds Lowri. 'Mine looks exactly the same. Toys, bags, wet wipes...'

Sally is obviously waiting for her to get to the point.

'So where do you go for a day out? For a picnic, or a walk?'

'I'm sorry, I'm not sure...'

Lowri swallows. 'Please,' she says. 'Just imagine if there were no green spaces to play in. Or rivers to walk beside. No castles to visit, no imaginary games playing princes and princesses...'

'Mrs Morgan... I know what you're trying to do, but this isn't about what I want, it's about what the law says. I can't tell a planning committee they categorically have to refuse an application just because a rare orchid is growing here. What I can do is advise them of its protected status and urge them to consider the potential problems development here would pose.'

Lowri stares at her feet. 'Sorry... I just...' She sighs. 'Never mind. Thanks anyway. It's really good of you to drop everything and come over.'

'I understand how important this is to you,' says Sally, rather more gently. 'This is a beautiful spot and given what you're trying to do here, if I were you, I'd be trying everything I could to stop the planning getting approval too. I will send off my report, stressing the importance of protecting this rare species, but all I can do is make sure the planning committee understand that if they wish to grant permission for the building works to go ahead, then the developer must include further specific proposals to mitigate any risk.'

'So they would have to change their plans?'

'Potentially, yes.'

'Which would presumably delay things, at least?'

'If the developer doesn't currently know about the orchids, yes it would. Although they should have had thorough site surveys done first.'

Lowri looks hopefully at Seren. 'And if the access they currently have to the meadow isn't suitable because it might be too close to the orchids, could the application be turned down on that basis? If no other access were available?'

Sally purses her lips. 'It might... I can't say for definite. That will be up to the committee to decide, I'm afraid. But I'd say it's your best bet. Like I said before, you really do need to find that contract.'

. . .

Elin is waiting for Lowri and Seren back at the gatehouse, with a huge pot of tea and a bag full of doughnuts. Her face falls the moment she sees them trooping through the kitchen door. 'These were supposed to be for a celebration,' she says. 'What on earth's happened?'

'The orchids aren't enough to stop the planning application going ahead,' says Lowri. She sits down wearily at the table.

'*What?*'

Lowri shakes her head. 'You tell her, Seren, I don't think I can say it out loud.' Ever since this morning, Lowri has had an almost unshakeable conviction that everything would work out. She doesn't know why, she just woke up feeling that Sally Wainwright would be their saving grace. But that confidence was obviously not enough. It seems her conviction was quite capable of being comprehensively quashed.

As Seren fills Elin in about the events of the morning, Lowri's eyes stray to the counter where Wren's card is propped. She made it the night before, presenting it to Lowri as she tucked her in to say goodnight. 'What's that for?' Lowri had asked, only for Wren to tell her that it was to cheer her up, because Mummy was looking sad again. On the front of the card is a drawing of a bunch of flowers, which Wren had coloured in, though the drawing itself is far beyond anything her small daughter could have done. Lowri has a very good idea who helped her.

'Oh, for goodness' sake, that's ridiculous,' exclaims Elin as soon as Seren has finished her recount.

'Yep, but there's nothing we can do about it,' replies Seren. 'And we were lucky to get Sally out in the first place. We just have to trust that what she says in her report will sow enough doubt in the minds of the planning committee.'

'So where's Huw?' asks Elin. 'Shouldn't he be here?'

'I have no idea,' replies Lowri. 'But he submitted our bid for grant funding this morning, so I imagine he'll be in a pub somewhere.'

Elin tuts. 'Lowri...' she admonishes.

'You know he was there earlier, don't you?' says Seren with a swift look at Elin which Lowri isn't meant to see, but does.

'Where?' asks Lowri, only because she knows if she doesn't, Seren will tell her anyway.

'At the meadow. He was standing close to the hedge line, pretty well camouflaged, but he was there.'

'And?'

'Lowri, don't be so down on him, please. He still cares about this place. Anyone can see that.'

'Then he shouldn't have lied,' she replies. 'Now can we please change the subject? I want to eat several of those' – she points to the bag of doughnuts – 'and I have a contract to find.'

Elin sends Seren another look, but she nods. 'Can we help? Where is it likely to be?'

'On his laptop, I'm guessing. Alun left no paper records of anything relating to Clearwater. I've already had a quick look but he used that laptop for work so there are hundreds of files saved on it. And none of them are obviously marked "Clearwater" – that would be far too easy. But he also had an email account I knew nothing about and there are a whole bunch of messages between him and Bridie. I'm hoping one of them has the contract attached.'

'Wouldn't the solicitor have it?' asks Seren. 'The one who set up the custodial arrangement with Bridie in the first place.'

Lowri shakes her head. 'He's retired. And there's nothing on file. Alun really didn't want anyone to find out about his connection to the place.' She grimaces. 'He probably used another solicitor, or used Bridie's, and she's not about to help, is she?'

'No, I guess not.' With a sigh, Elin begins to pour the tea. 'I don't know what to do now,' she says. 'After everything that's happened, I can't believe Bridie might win. She can't be allowed to build houses on that land, she just can't. I could cry.'

'Me too,' says Lowri, pulling Alun's laptop towards her.

'And, I'm sorry, but I wish Huw were here,' says Elin. She gives Lowri a look as if daring her to challenge what she's said.

But Lowri doesn't challenge her. Instead, her eyes fill with tears. 'So do I, Elin,' she says quietly.

'That's it,' says Lowri several hours later. 'If the contract *is* on Alun's computer, I can't bloody find it. There are hundreds of folders on here, and I've searched using keywords which he might have used to save the file, but none of them turn up anything. Of course, if he wanted to hide it, he could have called it anything he wanted. He could have called it banana milkshake for all I know.'

Elin wrinkles her nose. 'Banana milkshake?'

Lowri nods. 'His favourite. But, honestly, it's like looking for a needle in a haystack. I'm not sure it's even on here.'

'But why would he want to hide the file so badly?' asks Seren. 'I don't understand.'

'It's complicated. But like I said before, Alun wanted nothing to do with Clearwater. Partly because in his own way he might have been trying to protect me, but also because I think he was frightened.' Lowri flashes Elin a look. 'Elin's mum has a friend who was the local primary school teacher around the time Sorley went missing. She knew both boys and said that Alun blamed himself for what happened. That he'd wished Sorley dead. I think it's most likely that it was a childish spat, but I'm so sorry, Seren, I can't exclude the possibility that Alun *did* have something to do with Sorley's death. It would explain why he was so terrified of coming back here. Of having his name connected with Clearwater. The past doesn't stay buried for ever.'

Seren holds out her hand to Lowri. 'None of this is your fault. And I don't think for a minute it was Alun's either. It's just so incredibly sad that the past can have held on tight to so many of us, and for so long a time.'

Lowri nods morosely. 'And now Alun's gone, taking with him any chance we could have had to help find out what really did happen all those years ago.'

Beside her, Elin sits up suddenly. 'Hang on a minute...' She stares at them both, eyes wide. 'Try "Sorley",' she says, tapping the laptop screen in front of Lowri. 'In the search box, try "Sorley".'

Lowri looks up, her eyes meeting Seren's.

'It's as good a guess as any,' she replies. 'Not obvious, but not a name that Alun would ever forget either.'

Lowri licks her lips, and wriggles forward in her chair. She places her hands over the keyboard and types as all three of them lean closer to the screen.

'Oh my God...' The voice is Elin's. 'Click on it, quick!'

Seconds later, a document opens in full screen. A contract agreeing to grant one Bridie Turner right of access to the river meadow. Lowri swallows and leans closer still, eyes frantically scanning the details. Please, please, let it be enough. Let it show that Bridie's access isn't suitable.

'So what do we do now?' whispers Elin.

'We send off this contract to the planning committee and then we wait. And pray. And if naked incantations in the garden by moonlight will help, let's do those as well.' Lowri looks at them both in turn. Her friends. Her future. 'Our lives are in someone else's hands now.'

22
___

It's the most perfect day. The skies are high and wide, soft wisps of cloud all that break the blue. Without them noticing, April has slipped into summer and the sun is warm on the water, its heat raising clouds of mayflies in one last frenetic dance of life. They're a reminder to make the most of every day we have, their appearance so apt on a day when the past is being left behind and the future welcomed in.

Lowri has never done anything like this before, and a part of her feels silly, self-conscious and a little embarrassed. She's worried she'll say the wrong thing, ignorant of the little rituals that for Seren are as natural as breathing. Yet she also knows the very fact of her being here at all is the result of myriad synchronicities, all of which have brought her to this exact place and moment in time. It's a comfort that things are unfolding the way they should.

By unspoken accord, only herself, Seren and Elin will attend today's ceremony, and Lowri is glad of it. She has her own reasons for not wanting to see Huw, which have nothing to do with the inappropriateness of what Seren terms 'masculine energy'.

Lowri has hardly spoken to Huw for two days now, the fanfare which should have accompanied his submission of their funding bid, noticeable by its absence. It's a bridge she will have to cross at some point, but today is not about her, or Huw, and she turns her mind from it.

Just like Elin said she would be, Seren was incredibly moved by Lowri's suggestion to hold a memorial for Sorley and, after listening to her thoughts on how they might conduct it, declared it perfect. Popping home for a short while, she returned with a bunch of dried reeds from the river's edge, and showed Lowri how to make a simple woven basket. Lowri is carrying it now, down to the place where she first noticed Seren keeping her watching vigil from beside the millpond.

Seren is wearing a simple smock dress, one she made herself from unbleached linen. She's carrying a bunch of sweet peas and has more entwined in the shining copper curls of her hair. She looks up as Lowri and Elin approach, a broad smile brightening her face.

'What a beautiful day,' she remarks, turning her face skyward. 'Absolutely perfect for a long journey.'

Lowri smiles at Elin, feeling lumpen and awkward in her jeans and tee shirt compared with Seren's gentle serenity. She had fretted endlessly over what to wear, until Seren had reminded her the most important thing was that she should come as herself today, whatever clothes that meant wearing. Even so, Lowri had checked with Elin to see if she thought her casual attire appropriate. Elin had laughed, looking down at her multicoloured skirt and blouse, telling her at least she wouldn't be attending looking like a butterfly.

Kneeling on the ground, Lowri places the basket in front of Seren so she can see what it contains.

'I hope it's okay,' she says. 'I went wrong somewhere and it's a bit lopsided.'

Seren smiles. 'It needs to be honest, not perfection. But the most important thing for today's purposes is that it's bound tightly so it doesn't sink straight away. You've done a brilliant job.' She puts down her flowers and lifts a strip of material from the bottom of the basket. It's woven in bright shades of red and orange. 'This is beautiful,' she remarks to Elin. 'So we have earth represented by the basket and now in the cloth, fire.'

Elin blushes. 'I didn't have much time, so it isn't very big.'

'It couldn't be more perfect. The fire at Clearwater's heart.' Seren's fingers return to the basket. 'And now...' She looks at Lowri.

'I found it in the garden,' she replies, taking the feather from Seren and running her finger along its spine. 'I thought it might symbolise air.'

Seren nods. 'Do you hear them too? Every morning and evening. They're Canada geese, flying to and from their watering hole.'

'When I first arrived, I thought it the most horrific noise I'd ever heard,' says Lowri. 'But now I love it. Their honking is so exuberant, so vital. I used to commute to work by train once upon a time, and every morning and evening the same people sat in the same carriages, virtually silent and withdrawn. If only our daily commute was like that, I'm sure we'd have all been much happier.'

Seren replaces the feather in the basket. 'It's a brilliant symbol,' she says. 'The air and the feather working together to create flight. And with water from the pond, now all four elements are in harmony.' She picks up the bunch of sweet peas. 'Lastly, these are to say goodbye, and to thank Sorley for a lovely time... and we did have such lovely times.' She lays the flowers inside the boat.

Lowri looks down, embarrassed by her ignorance. 'So what do we do now?' she whispers.

'We give thanks for Sorley's life and we let the water take him where it will.'

Lowri nods. 'I wondered if I could say something? I feel I need to, only the thing is I'm not sure what *to* say.'

'There aren't any rules,' replies Seren. 'You can say whatever you like. Just go with what you feel.'

Lowri nods. She thinks for a moment or two and, finally, draws a deep breath. 'I didn't know you, Sorley,' she begins, 'but I know your sister, and I know how much she loves you. How she has watched over you, and waited patiently until she found you, but now that she has, it's time to set you both free. Seren will always be bound to you, but I'd like her to start living the life she was meant to before everything that happened when you were both so young. Sorley, you'll always be welcome here at Clearwater, it's been your home for so many years, but perhaps now the time has come for you to move on as well, and to take your final journey. I hope you find peace.'

When Lowri turns back to Seren, she sees her eyes are shiny with unshed tears. 'That was beautiful,' Seren whispers. 'Elin, did you want to add anything?'

But Elin can't speak, overcome with emotion. She rolls her eyes in apology, wiping beneath them as she shakes her head.

Tenderly, Seren lays the reed boat on the water and, with the lightest of touches, sends it on its way, watching as it moves slowly, spinning across the pond. Eventually, the current will take it, through the sluice gates and on into the mill race, past the wheel, and back out into the open river beyond. On to who knows where.

'Go gently, Sorley, in love and peace,' says Seren. 'Let the waters flow once more, and until it's time for us to play again, I'll always be your loving sister.'

For several minutes, no one moves or speaks. Tears are running freely down Seren's face, but Lowri knows they're good tears, the hurt she's carried locked within her for so long, finally finding its release.

Lowri is awash with differing emotions but the most

powerful by far is a sense of profound peace, and she lets it fill her up, pushing aside all else. There will be time enough to deal with everything that has assailed her over recent days, but the affirmation that she is exactly where she should be is strong, and never more welcome.

'I've stored up my tears for so long, I've felt bloated by them,' says Seren after a while. 'I've ached from the effort of holding them in. They need to flow, just like the river does. And rivers do need to flow, that's their purpose – from their birth in a tiny hole in the ground, to the moment they meet the wide oceans, their waters move, their energy flows. They allow us to harness their energy, the waterwheel is a fine example, but once it becomes blocked...' She smiles at both Lowri and Elin. 'I think fortunes will be better now.'

'Amen to that,' says Elin. 'I know things *are* changing at the factory, but I don't think I can go back there and carry on like I did before. It doesn't even seem possible that a few weeks ago I never gave my future much thought beyond what I would be having for dinner. Now... so much possibility exists. We have to get the funding, I don't know what I'll do otherwise.'

'You'll get it,' says Seren.

Elin sighs. 'Be lovely, wouldn't it? But how can you be so sure? There's every chance we could be turned down.'

'Then ask yourself why we're all here,' says Seren. 'Why now? I think our paths have been converging for a while. You're often not aware of it while it's happening, but you'd better notice it when it arrives.'

Lowri looks up. It's exactly how she's been feeling, as if everyone has been circling each other for a while, like stars in orbit around a sun. The brightness that is Clearwater.

'Well, that's it then,' says Elin firmly. 'You'll definitely get the funding now. How can the universe possibly pass up this opportunity?'

'And speaking of funding...' murmurs Seren. Her eyes are

still following the path of the basket as it floats gently towards the open sluice gates. 'Don't stay mad at Huw for long, Lowri, whatever he's done.' She gently squeezes Lowri's hand. 'Allowing the world to see his face after so long takes tremendous courage, and maybe you should think about why he suddenly feels that way. Allowing yourself to be truly seen by another person is one of the greatest gifts they can give you. If Huw is offering you that, don't turn him away.'

'But he lied to me. He's used me to get to Clearwater. He knew Alun years before he died, before I knew anything about this place.'

'And Alun also had lied to you.'

'Yes, but that's different, he—'

'Huw and Clearwater are bound by the past just as surely as Sorley has been. We don't always know why we do the things we do until hindsight provides the answer, but I don't think Huw has used you, far from it. I think he's trying to help you.'

'You know his story?'

Seren nods. 'I do, but I'm not the one who should be telling it to you.' Her look is direct, but kind, and she smiles. 'I think you'll find Huw might be the final piece of the jigsaw.'

'What do we do now?' asks Elin half an hour later. Seren has left for home and she and Lowri are wandering back up towards the mill.

'Elin, would you excuse me for a little while?' Lowri says. 'There's something I need to discuss with Huw. Only...'

'Three's a crowd?' Elin grins. 'No problem. I know when I'm not wanted. Besides, now you've got shot of Bridie, I can go back to work.'

'But what about the other women?' asks Lowri.

'Oh, don't worry, having Bridie gone will make the world of difference. Like you said, those that stayed have done so because they want to be here, so we have plenty to discuss. In fact, I'm really looking forward to it.' She grins with a gleeful nod. 'Now shoo, you and Huw need to go and... do whatever it is you want to do. I've seen the way he looks at you, Lowri. I'm surprised you haven't noticed.'

Heat blooms over Lowri's cheeks. Maybe she had noticed. But when exactly did she start noticing *him*? She gives Elin a sheepish look. 'Why didn't you tell me he was so good-looking?'

Elin shrugs. 'Because I forgot,' she replies. 'I think we all forgot.'

Huw is sorting through some of his belongings when Lowri arrives at the gatehouse, and just the sight of them flips her stomach. Would she really feel okay if he just upped and left? And could she blame him, given that she hasn't given him any reason to stay?

Yet despite how Huw must be feeling, he still smiles in greeting. 'How did it go?' he asks. 'You had a beautiful morning for it.'

Lowri has forgotten that Huw was well aware of this morning's memorial service.

'It was perfect,' she replies. 'At least it felt that way, you know... peaceful. Profound, in a way that's hard to describe, but it felt good. And I think Seren was right. I think it helped.' She pauses, watching as Huw folds a couple of tee shirts. 'I think Seren was right about a lot of things, actually.'

The hand holding the soft folds of cloth stills. But Huw remains silent.

Lowri doesn't blame him, but she doesn't know how to remove the barrier between them. And then she notices the suitcase on the floor. It isn't hers and it doesn't belong to Huw either. 'What are you doing?' she asks.

'Jamie's missus doesn't much like me,' he replies, 'but maybe no longer having this' – he puts a hand to his chin – 'means I'm less of a scary proposition. In any case, she relented, and the spare room's mine until the baby's born in a couple of months.'

'I don't think I knew she was pregnant.'

'No reason why you would,' he replies lightly.

Lowri's brows come together. 'You asked, didn't you? If you could stay with them when your boat sank, and she told you no.'

Huw's face is expressionless.

'So you literally had nowhere to go,' continues Lowri.

'I would have found somewhere.'

'Would you?'

Huw draws in a quiet breath. 'Maybe not. But I said how grateful I was for your offer of the sofa. I'm still grateful.'

'Huw, you saved Wren's life! What else would I have done?' She blushes. 'But that's not the only reason I asked you to stay. And you don't have to go now.'

'I think I do. I think it's time to find some work and plan how the rest of my life is going to look.' He drops his head. 'The insurers have been in touch. They'll only pay out half on *Pugwash*, and half of not very much is... not enough.'

Lowri looks at the meagre pile of possessions which surround him. It isn't much for a life and yet it strikes her that Huw would give away everything he had if someone else had need of it.

'But you have work, Huw. Once the restoration funding comes through, you're going to have work coming out of your ears.'

'And what if it doesn't?'

'It will.'

'Lovely though it is, optimism doesn't pay the bills, Lowri.'

'But if you lived here, you wouldn't have to pay any bills.' Lowri isn't quite sure what she's offering him.

Huw's stare is very direct. It's clear he isn't sure what she's offering him either. 'Thing is...' he says, 'I thought Clearwater was all I ever wanted. Turns out I was wrong and...' He lets the sentence trail away. 'Maybe working here wouldn't be such a good idea.'

'No! Huw, you can't say that. This is all you've ever dreamed about, you—'

'I've dreamed about a lot of things. Doesn't make them come true.'

'But what will I do if—' Lowri stops. The words 'if you go' are on the tip of her tongue, but she can't bring herself to say them. 'Please don't go,' she says instead.

Huw opens his mouth to speak, his eyes on hers. They're dark, hurt, and guilt blooms within her. He hesitates and, for a moment, she thinks he will relent, but then his face closes down again.

'I said Clearwater meant too much to me to ever be here under false pretences, and you've made it perfectly clear what you think.'

She drops her head. 'But you said you weren't here under false pretences and I should have listened to you. I never even gave you the chance to speak.'

'That's the trouble with anger. It pushes everything else to one side, determined to have its way. But it also speaks the truth.'

'It doesn't,' she says. 'Not always. Sometimes the truth it speaks is an invention in the head of someone who doesn't understand, someone who can't see what's in front of them, someone who doesn't listen.'

'Lowri, when you first met me I was drunk most of the time. I was holed up on my boat, wallowing in my own misery, not working, or at least not doing anything I was remotely interested in, or proud of. Did you never stop to think about why that might be?'

Shame washes over her. Because Lowri *can* think back, back to the day she first argued with Bridie when she reminded herself how much words matter. She remembered at the time how rude she had been to Huw and how she vowed to show him some understanding, some compassion, to care about his problems. She knew there was something, but she swept it aside, caught up in all that she was trying to achieve. Things grow if you tend them, he'd told her, and she hadn't listened to that either, let alone nurtured what they had.

'Being here must be the worst kind of torture,' she says.

Huw studies her face for a moment. 'At times,' he agrees. 'You know, when I first met you, with your hands on your hips, and your tongue sharpened to a point, you reminded me of Carys – your stance, the way she spoke.'

'I know, I... There's no excuse. I shot my mouth off then too, just like I did the other day and—'

Huw holds up his hand. 'But what I've learned since is that you're nothing like Carys. I've learned since that, invariably, the things you do are to make other people happy. If you want something, you go out and get it, but you never take it solely for yourself, you take it so that you may share it with others, and that's a big difference.'

'I'm not sure I deserve that,' Lowri says, feeling her nose begin to prickle. 'But thank you.' She looks around the living room. 'This place...' She holds up her hands as if gathering in the words she wants to say. 'I think everything I feel about it is so bound up in emotions about Alun that it clouds everything else. As if I'm the only one who's ever been betrayed, and yet I know that isn't true. You told me so yourself. What happened, Huw? I know this has something to do with Bridie.'

Finally, Huw puts down the tee shirt he's been holding and motions that they should sit. 'This has everything to do with Bridie,' he says. 'But I didn't realise that until it was too late.' He clears his throat. 'Just like when I first met Carys, I had no idea who she was either. It didn't feel like it at the time but, looking back, our romance was long on passion and short on detail –

very short, as it happens. Which is exactly how Carys wanted it. It never even occurred to me how little I knew about her, or her family, but by the time I did work out what was going on, no amount of knowledge would have saved me.'

'What happened?'

'I was incredibly naïve. I liked to think I was in love, but now I know it wasn't that at all. I was in love with the idea of love, with my dreams of Clearwater and, Carys, with all her talk of our rosy future, provided everything I thought I needed. I sank every penny I had into rebuilding this place – the gate-house, gave up my job so I could start work on the castle. So when Stephen died, when he left Clearwater to Alun and not Carys, when she dumped me quicker than you can even say those words, I had nothing. No job, no house, no money. Nothing.'

'And Bridie?'

'Carys's mum... and Stephen's ex-wife.'

Lowri nods as the last piece of the jigsaw slips into place. 'Of course,' she says. 'Carys's name is on the planning applica-tion. She's a director of the development company Bridie is working with to build the houses. But she has a different surname, so I never thought to connect her to Bridie.'

'No, she's married now.'

'Huw, I'm so sorry.' She can see it all now. How Bridie and her daughter had planned to get their hands on the estate. How Carys had wound her stepfather around her little finger, professing to look after Clearwater, promising to make her whole again, certain that one day it would be hers. But, instead, Stephen had left the whole lot to a man he barely knew, one he hadn't seen since he was a little boy.

'No wonder you thought I was history repeating itself,' she murmurs.

'Perhaps. To start with.'

'But you don't now?'

'No, I don't.' Huw looks at Lowri then, warm, and generous, and true.

She isn't sure how she could ever have doubted him. Except that, deep down, Lowri does know why. She doubted him because she doubted Alun, the one person she always thought she trusted. And if she couldn't trust him, then how could she trust anyone else? How stupid she'd been. How close she'd come to losing everything.

'So all this time, Bridie has thought Clearwater should rightfully belong to her. That's what all this has been about.'

'I've always thought so. When Carys dumped me, it became obvious she was only using me as a means to get this place. She needed my skills, but she also needed someone to give her authenticity, to make her seem like a worthy inheritor of Stephen's estate – someone who was settled, perhaps even with a family, who would do everything they could to uphold the traditions of the estate and pour love into looking after it. The reality was that the pair of them would have probably sucked it dry, ironically much like Bridie has succeeded in doing anyway.'

'So you had to leave the gatehouse too?'

'Yep, and after Carys and I split, Bridie did everything she could to make my life difficult.'

'But you hadn't done anything wrong!'

'Facts like that don't matter to Bridie, not when she doesn't get her way. No wonder Stephen divorced her. Except that now, of course, she's been busy taking back what she rightfully considers is hers, right from under Alun's nose.'

'So she was using him too.' Lowri shakes her head sadly. 'I've always wondered why Alun's uncle left Clearwater to him, but I guess it makes sense.'

Huw nods. 'I think perhaps he was trying to make amends – for Alun's childhood, destroyed by the actions of Stephen's own brother.'

'Alun was a little boy abandoned by his father, just as Seren was,' says Lowri, a wistful note creeping into her voice. 'But Stephen's kindness didn't have the effect he hoped. He didn't know Alun was terrified he'd had something to do with Sorley's death, and so instead of welcoming the chance to come back to Clearwater, Alun shunned everything to do with it. I guess I'll never know if his fears were justified. It's quite possible he *was* responsible, even if he never intended to harm Sorley. An argument which got out of hand or—'

Huw sits forward urgently. 'No, I know that's not true. Alun had nothing to do with Sorley's death.'

Lowri gives him a puzzled look.

'My mate Jamie... His surname is Armstrong. His dad's the local solicitor? And he's old enough to remember the night when Sorley went missing. He said it was a terrible business – that on the night Sorley disappeared they all went knocking on each other's doors, stirring up a search party. He knew Alun's mum and dad quite well, and though Anna and her sister might not have got on, Anna was still desperately upset she couldn't help in the search. And she couldn't, because she had to stay home and look after Alun – he was in bed with mumps at the time and really quite poorly. But Alun was also desperately upset because he'd promised to meet Sorley that night. They were meant to go for a ride on their bikes.'

'So Alun believed that if he *had* gone, if he had met him like they'd planned, Sorley would never have died. And he's blamed himself ever since.'

Huw nods. 'He was a good friend, that's all. He *cared*.'

Lowri stares at him, finally understanding what Huw is saying, not just by his words, but by his actions. Not only has he given her proof of Alun's innocence, but something else as well.

'You did that for me?'

Huw dips his head. 'I knew you had doubts about Alun. I knew he'd lied to you, but I also believe he had good reason and, more than anything, I didn't want your memory of him tarnished.'

Lowri's hand moves to her chest. 'I don't know what to say...' She takes in all the details of Huw's face, revelling in how little of it she could see before, but how every single part of it is laid bare before her now. It's such a wonderful metaphor for recent events, she can't help but smile. 'Why did you shave off your beard?' she asks.

Huw laughs. 'Is that all you can think of to say?'

'No, I just... I'm curious.'

Huw's eyes lock on hers. 'Maybe I no longer want to hide behind it. Maybe it's time to come out of the shadows. Time to let the world see me for who I am, warts and all.'

Except he has no warts. Lowri thinks he's the most beautiful man she's ever seen.

Her hand goes to the stone around her neck, remembering how Seren had told her it would let her see things for what they were, people too. 'Seren would say there's a rightness to all of this. That things have been out of balance, and until a wrong is put right, nothing can ever move forward. Do you think that you and I... that perhaps we've come together for a reason – to heal past wrongs?'

'To heal each other...'

Lowri reaches out a trembling hand to touch Huw's face, her finger tracing the line of his jaw almost in wonder. It's smooth and warm. 'So much you've kept hidden from me,' she says.

'So much I've kept hidden from myself,' he whispers.

'Will you stay?' she asks. 'Please. I can't do this without you.' She checks herself. 'I don't want to do this without you. Only this time there are no games, Huw. No schemes, no lies or deception. This time it's for real. You, me, Wren, and Clearwater.'

A slow smile works its way up Huw's face. 'I rather like the sound of that.'

'I was hoping you would.' She looks into his eyes, sparkling in the sunlight, seeing her own emotion reflected there. 'I'd rather like to kiss you as well...'

Huw's hand reaches up to gently slide around her neck. 'I was hoping you'd do that too.'

23

SIX WEEKS LATER

Lowri has hardly slept a wink. Not that this means she's had a lazy start to the day, far from it. Her morning began when it was still night, when her thoughts drove her from her bed, turning her, as she knew they would, in the direction of a once great building.

She stands in its shadow; yesterday, a ruin, a place of decay and lost purpose, a place of forgotten dreams and a shattered past. And today? Today is the day when all that could change. The day which could be the start of all their futures, of new hopes and dreams, just as the house she shared with Alun once was. And Lowri wonders, not for first time, if this still haunts her.

What if circumstances had been different and Alun *had* shared Clearwater with her? Would she be standing where she is now? What if they had decided to renovate the castle, would Huw be the one rebuilding it? What if they had decided to take over the textile business, would they ever have seen its real potential? *What if, what if, what if…*

But the truth of it, Lowri knows, is that coming here with Alun would never have worked. Because somewhere like Clearwater demands your heart, all of it, no half measures, and it began to cast its spell over Lowri the very first day she arrived. The difference was that she had surrendered to it gladly, whereas Alun would have fought it every inch of the way. It belonged to a past he could never quite outrun, but that wouldn't have stopped him from trying.

As Lowri watches, the first glimmers of pearl streak the lower edge of the sky. One way or another they will find out today what fate awaits Clearwater. Entropy or enterprise, it's as simple as that. One thing or the other. Black and white. If the government agency Cadw agree to fund them, their lives will be irreparably changed along with the landscape, but if they don't, then weeks and weeks of planning and hard work will come to nought and Lowri will be back where she started from. No, she corrects herself, not back to where she started. She's not lost, or fearful. And she's certainly not lonely.

Her mouth curves into a smile as she thinks first of Elin, the young woman who, even when she knew nothing about Lowri, offered friendship for no other reason than because she could give it. Lowri really doesn't know what she would have done without her. And now she has Seren too, who has so much to teach her, about so many things, not least of all about being a sister. But the smile stays on her lips for the longest time when she thinks of Huw, the man who has given so much to this project. A man with almost as many ghosts as she has of her own, and yet a man who has brought her something she never thought she'd have again. Hope.

A sound behind her makes her turn.

'Mummy, what are you doing?' asks Wren, rubbing her eyes. 'Couldn't you sleep?'

Lowri knows she should point out that Wren has strayed far beyond the point they agreed she was allowed, but this morning she lets it pass. Scooping up her daughter in her arms, she buries her face in the warm folds of Wren's dressing down.

'You're so snuggly,' she says, laughing. 'And so heavy!' She lets Wren slide down her body, taking her hand instead. 'One last cuddle before school?' she asks, knowing that Wren will readily agree. Leading her back inside the house, Lowri turns her thoughts to her daughter. To their new life.

Two hours later, there's still no sign of Huw. He said he had something he needed to do, and left not long after Lowri had taken Wren to school. But he promised he'd be back before lunch, and that time is rapidly approaching. Then again, like her, what would he do if he *was* here? Pace about, looking drawn and anxious? There are too many hours to fill on a day which, strangely, has little else to fill it.

Wandering back outside, Lowri goes where she often goes when she needs to find peace, the irony of its location only adding to its appeal. At one time, the mill was the last place she wanted to visit, but it holds no fear for her now. How can it, when it's brought them all so much?

Lowri breathes in the familiar smell, eyes closing as her head fills with images she's been dreaming for a long time now. All around her is the happy buzz of creativity, noise and bustle, and surrounding it, the water which gives life to it all.

'I thought I might find you in here.'

Lowri turns at the sound of Elin's voice. 'I was just thinking about what this place will look like once it's filled with industry again.'

Elin smiles. 'And? What *will* it look like?'

'Well, you'll be arguing over the chocolate biscuits for one, so good to see some things never change.' Lowri smirks. 'But it's good. It feels...' She inhales a deep breath. 'Like it was always meant to be.'

'Didn't I tell you?'

'You did. On the very first day I met you.' She holds Elin's look, suddenly overcome with a rush of nerves. 'God, Elin, what will we do if we don't get the funding?'

'We'll get it.'

Lowri rolls her eyes. 'But what if we don't?'

'Then we'll just have to roll out Plan B, that's all.'

Lowri raises an eyebrow. 'Do we even have one of those?'

'Nope. Which is why we'll get the funding – we have to.'

Lowri nods. 'Fair enough.' She closes her eyes a moment and then reopens them, grinning. 'I don't know whether to be scared and excited, or excited and scared.'

'Me neither. I can't settle at all. I've broken three needles already this morning, so Gordon sent me out for more biscuits before I bankrupt us.'

'That's not funny,' replies Lowri. 'What am I going to say if it all goes wrong?'

Apart from Elin, only two of the original team of staff are left, but that still means Lowri has responsibility for the livelihoods of three people, four if you include Gordon, and that's an awfully heavy load to carry.

'You'll just do what you always do and be honest,' replies Elin. 'Everyone knows where they stand. If it's a no today then we carry on as we were, a much smaller, but much better team than we were. Actually, what am I saying? We were never a team.' She smiles. 'But we are now. We're all here because we want to be, so if we get the yes vote today, then...' Her eyes are dancing. 'God, I can't bloody wait, can you?'

'It'll be a lot of hard work.'

'I know.'

'And I doubt it will go smoothly, these things never do.'

'I know that as well.'

'But we are doing the right thing, aren't we?'

'Ask me a sensible question.'

Lowri smiles and pulls Elin into a hug. 'What would I do without you?' she says.

Elin wrinkles her nose. 'It's no biggie, I'm only in this for the pay rise you promised me, I thought you knew that.'

Lowri snorts in amusement, giving her watch a quick check. 'I wish Huw would hurry up and get back. It's really not fair, leaving us to do all the thumb twiddling by ourselves.'

'I saw him earlier,' Elin replies. 'Said he had someone to see. Something about a promise he made? But I'm sure he'll be back soon.'

Lowri nods. 'He'd better.' She's about to add the rider that Elin should buy some more cakes while she's out, when the sound of a car catches her attention. She frowns and looks at her friend. 'We're not expecting anyone, are we?'

Elin shakes her head as the two of them automatically head outside. There's no mistaking whose car has arrived.

Lowri catches hold of Elin's arm. 'Come with me,' she says. 'I might need a witness.'

Bridie is out of the driver's seat and into the factory by the time they've crossed the short distance. Elin is about to follow, when Lowri stops her.

'Don't worry, Gordon will send her packing,' she says. Lowri's impression of him is rapidly turning around, and he's fast becoming a staunch ally. 'Besides, I want to say a few things to Bridie and I'd rather say them out here.'

Elin nods. 'Lowri Morgan, I never thought I'd see you openly gloating.' She grins. 'But you go for it.'

Lowri shakes her head. 'I wouldn't dream of it. But I would like to make her an offer.'

Elin looks puzzled, but Lowri simply smiles. 'You'll see,' she says.

Just as she predicted, it doesn't take long for Bridie to reappear, clutching a coat and a carrier bag, the remainder of her things she left behind. She barely acknowledges Lowri as she passes.

'Hi, Bridie.'

Lowri thinks she's going to carry on by, but Bridie turns at the last minute. 'I have nothing to say to you.'

Lowri nods. 'Fair enough. But I wanted to let you know that my solicitor will be getting in touch with yours. I have a proposition for you.'

'I'm not interested.' Her voice is flat, her hand on her car door.

'Not even if it means you won't go to prison?' replies Lowri. 'Or not yet, anyway.'

Bridie's eyes narrow. 'I don't know what you're talking about.'

Lowri takes a step closer. 'I'd like to buy the river meadow from you. I'd like you to have it valued, purely as a piece of amenity land, obviously, now that it's clear you can no longer build houses on it, and then I'd like to buy it from you.'

Bridie stares at her. 'And what on earth makes you think I would ever sell it to you?'

'Because it's worthless to you, so what's the point in hanging on to it? I'll pay you the going rate.'

'I think I'll pass, if it's all the same to you.'

Lowri nods. She expected as much. 'You could do the decent thing and just drop this ridiculous revenge thing you've got going on. Accept it, Bridie. Stephen never wanted you to have Clearwater, you or your daughter, and you're never going to get your hands on it. So why not be the better person and recognise that?'

'And let you have the river meadow?' She shakes her head. 'I don't think so. One has to have some pleasures in life, and withholding the meadow from you keeps me warm at night. We might not have got planning permission this time around, but who knows what might happen in the future. A different committee, one who can't be swayed by the ecological sob story your botanist friend laid on them. It's only a matter of time.'

'Okay...' Lowri pauses. 'Perhaps I didn't make it clear

enough. I'd like to buy the river meadow from you, and if you don't sell it to me, I will hand over to the police the file my forensic accountant is currently in the process of drawing up and let them handle the matter. You've been defrauding the Clearwater estate for years and I have proof.'

Bridie's mouth drops open. 'That's a very serious accusation.'

'Isn't it?' Lowri smiles. 'So what's it going to be, Bridie? Oh, and by the way, as well as handing over the file to the police, I will also make sure everyone around here knows what you've done. What will people say about the Turners then? All those people you know... They'll cross the street rather than speak to you. So I'm giving you the opportunity to save a little face, and quite possibly evade a prison sentence. Just sell me the river meadow and we'll consider things square.'

'That's blackmail.'

'Call it what you like, Bridie.' Lowri takes another step forward. 'But that's my offer. And it's also made on the understanding that neither you, nor your daughter, set foot on my estate again. You leave me alone, and you leave all my friends alone, because if you don't, I promise I will make trouble for you.'

'*Fine.*' Bridie is livid, despite her deliberately mild reply. 'I can see you're enjoying threatening me, but leave Carys out of it. This has nothing to do with my daughter.'

'Hmm... I'm not sure that's strictly true,' says Lowri, wrinkling her nose. 'Given that Huw has a recording of her pretty much confessing to scuppering his boat. Perhaps you'd be so kind as to pass the message on for me.' She smiles. 'Thanks so much.'

Bridie is desperate to have one last word, her eyes burning into Lowri's as she tries to think of a suitable comeback, but then she spins on her heel and yanks open her car door. Lowri knows she's made an enemy, but she's not sure what other choice she had.

Blowing out her cheeks as Bridie's car roars out of the car park, Lowri feels rather faint. But she's done it. She's said what she needed to. And if ever there was a perfect day to say it, today is it.

'Why did you just let her go?' asks Elin, watching the dust settle. 'She's a thief, Lowri, she's stolen money that belongs to you.'

Lowri draws in a deep breath. 'Because proving fraud is difficult. And it takes a long time. I could be fighting this through the courts for years, and that's time and money I don't have. Clearwater is what's important to me now. And I'm not passing up the opportunity we have just to settle a score with Bridie. I won't get back any money she's stolen, but what I *have* is far more important to me than what I don't have. Besides, people like Bridie, they don't go away. And I have a horrible feeling we haven't seen the last of her. I'd like a little insurance for the future, that's all.'

She looks at her watch, trying to find a smile. 'Listen, I was going to suggest you buy some extra cakes while you're out getting biscuits. I've already bought some, but I don't think I've got nearly enough for a celebration.' She does find her smile then as she thinks of what the rest of the day might hold.

Elin grins, looking back at the mill. 'Yes, boss,' she says. 'Leave it to me.'

Watching Elin drive away, Lowri scours the lane but there's still no sign of Huw. It could well be a couple of hours before they hear anything about the funding, but she just wants him here. She wanders back towards the gatehouse. Perhaps she can pass the time by cleaning something. Again.

Her heart almost bursts out of her chest as her phone trills from her pocket. Expecting it to be Huw, she peers at the unfamiliar number.

'Lowri Morgan? It's Rebecca Miller here, from the Heritage Buildings Capital Grant Programme, at Cadw?'

Lowri nearly drops her phone. 'Hi... hello... Um, yes, this is she.' She rolls her eyes at her sudden inability to string words together.

'I wanted to give you a call in advance of our official email. They don't go out until two thirty, but we always like to give folks a call if we can.'

Lowri nods. To let them down gently? Or to give them more time to celebrate? Her throat is so tight, she's not sure she can speak.

'And so in this case... I wanted to offer my congratulations. Cadw were hugely impressed by both your vision, and the level of detail in your bid submission. We've no doubt that Clearwater House will be an incredible addition to our historic environment.'

It takes a moment for Lowri to make sense of what Rebecca is saying. 'You're giving it to us?'

'Yes, Mrs Morgan. We're offering a full grant, for restoration of Clearwater House, to give it its official title, and the watermill also. Congratulations.'

Lowri can't help the noise which escapes her. 'Sorry,' she says automatically. 'I'm just... so absolutely bloody *happy*.' She feels as if she's floating, gently bobbing on the lightest of air.

'It's a lot to take in, you must have worked very hard.'

Lowri can hear the smile in Rebecca's voice.

'I need to sleep for a week,' she replies, adding, 'sorry, I'm rambling now.' She takes a deep breath, aiming for slightly more composure. 'So what happens now? What do we do?'

'The official email will explain all the next steps, but – basically – I'll be handing over your file to one of our project managers and they'll be your liaison moving forward. They'll be in touch shortly.'

'Oh God, thank you. Thank you.'

'That's quite all right, Mrs Morgan. Oh, and one last thing... Good luck.'

Lowri is left staring at her phone, wondering whether it's okay to scream and let it all out. Instead, she does an odd twirly thing, turning this way and that, completely torn over what to do first. She should let people know... the factory... no, Elin isn't there... maybe Seren, but what if she's there when Huw arrives back? She stops, the biggest smile on her face. There's only one person she could possibly tell the news to first, and suddenly Lowri knows exactly where he is.

The cemetery sits on a bank overlooking the town, with virtually the whole of St Merrion spread out below it. The view is spectacular and as she passes through the gate, Lowri stands for a moment, shielding her eyes against the sun. She traces the curve of the river as it winds its way through the valley, her gaze coming to rest midway along its length where a broken-down tower reaches for the sky.

Three months ago, she never dreamed she would find anywhere like Clearwater. She wasn't even sure if she could be happy, let alone find somewhere that felt so much a part of her she can no longer imagine being anywhere else. But it isn't just the castle making her feel like this, the tower, or the watermill. It isn't the river itself, or the woodland either. Instead, it's a gentle giant of a man, and Lowri doesn't know exactly where he is, but she's certain he's here somewhere.

Picking her way among the trees that dot the hillside, Lowri's heart lifts as she sees Huw's unmistakable silhouette, dark against the skyline. He's staring out into the distance, and she knows in her heart what he's looking at. Silently, she makes her way to stand beside him, slipping her hand wordlessly into his.

'Dad, I'd like to introduce you to someone,' he says, a smile lighting up his whole face. Lowri still can't get used to seeing it all without its covering of beard. 'This is Lowri... She's the one I've been telling you about.'

Lowri looks down at the gravestone in front of them. 'Morning, Mr Pritchard,' she says. 'Although perhaps you wouldn't mind if I called you Evan? That's quite some view you have there.' She raises her eyes to where the sun is glinting off Clearwater's tower.

Following her line of sight, Huw squeezes her fingers. 'Anyone would think he requested this particular spot. Damn near broke my heart when they buried him. So close, and yet so very far. Now... now I can't think of a better place for him to rest.'

'He'll be able to watch it all,' she says. 'Stone by stone until Clearwater Castle stands as she always used to. And he'll see his boy rebuilding it, just like he always promised he would.' She nods at the gravestone. 'And don't you worry, Evan, I'll make sure he does.'

'Be nice, wouldn't it?'

Lowri leans against him. 'Not nice,' she says. 'The future. I wasn't kidding your dad, Huw, I've just had a phone call from Cadw...'

Huw pulls back, as if to better see her face. She can tell his heart wants to leap, but he isn't sure what he heard, whether he's understood her right. Lowri nods, laughing softly.

'We got it, Huw. We damn well did it!'

For a moment they stand, eyes locked on one another's, full of emotion, and Lowri's filling with tears. She never ever thought she would feel the way she does now. And as Huw sees it, his tears come too, until the two of them are helplessly clutching one another. Lowri doesn't ever want to let him go. His arms are warm, and strong and soft, all at the same time. They are safe. And they are everything that is Huw.

They stay that way for quite some time, letting all the things they want to say flow between them. At this particular moment, there's no need for words.

Eventually, Huw pulls gently away, and they turn their eyes back to their future. 'It was one of the things I hated Carys for,' says Huw softly. 'That when I finally thought I'd be able to do for my dad what I'd always said I would, she took even that away from me too.' He lifts his head to look at Lowri. 'So I came here this morning to put all that behind me,' he adds. 'Whatever happened. Clearwater means too much to me to...' He breaks off, a gentle smile on his face. '*You* mean too much to me to ever let the past come between us. So a clean slate, a brand new beginning, and I want to start it untethered by what has gone before. I wanted to be sure there are no ghosts.'

'And are there?'

Huw stares out across the valley for a moment before turning back to look at her. His eyes are speckled gold in the morning sun. 'Not any more.' He reaches down and slides both arms around her again, pulling her close.

Lowri has to stretch, standing almost on tiptoes, to touch her lips to his. 'Then let's go home,' she says. 'To Clearwater.'

A LETTER FROM EMMA

Hello, and thank you so much for choosing to read *Secrets of Clearwater Castle*. I hope you enjoyed reading it just as much as I enjoyed writing it. If you'd like to stay updated on what's coming next, please do sign up to my newsletter here and you'll be the first to know!

www.bookouture.com/emma-davies

For those of you who follow my writing (a huge thank you!) you'll know that *Secrets of Clearwater Castle* sees a return for me to writing romantic fiction, very different from my last four books, which were cosy mysteries. They were books I really enjoyed writing and, as I'd been wanting to write them for such a long time, truly scratched an itch. However, when the time came to think about what could come next, I was torn. Readers have so generously taken the time to tell me how much they've loved the Adam & Eve Mysteries, so I knew that continuing with this series was a real possibility, however, something within was telling me it was time to return to writing stories which lift hearts as opposed to sticking cake slices through them!

And I do so love writing feel-good fiction. I love reading it too. Increasingly, the world seems a far more hostile place than it ever was, and at times, if you let it, it's hard to remind oneself that good things and good people do exist. I have always loved writing about community and friendship, the triumph of kindness over hate, the small things we can do for one another which mean more than can ever be expressed. And the world is full of such examples, if only we care to look. I like to think the world *is* the same, but with so much access via the news and social media to the more negative aspects of our lives on this planet, our perception of it has changed. So, I determined to make *Secrets of Clearwater Castle* a place to draw comfort from, a place to make new friends, and a place to lose yourself for a while.

As always, there are many people to thank for their help while writing this book, and this is one I truly could not have written, were it not for my incredible children. We've had a tough couple of years, and recently suffered a devastating loss, but although our song will be a little quieter for a while, I know we'll keep singing. So, truly, thank you.

I'd also like to thank our marvellous frontline workers, particularly in the NHS. Your generosity, hard work, grace and humanity in the face of increasingly hard working conditions has not gone unnoticed. I could not work with my hands tied behind my back, but it appears that we expect you to do so, and I truly hope for better. I personally salute you and thank you for all that you have done, and continue to do.

In the writing of my books I'm also incredibly grateful to my wonderful publishers, Bookouture, for enabling me to bring you these stories and for their unfailing support. Thanks also to my wonderful team of editors and, in particular, Susannah Hamilton for her sage advice.

And finally, to you, lovely readers, the biggest thanks of them all for continuing to read my books, and without whom none of this would be possible. You really do make everything worthwhile.

Having folks take the time to get in touch really does make my day, and if you'd like to contact me then I'd love to hear from you. The easiest way to do this is by finding me on Twitter and

Facebook, or you could also pop by my website, where you can read about my love of Pringles among other things.

I hope to see you again very soon and, in the meantime, if you've enjoyed reading *Secrets at Clearwater Castle*, I would really appreciate a few minutes of your time to leave a review or post on social media. Every single review makes a massive difference and is very much appreciated!

Until next time,

Love, Emma xx

www.emmadaviesauthor.com

 facebook.com/emmadaviesauthor
twitter.com/EmDaviesAuthor

Printed in Great Britain
by Amazon

33438742R00189